THE
RESCUE

T. JEFFERSON PARKER

THE
RESCUE

TOR PUBLISHING GROUP • NEW YORK

THE RESCUE

Copyright © 2023 by T. Jefferson Parker

A Forge Book
Published by Tom Doherty Associates / Tor Publishing Group
120 Broadway
New York, NY 10271

www.tor-forge.com

Forge® is a registered trademark of Macmillan Publishing Group, LLC.

The Library of Congress Cataloging-in-Publication Data is available upon request.

ISBN 978-1-250-79356-0 (hardcover)
ISBN 978-1-250-79358-4 (ebook)

Our books may be purchased in bulk for promotional, educational, or business use. Please contact your local bookseller or the Macmillan Corporate and Premium Sales Department at 1-800-221-7945, extension 5442, or by email at MacmillanSpecialMarkets@macmillan.com.

First Edition: 2023

Printed in the United States of America

0 9 8 7 6 5 4 3 2 1

*For Jasper, the Mexican street dog who gave me this story,
and for the fine people of the Fallbrook Animal Sanctuary,
who brought him to us*

THE
RESCUE

1

Night in Tijuana, light rain from a pale sky.

Inside the Furniture Calderón factory and warehouse, the Roman follows his mongrel dog as it noses its way through the cluttered workstations, sniffing and snorting the chairs and sofas and barstools and bed sets in varying stages of completion.

The dog stands on its hind legs to smell the table saws and sewing machines, the measuring tapes and clamps and glue pots, then drops back to all fours again to sniff the fragrant bundles of hides and the colorful bolts of fabric piled high like treasures looted from a caravan. Between stops, it covers ground swiftly, nose up, nose down. Its short, four-count breaths draw the air both into its lungs and across the scent receptors packed within its muzzle.

The Roman is in black tactical couture all the way from his polished duty boots to the black ski mask snug to his face and head. Black socks, a loose black kerchief for that band of neck below the mask. The dog's black leash is bunched in one hand. Behind the Roman are some of his business associates—four militarized soldiers of the Jalisco New Generation Cartel, and four men in humble street clothes instead of the khaki-with-green-trim uniforms of the Municipal Police, their official employer. They all carry late-model automatic weapons, some laser sighted and some with traditional iron sights.

Sullen and alert, these men trail the Roman and his dog, respectful of their sizable skills and reputation as a cash-and-drug-detection team. The Roman has never told the men his real name, only his nom de guerre, the Roman. So to them, he is simply Román.

The dog's name is Joe, and he looks more like a common street dog than a cash-and-drug-whiffing savant. Joe is a trim fifty-five pounds, short haired, long legged, and saber tailed, with rust ovals on a cream background. He is terrier-like and dainty footed, but his gull wing ears protrude from what could well be a Labrador retriever's solid head. To these heavily armed men, accustomed to the burly German shepherd dogs, Malinois, and Rottweilers favored by the DEA and Federales— and the pit bulls adored by *narcotraficantes*—Joe looks amusing and almost cute. The Roman, on the other hand, is simply *loco*. But the Roman and his dog always find and deliver.

Joe's snorts sound softly in the still, cavernous factory. His gently up-curved tail wags eagerly. He wheels and feints his way through the river of smells. Cuts right, then left, then right again, but moves forward, always forward. His ears bounce. He loves his job.

The Roman, through his ski mask, also smells the leather and the lumber and the faint dust-smoke of the incandescent lamps above. He marvels once again at Joe's ability to experience these strong, obvious scents but also hundreds of others that he, a mere man, can't smell at all. And not only does Joe gather exponentially more than any human, he instantly distinguishes these smells from the chosen few that are his purpose and his passion: fentanyl, heroin, cocaine, methamphetamine, marijuana, and currency.

And, of course, small animals.

Joe breaks toward a slouching stack of boxes, snatches a mouse off the floor, dashes it twice against the concrete—*rap, rap*—then looks proudly at his master.

Whispers and grunts and the metallic unslinging of guns.

"Joe, *down, you* sonofa*bitch*."

Then laughter.

Joe plops to his belly, head up, ears smoothed back in submission, staring at the Roman with eager penance. He doesn't know what *sonof-abitch* means, but he knows what the Roman's tone of voice means.

"That's one of the reasons they retired him," the Roman says to no one in particular. His Spanish is good but accented by English. Learned in school, by the sound of it, not border Spanglish picked up on the job. "He's got a lot of terrier in him, and some things he can't control. Won't control."

"*¡Un perro terrible!*" says a policeman.

"*¡Muy rápido!*" says a cartel soldier.

"Come," orders the Roman. Joe bolts to his side and sits, looking up hopefully. "Steady, Joe. Steady, boy. Let's try this again. Okay, *find!*"

In the back of the vast warehouse, Joe alerts on a dented metal trash can overflowing with scraps of cloth and leather and wood.

He sits in front of his perceived find, as he has been trained. He looks first at the Roman, then at the trash can, but with a very different expression from his please-forgive-me-for-killing-the-mouse look. Now his ears are up and his eyes are fixed on the object of his alert. A quick glance at his master, then back to the business at hand. He's trembling.

Two of the policemen quietly tip over the container while a third, on his knees, rakes out the trash.

"Ah . . . aha!" he says, pulling a green steel ammunition box from the mound of trash, then another, and another.

The Roman can smell the gasoline that the ammo boxes have been wiped down with—a standard dumb idea for confusing a dog. He's seen hot sauce, cologne, mint-flavored mouthwash, cat urine, bleach, and antiperspirant used too. Most traffickers don't know that dogs don't smell the combined odors within a scent cone; they smell individual ones. They separate and register each component of the whole. A book of smells, each smell a word. So no matter how you try to disguise a scent, the dog is rarely fooled or repelled. The dog knows what's there.

The Roman knows the only thing that works against a good narcotics-and-currency dog is perfect packaging, but Joe has the best nose the Roman has ever seen. The much surer solution would be to keep your stash far away from dogs like Joe, maybe on another continent. Or to bribe the dog's handler, or the handler's handler. Money solves most problems.

A squat cartel lieutenant whom the Roman knows only as Domingo kneels and pops the heavy latch on one of the steel cases. It's a standard US Army–issue ammunition box—twelve by six inches and seven and a half inches high—and the former contents are stenciled in yellow on a lengthwise flank: 100 CAL. 50 CARTRIDGES.

As the rain begins to pound the metal roof high above, Domingo removes an open package of fragrant naphthalene mothballs from inside the box, then six neat vacuum-packed bricks of US twenty-dollar bills. The Roman knows that the old-school Sinaloans from whom he is stealing weigh-count the bricks to exactly one-half pound, which means this case contains $28,800. And he knows that $9,600 of it will soon belong to him and Joe, who is watching all of this with shiny-eyed pride. From one of the many pockets on his pants, the Roman gives him a cube of steak.

The other two ammunition boxes contain identical treasures, for a gross total of $86,400 for the Jalisco New Generation Cartel and the participating Municipal Police officers who have helped make this possible.

And $28,800 for himself, the Roman, and for Joe, man's best friend.

But the raindrops suddenly turn into footsteps, faint but fast.

The Roman and his little army dive for cover, machine guns chattering away at them. Domingo, closest to the loot, goes down with a cry and a wobble of blood.

The Roman calls Joe but the dog has vanished in the horrific noise. The compadres return fire, their bullets clunking home or twanging in ricochet. The Roman knows he's in a numbers game, and the noise actually sounds encouraging: four shooters, six? But this is the Sinaloans' warehouse and they know it better than he and his men do.

"Joe, come! Joe, *come!*"

The Roman draws his sidearm, a .40-caliber Glock 35 with a laser sight that holds twenty-two rounds and will not jam. He calls Joe again but the dog is gone. The gunfire subsides while footsteps land in the smoky silence. The Roman runs from his cover toward the rear exit of the warehouse. Then a volley and a high-pitched *yipe* from Joe. The Roman strides straight toward that yipe, shoots down a slender *sicario* in a white cowboy hat and a Shakira T-shirt, turns and center-shoots another man, twice—*boom, boom*—the bullets slamming into the far wall before his body plops to the floor. The Roman is a big man; he knows he might take a bullet someday doing shit like this.

But he loves it.

You wear the crown, you wear the target.

Joe whimpers to his left and the Roman charges the sound, zigzagging down a long aisle lined with mile-high shelves like a big-box store, and the Roman senses the enemy behind him, turns, and blows him down with three shots, the *sicario's* machine gun clattering to the concrete.

The Roman and his employers press the running battle toward the rear exit and the loading docks and the street. The Sinaloans are fewer, just as the Roman had thought. They're running hard for the steel sliding door through which they entered; it is still cracked open. Two escape, but the Roman and his confederates cut down two others as they try to squeeze out.

Followed by Joe, who clambers over the bodies and limps crookedly through the door and into the night.

"Joe, come! *Come!*"

Outside, the Roman scans the dark barrio with his pistol raised, trying to watch the cars and the houses and the buildings and the street, trying to keep from getting shot, trying to see his wounded dog. The Sinaloans have apparently taken off. Two boys run down Coahuila Street, oversized athletic shoes splashing potholes filled with rain. Sirens wail and citizens stoically observe the Roman from behind windows and cracked doors. They've seen this before—their city among the most violent cities in a violent country in a violent world.

The Roman calls out to them in anguished Spanish: "Where is my dog? Where is my dog?"

No one answers.

"Joe! Here, boy! Come!"

The Roman searches the sidewalks and beneath cars, under the festive furniture on the porches and the tiny front yards, even the gutters running black and throwing up wakes over pale sandbags that just maybe could be Joe.

The sirens force him away.

He's the last to pile into the white-and-green van parked on a side street. It's the one with the Ciudad de Tijuana Policía Municipal emblems on the sides and the orange light on the top and the three green cartridge cases on the floor beside the badly wounded Domingo. The driver runs the wet city streets fast, no warning light and no siren. Just the high beams. And the stink of blood and fear and gun smoke, and the pounding of the Roman's heart.

Five minutes later the van pulls into Superior Automobile Repair and Service, and the motorized wrought iron gate with the big sign on it rolls closed behind them. The compound is surrounded by an impregnable ten-foot concrete wall with broken bottles cemented to the top. A man in street clothes waves the driver in to the high bay and the repair stations inside.

Domingo has died, so the others climb over him and out. The Roman is first among them, carrying one of the three ammunition cases, his pay for the night's work. He loves the feel of $28,880 in his hand, but his heart aches with the loss of Joe.

Another man in street clothes walks the Roman to his car.

"It is terrible what happened, Señor Román."

The Roman has rehearsed a lifetime for what just happened. Which prepared him poorly for it. He's killed three men just now. His first, not counting war. He feels gutted and surprised.

"Fuck off, Amador."

The Roman's car is a green Maserati Quattroporte parked over a platform jack in one of the repair stations, as if to be worked on first thing in the morning. The Roman sets the ammo case in the trunk and tosses the ski mask beside it. Runs his hands through his short blond hair.

Behind the wheel now, he nods to the man, who throws a toggle on a cabled control box. The platform jack shudders and lowers the Maserati into the ground. The Roman looks at himself briefly in the rearview as the darkness claims him, blame and anger in his bloodshot gray eyes. Blame and anger. He thinks: *Joe. I'd go back and look for him if* la colo-nia *wasn't crawling with cops, some on cartel payrolls but some not.*

Five minutes and a slow mile through the dark underground tunnel later, the green Maserati rises from its grave, safe within the high spiked walls of Platinum Foreign Car Specialists in Otay Mesa, California.

The Roman waits as the gate swings open, then drives through it into the California night.

35 Days After the Shoot-Out . . .

2

Joe lies on his pad in the Clínica Veterinarea San Francisco de Asís, looking out from his ancient rock-and-iron-grated cell at the blustery winter day.

The clinic director, Dr. Félix Rodríguez, has named him El Perro Disparado, Shot Dog, because, well, he's been shot, and Tijuana street dogs don't have name tags, and he has to call the dog something.

Joe has named the doctor Good Man. He understands that Good Man brings the food. He understands that Good Man has done something mysterious to him. That he has a good face. That he scratches good—under the throat and behind the ears—like Teddy and Dan.

On his belly, head resting forward between his trim front feet, his saber tail curving along his hind legs almost to his chin, Joe watches and listens and lets the smells of the world drift past.

The clinic door opens with its clunk and long squeak. Through the rusting bars of his cage, Joe sees Good Man enter the row of kennels. With him is a Woman he has not seen before. From their expressions and bodies, Joe sees that they are not a Team.

Joe has no concept of luck, but the doctor knows that this animal is fabulously lucky to have been brought here by a boy, who, smeared with the terrified dog's blood and intestinal fluid, carried him over a kilometer in the rain.

But the doctor also knows that luck has two faces: Shot Dog's miracle rescue and touchy surgery have landed him at the end of his allotted thirty-day adoption period, which expires today. Baja California state policy, beyond the doctor's control. Shot Dog will be euthanized in the morning unless he is adopted before then, odds that Dr. Rodríguez knows are smaller than small. Not a single prospective dog owner has come by today, and the expected rain bodes ill for a late-hour miracle.

Last week, an elderly man was interested in Shot Dog but had no money. When the doctor offered to waive the modest adoption fee and give him a week's worth of food, a leash, and some good flea-and-tick pills, the man had promised to return the next day but never came back at all. Rodríguez turns away dozens of dogs every week because his clinic is 100 percent full. He's even got portable crates set up inside the hospital and lobby, but these, too, are full of yowling, hopeful, pathetic dogs.

It's been a long thirty-something days for Joe. No Dan. No Team. No work. No play. No meat treats. No sleeping on his couch in the living room or in Dan's bed when the women aren't there. No swims in the pool. Sure, his pain is mostly gone, and the itchy stitches, too, and so is the slobbery plastic cone once tied around his neck. But these are small things compared with the immense sadness that seems to run through every part of him. There are memories and there are dreams, dreams of memories and memories of dreams. They are one story. His dog mind is never fouled by time, beginnings, middles, and endings. He knows that Dan will return and they will be the Team again, but the long hours in the cell are wearing him down.

Good Man and Woman come down the walk between the facing rows of cages; then Woman stops. Joe does not like women, because they get Dan's attention and sometimes even his bed. The Team Bed. The women are not part of the Team. The Team is Joe and Dan.

Now Woman plants a shiny, three-legged tree and screws a black thing onto its flat top. Joe is familiar with these. People have them all the time, mostly to talk to. Sometimes they make sudden strong light. People used to point them at him and Aaron, who was the leader of his Team before Dan. People used to point them at him and Teddy, his first Boy. Teddy then Aaron then Dan. His Teams.

Thirty feet downwind of the humans, Joe registers the familiar bleached-white-coat smell of the doctor, the leather of his new athletic shoes, his musky cologne. He smells the woman's flowery hair, her female sweat and perfume, and the strong, nose-quivering powder that Dan puts into his morning cup. All of these join the ambient river of scents that has flowed past him for thirty-plus days here at the clinic: car exhaust and street-vendor foods, trash and tire burns, diesel smoke, dog pee and feces and disinfectant sluicing down the walkway slot that runs between the cages, the restaurant food that makes his stomach growl, the climbing roses on the rock wall that separates the clinic from the auto repair shop next door. And much, much more.

Woman aims the black thing at Good Man, then stands beside him. Joe can see that the doctor is worried by the black thing, or it might be Woman who worries him. Not very worried, but a little. Dan is never worried or afraid.

Joe hears their words very clearly, and recognizes some of them, but not nearly enough to understand what they are saying. He never stops trying to understand. His ears are good and he listens to humans very closely. He watches their faces closely too. Woman's voice is calm. They talk the language of Dan, not the language of Good Man:

"Bettina Blazak here, with Dr. Félix Rodríguez of the Clínica Veterinarea San Francisco de Asís in Tijuana, Mexico. Dr. Rodríguez, thank you so much for sharing your time with *Coastal Eddy*."

"I am happy to be here, Bettina."

"Tell us about the clinic."

"Yes, of course. Mexico loves dogs. We love them so much that twelve million of them run free on our streets and parks and beaches. They have no owners. No one cares for them. Without government sterilization programs, they breed. Many die of starvation and disease and, in my opinion, of sadness. We have a name for them, *perros callejeros.* 'Street dogs.' All these animals here come from our streets. Our purpose is to find for them a home. This is a great challenge because there are so many dogs."

"What exactly what is a Mexican street dog? What breeds do they comprise?"

"We like to say they are not a pool of genes but an ocean of genes! Terriers and retrievers of all kinds, collies, boxers, and German shepherds. Spaniels, huskies, Dobermans, Lacy dogs and vizslas, basenjis and pit bulls. Greyhounds, of course, because they race here and later are sold as pets, and what do they do when you get them home? They either sleep or run! There are many small and toy breeds especially popular in Mexico—Xolos, Chihuahuas, papillons, miniature dachshunds and poodles. Even the genes of the legendary Korean hunting dog, the Jindo, have been found in dogs here."

"What's the first thing you do when someone brings in a street dog?"

"Food and water. A dog starved once is always hungry. Then medication for fleas and ticks, and a thorough medical examination. Vaccinations. Sterilization is performed. Decayed teeth are removed. We bathe them so they are clean for a possible owner and a home."

"What do your examinations usually reveal?"

"Starvation and dehydration. Parasites, *Erlichia*, many viruses. Canine influenza. Skin disease is common. Some dogs have been on the street so long that their toenails have grown through their feet because of no trimming."

"That's awful."

Good Man nods his head and makes a sad face. Joe has recognized the words Dog, Beach—because Dan takes him there—Street, Food, and Water, and he thinks that the word *home* might mean Crate. Other than that, these two humans might be talking about anything. He understands from their voices that Good Man is serious, and Woman is becoming unhappy.

"It must be very expensive to do all this medicine on so many dogs," says Woman. "How does the Veterinary Clinic of Saint Francis of Assisi survive?"

"We are partially sponsored by a major North American pet company, and we receive a small amount of funding from the state and city. We ask for a donation when we place a dog for adoption."

"How much?"

"Whatever the person can pay. We recommend twenty dollars, which includes food, the collar they are wearing, a leash, and one toy."

"How many dogs do you rescue and place for adoption each month?"

"Adoptions are slow in January, February, and March because of the Christmas dogs whose owners have become tired of them. So they take them somewhere and let them go. No one wants another dog then. In September, when the hot weather is leaving, people want dogs. We place many dogs through December. As presents to make the children happy."

Joe has no idea what Good Man has said, other than Dogs, Dog, Dogs, and Dogs. The man's tone is not clear.

"How can our readers and viewers in the United States help?"

Good Man smiles and his tone of voice becomes happier. "There are two things they can do—send donations to us or come to Mexico and rescue one of our beautiful dogs. We take care of all the adoption paperwork right here, and send them home with all their shots. And the little things, the food and the toy. Your readers and viewers will receive a healthy, loving, and grateful rescue animal. They are intelligent, humorous, and very good learners."

"Dr. Rodríguez, can you introduce me to some of your dogs?"

"Yes, of course."

Woman removes the black thing from the shiny three-legged tree. They go from cage to cage. When Woman kneels down in front of one, a tan muzzle with a black nose appears through the bars and Woman makes high Woman sounds. She points her black thing at the cage.

"Oh, look at *this* little cutie!"

Again, her words are lost on the dog, but her meaning is very clear.

And to Joe—as well as to his ancestors lying by the fires that first lured them into the world of men—meanings are always more important than words.

Now Good Man and Woman stand outside Joe's cage, looking down at him.

"This is Shot Dog."

"What a terrible name."

"It is more a description."

"How did he get shot?"

"I don't know. He was shot and a boy brought him in and I performed a dangerous but successful surgery."

Woman points the black thing at Joe as she talks: "A boy saved his life. A boy and you, Dr. Rodríguez. This dog has been very lucky."

"Some people shoot the street dogs for sport. Rather than feed or help them."

"My readers in California will want to know that," says woman, still pointing the black thing at him. "They'll be horrified. Could this have been an accident?"

Good Man's expression softens and so does his voice. "Anything is possible."

"Has anyone shown interest in adopting him?"

"An older man, but nothing happened."

"He's really cute. The way his ears stick out. How long has he been here?"

"More than the thirty days that I told you about."

Joe watches Woman lower the black thing. Her expression has changed. She looks at Good Man, then back to him. Her face is sorrow. She does not need words for Joe to understand that something very bad is happening.

"It breaks my heart, too, Miss Blazak. He is already past the limit. It is the policy."

"Just leave him where he is. In this cage. Simple."

"Injured dogs are considered bad luck."

"With all he's been through!"

The woman kneels near the bars. Joe smells the cinnamon and coffee on her breath and a spilled drop of hot sauce coming from the knee of her pants. He's used to finding valuable smells, but these are not valuable. He rests his head on his front paws and sighs.

"Excuse me, Doctor."

Woman walks briskly to the clinic building, turns, brings a hand to her mouth, and looks back at Dr. Rodríguez and Joe. Who understands that Woman doesn't know what to do. Dan always knows.

Then she's back.

"May I open the door?" she asks.

"Allow me."

Joe rises and stretches, then limps out of his cage and into the noose of the doctor's expertly dangled lead. Joe is long legged, long tailed, and concave like a whippet. He sits before the kneeling Woman and they are almost eye-to-eye, Joe's brown and Woman's blue. He reads her face for meanings as best he can. He can't understand them as he does Dan's, Teddy's, or Aaron's, or other people he has spent more time with. He has never known a Woman well, and never liked the way they take attention away from him. Away from Dan and him, the Team. Same as when he and Aaron were the Team, and when he and Teddy were the Team.

Woman is sad but Joe doesn't know why. The sadness began when Good Man said *thirty days*, but Joe doesn't know what those words mean. Dan is almost never sad. Dan is strong, and fast moving for a human. Sometimes angry, sometimes happy. But not sad. Joe smells her breath and body, under her arms, her legs, her feet and sandals.

She reaches out her stranger's hand slowly, palm down. Joe decides not to bite it. He has been sore and sad since coming here to the clinic, but his training is to bite only on command. He lets her pet him under his chin. He holds her gaze, and his eyes narrow at the pleasure. Then she strokes his throat, and behind his ears, and gently rubs the raised scar inside his ear flap. On her face Joe sees Woman's sadness change to something else: happiness. He smells her tear forming before it rolls down her face.

"Señor Rodríguez," she says. "I came here to do a story on your clinic and adoption center. It will be a good story. And I want to adopt Shot Dog. I will not let him die here. I want to help him heal and get him off these streets forever."

Good Man looks at Woman, his face filled with happiness. Joe knows that these two people have gone from sadness to happiness very quickly. He taps his tail once, looking at Woman. He thinks he understands what all this happiness means: Dan is coming to get him. They will be the Team again. What else could it be?

"Señorita Blazak, you have just done a wonderful thing for one of God's own creatures! You will be blessed forever by the Holy Mother."

"Let's do the paperwork quickly, before I change my mind. I have to be back in Laguna by late afternoon, and the border will be awful. I'll make a donation to your clinic, beyond the twenty dollars."

"I am a very happy *médico veterinario* and I know Shot Dog will be happy too."

"I'll probably change his name."

"This is your right."

"I need video of us together."

In the office, Joe lies under the big wooden desk, his leg hurting but not badly. He's leashed at Woman's feet, her bag on the floor beside him. He smells the leather of her sandals, the woman skin of her feet, a medley of flowery smells flowing from inside the bag, and one of the very valuable smells he's trained to track. He listens to her making pleasant talk with Good Man, and scratching something on paper. From the man's side of the desk come the same sounds that Dan makes at home when he uses the black slab on his desk. Woman's hand descends and takes something from her bag on the floor beside him, and Joe smells the money. There isn't much. Dan would not be happy.

Two men walk in. From under the desk, and judging by their shoes, Joe sees that one is big and one is small. He knows people like these, their jangling metallic sounds, their commanding voices, their smells of leather and gun oil and solvent. They always do what Dan says. Joe does not like police, because they take Dan's attention away from him, just like women do. They are not part of the Team. So Joe stays where he is, listening, out of sight under the desk where Woman and Good Man sit. He understands none of their fast, unfamiliar language.

"What do you want?" asks Good Man.

"We are looking for a dog that ran away in the North Zone last month. There was a dispute and he was shot."

"Was it the narcos, or men just shooting dogs for fun?" says Good Man.

"It is under investigation."

"We have no such dog."

"We will search the kennels."

"Of course. Take your time."

When the police have clanked from the room, Good Man says strong, fast, quiet words to Woman. Dan sometimes gives orders in this tone. It means *now*. It means *important*.

Joe hears clunking on the desk, feels a firm tug on his leash, and follows Woman out of the clinic and into the bustling Tijuana streets.

He understands that his world has just changed.

3

Bettina Blazak steers her red Wrangler down Calle Benito Juárez toward the port of entry at San Ysidro. She doesn't want the policemen from the clinic to see her, but she can't exactly gun it in the heavy Tijuana traffic. Bettina keeps her eyes on the mirrors and her hands at ten and two. The potholes still hold last night's rain.

The wait at the border is long and the air is humid and dirty. Vendors weave their way through the waiting cars with churros and foil-wrapped tacos, huge paper flowers, guitars, bright pottery, piñatas, statuary, acrylic blankets with images of pop singers emblazoned on them. Bettina buys a beautiful yellow vase with red roadrunners on it and a large cold bottled water. Gets the dog into the front seat, where he can drink from this morning's coffee cup.

The dog laps, his tongue rasping on the paper.

"Hey, pooch, what am I going to call you? I wish you could tell me your name. But it's possible you've never had one. The Dog with No Name? Nah. Guten Doggen? Mom called all our dogs that because she was part German. Nah. Can't believe I came down here for a story and am going home with you. I'm a dog person, don't get me wrong. When I was a girl, we had Labs and terriers. The Labs were for quail hunting, and the terriers roamed around killing things. We lived in an old house and had a barn and some acres we leased out for grazing."

Bettina thinks of her mom and dad, still there in Anza Valley—Gene, a water district hydrologist, and Barbara, an English teacher at the high school.

One older brother up in the Bay Area, raising kids; another in Nashville, waiting tables and making music. All living somewhat distant lives but always in touch.

She doesn't think of her youngest brother right now.

Has to pick her moments for Keith.

"Water?"

She pours the dog a refill, and when he's done he glances at her, then puts his nose out the window.

"Of course, you're dying to know something about me," says Bettina. "But maybe I shouldn't make 'dying' jokes to a dog that's been shot and almost got euthanized. If someone shot you just for fun, then he's going to a very hot place in hell. I'm hoping it was an accident. From the narcos going at it again. That big shoot-out last month in Tijuana made the news in California. Were you there?"

Bettina starts the engine, creeps forward, turns it back off. A vendor comes by with a painting of calla lilies that's really quite pleasant, but the walls of her apartment are already crowded with pictures and paintings and the California Native baskets she collects. The old vendor stops and holds it closer. His face is dark as a roasted almond and he has even white teeth.

She shakes her head no.

"Almost free," he says.

"It's very nice but, no, thank you."

"How much can you pay?"

"No gracias, señor."

"Fifty dollars? Okay. We have a deal." He hoists up the painting to give her a better look. "Forty."

She shakes her head and looks away and the man moves on.

Then she turns to the dog. She always talked to the family dogs when she was a girl and always answered back for them. Gave them words.

"So, pups, my name is Bettina Blazak."

When he looks at her, she taps her sternum with a forefinger and repeats her first name three times. The dog watches her but his expression doesn't change.

"I'm Polish-Irish with dabs of French, German, and English—and way back, some Cahuilla Indian. A mutt, like you. I grew up in a small town in California's desert. As soon as I could, I moved to Laguna Beach. That's where we're headed. You'll love it. I'm twenty-six years old and plan to stay that age forever. Not everyone gets my jokes. I don't know how old you are, but Dr. Rodríguez said five to seven years."

Bettina tells the dog about the weekly Laguna Beach newspaper she works for, *Coastal Eddy*. She writes and photographs for the paper—both print and digital editions—and makes videos that post to *Coastal Eddy* subscribers through a web page, email, and social media. Coastal Eddy is not a man, she explains to the dog, but a wind pattern that causes cloudy mornings along the coast. The dog curls up on the seat and looks at her, head on his paws, his button ears relaxed.

Bettina likes it when someone—even a dog—listens without interrupting. With three brothers plus Mom and Dad, Bettina, the baby, could hardly get in a word.

"Readers love dog stories," she says. "And pictures and video of dogs. You will soon be momentarily famous in a small way. I try to do good reporting about things that matter, even if they don't all happen in Laguna. A story has to matter. Like this one. Millions of dogs that nobody takes care of? That matters. I also want to get myself onto the *Los Angeles Times* someday. And win a Pulitzer too."

She checks her messages, plugs in the phone to charge.

Again, Bettina starts her Jeep and moves into the new gap before her. The dog sits up and looks out, ears erect, tips flapped over. For a while, the line of vehicles creeps along a little faster. She sees the dark clouds to the north.

"Doggen, you listening? I love horses, trapshooting, surfing, cycling, and writing. I'm going to level with you. I like clothes and beauty products and good food too. I'm told my best feature is my hair, which is dark brown, though from what I've read, you probably see it as very dark gray. So here I am. Your turn. Tell me about yourself."

The dog curls into the seat again, muzzle between his front feet, furrows his brow, and closes his eyes.

Bored, Bettina thinks. She wants to talk for him but she can't. She knows almost nothing about him. No name, no exact age, no breed or parentage, no history, nothing except Tijuana and a bullet.

He's a mystery, and she loves that about him. She's a born storyteller, and she wants to tell his story. She's glad to be part of it now.

Curled up on the front seat, his long saber tail wrapped all the way to his chin, Joe listens to Woman. He understands that she's talking to him and he likes that. Her voice is pleasant and happy. She sounds excited when she says words he knows—Good, Dog, Water. Other words like Pulitzer and Cahuilla are new to him. Many he's heard before and doesn't know, but her emotions register clearly through her voice. Her face is happy but not excited.

He sits up and watches the world go by, and the window goes down but not far. Puts his nose out there, smelling the very different world from his home with his Boy Teddy, and later his home with his Man Aaron, and later his home with his Man Dan.

Different Teams, different places, different smells.

Joe feels sad, but Woman is maybe good like Teddy's mom was good.

They stop at one of the big pet stores off the interstate, where Bettina is surprised that the dog knows his leash manners perfectly. Limping slightly, he keeps to her left, just a nose length ahead even when cornering the aisles, adjusting to her pace, sitting when she stops. He sits and downs on command. In English! Bettina wonders where a Mexican street dog learned all this. The pet store clerk gives him a treat, which the dog accepts tentatively. Her dog is leery and aloof, not just with strangers—human or canine—but with Bettina too. She doesn't buy a tag, because she's not sure what to name him.

Such a funny-looking thing, Bettina thinks as he walks the aisle at her side. A deep street mix, like the doctor said. Curvy, big headed. Slim loins but big thighs. She guesses Lab and whippet in him, Jack Russell, maybe Chihuahua or Xolo. There's something almost undoglike about him. Wallaby? Jackalope! And those ears, randomly articulating with his senses—one moment they're button, the next rose, the next gull wing or a combination. She can feel herself falling more in love with him by the minute. It doesn't really matter what he's made out of. He's what he is. She figures a DNA test would be uselessly crowded and inconclusive.

From Laguna Canyon Road, she heads up Stan Oaks Drive, parks in a carport under the Canyon View Apartments. The apartments are affordable on a small-town newspaper reporter's salary. Pet friendly too. The wood-and-glass building rises from the flank of the canyon on imposing concrete caissons.

Bettina leads the dog up the stairs to her veranda, lugging a collapsible crate in one hand, glad to be home. Looks forward to her windows and good views. Her Canyon View neighbors are sometimes noisy but basically cool, and they look out for each other, observing Canyon Cocktails nightly around the pool and the communal firepit.

Inside, she gets him water, trades out his dirty collar for a new blue one, and tosses him a new chew toy turkey she thinks he'll like. Then shows the dog her place. Downstairs: the living room, kitchen, breakfast nook, and office/studio where she writes and makes her videos. There's a beautiful blue six-foot-eight-inch swallowtail surfboard in one corner of the living room. And a sleek white Cannondale road bike she rides with her club, the Biker Chicks, propped against one wall in the office, her helmet dangling from the saddle. Her trap guns are locked in an office gun case that she and her dad made when Bettina was twelve. Upstairs is the bedroom and a bath that has a shower with an eye-level window and an ocean peek, and great views of Laguna Canyon.

Back in the kitchen, Bettina pours a cup of premium salmon kibble into a bowl and sets it on the floor. The dog sniffs it, then goes under the breakfast nook table and lies down, resting his unhappy face on his front paws. Gets his furrowed expression again, eyes looking up at her as if she has taken away everything that ever mattered to him. Offers him the chew toy turkey again and he ignores it again.

That evening she takes him to Canyon Cocktails, introduces him to the neighbors. He's standoffish and draws mixed reviews. Bettina tells them about his close call on the streets of Tijuana, his recovery, and her falling in love with him pretty much on sight. Of course, they've got name ideas:

Lucky.

Ears.

Bullet.

Dodger.

Spots.

Coastal Eddy.

How about just Eddy?

Bettina tells them she'll think it over. She sees by the dog's face that he's unhappy here, doesn't want to be looked at by strangers.

Later she invites him into her office where she starts her story about the Saint Francis animal clinic and shelter in Mexico. "The Story of Shot Dog" by Bettina Blazak. He curls up on a rug and is soon asleep.

She pours the last of her bourbon into an old-fashioned rocks glass, adds an ice cube and a splash of water.

One page in, Bettina realizes that she needs more medical details on the operation, and whatever else the vet can tell her about the dog's condition that night. And she could use some background on what life on the street had been like for him.

She calls the clinic, and, predictably, it's closed.

But Rodríguez gave her his home number, and Bettina gets his wife, Señora María Lucero Obregón. She is very upset. She says the doctor was taken away by the police for questioning and allegedly released from custody only three hours ago. But Félix has not come home.

"He loves his home," she says in rapid Spanish. "He is not with our children. He does not have a lover. The police said he walked out of the station, turned right on Cristóbal Colón, which is the direction home. They haven't seen him since. I walked and drove the streets from the Zona Norte all the way home, for two hours, and there is no sign of him."

Bettina's Spanish is college-good, but it's still hard to get her own tone right with a native speaker. It's hard to be subtle.

"I'm sure he's fine, señora," she says. "Maybe he got lost. Or stopped for a drink." An awkward pause, then: "I need some more information on my dog."

"How is he?"

"He's sad and a little afraid of strangers."

"Have you named him?"

"Not yet. Señora Lucero, while I have you on the phone, can you answer some questions about the dog?"

"Of course. I am a veterinary doctor myself, and I helped with the procedure. But it's Félix who has the gift of surgery, not me."

She goes on to describe the abdominal entry wound of the bullet and its exit through the muscle high on his left thigh. It had broken open his intestine and nicked an artery, and the bleeding would not have stopped without a repair, which her husband did beautifully. The intestine was leaking waste fluids and had to be tightly sutured and drained as well. The muscle damage was substantial for just one bullet, and the doctor speculates that it may have bounced off the street and expanded up and through the dog. Tremendous doses of antibiotics were required.

"Do you know if he was shot for sport?"

"I think it was an accident. That night there was a large shoot-out between rival Tijuana cartels. It is a war between the New Generation Cartel and the Sinaloa Cartel. Everyone in Mexico knows this. It has been going on for many years. The Sinaloans are trying to hold their plaza in our city, and the New Generation is trying to take it. They were made brave when El Chapo was arrested. This battle took place in a furniture factory. Many shots were fired and six men died."

Bettina's fingers fly across her keyboard as she makes notes. She can type almost as fast as Dr. Lucero talks, though the translating slows her down as her memory struggles for the words.

"Did you know that the dog is almost perfect on leash, and knows his basic commands by voice? Not only in Spanish but in English as well?"

"No. That is unusual. But we noticed he was obedient off the leash, which is unusual, too, for a street dog."

"Can you tell me who brought him to the clinic?"

"A boy from downtown, where the gunfighting took place. He knew of our clinic."

Bettina's head is spinning with a great new story idea about the boy who took the shot dog to the clinic. Thereby saving the dog's life.

"Do you know the boy's name?" she asks the doctor.

"I'm sorry. We were in such a rush to save the dog, we hardly thanked him."

"Doctor, what is life like for a street dog in Tijuana?"

"Hunger, dehydration, disease, ticks. Violence from men and other dogs, and coyotes. Giving birth in alleys and gutters. No love. No kindness. It's a terrible life."

A cold shudder issues down Bettina's back as she considers the former life of the dog she has rescued. He's looking at her doubtfully. She hasn't realized until now what a miracle she's performed for the dog. What a miracle the boy who carried him to the clinic has performed. Most of all, what a miracle that doctors Drs. Félix Rodríguez and María Lucero have performed.

She gets a sudden inspiration and takes a deep breath. "Señora, I want to name the dog Felix. For the man who saved him."

"Félix is a good name. It means 'lucky' and 'happy.' My husband, Félix, and the shot dog are both those things."

Bettina thanks María Lucero and tells her that her husband will be home soon. "I'm going to call the Tijuana Police right now and get to the bottom of this." She hears the worry in her own voice.

The desk sergeant says that Rodríguez voluntarily came in for an interview about possible irregularities at his veterinary clinic.

"What irregularities?"

"Oh, I cannot answer this. But it was routine. He talked to our detectives and left the station at approximately four in the afternoon."

"Were you on duty?"

"I was right here at this desk. I watched him go."

"Which way did he turn on Cristóbal Colón?" Bettina asks.

A pause: "*A la izquierda.*"

To the left, notes Bettina.

"Are you sure?"

"Surely, yes."

"Thank you for your time."

The cops can't even get their directions right, thinks Bettina, reading through her notes on the monitor. Do they not agree on what they saw, or are they hiding something? There's something ominous in the doctor not coming home.

Later that night, Bettina almost finishes the story. She'll write that last graf in the office tomorrow morning. She's a fast writer, tries to be clear and accurate rather than stylish or poetic. She thinks her editor at *Coastal Eddy* will love it, and be glad she let Bettina wander so far from Laguna for the story. The pictures and video she took with her smartphone are good.

Then she edits and over-voices her video, "Felix: The Rescue of a Mexican Street Dog." Her viewers will learn some of Felix's misery on the street and get a real feel for his cold, lonely Clínica Veterinaria San Francisco de Asís days. They'll be delighted that his name is now Felix, not simply, gruesomely, Shot Dog. There's a lot more to him than just getting shot, Bettina thinks.

She edits and retouches the video so Tijuana looks cold and forbidding, and the poor dog looks miserable. Not hard to do. But her viewers will also see that Dr. Rodríguez is a good soul, and how lucky the dog is to have survived possible cartel violence. She makes sure they know that Felix was one of twelve *million* dogs living on the streets and beaches of Mexico. She loves it when her stories point out a problem that people can do something about. In the video, Bettina thinks that she looks composed, capable, and borderline pretty. She's never done a story this personal. It's a little weird to be reporting on yourself.

She sends the story and video to her *Coastal Eddy* editor, Jean Rose.

And later sits cross-legged on the bedroom floor in her robe and slippers, with Felix lying against one thigh. She strokes his face and neck and ears. Rubs her thumb gently inside the warm triangular flaps, feels the raised bump of what must be an old wound. A street fighter's scar, thinks Bettina.

She tosses and turns some of the night, patting the mattress for Felix to come join her, but he stays in his new crate beside the bed.

She's exhausted, but she can't stop her thoughts.

Typical, she thinks, and of course the bourbon's gone.

Always the story hound, Bettina Blazak wonders as she begins to drift off how a Mexican street dog has not only been obedience-trained but trained in English besides. Has he spent some of his years *not* living on the streets of Mexico? And she wonders if the bullet that almost killed him was no accident but happened during the cartel shoot-out—and for a reason. The timing sure looks right. Why were the Mexican police looking for a shot dog? Why interrogate the veterinarian who saved him? Why couldn't they agree on which direction Rodríguez went when he left their station in the Zona Norte? And where is the doctor now?

The boy, she thinks: I need to talk to the boy who carried a dying dog half a mile through the rain.

He should be next:

The Boy Who Saved Felix
By Bettina Blazak.

4

Five years and three days before Joe was wounded and carried to the clinic by the boy, Joe's sire—a nameless little street mutt—began another of his journeys from Tijuana to the McDonald's in Otay Mesa.

It was a February Sunday, and Street Mutt was—as always—in search of food, water, and a mate. Early morning, still dark.

He followed his usual trail along the Tijuana River, swollen as it was by last night's rain. Trotted through the towering, windswept Arundo reeds and swam across the wide cold current, shaking himself off on the other side and sniffing his way along the bank until he began to pick up the scents of one of his many food places.

He was very hungry, pushed by his memories and pulled by his senses. He smelled the coyotes not far from here and heard them yipping beneath a fading crescent moon. He went faster. The coyotes smelled big and he had seen what they can do to a dog.

The path led through the estuary to a tall rusting fence that ran along the brightly lit tarmac of Tijuana International Airport. The asphalt prairies of the airport stretched as far as Street Mutt could see, the big terminal glittering in the distance.

He stopped once to look through the chain link at the incomprehensible world on the other side. But only once and only briefly. He knew that movement means life and stillness means death. Such as when his friend the dark dog froze in the middle of the street and was hit by a white car. Or when the big dog stopped to fight the coyotes instead of running and they got behind him and tore at him. Street Mutt's mind is a kaleidoscope of images going back nearly seven years. Thousands of them. Like all dogs, he had experienced his world through his senses but he had no words to communicate or to order his images. His memory is keen and the images reappear clearly when triggered by his senses, and sometimes when they are not, as in dreams.

Soon Street Mutt was back on his small-footed trot into the first light of a Sunday morning. There was some whippet in him—which made him sleek and built for speed, and gave him his expressive rose ears. But there were scores of other breeds in him as well: small terriers and pointers and spaniels. A trace of German shepherd from generations ago, a hint of Labrador, and golden retriever too. More small breeds than large, for sure: Chihuahua and Xolo and Parson Russell and toy poodle. Traces of everything. Beagle. Bichon frise. Greyhound. Akita. Collie. Dachshund. Papillon. Chow. In some ways, he had the best of all of them: whatever worked, whatever allowed him to survive.

He half circled the airport, keeping to the edges of things: the brush along the culvert, the dry tumbleweeds collected along the chain-link fence, the hedge of failing oleander. A huge bird boomed into the sky, climbing.

It wasn't hard to follow his nose to the hole under the fence, well marked by himself and others. After crawling through, he sat and looked both ways for cars. Looked again. Then hustled across the road into a streambed, along the eucalyptus windbreak, around the brightly lit customs buildings and the inspection grounds, his hunger driving him into the new light.

As the sunlight grew, Street Mutt saw his familiar food place. He saw the yellow arches against the new blue sky, but the rest of the building was only shades of gray, black, and white. The scent all around him was overwhelmingly good and strong, mixed with the smells of exhaust coming from the cars in the drive-through line, of burning jet fuel, of standing water and eucalyptus, the oily gravel beneath his paws, bleach and disinfectant wafting from the open rear door, of the rat poison coming from the traps anchored along the walkway of the building. He has cataloged hundreds of smells and attached meaning to them. Many of them are food places.

As fragrantly demanding as the dumpsters were, Street Mutt knew he couldn't get into them. So he learned long ago to employ humans to get what he needed. He found that he could stand just outside the propped-open rear door of the burger emporium, framing himself in the light from within, and give the humans what they wanted from him: ears up but not aggressively, tail wagging, his face calm and his eyes imploring. Eagerness. Friendliness. Compliance. All of which he'd learned early in life, from the human faces and tones of voice, and from their ensuing behavior. These were easy lessons because a human face is easy to understand, and because Street Mutt had always wanted to have a human of his own. He had that common dog need to give one human everything. But some dogs get humans and some do not. He had no word for *love*. Just as he had no words for being kicked, or being hit with sticks and rocks, or being left tied up and hungry.

A boy pushed a clattering wheeled bucket through the back door and stopped when he saw Street Mutt standing handsomely in the light. The dog had not seen this boy here before. His face looked friendly. Street Mutt sat and twitched the end of his tail twice on the cement.

"Who are you? You look like you snuck in. No collar. Do you bite?"

The boy—who in Street Mutt's eyes was wearing dark pants and a light shirt and a yellow-and-gray hat of some kind—stood the handle of his mop straight up in the bucket and knelt.

The dog rose and wagged his tail humbly, walked over, and sat. Smelled frying oil and meat smoke and milkshakes. And the bleach on the boy's shoes, and his body odors, and the soap on the boy's hand as he licked it. The dog remembered a boy who once did this, then choked him. That was a long time ago, so now Street Mutt was able to control his fear and let the boy's hand go to his throat and scratch. He was a good scratcher, this boy. Street Mutt stood and let the boy scratch, then pat his haunches. He would have been this boy's dog if the boy wanted him to be.

"Wait here."

Street Mutt sat and waited. He heard the big ceiling fans inside, the sudden uproar of boiling oil, and the people talking into the big box that had food pictures on it.

The boy came back with a black plastic dish and half a foam clamshell, which he put down.

Street Mutt was all over it. The half clam was just water, which he ignored at first, but the black dish was piled with bits of sausage and scrambled eggs and hash browns and pieces of bread. There was ketchup and salt and pepper.

The black dish skidded along the ground and the dog nosed it against the wall but the food was gone. Still, every lap of his tongue brought treasures to his nose.

He turned and looked at the boy, who was upending the wheeled bucket over a drain.

"More?"

The dog knew no English, of course, but he knew the word's tone so he wagged his tail and sat again.

Two minutes later he finished his second big plate of scraps and felt the bloating satisfaction inside. He drank the water, then sat by the empty plate and looked at the boy with his very best, most hopeful, most friendly expression.

But the boy wheeled the bucket over, picked up the plate and the white clamshell.

"I got to go back inside. Don't follow or you'll get kicked. The manager hates dogs."

Half an hour later, on his way back to Mexico, Street Mutt suddenly registered the distant scent of a female in heat. It hit him like an old friend, throwing that switch inside him. Next to food, this was his most important smell. His most primal. If he had words, he would have described it as urgent desire, pleasure, maybe even a quest to experience beauty.

It took him another few minutes to find her, following a shallow drainage ditch and narrowing her scent cone to the backyard of a house on Marconi Court. He saw her through the chain links of a tall fence, lying in a patch of sun on her patio. She was pale, much larger than he, and beautiful. A full-bodied beauty. The tag on her collar caught the sun.

He yipped, raking dirt furiously. Pale Beauty came over and paced, watching him. In less than five minutes, Street Mutt excavated a body-sized cavity under the fence. He dug with the efficiency and strength of a machine. Soon as he wriggled under, Pale Beauty bolted for the back door of her house, and when Street Mutt tried to climb her, she threw him off and raced around her home. Then around it again, and again. She was fast and cornered well. So Street Mutt reversed himself, crashing into her head-on at the doghouse entrance. She was heavy enough to knock him inside. He scrambled out and was on her tail again by the time she got halfway across the yard; then she cut and ran back across the grass. Suddenly she wheeled and nipped him, but quick and nimble Street Mutt was behind her in a flash.

Street Mutt finished in a dizzying rush, then got himself back under the fence and out the way he'd come.

He drifted toward sleep in the shade of a decorative hedge lining the McDonald's parking lot. Lost in the same enjoyable haze he's been lost in many times before. Dreamed of getting a good lunch when he woke up.

After a nap, Street Mutt went around to the back door again but it was closed. He put his nose to the air and started back for Mexico.

He hadn't gone far when he picked up the scent of grilling meat and followed it to a backyard barbecue on Siempre Viva Road, hopes high.

Five Days After the Shoot-Out . . .

5

Apex Self-Defense sits in a tangle of streets, overpasses, power lines, and light rail tracks that link the San Diego Convention Center, downtown, the airport, and the Transit Centers. Some of the buildings are old, some new, and from certain heights the graceful blue span of the Coronado Bridge can be seen reaching across to land. From other angles, it's all steel and concrete, bright sun and shadow, unhoused people strewn upon the ground like rags.

Apex Self-Defense is a brick industrial structure built in 1938. There is no exterior signage except for the ancient rusted emblem of the former owner, hanging over the dated front door: San Diego Sandblast.

Dan Strickland is hard at work here now, deep in the basement gun range—six stations, motorized target pulleys, walls and ceiling all baffled with soundproof batting. Its far end is a concrete wall faced with railroad ties and hay bales. Despite the earsplitting handguns deployed inside the range, from outside it is silent, thanks to the City of San Diego's strict noise codes.

Above him is floor 1—the office, combat ring, wrestling arena, weight room, lockers, and showers.

Floor 2 is classrooms, lounge, gaming arcade, lunchroom, and dormitory.

The first two floors have a drab, not-new feeling; furnished for utility and value.

But the remodeled floor 3 is Strickland's lair, his pride and joy—a steel-and-glass penthouse, all hard lines and right angles, with views of the city, the Coronado Bridge, and the Pacific. One big room with everything he needs. A space for contemplation, books, art, music. For a gigantic TV. A good kitchen and a big firm bed.

Joe's crate is in the bedroom, heaped as always with his blankets and pad, his chew hooves and antlers, the plush toys that he preserves rather than destroys. His pink bunny. His chimp. Here at home, Joe was all puppy, even as a retired narcotics and currency specialist. His food and water dishes are on the slate kitchen floor.

Earlier this morning, Strickland looked at all of Joe's things and wondered again how to get through another day without him.

His heart ached because he loves Joe and he loves the money Joe makes him.

Strickland has been waiting for one of his business associates south of the border to message him with good news: Joe has been found. Joe is alive. Joe was wounded but it was not serious. We have him. He's waiting for you at Platinum Foreign Car in Otay Mesa.

But only silence from south of the border. Which to Strickland means that the worst has happened.

Now he watches his current undergraduates blasting away in the basement. There are six students, his maximum per class. The course is ten weeks—one day per week for eight hours. He's booked four days a week with four concurrent courses, well into the year.

Strickland stands behind the firing line with his arms crossed. He's wearing foam ear inserts and a good sound suppressor but he feels the gunfire in his body, a steady, concussive *whop, whop, whop whop whop*, that is really not like any other sound on earth, he thinks. From a distance it might sound like firecrackers, but close like this it's another dimension of sound altogether. It goes through you, just like the bullets would.

Overall, this is a pretty good class for four weeks in, he thinks. He watches Edward trying to keep his rounds in the kill zone of the paper target—a life-sized human torso—ten feet away.

Then there's Molly, the high school teacher, her glasses starting to fog up again as she inexplicably places another tight group, all in the black, from twenty-five feet out.

Next to her is Kim, who owns a jewelry store in La Jolla, also a good shot.

And Mario, the Starbucks manager, and D'Andre, the nightclub owner, and finally Tucker, the actor from up in Silver Lake.

Strickland doesn't issue diplomas or certificates but he does promise that each graduate will have the training necessary to effectively defend against a life-threatening attack. If graduates don't have confidence in their skills and the equipment they've bought, then they can take the course again for free. The ten-week course runs $2,000 per person, earning Strickland roughly $480,000 a year for four days of work per week, and twelve weeks off. His business is a great laundry for his jobs with Joe. This is Apex Self-Defense's fourth year. The only people who have tried to take the course again for free were a woman and, later, a man, both of whom ended up making sexual propositions to Strickland and dropped out shortly thereafter.

He offers training of attack dogs and their owners, but few people will accept the liability for a lethal animal, where a simple verbal miscue can unleash otherworldly violence.

Guns are much easier. He helps his graduates apply for concealed-carry permits, still not easy to get in California, but doable if you have connections in the county, which Strickland does.

He likes this work and he loves not so much the money but what the money buys.

He's thirty-three years old.

He moves behind Edward, and of course, he has to shout to be understood.

"Edward, keep your elbows in and bend your knees! Relax! Breathe evenly! It's not about muscle."

Edward's life-sized torso target is only ten feet away, but Dan Strickland knows that ten feet is farther than it sounds when your adrenaline is pumping and you've got a heavy gun in your hands. Edward is midway through his course but only half his shots this close are hitting the kill zone. Edward is a young gym manager who lives in a rough part of San Ysidro and sometimes sees gang activity in his neighborhood. Sometimes he has to carry cash from the gym to his car. He's got a wife and a daughter. Strickland knows that because Edward is a bodybuilder, he thinks large muscles will make him powerful, but Edward strangles his pistol and the strain shivers the barrel, ruining his accuracy and jacking up his stress. Edward finishes his rapid volley, lowers his gun to the bench, and looks at Strickland through his shooting glasses, eyes bugged and sweating hard.

Strickland toggles in the well-perforated target, replacing it with a fresh one. "Let's try ten feet again, Ed. You can't be missing these shots. You've got to be perfect inside ten feet, great at twenty, and good at thirty. You're still up from last week, so, right direction, Ed. Now, address the threat with calm and cool."

The most valuable thing that Dan can do for his students is to make them positive and confident, but still aware of their weaknesses. The first is easy. By the time they've made it through eighty hours of shooting, hand-to-hand fighting, bear spray applications, weapon-retention, reaction conditioning, and fitness training—they'll be positive and confident, all right. But if they're not truthful about their weaknesses, those weaknesses might get them killed. *You're only as strong as your weakness*, he tells them. *Your goal is to walk way. Your goal is to stay alive.*

From the moment his applicants sit down across from him in the Apex office, Strickland probes them for weakness. He senses it by their bodies, expressions, their words and clothes, their complexions, their smells, even their handwriting. After their first day of evaluation and training, Strickland knows exactly what these mortals must do to survive the things they fear. His job is to make them do it, and equip them.

Edward needs to fire another thousand rounds at ten feet into the paper torso.

Molly, the English teacher, needs eye surgery. She's a natural with a pistol, shoots tight groups at ten feet and is capable at thirty. But she wears glasses, and her heavy lenses steam up when she's under exertion, and she won't wear contacts, and she doesn't want some guy cutting into her eyes. Strickland has been cajoling her for four weeks now on the merits of LASIK. Some of his students have had it, all agreeing it's the best $4,000 they've ever spent. Molly wants good eyes and she wants to please him. He's offered to help pay for her surgery.

He stands behind her and watches. When she's emptied her pistol, she turns and smiles at him.

"You're killing them today, Molly."

"Yes, I am. I hit the public range twice this week."

"I see those glasses are a bit steamed up."

"It's like shooting through fog."

"Get the surgery, girl. It could save your life."

"I'm leaning in that direction but I will not accept one penny from you."

"As you wish. Just do it."

"I'd accept a cup of coffee or a beer, though. When this is over. When I graduate."

"Let's graduate you first."

Her expression cools almost imperceptibly.

"You call the shots, Dan."

After shooting is lunch, twenty minutes of meditation, then two hours of hand-to-hand, an hour of situational weapon retention, and another hour of de-escalation. Bear spray comes last, always last, showers optional.

In the hand-to-hand, short, slender Molly kicks and hits him *hard*. As instructor, Dan is padded up, but a mule kick to the balls is still a mule kick to the balls. The eye-rakes still smash the catcher's mask into his face, as do the palm-heel nose blows thrown with a pivot of the hips. Dan has chosen the quickest and most debilitating moves from the several martial arts he knows. The only thing he'll teach but won't let them practice on him is biting.

His students end the day with a rough hour of weights and stretches and leave Apex well after dark, mentally and physically exhausted.

Dan stands by the door and shakes their hands as they leave. Then climbs the stairs to his penthouse, exhausted too.

He sits down at his computer and calls up his favorite Tijuana newspapers, searching their pages for any mention of a dog found dead or wounded at the Furniture Calderón shoot-out. Tries the gruesome, anonymously operated *Blog Narco*, always a good bet.

Nothing about a dog that night, shot or not. Of course not, thinks Dan. Tijuana is full of dogs. Why should even a wounded one make the news?

In the bedroom he gets ready to shower, looking down at Joe's crate and all the dog's beloved stuff. Joe loves plush toys. Dan has yet to know another dog that would leave the squeaker working in a plush skunk for months on end.

Joe.

Strickland checks his phone.

It's Héctor:

?????

And a picture of a dog on the shoulder of a dirt road. It's not Joe, but Dan's eyes burn as he steps into the shower, and it's not from the bear spray.

6

Bettina sits in her window cubicle at the *Coastal Eddy* offices in Laguna, looking out at Coast Highway. The last paragraph of her story on the rescue of Felix is done. The winter morning is bright and cool and the Pacific glimmers like a mirror. The cars on the highway glide.

Felix lies in a patch of sun beside her desk. He seems less fretful than yesterday, and slightly more curious about his new human.

Jean Rose, Bettina's editor, bustles into the cubicle. "Betts, incredible—we put up the dog story two hours ago, and the views are incredible! *Coastal Eddy* has never seen this kind of engagement before. Messages still pouring in, and pictures of other dogs that look like our hero. Great work on the print story too."

"I'm glad you like it."

"Just a few questions."

Jean Rose is a bright, optimistic woman, mid-sixties and always dressed more up than down. Tasteful jewelry, light makeup and lipstick, hair casually perfect. She treats Bettina as a promising, in-the-rough underling, but in a gracious and helpful way. She offers Felix a treat from the jar on Bettina's desk and the dog politely takes it. Jean sits opposite her reporter.

"I had standard poodles in my dog days," she says. "I miss them."

"Get another one, Jean."

"Too much work."

"Get a lazy one, like a retired greyhound or something."

"No, I like my freedom. Now, your print story—what about the boy who saved Felix? Can we name him?"

"Not a good idea if cartels were mixed up in Felix getting shot. Dr. Rodríguez didn't get the boy's name. The doctors didn't even have time to thank him. Because of how serious it was."

Jean Rose nods, purses her lips. Bettina thinks that she'd someday like to have what Jean has: brains and class. To be an arriver, not a striver. Arriving at yourself and liking what you find.

"I'd like to go back down there, find the boy, and get his story," Bettina says. "I know where the shoot-out happened and I can ask around. Someone will know who he is. I'll keep his name out of it. No pictures."

"You know, Bettina, that's worth pursuing at some point," says Jean. "But first I'll need the council wrap, and your summer festival preview. And, of course, the calendar. We *are* a community newspaper, after all. Not an international one. Which, I think someday would be a good place for you."

Bettina thanks her, and Jean smiles, but Bettina feels her usual annoyance with the boring city hall stuff, the puff pieces on Laguna's several art festivals, the tedium of the weekly entertainment calendar. Just as she told Felix during their long wait at the border yesterday, Bettina likes stories that *matter*.

She follows her boss's gaze out the window, to where LBPD officer Billy Ray Crumley is pushing his patrol e-bike toward the *Coastal Eddy* front door. He's got on his helmet and his navy-blue Bike Team uniform: shorts, a shirt, and a blue LBPD windbreaker.

"Here's Billy, right on time." Jean Rose winks pleasantly and rises.

Bettina hears him out in the lobby, greeting Marin, the receptionist. Billy has a pleasantly forceful voice and he's a talker if there ever was one. She can't hear his words, but she tracks his movements just by their sound: first a greeting to millionaire *Coastal Eddy* publisher Herb Sutton in his private office; then brief newsroom chatter with the city editor, the sports and business writers, then the arts and entertainment editor, Bettina's own Jean Rose. Bettina's cubicle is down the hall, on advertising row, because she's the latest hired and the editorial newsroom was full. Which to her was a good trade for the views of the city and the snippet of ocean beyond.

Billy works his way down advertising row and spends extra time with Allison, whom Bettina believes is secretly crushing on him, and finally, he's here, balancing his bike on her cubicle partition as his soft brown eyes behold the dog, who wags his tail.

"I just *got* to meet Felix, Bettina."

"He doesn't care for strangers, but sure."

Billy Ray, tall and rangy, balances his patrol bike against the cubicle wall, hangs his helmet on a handle bar, covers the space in two strides, and kneels in front of the dog.

Felix sits and looks him in the eyes. It's an interesting face-off; then it's Billy, not the dog, who cocks his head. Then the dog goes closer and lets Billy pet him. Bettina watches his fingers working the dog's throat and chest. Felix squints with pleasure, leans into it.

"He likes you," says Bettina with a twinge of jealousy. Wonders if gregarious Billy Ray Crumley likes that everybody likes *him*.

Billy gets one hand behind each ear, jiggles them gently, flaps relaxed and flopping. Felix aims his pleasure-squinted eyes into Billy's.

"Yeah, boy," says the Texan. He breaks his gaze with the dog to look up at Bettina. Billy Ray has this way of looking right into her, and Bettina takes it in. She's pretty sure she looks into him too. He's always pleasant. Always here. Some of the *Coastal Eddy* staff tease her about him. He's dark haired and good looking and five years older than Bettina. He's rumored to have left a bad marriage back in Wichita Falls, Texas, but he's never once shown any interest in seeing Bettina other than right here, on his Coast Highway Bike Team rounds. So she might just be part of the furniture.

"Bettina, this is one fine dog. You did good. Your video is going crazy, so now this little street dog is famous."

Billy stands and gets a kibble from his windbreaker pocket—lots of dogs in Laguna—and lures Felix back to his place in the sun with it.

"Well, Bettina, it's really fine to see you again."

"And you, Billy."

That look of his.

"Rain later this week," he says. They always note the weather.

"Cool too."

"Spring's just a couple of weeks away."

"That means orioles on my bird feeders, and tourists crowding into town," says Bettina.

He puts his helmet on, leaves the strap undone, and rights his bicycle, its saddle knocking against the gun holstered high on his hip. He tips the helmet visor with one hand, like a movie cowboy, which Bettina finds funny.

"I'll drop by tomorrow, if that's all right."

"I have interviews in the morning."

"Afternoon, then."

As the man with the Bike departs, Joe smells the familiar scents of men's shoes and socks and the sweet, attractive smell of gun oil and leather. Hoppe's is not in Joe's vocabulary, only in his immense, evolving encyclopedia of smells. It's the same gun oil Dan uses. A sweet, comforting smell. He wonders if Dan knows this guy.

He thinks that her name is Bettina and his is Billy.

After grinding out the calendar and city hall stuff and setting up some Festival of Arts interviews, Bettina uses her work computer and *Coastal Eddy*'s fast internet to get the Tijuana newspapers.

Tijuana is a big city, awash in newspapers and tabloids. There's *Frontera*, *La Crónica*, *El Sudcaliforniano*, *La Voz*, *Razón*, *Zeta*. There are dozens of online publications, too, from *Restaurant Week* to the *Gringo Gazette*.

Her favorite is the daily *Sol de Tijuana*, for its handy translation button and good archives.

She goes back to the second of February, the day after the boy took Felix to the clinic, but the story of the shoot-out happened too late to make the edition.

But there it is on February third, the lead article:

Deadly Gun Battle Kills Six

Six men were left dead Wednesday night in a bloody gunfight that started in the Furniture Calderón factory downtown.

"Some of the victims appear to be Sinaloan Cartel soldiers while others are members of the New Generation Cartel," said Municipal Police captain Benecio Zumbaya Bertrán. "It appears that the Tijuana narcos were attempting to steal drugs and cash belonging to their rivals. This inter-cartel fighting is increasingly deadly. This is part of the reason Tijuana is the bloodiest city in Mexico."

Bettina knows that Tijuana was the murder capital of the *world* just two years ago, and is on track to regain its title in this still-young year.

The Calderón shoot-out pictures of the dead are unpublishable by US media standards—bodies shot to ribbons, blanched and bloody in the camera flashes. Two on the street. Four in the factory. The details aren't great, but four of the men are dressed in street clothes and two in military-looking tactical wear.

Zumbaya himself is a grim-faced man with fierce black eyes and pock-marked cheeks. His coat lapel is studded with stars and decorations.

She reads on:

Captain Zumbaya stated that no drugs or other contraband were recovered and that four automatic rifles of North American manufacture that were left behind have been confiscated as evidence.

"We believe that several of the gunmen escaped in a white van that was parked on a side street west of the factory," he said. "Increasingly, automatic weapons are being used in cartel violence against each other and against law enforcement. The cartels have more firepower than we do."

Witnesses say that the shooting began inside the Furniture Calderón factory and warehouse, and soon spilled into the downtown streets. No bystanders suffered injury. The factory itself sustained bullet damage, and several chairs and sofas were riddled, according to owner Juan Calderón.

"Nothing like this has ever happened here before," he said. "This is a peaceful neighborhood. Furniture Calderón has been here for forty years."

Bettina figures that the police found no drugs or money, because the victors took it all away in the white van. She wonders, with her reporter's suspicion, whether Juan Calderón had been questioned, and how Captain Zumbaya knew it was the New Generation ripping off the Sinaloans, and not the other way around. Did it matter?

Bettina finishes the article, but it says nothing about a dog or a boy.

She has no better luck with *La Crónica, El Sudcaliforniano,* or *Frontera.*

Nothing anywhere about a boy and a shot dog or a veterinary clinic.

Which makes sense to Bettina: Why would the boy talk to the press about a cartel gun battle? The cartels are famous for killing and disappearing witnesses to their crimes. Running through the streets with Felix, the boy was probably scared, but maybe even more so as he lay in bed that night and thought about what he'd done.

She calls the Veterinary Clinic of Saint Francis of Assisi, and gets Dr. Lucero.

"He came home late last night," she says in her rapid Spanish. "He was never taken to the police station. He was held in a small apartment in Agua Caliente. He was interrogated and beaten and driven to Chapultepec Park, where they let him out. He was disoriented and got lost in the forest. He was mugged, but finally someone gave him a ride home."

It takes Bettina a moment to process and organize her words in Spanish. Wasn't all this violence at least partly her fault, for taking Felix from the clinic, right under the noses of the policemen? Maybe she should have just kept to her gringa business and stayed here in Laguna to do her city council and calendar stories. Stories that *matter*? Such as a veterinarian who saves a dog's life and gets beaten by the police? Yes, Bettina thinks. This is exactly a story that matters. A lot.

But at what cost? Her voice is a trembling whisper. "I am so sorry. I'm so sorry. Is the doctor okay?"

"He is angry and humiliated but he is fine."

"May I speak with him?"

"Surely."

"Buenos dias, Señorita Blazak," says the doctor, his voice soft but re-solved. He says the police were interested in two things: Who had ad-opted the shot dog that the clinic treated in early February, and which sedatives and painkillers was he dispensing at the clinic perhaps for people, not animals? Of course, the veterinarian explains, he is not a drug peddler. And he told them nothing of Bettina and the dog. He destroyed the adoption forms as soon as he got home. But the doctor plays down the horrors of last night, sounding more embarrassed than anything.

"I am honored you gave him my name," he says.

"I'm so moved by what you did. And the price you have paid."

"It was a terrible thing," he says. "But maybe a small good came of it. When they were beating me and asking questions, I tried to ignore the pain. Let my mind go free. And when they asked again about the dog, I remembered that you wanted to write an article about the boy who brought him in. And through the pain, I remembered the boy told me he lived on Coahuila Street, across from Furniture Calderón. Surely you could find him, but you must now realize how dangerous it is to do anything in Tijuana. Anything, even good things. If you write about him, you and the boy could both pay a large price for a small story. You should consider not writing it. I would not write it if I were you."

Bettina Blazak—always up for a fight when told what she can and can-not do—feels a familiar spark beginning inside her. She's had that spark ever since she can remember. She likes it. Considers it a genetic plus, a Polish-Irish thing. And it can become a flame in the blink of an eye. Then a fire. The fire that made her fight her brothers when they turned on her, the fire that forced her to outshoot everybody on the trap range at the Olympic team tryouts, the fire that sends her down Coast Highway on her road bike at forty miles an hour, that makes her paddle hard to drop in on a hollow five-foot wave at Brooks Street beach in Laguna. She likes the fire.

But she knows that Rodríguez is right: she'd be putting the heroic boy in danger if he were seen talking to her by the wrong people.

"Yes, I understand," she says.

"How is he, Felix?"

"He's warming up to me and his new life. I think he likes me a little more than he did yesterday."

"I saw your video. It is very good."

"Thank you, Doctor."

"You and your dog will be wonderful together. Tell him Dr. Rodríguez says hello."

Before leaving the office, Bettina checks her *Coastal Eddy* mail and media feeds again, sees another batch of Felix look-alike pictures. Some are from Mexico, but most are from the United States. She had no idea how many "relatives" her Mexican street dog has.

Also, scores of messages. Many of them are accounts from other dog rescuers. Many say how lucky the dog was; others how lucky Bettina is. Some congratulate her. Some warn her about the terrible diseases that street dogs often carry. Others say she should adopt more animals and bring them to the United States for adoption. Some tell her she should have left the dog south of the border, where all Mexicans belong. There are plenty of American dogs that need help.

And an interesting email from someone calling himself Teddy Delgado:

Dear Ms. Blazak,

Felix's real name is Joe, and I raised him from when I was ten. It was the best time of my life. When my parents died, Joe was taken away from me. I said goodbye to him and have not seen him since. Then today I saw your video. I am very sorry what happened to him. But so incredibly, incredibly happy that he's alive! Do you mind if I come to Laguna Beach to see him? I don't have a lot of money but I want to buy him from you. I love him more than any living person or thing.

Sincerely,
Teddy Delgado

Bettina thinks before answering. That last sentence from the boy is among the most beautiful and—given Teddy's circumstances—saddest she's ever read. On the other hand, what if he just made this story up? He could be an adult, a bad actor, delusional. Or just mistaken. Look at all the look-alikes! But his story really is fantastic.

Bettina would like to hear more of it.

Dear Mr. Delgado,

You can visit Felix and tell me your story, but I won't sell him to you or anyone else. Before you come here, I need to know more about you. I want you to write me again and tell where you were living when your parents died, and how they died. And why Joe was taken away from you. And where he went.

Teddy gets right back:

I will do that and call you when I get to Laguna. It might be a while. I'm trying to do well in school, and I can't drive yet.

Teddy's mention of the death of his mom and dad is much more than just sad and intriguing to Bettina Blazak.

It's a powerful, mainline connection to Keith, her youngest older brother, dead at age twenty from a fentanyl-laced vape pen. Jobless and homeless. Living under Highway 163, near the zoo in San Diego. An achingly sensitive boy and man. Once a writer of poetry. Former student, former bass player, former horseman, former janitor, former dishwasher, former carpet cleaner, former drug dealer. Once described himself to Bettina as a "former human." Prone to bad decisions, alcohol, and strong pharmaceuticals.

Older than Bettina by thirteen minutes.

Her beautiful, quiet, tortured twin.

Beena and Keefo: their names in their small, private language.

Which their mom, an English teacher, called cryptophasia, and forbade in the Blazak home, warning that it would slow down their English language development.

Which of course Beena and Keefo found extremely funny, given that their English was just fine.

Sitting in her office on Coast Highway, Bettina gazes out the window and remembers when they were five, Keith saying his book, *Turtle Splash! Countdown at the Pond*, was way better than her book, *"Let's Get a Pup," Said Kate*.

There was another book back then, in the You Read to Me, I'll Read to You series: *Very Short Stories to Read Together.* They agreed it was very good and read the stories to each other.

She smiles slightly. Six years ago, when Keith left on his next journey, Bettina made a deal with him and herself: she would remember only his goodness, not his pain.

7

That evening at sunset, Billy Ray Crumley leans against a streetlamp outside the *Coastal Eddy* building, watching the front door, nervous as hell. He's fresh from the PD showers, his best mother-of-pearl snap-button western shirt on—white with black piping on the yokes—and jeans he ironed himself the night before. Lucchese boots, a boxy brown blazer against the chill. It feels weird to dress up for somebody who isn't Lorna.

Through the windows, he tracks Bettina as she passes the cubicles, her leash hand extended. A blue bag over one shoulder. She's got on that red satin blouse and black jeans and her black duster. She's a big woman and pretty, and watching her now, his heart does a little hop. It's been a long time since he's felt like this, and he's not at all sure if what he's about to do is right.

The leash in one hand, here she comes through glass front door.

He holds open the door for her, sees the surprise on her face. Felix sniffs his boots as Billy and Bettina retreat from the sidewalk pedestrians. Felix sits and looks up at her.

"Bettina, I was just wondering if you might like to get a cup of something or a drink maybe, sorry to just surprise you, but my shift started early today, and I covered for Hanson yesterday, so, it was all, you know, it worked out perfect so I had this free time all the sudden and . . ."

Billy feels this whole thing spinning away from him. He can never just shut himself up when he gets enthused about something. Felix senses his excitement.

"Yeah, Billy, sure," says Bettina. "A drink after work is a good thing."

"Oh man, this is great. Thanks, Bettina."

"You bet. The Cliff is dog-friendly."

"I love that place."

They take two stools at the end of a long narrow table that spans the entire length of the restaurant. Felix lies down under the table, between them. Bettina gets the water bowl from her bag, and the waiter fills it from a sweating steel pitcher. They order drinks and he leaves menus.

The western sky is a cloud-jam of gray and black, illuminated by orange from beneath. Billy's glad he's sitting next to her instead of smack-dab in front of her, where he'd look at that face and just say one stupid thing after another. He knew upon meeting her those several weeks ago that she was intelligent, much more intelligent than him, making her both attractive and scary.

Billy talks about growing up in Wichita Falls: a family of five. Mom a school librarian and Dad a deputy, both Wichita Falls High School jocks—Mom fastpitch softball and Dad baseball. Billy threw his first baseball at age three. Went through a living room window and landed on the lawn, but Billy was already in love with the game. By the time he hit high school, he had an easy natural delivery and an unnaturally live fastball. His brother Arnie caught him, not an easy thing to do, with that velocity and the ball veering, dipping, sailing. College offers but he signed with Kansas City out of high school. No agent—dumb, Billy admits—got a small bonus, spent two solid seasons in Triple-A before they called him up. He made twelve appearances in middle relief, gave up buckets of runs on hits and walks. Lots of strikeouts, though.

"It was always the control," he says. "Even back as far as Little League. Not wild. Just fractions of an inch. But you get up to the pros and they'll just wait for the mistake and if you make it, you will pay. And I always made it. They sent me back down and I played out the contract, then went to college back in Wichita. I was a major-league hero in town but I felt like a loser. Took me a while to shake that off."

They drink beers and eat dinner and watch the heaving, twinkling Pacific.

Billy hopes he doesn't sound self-pitying, because he isn't. He's just a little touchy about it—MLB—and he doesn't follow the Show at all now, doesn't keep up with his friends who still play, doesn't talk or think about it much except when he must, like right now.

"I still get to play, though," he says cheerfully. "They got this Southern California Amateur League, and we have us a time."

Billy is relieved when Bettina starts talking about herself. Not just relieved, *happy*. He likes that her family in Anza was close, kind of like his was, that they had horses and hunted birds with dogs, and her getting invited to try out for the Olympic trap team proves she was as good at shooting as he was at baseball. Heck, maybe better.

Billy's phone rings and he sees who it is. Bets this isn't a social call.

Apologizes to Bettina, steps away from the table, and finds a place between the little shops where he's away from the crashing sound of the waves.

"Arnie, what's up?"

"Just checking my feeds here and I see that your reporter friend posted a dog story last night. Everybody here's talking about it."

Billy isn't so sure he should have mentioned Bettina to his professionally nosy older brother. Too late now. "Yeah, so?"

"Well, I want to know when and where that dog was shot."

"Then read the story."

"It's not in the story. The veterinarian speculates about a shoot-out, and the police aren't sure."

"Why do you care?"

"You know damn well why, Billy—because I take my territory seriously. I need to know exactly when and exactly where. If she knows, maybe she'll tell you, Romeo."

Billy has to think about this, but he already knows he'll do what he can for Arnie. Because he's my brother, Billy thinks. Because Arnie doesn't ask for favors lightly. Because he's DEA and serious as a heart attack.

"If she knew when and where the dog got shot, she'd of put it in the story," Billy says.

"Please ask her. Don't say anything about me and what I do. I really appreciate this, little brother. Hope it doesn't put you in a spot. I'm going to call you back in one hour."

"Okay. She's cool. We're cool."

After dinner they head north on the Main Beach boardwalk, past the lifeguard stand, toward Heisler Park.

"Bettina, do you know where and when Felix got shot?"

"Who wants to know?"

"Just me, curious is all."

"Don't bs me, Billy."

He feels stupid he can't get away with a simple white lie. "That was my brother, Arnie, on the phone. He saw your video and liked it."

She looks at Billy skeptically. "The answer is no—I don't know exactly where or when. Only that the boy brought the dog to the clinic, which was February first, like my video said. There was a big cartel shoot-out that night in Tijuana. I read every newspaper account I could find, and there was nothing about a dog being shot. Not that there would be, with six human beings dead. Why does your brother want to know, Billy?"

Billy feels trapped between Arnie and Bettina, but he also feels like he owes her some basic honesty. He tells her what Arnie does for a living.

Bettina comes to a stop on the boardwalk, and Felix sits immediately and looks up at her again. "Strange," she says.

"How so?"

They leave the boardwalk for the shoreline, and Bettina tells Billy all the odd things about Felix: from his unknown life on the streets of Mexico that left him likely uncared for yet neutered; to his mysteriously inflicted and near-fatal wound, possibly not an accident, possibly sustained during a cartel versus cartel shoot-out; to his miracle rescue by an anonymous boy and the good doctor Rodríguez; to the Tijuana police, who were looking for a shot dog thirty days later, on the very day that she adopted him at the clinic; to the same Tijuana police who brutally interrogated Rodríguez about the dog, then lied to his wife and to Bettina about it; to Felix's fine off-leash behavior and his perfect understanding of English commands.

She tells Billy about the message from Teddy Delgado, a boy claiming to have raised her dog, whom he called Joe, from puppyhood, and who of course wants him back.

Now the DEA is suddenly interested.

"That's a lot of mystery around one little dog," says Billy.

"I want to interview the boy who saved him. He'd be able to explain some of this, and he'd make a great story."

"You know where to find him?"

"I can find him."

"I'm not so sure how far you should go, poking into this, Bettina. Anything to do with drug cartels is bad news."

She stops again and Felix sits and looks at her. Billy smiles welcomingly but Bettina's voice goes sharp.

"Billy Ray, anytime someone tells me what I can and cannot do, that makes me mad. And I will fight and I do fight."

"I'm not telling you what to do. I'm saying it's dangerous to be asking around about cartel crimes in Mexico. That's all."

"I'm not stupid."

"You're smart. But I see the other side of things. From being a cop. I'd just hate to see you and that boy mixed up in trouble."

"The dog is mine and his story is mine."

"Well, okay, Bettina. I'm telling you to be careful, so if I have to fight you just to say that, then I guess I will. Be careful, woman."

She gives Billy Ray a look he can't read. He feels examined.

"I will, Billy. And if you're that worried about me, maybe you should come too. Down to Tijuana to find the boy and get his story. It matters. We can't be seen talking to him. We can't name him or show him on video or in pictures. But I want to tell his story."

Truth is, Billy Ray would follow this woman to the gates of hell if that's what it would take to save her fool ass. He's felt this way about a lot of people in his life, from family to friends to the general public he has sworn to protect and serve. His father told him a lot of cops feel it, this need to be of help. Which, of course, occasionally gets them killed.

"I'm off Tuesdays and Fridays."

They climb the concrete stairs to Heisler Park. Billy likes riding his bike up here on patrol. The Pacific is different every day, sometimes gray and solemn, other times chipper and sparkling, still others pale green and churning with whitecaps. He thought Wichita Falls was beautiful until he came here. Tonight, the Laguna Art Museum is lit up and the path through the rose garden has only a few late-winter tourists.

Billy and Bettina stand at the gazebo railing, looking out at the ocean. Waves slam into the big rocks below, and the spray rises white against the dark sea. Felix sits between them. Billy pats the dog's head and sneaks a look at Bettina in profile.

On the railing, her little finger touches his little finger, an event as emotionally charged as any that has happened to Billy Ray Crumley in some time.

"Tomorrow is Friday," notes Bettina. "Can you go on short notice?"

"I can and will."

A wave of gratitude breaks inside her.

"Sorry," she says. "But I need to know this boy's story—the boy who ran Felix through the rain. Billy, I hate being told what to do. And I will fight. I have this spark that leads to fire. I'm not saying it's good. But you should know."

"Peace, Bettina."

"Peace, Billy."

Back home, after Bettina turns off the lights, Joe waits for a while in his beloved Crate, with the blankets and plush Toys and chew things Bettina got for him at the big store that lets dogs in.

When he hears her breathing change, like people do when they stop moving at night, he rises and stretches and goes downstairs to the living room.

The security floodlights down in the parking garage throw a pale light through the sliding glass doors. Joe smells the big rug on the floor, its dust, and a sharp chemical deodorant that stings his nasal passages. He follows his nose along one wall: a mouse not very long ago; floor cleaner like where he grew up with Teddy, one of the many scents of Woman. He stops where one of those bugs with pincers has recently left his smell, a good smell but not to eat.

To the leather sofa with its animal scent, then under the small glass table on wooden stumps that smell like trees, to a splendid blooming kernel of popcorn like Teddy and Dan sometimes give him, which crunches deliciously on his molars. In one corner of the living room stands a tall thing with a smell that Joe recognizes but has no word for: the coconut in the surfboard wax that sits in clumps on the top and is rough and salty on his tongue.

The kitchen tile is cool on Joe's feet as he hunts crumbs around the refrigerator and under the counters, nothing much here but the floor cleaner again and some fine sand. In the room where Woman sits and does things, Joe smells the piquant tires of the big-wheeled thing like Billy had in Bettina's room in the city. Possibly a Bike. And there's a tall wooden box, from between the doors of which comes the Gun smell that was always very strong on Aaron and sometimes strong on Dan, too, and that Billy has.

Back upstairs, Joe sits on the floor and rests his snout on the bed, drawing in the smells of the Bettina, who breathes steadily just a few feet away. He can see one side of her face, but the rest of it is buried in the pillow. She has many scents and he likes them all. Bettina is a long name to remember. On the bedstand is an empty glass that smells similar to Aaron's many empty glasses and a book that smells old. Joe touches his nose to the small, flat, angled piece of ribbon that protrudes from between the pages. He sniffs down where the bedspread almost meets the carpet: old dust.

Joe lies down next to the bed, where the smell of Bettina is strong and good, sets his head on his front paws, and thinks of Dan, who was very happy when Joe found the drugs and money. Who took him to the beach. Then Aaron, who was sad when he didn't find enough drugs and money, no matter how hard he tried. Then he remembers his happiest times of all: wrestling with Teddy when he was a puppy, and the way Teddy taught him to find things.

The Teams.

Almost Five Years Before
the Shoot-Out . . .

8

Street Mutt's pups were born on Sunday, April 9, in a big crate on the floor of a bedroom belonging to a ten-year-old boy named Teddy. Teddy named his favorite pup Joe.

Joe's was a dark, warm, hungry world, and he knew only the sweet thing that came from his mother and the strength of the creatures all around him trying to get the sweet thing too.

Joe couldn't know that his mother's name was Mabel, that she was petite for a Labrador retriever, almost white, with a cute black nose, a pleasant disposition, and a passion for tennis balls. To him she was just the warm large thing that fed him and licked him and let him sleep up against her always thumping, gurgling belly.

Joe couldn't know, either, that giving birth had been an urgent ordeal for Mabel, leaving small bloody dogs all over her crate pad to lick clean and feed with her swollen, tender teats. The little beasts jostled for position along her underbody, never satisfied, moving from nipple to nipple and sucking hard for more.

At three weeks old, Joe had become bossy and got whichever nipple he wanted and could out-wobble his siblings across the floor to Teddy when he came to play with him, which was often.

Joe loved the way Teddy looked at him and held him. As his eyes grew stronger, Joe studied Teddy's face. He was like a god, though Joe had no concept of God and never would. When Teddy lifted him to his chest and kissed his nose, Joe could feel the boy's heart beating and smell the wonderful smells of his mouth. Being high in the air like this should have frightened him, but in Teddy's arms it didn't. Joe's trust was instinctive and unconditional. If he jumped, the boy would catch him.

Later, when Teddy began giving him meat, and Mabel was spending long hours away from the crate, and his siblings were vanishing one by one, Joe gave himself to the boy and took the boy for himself. The emotional exchange was sudden, automatic, and complete. It was easy to understand: Teddy and Joe were above his mother and siblings now. Joe couldn't articulate it, but his mother and siblings mattered less. His decision was final. And though Joe couldn't know it, this would happen again in his life, three times.

Now Teddy was his world. Teddy was his Boy. He was Teddy's Dog. Those were Joe's first four words: Joe, Teddy, Boy, Dog.

Joe didn't know the word Team yet, though before long he would understand that Teddy and he were a Team.

That night he slept in what he would someday come to call the Team Bed.

At eight weeks, Joe began to learn things from his Boy. They started with the leash in his backyard and in the house, always a reward from Teddy's pocket when Joe did something right.

Sit. *Treat.* Stay. *Treat.* Come. *Treat.*

After dark, the Boy held him on his lap on the floor in front of the TV, where a small man spoke words that didn't seem to come from him, and a small dog seemed to understand him. It was hard to tell where the small man and dog were, and they moved strangely. Joe knew that his Boy wanted him to do something, but he didn't know what. So he wagged his tail briefly. Sniffed the boy's pockets for treats. Teddy watched the TV very hard, though, pointing at it, and talking to Joe. His Boy also had a book with a girl and a dog on the front.

During training—at all times, in fact—Joe naturally watched Teddy's face and hands, and listened to his voice, then tried to do what his Boy was telling him. If it was the wrong thing, try another. Sometimes Teddy would help him: push down on his rump and pull up on the leash for sit; pull on the leash for come; tie the leash to a doorknob for stay. Joe learned fast because he wanted that kibble.

When Joe was ten weeks old, he squeezed out of his crate and followed the smell of kibble to a small room that was near where the people ate. It had swinging doors that looked like he could get through. He could hear Teddy outside the house. The Big People were gone. The kibble was somewhere in here, though, so he nosed his way in the pantry. There were shelves of food and food-like things. The smells came to him strongly and namelessly: potatoes, white onions, cheese snacks, oranges, bits of mown grass on the floor, tracked in from outside. And, of course, the mouthwatering kibble, up high and out of sight.

He pulled himself up on the lowest shelf, scratching with his hind feet for purchase, reaching blindly with his front paws, but they landed in something smooth and heavy that slid free and sent him to the floor on his back. The thing landed on top of him, clear, cold, and hard. When Joe scrambled upright, it fell to the floor and made a bonking sound. He could see it and see through it at the same time.

He tried again and fell on his back again, a long thin container landing on him this time. It wasn't heavy like the other. Joe righted himself quickly and investigated the unusual thing. Its top had come open and a sharp-toothed blade pricked his nose. He found a tube of metal paper inside that came off in tangy metallic bits in his mouth.

Joe got the tube out and went to work, holding it still with his front paws, tearing at it patiently until he was lying in a field of shiny metal bits. Then somehow the tube rolled away from him until there was no metal paper left, only a hollow tube that Joe chewed to shreds in less than two minutes.

He fell asleep in the mess, still smelling the kibble way up there and out of sight. Which is where Teddy found him a few minutes later.

"Bad dog, Joe. Good thing I found you, not Dad."

Even at ten weeks, Joe understood Teddy's tone of voice very clearly, most of the time. He cowered and looked at the floor and not at Teddy. Teddy scolded him in a low voice and Joe peed, instinctively sensing that this would not make his Boy happy.

Teddy ordered Joe to come and went down the hallway to his room.

"Crate up, Joe," he said, and the puppy looked at him, then walked into the cage. "Why did you go in the pantry, Joe? What were you looking for?"

Teddy latched the door and left the room, and Joe felt a terrible sadness inside because he had made his Boy unhappy. It was a crushing feeling, and his Boy's unhappiness was something Joe wanted to take away. Lick it away, chase it away, bark it away, or bite or chew or whine it away. Joe heard him going down the hall and into the place where the people ate and then he heard the doors open on the Kibble Room. He could hear the crackling of the metal paper. And the thump of the heavy glass dish that had landed on him, being lifted from the floor.

Footsteps and his Boy was back.

"It was the kibble, wasn't it?"

Joe certainly understood Kibble, and he wagged his tail.

"Did you smell it from all the way in here?"

Joe had no idea what Teddy was saying but he wagged his tail again. He could see that Teddy wasn't unhappy anymore, so he went to the crate door but his Boy did not let him out.

Instead, for the next few minutes, Teddy hid very small amounts of kibble—just a bit or two—all around the house.

Then let Joe out of the crate, leashed him, and waved one small kibble in front of the puppy's nose.

"Find," he said. "Joe, find kibble."

Puzzled, Joe sat.

"*Find kibble*," said Teddy, holding the food under the dog's nose again. Find?

How about . . .

Joe led the way, his Boy just behind him, down the hallway and into the pantry. Here the smell of his dog food was strong as before. Joe lifted his nose into the rich meaty river of scent. Wagged his tail and sat, looking into the smell. He still couldn't see it, but he knew it was there.

"Okay, Joe, that was easy. Now let's try this."

He led the dog into the dining room and held out some food again and told him to find it.

Joe wasn't sure what *find* meant, but finding the kibbles made Teddy happy, so Joe followed his nose to the two small nuggets in the far corner. Ate them fast as he looked at his Boy.

"Good dog, Joe!"

Teddy's voice was so pleased. His face so happy. Joe pushed his small plump body against Teddy's leg.

There in the dining room, Joe found two more treasures under the table, and one in a wadded-up paper napkin on the seat of a chair.

Which led him into the adjacent foyer, where he discovered one nugget beneath the hat-and-coatrack, two under the mat, and one under the bench.

Then to the living room, where kibble scent streamed into him from under a couch cushion, behind the TV stand, inside a drawer, beneath the throw rug, under the cushion of the big skin-smelling chair.

"You only missed two, Joe!"

Joe charged his Boy, grabbed one of his shoelaces, and shook it back and forth with all his pudgy might.

That evening, Joe watched Teddy at the computer, the light from the monitor faint on his beautiful, expressive face. Teddy seemed to be very interested. Joe tried to stay awake but he drifted in and out of sleep, dreaming of his mother's milk while, unknown to him, his Boy read online articles on how to train dogs for search and rescue, or to detect just about anything—bombs, guns, drugs, cash, even truffles, cancer, depression, diabetes, and bedbugs!

———

By the time he was six months old, Joe weighed twenty pounds and his adult form had taken shape. From his Labrador mother, Mabel, he inherited a blockish head, an intelligent face, a long tail, and her pale skin and coat. He got Street Mutt's slender torso, long legs, tan ovals, and the jaunty terrier button-rose ears.

Day after day, he became more adept at finding the very small amounts of whatever Teddy hid around the house and in the yards and garage: dabs of peanut butter, a clove, orange seeds, a piece of toilet paper brushed with alcohol and allowed to dry, scraps of flavored dental floss, chips of bath soap, dandelions from the yard, single flakes of breakfast cereals. New things every day.

Once Teddy had given him a good whiff of the target item and said, "Joe, *find!*" the dog would set off, drop his nose low, and begin quartering the area—sidling oddly, switching back, veering suddenly, then switching back again. And when he stopped and raised his nose to the air, it meant he had entered the scent cone, and his motion would become more direct, with fewer changes of direction and longer angles as he quartered, narrowing the cone, following the smell to its source.

Joe enjoyed this game almost as much as chasing tennis balls or chewing cow hooves. He was always so happy to see his Boy smile, and to get that treat. Simple: all he had to do was take the target scent into his dense, copious, detailed scent-cataloging memory, then follow his nose to the thing. Some things took longer because their scent was weaker. Some took longer because Teddy tried to confuse him with hot sauce, vinegar, mouthwash, milk, mustard, ketchup, deodorant, mothballs, and the scented fishing bait that Teddy and his father used at the beach. But the smells that his Boy put with the target smells only added to Joe's voluminous capacity to detect and isolate and find. Joe had no idea what scent receptors were, or that he would have three-hundred-plus million of them when he grew up, or that great Teddy, his Boy, would have only six million.

One day, Joe was excited to have Dad join him and Teddy for a game of finding things. Joe liked Dad, but Joe couldn't make him happy. His face rarely changed, even when he talked. He was calm and tired and sometimes looked and smelled like he wanted to bite something or somebody. Dad left home every morning and came home in the evening. He wore dark pants and a light shirt with a patch with a word on it, but Joe had no idea what *Tony* might mean. He drove a large white thing with a picture of a man who looked like Dad running fast with a box in one hand and a tool raised in the other. Under the picture were more words that meant nothing to Joe, and never would:

Delgado Heating and Air—Call Us First!

That day Joe found the hidden things very easily. It seemed like his nose was working better, or maybe Teddy had chosen stronger smells.

When the game was over, Joe laid himself down and listened to Teddy and Dad talk. Their voices sounded hopeful and excited, made him feel good.

Ted, I think Wade Johnson should see Joe in action.

He'll be amazed, Dad.

Joe, of course, understood only his own name and that good things were going to happen.

9

Dan Strickland can't believe what he's seeing on his phone.

Heart pounding, he watches the *Coastal Eddy* video of Joe, not dead, not injured, but looking healthy, though a little subdued.

"Felix: The Rescue of a Mexican Street Dog," has come to Dan from one of his graduates, a Newport Beach woman who remembered Joe from her time in Dan's penthouse, and hadn't minded at all if the cute dog joined her in Dan's bed after she was finished with him.

Strickland watches the video again. Joe looks kind of stunned, really, but whole and alert. The doctor talks about what the bullet did and how he had to suture the intestine and seal the artery and follow up with strong antibiotics. Dan witnesses the reporter lady—very attractive—falling in love with Joe over the five-minute segment. It comes as no surprise that she takes him home. Dan looks at the closing clip of Joe in his new home in Laguna Beach with a joyous but troubled heart.

How is he going to get Joe back from his new and obviously devoted owner? He can't exactly tell her what Joe was doing the night he was shot. Certainly not what *he* was doing. Reporters can always pry into and expose you. That's what they do. But no matter how believable and sympathetic Dan's cover story might be, he knows the reporter would never let him have Joe back.

It takes Dan Strickland all of two more seconds to realize how to get Joe back: drive to Laguna, find the *Coastal Eddy* offices and where the reporter lives, and wait for Joe to be alone. Then leash him and trot him to the Maserati and let Joe leap in, as he loves to do. Drive home.

Simple, clean, and easy. Bettina Blazak will never see him, and Joe will be happy, and the team will be back together for some much-needed profit in romantic old Mexico!

He hires two of his former associates to teach his next week of classes.

He wonders who else has seen the video and would be able to link the dog to him. Only one other man in the United States knows of his moonlighting, or of Joe's adventures south of the border. Not even Aaron knows exactly what Strickland is doing with Joe. But there are Strickland's associates in Tijuana—the New Generation Cartel, a handful of Municipal Police, and of course the Sinaloans they steal from—who know that a button-rose-eared apparent street dog has so far cost them $1,500,000 in cash, five uncut kilos of Mexican-made fentanyl, seven kilos of Mexican brown heroin, and over twenty pounds of top-grade Columbian cocaine for a total street value of . . . well, Dan has no damned idea except that he gets one-third of everything Joe finds. One-third of the currency, and the cash value of one-third of the drugs' wholesale value. Dan trusts the New Generation to do the math fairly. He counts the cartel's Tijuana faction leader—Carlos Palma, who accepted him as a partner in this risky venture—as a friend. As he does Tijuana Municipal Police captain Benicio Zumbaya, who protects and answers to Carlos. There is indeed honor among thieves.

Success breeds loyalty, Dan thinks as he packs. His secrets are safe with them as long as he's taking the risk and making them mountains of money. Mountain *ranges* of money.

That evening, just after sunset, Strickland sits in the curbside Havana Café, directly across Coast Highway from the *Coastal Eddy* offices in Laguna Beach.

Glancing at the intro of "Felix: The Rescue of a Mexican Street Dog" on his phone, Dan confirms that Bettina Blazak and Joe are now coming out the glass front door held open by a young man in shiny cowboy boots, pressed jeans, and a dumpy yoked blazer.

Joe looks great: composed, and even at this distance and through the hectic two-way traffic on the busy highway, Dan can see that Joe is attentive to the woman. He limps but not badly. Bettina Blazak is larger than Dan had expected. Probably six feet, he guesses, which, in her heeled boots makes her almost as tall as the Cowboy in the bad coat. Her dark brown hair has nice bounce, and it shines in the streetlight. She reminds Dan of his Newport Harbor High School art teacher, Miss Waters, who drove him utterly bats and damned near got him expelled and herself arrested.

Strickland leaves plenty of cash on the counter and parallels them up Coast Highway north, cars whizzing past, a river of headlights and taillights. He pulls his snap-brim fedora low, keeping one eye on Joe and his captors. At the lights he pulls almost even with them and thinks of crossing here at Thalia, but the Cowboy beats him to the crosswalk button. Dan turns his back on them as they approach, drifts into a clot of tourists looking through the Thalia Surf Shop window, noting Joe's progress reflected in the glass. He loves the way Joe's ears flap as he trots. Just incredible you can get so attached to a dog, he thinks. Irrespective of the money. Part of the sidewalk crowd, he follows them north again to the Cliff Restaurant, where a congressman whom Dan once protected from a death threat liked to dine and drink. Easy money and good food, Dan remembers.

Watching them enter the little village of shops and galleries that surround the Cliff, Dan sees that the Cowboy and the reporter don't know each other very well. The guy is as attentive as a butler, while she has the straightforward economy of movement enjoyed by people who know what they want. The man is also alert and protective: cop-like.

Strickland walks past the jewelry shop and the art galleries and the bead-and-necklace boutique and the classic longboards shop. He keeps plenty of distance because if Joe smells him, he'll likely come charging over, and that might be a little difficult to explain. Bettina leads Joe and her date to the far end of a long communal table that overlooks the swelling black sea.

Dan sits at the bar behind the diners, in the very place where he'd kept an eye on the congressman and his wife. Those were his protection days—Strickland Security.

Dan has a rear view of Bettina and her suitor. Joe is in the darkness under the table. Dan can see that they're in a meaningful conversation, and again, from their postures and the cant of their heads, don't really know each other. They're a little formal. *Getting* to know each other, Dan thinks. The lucky Cowboy.

He lays his phone on the bare table and cues up the Felix video again. Mutes it and watches Bettina Blazak on-screen, kneeling before a cautiously appreciative Joe, scratching his chest, smiling at the camera, and talking to her viewers. Dan likes the way she touches Joe. She's been around dogs.

Something odd now stirs in Dan Strickland. He hasn't felt it before and he's not even sure what it is. With women he has always accepted what is given, and over his thirty-plus years, he has been given much. But he has never given back; neither his nature nor his nurture seems to allow it. He's not really sure how you do that. Now, this odd feeling of generosity. Wanting to give her something good. It's new. Bettina on the screen is still talking, as Bettina here at the Cliff shakes her shiny hair and turns to look in Dan's direction.

He sweeps the screen to cut the light on his face, and looks down.

Dan tails them back south on Coast Highway, still plenty of highway between him and Joe, and plenty of pedestrians for cover. Joe, Bettina, and the Cowboy go down steps to the parking garage under the *Coastal Eddy* building. A moment later the Cowboy comes out on foot and continues on south down the sidewalk, sizing up the world around him. Definitely a cop, Dan thinks. Notes the lump under the frumpy, practical coat.

A red Jeep comes up the ramp and waits while the gate arm rises through the headlight beams. Dan can see Joe in the front seat, face observant, and Bettina's long look down Coast Highway before making the turn.

He gets into his car and follows the Jeep three cars back to Broadway, which becomes Laguna Canyon Road and will lead inland, Dan knows, to the freeways. But soon Bettina signals and turns right on Stan Oaks, into a small retail village tucked beneath towering eucalyptus. Dan slows and turns in without a signal, parks in front of an antiquarian bookseller, keeping an eye on the Jeep as Bettina ferries Joe through the lot. At the far end, she heads up a narrow drive leading to Canyon View Apartments—says the sign—built on caissons along the steep flank of the canyon.

Through his good Leicas, Dan watches her take one of the covered stalls that run beneath the back of the building. Bettina does whatever it is that takes women so long to do before leaving their vehicles. She and Joe finally get out, climb the stairs, and disappear, Joe perfectly fitted at her left calf, no chance he'll pull or drag her into a fall. Dan watches, wishing he were Bettina Blazak, leashed to his beloved Joe— and wishing he were Joe, leashed to Bettina Blazak.

In his rearview he sees the police radio car turn into the little shopping center. Dan slides the binoculars under the seat and takes up his phone. Watches as the cop car slowly makes its way along the shops, all closed, and only a few vehicles here this late.

It stops behind him, and Dan, phone to his ear, watches the spotlight seize his dashboard and flash off the mirror. He tells the phone he sure hopes this fucking cop will buzz off.

A moment later, the light vanishes and the radio car moves along, loops the lot, and exits onto Laguna Canyon Road, headed back to town.

Dan gets a room at the Laguna Montage for a week, where he'll blend in with the affluent tourists. From what he's seen of Bettina's work and living arrangements, it might take some time to steal Joe without getting caught.

He stands in his stupidly expensive room overlooking the twinkling black Pacific, wondering what it would be like to meet Bettina Blazak. What it would be like to be close enough to really *see* her.

And when she wasn't looking, of course, jack the dog.

10

Bettina and Billy Ray step around the potholes on Coahuila Street, where the bloody cartel shoot-out took place over a month ago.

Leading them is Luis, an old man they've just met, who knows the family of Fidelito Camacho, the boy who took a wounded dog to an animal hospital one night last month. He's well dressed and walks with a sprightly limp.

In the Coahuila barrio, he says, everybody knows everybody.

Luis speaks little English, so Bettina explains in Spanish that she and Billy are researching a story for a small newspaper in California, *Coastal Eddy*.

"I will protect Fidelito," she says. "But I need to tell his story because it matters, because that boy risked his life for a street dog."

"Fidelito will not talk to you, because the dog maybe was shot by the cartels," Luis explains in his native tongue.

"I will not use his real name. I want to talk to him privately, where we won't be seen."

"Everything is seen. They will see me talking to you, but I am old and without value and I do not fear them."

"We don't need pictures or video," says Bettina. "Only to hear his story."

"I will explain this to his father and mother, but they are pious and proud. They won't let you inside."

"Please tell them we are honest reporters who believe in God," says Bettina with a guilty current of sacrilege coursing inside her.

A Tijuana Municipal Police cruiser rolls by.

A street dog who looks like Felix hustles across the street in front of it, well out of range.

Luis tells Bettina to stay here while he talks to Fidelito's mom and dad.

"Wait," she says. "If Fidelito's parents won't let him talk to me in person, maybe they'll let him talk by phone."

"Maybe," says Luis. At Bettina's suggestion, Luis accepts her number on a small scrap of her notepad paper. He gives her a conspiratorial look.

Bettina and Billy watch from a small *zócalo* featuring a leafless sycamore tree and a flock of pigeons competing for food from an old man on a bench.

Luis knocks on a side window of a squat pink house on a dirt road intersecting Coahuila. The glass slides open and Luis talks to the screen.

A moment later Luis disappears around the back of the house.

Five minutes come and go, then Bettina's phone rings with a number not in her contacts.

"This is Fidelito but you can't use my name. My father has allowed me to talk to you only on the phone."

Fidelito's voice is high and sweet, and he mixes in some English with his Spanish.

"This is Bettina. I'm a writer. I will change your name and not take your picture or video."

"Do you have the dog? I saw him two weeks ago at the clinic and he looked good."

"I adopted him and took him to California and named him Felix. I want to write about you for my paper. I want to present you as a hero."

"I heard God's voice tell me to save the dog. He ran under a car in the back of Factoría Calderón. It was dark. Is that you in the *zócalo,* with the tall man? I can see you through a window."

Bettina waves. "Yes, Fidelito, I'm right here."

"If you look down Coahuila behind you, you will see the furniture factory. There is a back door and a loading dock. That was where I first saw the wounded dog running."

"I'm going to walk over there so my assistant can shoot some video."

"I was hiding behind a house. I heard many bullets. I saw two men run from the building, and two men who were lying in the doorway. And the dog, he climbed over the dead men and he ran. He was limping."

They approach, Billy shooting video and stills on his phone. The factory is old and the plaster and bricks are crumbling and patched over. It's kind of ominous, she thinks, a place where bad things could happen. Her viewers will see that. Billy shoots another police car going slowly past. The driver rests his elbow on the window frame and looks at them through his aviators, then smiles and waves. Bettina waves back.

"We need basic establishing shots for 'Hero Without a Face,'" she tells Billy.

The pedestrians give them a wide berth and study Bettina with stoic calm. Billy Ray gets some video of the back side of the factory. Bettina notes Billy's tight expression. Wishes he could relax some. Fidelito tells her about that night, the rain cold and some wind too.

Tells her that his father used to work in the Factoría Calderón.

They circle the building back to its entrance and go inside.

"We're inside," she tells him. "Excuse me while I talk to this man. Don't hang up. This will only take a minute."

Señor Juan Calderón greets them with a smile and a suspicious glance at the phone in Bettina's hand. Bettina tells them who they are, and explains the story they're doing about the dog wounded in the shoot-out back in February.

"Please to not take pictures here," says Calderón. "It is proprietary."

"Of course, sir," she says. "I understand."

The factory is well lit, with high ceilings. Tall racks of lumber and hides and cloth line the four walls, and the workbenches are fitted with power tools. Bettina sees the bedstands and the armchairs and the dining sets and the sofas, dozens of them, some apparently complete and others in progress.

She thanks him, looks at the workers at their stations, who watch her back, this gringa wearing a knit suit and white tennis shoes. Señor Calderón is clearly uncomfortable.

"We have never had any problems here before," he says, echoing what he had told the newspaper *El Sol de Tijuana*. "We have been here forty years."

Bettina surveys the big open factory and warehouse as best she can, itching for pictures and video. She looks at all the boxes of supplies and the tall walls for bullet holes. Thinks she sees some high up by the ceiling fans, but at that distance they might just be chipped paint or flies.

Back outside, she asks Fidelito if Felix came to him when he called out to the dog under the car.

"He was in the gutter near the back tire," Fidelito says. The call breaks up, then clears. "He was licking his belly, near his hind leg. I was on my hands and knees right there, looking under the car so I could see him. He looked at me only once. That's when I saw the blood. He whined. He looked afraid. He was patiently licking. There was still shooting from the factory. Men screamed and machine guns fired. I had a dog when I was little. He disappeared. A feeling came over me. The voice of God told me to take the dog to the clinic. Everyone knows the clinic is good and doesn't charge money."

"But he didn't come to you?"

"He was afraid. I pulled him out. He yipped and closed his teeth on my arm but he didn't bite hard. I thought he was thanking me. He let go and I ran with him all the way to Vía Rosa to get away from the guns. I didn't know if maybe who shot him would come after us to finish killing the dog. When I was far down Vía Rosa, I was able to slow down. The dog was hard to carry because he was very heavy and wet, and I held him in both arms like a baby and he curled into me and licked himself. I knew the fastest way to the clinic. And I kept looking back to see if men were coming after us, and I saw people in the darkness. I thought maybe the bullet hit the dog by accident and nobody even knew that he had been shot. God told me to run or the dog would die. The dog whimpered as I ran. The rain got heavier and I kept running and I timed my breaths to my steps. The streets and sidewalks were slippery. When I got to the clinic, I saw there was a light on in the office. There was a bell and a man finally opened the door."

Fidelito verbally coaches her down Coahuila Street to Vía Rosa, then sends her down two alleys that bring her to within eyeshot of Dr. Rodríguez's *clínica*.

"I can see the clinic, Fidelito! It's a harrowing story, Fidelito," says Bettina. "But you saved his life!"

"I only carried the dog. God saved his life. God and the doctor."

"You're too humble. You should be aware of your unselfishness and true bravery. When people read this story and see my video, they're going to be inspired by your courage. But I will never say your name or show your image. All because of what you did. You will be a hero without a face."

"Gracias, Señorita Blazak."

Bettina and Billy set off down Vía Rosa to retrace their steps to the Factoría Calderón. At the corner of Avenida Revolución, a rough-looking young man in a ratty silk sport coat right out of *Miami Vice*, wearing a belt with an enormous silver-and-turquoise buckle, offers to show them his cocaine, pure from the Sierra Madre, or his highest quality "super-ice" meth—both containing a safe amount of fentanyl, both on sale today.

Billy Ray badges him. "Can I help you?"

The young man backs away, then wheels and runs into the busy Avenida Revolución sidewalk.

Bettina and Billy continue on Vía Rosa, but two blocks later, the drug peddler and two beefy associates are coming up the sidewalk from behind them. Billy with his cop antennae spots them first. He gently ushers Bettina into a narrow curio stall filled with hanging blankets, serapes, hoodies, guitars, dresses, and chino pants. Steers her deep into the garments.

"I know you don't like being told what to do, Bettina, but stay here. I mean it."

He's gone before she can answer.

Through the hoodies and blankets and hanging guitars, she can see him in the open doorway of the shop, his back to her, feet spread, arms crossed.

Sees the three men confronting him, Billy shaking his head, hands at his sides now. Leaning into them, leading with his big open face. From Bettina's perspective, all four men seem to be talking at once. Billy steps through them toward the street, one hand waving high as if hailing a cab.

Which is exactly what he does.

Then he turns and waves Bettina out to the sidewalk, where he shepherds her into a clean white-and-orange Taxi Libre while the original drug seller curses them in loud foul language that Bettina understands.

The driver U-turns and barely misses the drug men, who follow the taxi down the street. He berates them through his open window, shaking a fist and calling them names and also trying to apologize to his fares in English.

He swiftly delivers them to Bettina's Jeep, parked not far from Factoria Calderón and now of interest to two uniformed Municipal Police officers. Two green-and-white Policía Municipal vehicles—one a sedan and the other a pickup truck—are parked on the sidewalk. Two more uniformed cops lean against the truck and watch her.

Bettina, rattled by the dealers, takes the offense in her passable Spanish, telling the police to get away from her Jeep as she digs into her purse for her key. She tells them that she learned Spanish in college and understands every word they say. At which the stocky sergeant laughs, and his beanstalk-thin officer smiles, further provoking her.

Billy tries to intervene, his LBPD badge wallet in hand, his voice in full Texas hospitality mode, but the thin cop takes him by the arm and draws his club. Billy yanks his arm free with a loud *Hands off!*

Which penetrates straight into Bettina's sprung temper, and, pulling angrily on her wad of keys, she spills half the contents of her purse onto the sidewalk.

The sergeant grabs up her phone and barks an order at his officer. The man lets go of Billy, belts his baton, and strolls to the prowl car.

Bettina follows the sergeant as the two men leaning on the truck come forward as if to intercept her.

"Do not return to Tijuana to purchase narcotics," says the sergeant, poking the phone at Bettina. "You will be arrested and charged."

"Give me that!" she barks in Spanish.

"Evidence," says the sergeant.

Bettina reaches for her phone, and the burly sergeant backs away toward the now idling prowl car, where the skinny officer waits behind the wheel.

Bettina has traveled in Mexico enough to know that local cops shake down gringo tourists all the time. She manages to get both her emergency hundred-dollar bills from her wallet, and, hands shaking, now advances on the cruiser.

The intercepting officers stop short, hands on their clubs. She holds out the money to the sergeant as the big man climbs into the car.

He slams the door and looks at her without expression. The driver guns the car off the sidewalk and bounces it into the traffic, lights on and siren blazing.

Billy's already behind the wheel of the Jeep, says he'll drive.

"Follow them to the cop house so I can get my phone back," snaps Bettina.

"No," says Billy, pulling into traffic. "The last place you need to be is in *their* cop house."

"They can't rip me off."

"They don't want your phone, they just don't want you using it."

"There's a Camacho number on the incomings," she says.

"The police can't break into your phone without a code and password," says Billy. "Don't worry. The video and pics are on mine."

Bettina can only think of one appropriate thing to say: "Son of a fucking bitch."

"Yes, ma'am. We're getting out of here now. We're lucky they let us go."

"Son of a . . . son of a . . . son."

"There's another police car behind us right now."

"Get us out of here, Billy."

"Bet on it."

Bettina stays turned in her seat, glaring at the cop car all the way to the border in San Ysidro. She's furious and frustrated, her least favorite emotional cocktail. If she had her phone, she'd be shooting video and taking pictures of these surly bastards. If she had her trap gun, she could shoot out their front tires. Instead, she uses Billy's phone and calls her landlord, who had volunteered to dog-sit. Felix has been very good, he says, sleeping most of the time in his crate, out by the hot tub.

She calls Jean Rose at *Coastal Eddy* with the news that she had some problems down in Mexico today but don't worry, I'm almost home now.

"I'll write the 'Hero Without a Face' story tonight, and put together the video tomorrow. I've got some decent location video, of where things happened the night Felix was shot, and how he got to the doctor, and a terrific account from the boy who saved him. It's going to be strong, Jean. A brave boy and a wounded dog."

Jean Rose says she fully understands, then tells Bettina that she's had some complaints from *Coastal Eddy* readers that the Felix story and video were too violent and don't really matter to people in Laguna Beach.

"Don't matter to *what* people?"

"They employ us."

Bettina rings off, sets Billy's phone in the cup holder.

"I guess I'm not just telling a story about a dog and a boy."

Billy considers this as they grind to a halt a quarter mile from the crossing.

"They're only parts of a bigger story, Bettina. Or what happened just now would not have happened."

"What's the bigger story, then? What am I not seeing?"

He looks at her with his open face, his soft eyes. "Bettina, I wish I knew.

But you got yourself a good dog and a couple of good stories out of him, so maybe you should just move on."

"I'm not moving on, Billy."

"I know you're not."

"I'm digging in."

At home that evening, Bettina writes her story, "Hero Without a Face," but with no pictures or video of Fidelito himself. With no recording of what he told her, it's very hard work. She has to put Fidelito's eleven-year-old, simple, expressive Spanish into her own dispassionate reporter's English. Yet make the reader feel the fears of both boy and dog as Fidelito—she names him Julio—runs through the night, clutching a wounded dog to his chest. How can that ever, in a thousand years, not matter? Finally, she finds a voice that sounds like Fidelito's and manages to remember some of his phrases too:

There were many bullets . . . and the dog he climbed over the dead men and he ran . . . men screamed and machine guns fired . . . here on my knees I pulled him out . . . he closed his teeth on my arm but he didn't bite hard . . . I had a dog when I was little . . . The voice of God told me . . .

Felix seems to sense her tension, dozing near his crate, sometimes looking at her with a placid expression and worried eyes.

"Who are you?" she asks out loud.

He cocks his head and his ears rise, but only one flap is down. She loves the way his ears often act independently, giving Felix a random cuteness that makes her smile.

"Did you lose some of your courage when they shot you? That would make anyone sad. And cautious."

He lays his head on his front paws and looks up at her.

Bettina knows he's missing someone. Teddy? The person who trained him in English commands? Or his Spanish commands? Are they one person or two, or three? Is Teddy even real? Did you really have a home once?

Four and a Half Years Before the
Shoot-Out . . .

11

Six-month-old Joe was wired with excitement there at the Excalibur K-9 Training Center with Teddy and Dad and an old man they called Wade. Joe had never felt energy like this. He was forty pounds of energy and happiness, with a seriously wagging saber tail.

Dogs everywhere! Some in cages with people ordering them to do things—almost all fun things that he could do very well, thanks to Teddy. Other dogs were running free in a big field of grass, playing with toys, barking. Some of them leaped through the air and bit people with pillows on their arms and legs! Whistles blew and clickers clicked and guns popped and the people voices were loud and clear. Then their voices become higher-pitched and full of kindness: *Good girl Susie. Attaboy, Dismas. You're the best, Doll!*

Joe saw that these dogs were all bigger than he was, some of them by a lot. No matter. He knew he could do anything better than them and with his long thin legs he was faster for sure, and Teddy and Dad were here to rescue him if something bad happened. He had never felt this much desire to run fast and jump high and bite hard, then play and wrestle with other dogs in grass alive with scent. He hoped he'd never have to leave this place, except to eat at home and to sleep in the Team Bed.

On leash, Joe followed Teddy, who followed Wade and Dad into a big gray building. Wade was higher than Dad and wider too. Joe saw that Dad and Wade knew each other but they were not a Team. Wade had deep lines on his face. His face had the hard thing that men got when they gave a command. Not meanness but not happiness. Joe knew no word for it but he knew what the lines on Wade's face meant.

They went into a place that looked to Joe like his garage at home but bigger and less crowded: a concrete floor, two shelves of boxes, a tool bench, bikes along one wall, a weight-lifting machine, bags of golf clubs propped up in one corner, a small desk. There were pasteboard boxes here and there, some closed and others overflowing with rags, wadded newspaper, human toys, and food containers.

Joe sensed that Teddy's excitement was almost as great as his own. His Boy asked questions and Wade answered them with strong, mysterious words, a few of which Joe understood. He still listened intently because he knew from their tone that these words were important:

"Just to introduce us, Teddy, we're Excalibur K-9, and though we train obedience to pet owners, the primary focus here is law enforcement and private protection dogs. We train the handler, too, if need be. We've been around for thirty years, so we know what we're doing. We're one of only two private canine academies contracted to train for the police and sheriffs of San Diego. The dogs we train for agencies are handpicked by me. We have four base models: detection, security, patrol, and protection. We train every dog as an individual. One approach won't work on all of them. Some dogs nothing works on, so they flunk out fast. We're all about obedience and control. Perfect obedience and perfect control. We won't place a dog that has anything less."

"That's really impressive, sir. Do you love dogs?"

"I love a tool that works, and dogs are the best tools man has ever made."

Joe registered uncertainty on Teddy's face. But he'd understood two words of Wade's last sentence: Dogs and Man.

"Teddy," said Wade. "Your dad tells me that Joe here has some pretty special talents."

"Only one, sir—he has a really, really good nose for whatever you want him to find."

"Is that so? Do you think Joe would find those things for me?"

"He's pretty wound up right now, but I'm pretty sure he would."

"What's your prompt?"

"I let him smell what I want him to find. Then I say, find this!"

"Ah, simple and clear. I hid some things around this room a couple of hours ago. Let me give Joe a try."

Teddy walked Joe over to Wade and gave him the leash. Joe registered the change through the light, strong nylon: Teddy gone, Wade now.

Joe sat and stayed at Wade's command and watched the man take something off a shelf. He brought a folded napkin back to Joe, opened and held it just outside Joe's extended nose. Joe knew the smell immediately. Teddy used it. It was a very strong one and very good to eat.

"This morning's bacon," said Wade, unleashing the dog. "Joe—*find this!*"

Joe lowered his nose and sniffed the floor with his instinctive inhale that divided the air into his lungs and his sensors.

No, he thought. Then lifted his nose into the air.

Yes, but far. Yes, but small.

He eased into this lake of smells, nose still up, quartering the room and stopping to test its objects, the scent subtly strengthening, weakening, strengthening.

He weaved and sidled, sidled and weaved. Teddy used to laugh at this but Joe wasn't thinking of Teddy now.

The box of newspapers, no.

The bicycles, no.

He stopped, raised his nose and waited, his breaths short and fast, his black nose twitching, snorting softly through his girthy Labrador's muzzle, drawing the smells in.

The box of human toys, no.

The far side of the desk, no.

Tools, no. Shelves no.

Stop then. Air smell, yes.

Air, yes, bigger.

Go.

Air *big*.

Joe followed the narrowing, strengthening scent cone to the tall bag of sticks propped in the corner. Touched a small zippered pouch with his nose. Looked at Teddy then Wade then whined piteously and touched the pouch with one paw. Joe had no word for bacon, but he had cataloged the smell of it when he was two months old.

"One minute and forty-eight seconds," says Wade, but Joe barely heard him. His full attention was on the pouch of this golf bag. Joe knew not what golf was, only that this pouch contained his purpose and his desire. It was the treasure that he has been asked to find.

It will make Teddy happy. They are a Team.

"Is that a respectable time?" asked Dad.

"Very," said Wade.

Joe needed only fifty seconds to find the toothpaste; forty-six seconds for the brick-thick bundle of dirty dollar bills; twenty-four to locate the unopened packet of sunflower seeds; and he trotted a straight, eight-second line to the pinch of dried oregano in a sealed plastic bag stuffed into an athletic sock in the bottom of a box on a shelf.

He'd smelled all of them before, on his way to the bacon, separated and collated them in his perfect encyclopedia of smells. Like the bacon, he recognized the sunflower seeds and dried oregano from Home.

This room is easier than Home, Joe thought. Wade happy and Teddy happy.

"That was pretty good," said Wade. Joe heard the joy in his voice and saw it in the lines of his old face.

"He found kibble inside an inflated bike tire," said Teddy. "I cut a hole in the inner tube and put the kibbles in and patched it and blew it up. And put it back in the tire and the tire back on the bike. Once, he smelled a wart on my foot before I could even see it. He smelled it and licked it over and over. I didn't know why until the wart came out. He smelled Mom's tears once before they happened; he got up in her face and licked them when they started up."

Joe sat and panted softly, enjoying the wonderful sound of good words that were clearly about him. Wondered if he'd get some Food.

"His mother is a papered Lab, you say?"

"Yes, Mabel," said Dad.

"But you don't know who sired him?"

"I think it was a street dog," said Teddy. "A skinny one shaped like a terrier and a whippet but small, like he had Chihuahua in him. Funny ears, like Joe's. I caught him looking at her through the fence two different times. He must have snuck across the border. I've seen them where we live."

Joe lay down and set his head on his front paws, eyes alert, tracking the mostly meaningless words. He knew Street, Dog and his own name, which was coming up a lot here, and always in a good way.

Wade put the leash back on him and led Joe through a basic obedience test, prompted by voice commands or hand signals. Joe's favorite was the roll over. He trotted beside Wade, who took bigger steps than Teddy, keeping his right shoulder even with the man's left calf like his Boy taught him.

When they were done, Teddy gave him several kibbles from his pocket and petted his head the way Joe really liked.

Outside again, he saw the dogs running and jumping, sitting and staying; saw a big dog biting a man with his arm in a pillow; heard the commands shouted out and the sharp pop of a gun going off; watched the dogs on the grass fetching toys and throwing them in the air. Just seeing and hearing and smelling all of this, Joe became wired with excitement all over again.

They went to a shady place on the grass and Wade released him.

Joe sprinted into a boiling cauldron of dogs who immediately knocked him down and kept running, but in a blink he was after them, no way they could outrun him, not with those long legs.

Out of Joe's earshot, the people discussed him:

"He's got a good nose," said Wade. "And he's only six months, so it's going to get stronger. If he knew his target odors and his discard odors, he'd be even better. He's obedient and controls himself. The question is, what do you want me to do with him, Teddy?"

"Make him a detection dog and train me to handle him. He can find anything. He can help people find things they've lost. He can help find bad guys."

"He's small for K-9 work," said Wade. "Detection, maybe. Security, patrol, or protection—no. Takes more dog than Joe to deal with a two-hundred-pound criminal high on meth."

They watched Joe on the grass with the other dogs, all larger than him. If any of them had belligerent intent, none showed. Joe rolled and tumbled and sprinted and cut. An enormous black-faced German shepherd knocked him down, then ran off in victory, hotly pursued by Joe, shrieking, gull wing ears flapping.

Twenty minutes later, Wade called Joe in and took him to the water nozzle. When he was done drinking, Joe crashed onto his side in the shade, flank heaving rapidly, tongue on the ground.

"Tony," said Wade. "I'm willing take on both your fine son and Joe. As a favor to you and to your father. I miss him and I know you guys do too. And to be truthful, this little dog has potential. Can you tell me, Teddy, what you'd like to see in your future with Joe? You're eleven now. Your dad tells me you're thinking of law enforcement."

"I want to work with Joe someday," he said. "Be his handler. Let him find important things. Like drugs and bombs and missing people."

"Yes, but the soonest you could work with Joe would be seven years from now. He'll be ready to retire by then."

Joe saw and heard Teddy suddenly go sad.

"Yeah," said his Boy. "I know. I wish we could do it right now. I want Joe to do what he's so good at."

"You don't mean you'd give up your best friend for training, and for work, do you?"

"No, sir. Never. I can't give up Joe."

Joe lifted his head at the sad tone of his own name just now. Teddy almost never sounded like this. Matching that unhappy voice were the tightness of his face and the glistening of his eyes. Joe wondered what was happening, felt wrong inside. Things were suddenly so bad. And he was a bad dog.

Joe clunked one side of his head down on the grass again, still panting, still listening to the words that he understood were important.

"I have an idea, Teddy," said Dad. "Let's do the fun part. We can bring Joe here on the weekends for basic training, and they'll show you how it's done, and how to work with him. Someday you may get certified as a K-9 handler, if that's still what you want. Joe will be your dog the whole way through training, and you'll get another dog to work with when you're old enough. Everyone wins."

Joe lifted his head again when he heard Another Dog. He understood Dog, but this word, *another*, worried him. Teddy's face was still not happy. So Joe was not happy. All the joy he'd brought to his Boy earlier today seemed to have changed into something else.

"Yeah, okay," said Teddy. "Let's do the fun part. That would be good."

Joe heard some happiness back in his Boy's voice. Humans could go from sad to happy very fast.

He would have said that it makes a dog tired, keeping track of mysterious emotions, but he didn't know a single one of those words except Dog.

He felt them, though, deeply and clearly.

12

"Bettina," says Marin, the *Coastal Eddy* receptionist, sticking her head into Bettina's cubicle. "There's a Dan Strickland here in the lobby to see you. "Somewhat hot."

Felix sits suddenly, faces the open doorway to the cubicle, ears up, tips out and alert.

"That got his attention," says Marin.

"It sure did."

"Shall I show him in?"

The dog studies Bettina with his full attention.

Bettina studies him back. "I'll come to the lobby. Felix, kennel-up."

The dog whines softly but goes into his crate. Bettina hooks the door closed.

The *Coastal Eddy* lobby is small and well lit, with a Scandinavian sofa and chairs in blue leather and steel, glass tables, and windows facing Coast Highway. Two of the interior walls are mostly glass, giving open views of Marin at the front desk and beyond, to the editorial, sales, and production areas.

There's only one other person here, a blond guy in tan cords and a black sweater with the sleeves casually hiked. Polished brown boots, gold watch. He stands, cants his head, and offers a polite, post-pandemic spread of hands from six feet away, which Bettina answers with her own.

"I'm Dan Strickland and I'm really sorry to barge in on you like this. But I wanted to meet you in person. I absolutely loved your dog video, and the story in the paper. I sent a donation to the clinic. Your stories really moved me. And I don't move easily."

He's half a head taller than she is at six feet, which puts Bettina at ease. His face is lean and closed, the opposite of Billy Ray Crumley's. Gray eyes. Thirtysomething. Handsome. He reminds her of Nick, her oldest brother, up in San Francisco, raising a family.

"Well, I'm happy you like the stories, Mr. Strickland."

"I love them. The clinic video, that poor dog. The doctor. The boy who carried the dog through the rain. Wow—it's a story with meaning. I'm familiar with Tijuana, too, and I know how violent it can be."

"What do you do?"

"I'm a self-defense instructor. I have a school down in San Diego."

"A dojo?"

"Part dojo, part gym, part shooting range. Classrooms, a lunchroom, kitchen, showers and locker rooms."

"Serious stuff."

"I take it seriously."

"I like to shoot trap," she says, wondering why.

A small smile. "No room for a trap range. Sorry."

"What can I do for you, Mr. Strickland?"

Bettina tries to read his expressions but she can't sort them out: reluctance, hesitation, determination? What *can* she do for him? she wonders. He's got the air of a man who gets what he wants.

"Felix's name is Joe," he says. "He's a washed-out DEA detection dog that the agency placed with me after his retirement. He ran away from home six months ago. They said he was a wanderer, and they were right. I'm astonished that he's still alive. Especially after being shot, down in Mexico."

"My God—Felix was yours?"

"Well, Ms. Blazak, that's why I'm here. Because Joe *is* mine."

"No, he isn't, and you can't have him."

This Strickland looks surprised. "Can I see him?"

"Absolutely not. I rescued that dog from the needle. I paid good money to the clinic. He likes me and he's happy. He was shot on your watch, Mr. Strickland. I don't think he needs a reminder from his past. He needs to move forward into a new life. Your part of his miracle is to let him go. You can't prove it anyway."

"Nonsense. He's my dog who wandered off."

"But he's mine now."

Strickland gives her a sympathetic look, takes out his phone, sits on the long blue leather-and-steel sofa. Bettina sits four feet away from him, staring unhappily out the window at Coast Highway. Her heart pounds with contradictory emotions: If Felix was really this guy's Joe, am I morally required to give Felix back to him, or am I permitted to keep him?

Furthermore, Teddy Delgado claims that Felix was *his* Joe, so can they both be telling the truth?

The man leans forward, then sets his phone on one of the glass tables with the potted succulents and stacks of *Coastal Eddy* hard copies tastefully fanned out in reverse chronological order.

"I'm sorry," he says as she picks up the phone and studies the pictures:

Strickland and Felix sit on the tailgate of a pickup, both facing the camera.

Strickland and Felix in a swimming pool.

Strickland and Felix, face-to-face, the dog smiling in that way dogs have, all tongue and teeth and joy.

Strickland and Felix in a good close-up portrait.

Felix asleep in a square of sunlight, ears relaxed, eyes slits—a picture taken with love.

It's Felix, all right, Bettina knows, unless he has an identical twin. Which she also knows is possible, but extremely rare. Technically he and his siblings are fraternal twins, but there's plenty of variety in litters. Especially in street dogs composed of varied ancestry.

"He has a scar inside his right ear, kind of raised and rectangular," says Strickland. "You've probably noticed it. His manners are very good, both on-leash and off. He likes to lie on his stomach, put his head on his front feet, furrow his brow, and watch you. He's thoughtful. He's faster than greased lightning, chases his tail in a blur, and he's a world-class napper."

"You can't just come in here and take him."

"I didn't ask to take him. I asked to see him."

"Do you think that's fair to him? To interrupt his new world?"

"I do. And I think you are ethically required to let me see a dog that I spent well over a year with, and you've had for less than four days. If our positions were reversed, I would let you see him. I would be happy to."

"Don't tell me what to be happy about."

"Is he here with you now? I see a short white Joe-style hair on your sweater."

"He's with a friend today."

Bettina sets the phone back on the table and Strickland takes it, glances at the screen, swipes up. A small nod and smile. No joy in him. The pain of memory? Longing? Being close to what you cannot have?

"If I were a writer," he says, "I'd like my dog at my feet while I work. In fact, that would be my dream job—to write good stories with Joe nearby. Unfortunately, I have none of the talent you do. In my self-defense classes Joe hangs around and socializes but play-bites people's toes sometimes."

"Felix is a sweetheart," says Bettina, her disappointment collapsing down into itself like a dynamited building.

"Would you consider money?" asks Dan Strickland.

"I will not sell that dog to you."

"No, money to see him."

"I'm not that cold."

"I just want to see Joe."

"I wish you had never walked in here."

"Just wait till you get to know me." Then, of course, the man-who-gets-everything-he-wants grin.

"I can wait."

Strickland stands and pockets the phone. "I could be wrong, but I think Joe is just a few yards from here, in your office."

"It's a cubicle."

Strickland walks away from Bettina and looks through the glass wall as if he'll spot Joe in the interior bustle of *Coastal Eddy*.

Bettina is angry and refuses to check out his hindside. More than angry. She loves Felix and hates herself for being defeated. Hates having to do the right thing.

"Follow me, Mr. Strickland."

"Just Dan."

When Bettina opens the crate, Felix tears to Dan Strickland's side and sits, looking up into his face with adoration, whimpering. Strickland kneels and pulls the dog's face to his own. Lets Felix lick him while muttering "Joe" over and over. Felix stands and keeps licking, his entire body wagging.

"You still can't have him," says Bettina.

"I'll pay you five thousand dollars for him."

"I won't sell him for any price."

"Ten thousand. Think what you can do. Give it to the Assisi clinic and save hundreds of dogs. And get a puppy you can bond with in the eighth week of his life. You'll never have that with Joe. Even I didn't."

What kind of man blows ten grand on a dog? she wonders. In love or just nuts?

"If you try to walk out of here with him, I'll call the police."

Strickland gives her a sharp look.

"I have papers to prove ownership, vaccines, everything," she says.

"I understand that he's legally yours, Ms. Blazak."

"Now we're getting somewhere. Felix, come."

Felix hesitates, then goes over to Bettina, looks up at her with a doggy smile, still wagging his tail. Bettina sees that Felix adores his former owner, but he likes *her*, *Bettina*, too. She wants to kneel and let him lick her, but she doesn't want Dan Strickland's know-it-all manly fucking germs all over her face.

"Can I arrange a play date for him?" he asks. "With me, I mean."

"You cannot be serious."

Dan Strickland looks serious, though.

Bettina kneels to pet her dog's head, gets her fingers behind those expressive button ears—or are they rose ears or semi-pricks? It all depends on what he's feeling. Mood ears. Not even always symmetrical. But he loves getting petted there, Bettina knows. She's hugely surprised and deeply thankful that Felix likes her, even with his previous master in the same room.

"I don't joke," says Strickland. "Life is too short for jokes. I want to see Joe again."

"I don't trust you to bring him back."

"I won't take him away in the first place. I mean you too. The three of us."

"God, no."

"Why not?"

"It's just a bad idea."

"How am I not trustworthy?"

"I don't know exactly. It's just too . . ."

"Too what?"

"Much. It's too much."

"It's not much at all. A simple walk on the beach. Or maybe at the park at Top of the World, or Heisler. It can be anytime you like. Any hour of any day. Joe, you, and me."

"Felix. He's mine."

"But *you* have an ethical obligation to let him be mine again. At the very least to share him with me. You can't just barrel in and take a man's dog away."

"Oh yes, I can."

"Think about what you just said."

"Do not. Tell me. What to do."

He puts his hands on his hips and stares at her.

She sizes him up as best she can. He seems calm and *maybe* trustworthy and she senses no meanness in him. Nothing out of plumb, as her dad would say. He's possibly intelligent, seeing the dog hair on her, and not falling for her fibs. His face is difficult to read and his gray eyes look hard as stones. He teaches people how to shoot and beat up other people. He looks like a guy in a pickup truck commercial but without the truck. Better dressed. Like her Nick again: something of the boy in him, but resolute and inadvertently likable.

However, Felix was in Strickland's care when he got shot and almost killed. Strickland might have tried to find him, but how hard did he look?

Bettina won't trust Felix alone with this guy for even one second, but that's not really the question here, she reminds herself. The question is, could she tolerate Felix and her seeing this guy again, on his terms, under any circumstances?

"I'll consider it. You can get me through the *Coastal Eddy* directory."

Dan Strickland smiles widely now, changing his whole stern countenance. The boy comes through when he lets his emotion show. He offers his open hands toward Bettina as he did in the lobby, but makes no move toward her. Bettina does likewise. Strickland kneels down again to hug Felix.

"You made my day, Ms. Blazak," he says. "I can't wait to see you two again."

"Down, boy," Bettina tells him.

At home that night, Felix on the floor beside her, Bettina does due diligence on Dan Strickland.

Her truthmatters.com service spits out the basics:

> *Daniel Knowles Strickland, 33 years old, LKA 521 E. Cedar St., San Diego, CA.*
>
> *Son of investor Dyson Strickland and attorney Jennifer Knowles-Strickland.*
>
> *Sister Allison Strickland-Stewart, 26, of Greenwich, CT.*
>
> *No criminal record or current warrants; Newport Harbor High School graduate 2008; one semester Orange Coast Community*

College 2010–2011; Marine Corps service 2012–2013, one tour of duty in Afghanistan; Silver Star awarded 2013.

San Diego Police Department 2013–2014.

California Private Investigation certification 2015.

Strickland Security, LLC, 2016–2019.

Apex Self-Defense 2020 to present.

Bettina finds Dyson Strickland and Jennifer Knowles had combined assets of $145 million at the time of their recent divorce. Dyson now residing in Newport Beach, CA, and Jackson, WY; Jennifer in New York, NY.

Apex Self-Defense, including the building, is valued at $2.1 million. Dan Strickland is sole proprietor; no liens or judgments.

"Boy, that former master of yours sure goes fast," she says, looking at Felix, who cocks his head and lets his ears rise as if he's trying to catch every syllable. "One day he's graduating from high school, and eight years later he's been to college, gotten the Silver Star, been a cop, a licensed private eye, and has his own security company. One thing to another. With years off, in between. What was he doing? Not marrying, not having kids. Estranged from Mom and Dad. Estranged from sister."

She finds the social media slide on truthmatters.com, but Strickland doesn't do social media. He comes up on an old SDPD website photo of young officers, then she sees the same picture way down on her Pinterest SDPD search.

"Maybe he gets bored," she tells the dog. "Maybe he's got ADHD. One semester of college? Who drops out of college after one semester? He seems calm and reasonable. Maybe that should worry me—the 'seems' part."

On the real estate / residence slide she finds seven former addresses, all in Southern California. When she calls them up with Google Maps, they're modest-looking places, small single-family homes, usually in coastal towns.

Apex Self-Defense, which apparently is Daniel Strickland's residence as well, looks like an old brick warehouse beneath an overpass and surrounded by taller structures, older and newer. A tangled urban mess, Bettina thinks. No sign on it, no clue that there's shooting and hand-to-hand combat going on inside. Not many windows, except for the third floor, which has big, new-looking windows all around. Still, thinks Bettina, not a place I would want to live.

She pictures Felix inside that building, mixing it up with the shooters and fighters.

Truthmatters.com tells her that "Private Strickland was awarded the Silver Star for gallantry in action against the Taliban in Helmand Province in 2011."

Leaving Bettina curious about what he actually did to earn the Silver Star. She'd ask him that herself, on the small chance that she accepts his offer of a "playdate" for Felix. The very small chance. It intrigues her that Strickland has been trained to kill, and now trains others how keep from being killed.

She's always been interested in people who accept—and even welcome—danger. She's written and posted about a police officer who survived an on-patrol shooting and returned to duty as fast as he could, and a decorated soldier back from his third tour of Afghanistan, and a married couple whose business is taking people down into the ocean to view great white sharks. She has also interviewed her idol, surfer Bethany Hamilton, who survived a shark attack and continues to surf professionally with only one arm. Try paddling out on a ten-foot day without *that*. What draws her to these people is her own willingness to go fast and fall hard: barrel-racing horses, surfing waves taller than she is, road-biking up and down the hilly Southern California coast at breakneck speed, asking questions in dangerous places—such as in Tijuana with Fidelito and the mean cops. Even her trapshooting as a teenager had an element of danger in it, guns being instruments of death.

Bettina likes the risk of danger and the excitement of being close to it. The excitement of *beating* it. Her mother is that way; her father is not. Only one of her brothers sides with her mom—Nick is a high-risk guy, joined the Army and came back decorated. Connor was his opposite, as was Keith—cautious and measured.

Now she considers a USMC photo of Strickland being presented his Silver Star. Even with the buzz cut and the desert camo, he's good looking. A strong chin and nose. Clear gray eyes. No emotion. Calm but ready.

There's a story in this guy, she thinks.

For her, a problematic one. She can't profile a San Diego self-defense wizard in Laguna's *Coastal Eddy*. Jean Rose would shoot that idea down in a heartbeat. Going to Tijuana for the dog rescue sanctuary and the Fidelito follow-up story were hard enough for Bettina to pull off. She's not going to get freedom like that now. Not with the timid readers complaining that the Felix and Fidelito stories are violent and don't matter in Laguna Beach.

However, Bettina thinks, a good story is a good story. It has value. Not every one of them has to be written.

Just lived.

The most interesting thing of all about Dan Strickland is he's the second person to have identified her dog as Joe, and claimed to have owned him for a year, and wants to see him and buy him back.

First Teddy Delgado's Joe, and now Dan Strickland's.

What are the chances that even one of their stories is true?

Or both?

Later she gets another email from Teddy:

Dear Ms. Blazak,

It will be a while before I can come get Joe in Laguna. I have a job at a bowling alley called Rock and Bowl, and there's only two dishwashers and I'm one of them. We are very busy. Plus school. I made honor roll but I've been truant and the principal is mad at me.

You asked about some stuff. We were living in Otay Mesa when Mom and Dad died. Uncle Art and Aunt Nancy adopted me but not Joe because of allergies. I haven't seen him in four years.

I hope to see him soon. My boss here doesn't give dishwashers time off, but I don't want to just quit.

I watch "Felix: The Rescue of a Mexican Street Dog" over and over. I like what you say about him and how you pet him. He loves to wrestle on grass. Joe was not a Mexican street dog when he lived with me. I named him.

Will you at least think about selling Joe to me?

Sincerely,
Teddy Delgado

13

Late the next morning, Bettina meets Billy Ray Crumley and his brother Arnie at the Cliff restaurant. At Arnie's request, they get seats way at the end, out of earshot. Felix accepts ice water from a waiter, then curls up under Bettina.

Arnie is a shorter, thicker version of his younger brother, Bettina notes, the stout boyhood baseball catcher of future big-league, kid-brother Billy. They have similar open, easy-to-read faces and pretty brown eyes under heavy brows.

But Bettina knows from Billy that Arnie is a special agent for the Drug Enforcement Administration, working the border beat from Imperial Beach to Yuma. Apparently not an office gig: Arnie is casually dressed in jeans and scuffed cowboy boots, an open-collared white shirt and a worn black corduroy sport coat. A chain with a cross around his neck, a bulky gold watch. He needs a haircut and a shave. Sets his beat-up black cowboy hat on the table crown down and Bettina—an unapologetic hat girl—checks the label: Atwood Marfa, just as she thought.

After some small talk, Arnie gets to his point:

"A dog that looked a lot like yours worked for us a few years ago," he says. "He was small for a detection dog, but a good nose. No, I mean a *great* nose. Ran up some impressive numbers that I wish I could share with you. They nicknamed him Midas. His real name was Joe."

Which hits Bettina like a punch. Reminds herself to inhale.

"You're trying to tell my Felix is your Joe?"

"Oh, he's DEA's Joe, all right."

Felix sits up and cocks his head at Arnie. He hasn't looked this focused since leaping onto Dan Strickland.

"Good boy, Joe," says Arnie with a smirking glance at Bettina.

First he's Teddy Delgado's dog, she thinks, then Dan Strickland's. Both named Joe! Now he's the DEA's Joe. Who's next?

"Cool," she says, then waits for Arnie to continue, thankful for her sunglasses and native acting skills.

"What's cool?" says Arnie, taking a sip of his Bloody Mary. "I never worked with Joe directly, being UC. We retired him after four years of work, about average. When I showed them your video, everybody thought Felix was Midas. They sent me to confirm because you're a friend of Billy's. Joe would be easy to ID from the number inside his ear."

"Like I said on the phone, there is no number on his ear," says Bettina. "Just a scar. I'll show you."

On Bettina's command, Felix sits up and she scratches his ears for a while, then lifts the flap up to reveal the scar.

"He was billed as a Mexican street dog by the clinic vet," says Bettina, grasping at straws. "That's where a boy found him, literally, on a street in Mexico. Not a drug-sniffing dog at all. Impossible."

"He's DEA property," says Arnie.

At DEA, Joe looks to Arnie again, all attention.

Arnie shrugs. "Joe looked like a street dog too. Same ears and head as Felix. Same body type. Long legs and tail. Same coat and coloring. In fact, the people who trained him for us speculated that his sire *was* a Mexican street dog that snuck across the border in Otay Mesa. Which is where Joe was born. They do that all the time, the street dogs. Raid the trash cans and get water from the creek. Knock up the gringa bitches."

Bettina notes Billy's sharp glance at his older brother.

"So you're trying to tell me that Felix might be Joe?"

"Oh, it's him, all right."

"Hey, Arnie," says Billy. "Stop being a jerk and tell us what's going on."

"Sure, little brother." He fiddles with his phone, hands it to Bettina, who shades it with her free hand and looks at the pictures.

"Scroll down," says Arnie. "There's six."

Bettina takes a good hard look at each picture, but she can tell by the second one that her doubts do not apply.

Felix is Joe, all right.

Again.

Her first instinct tells her that Arnie Crumley of the DEA might like to know that a boy named Teddy Delgado raised Joe for the first year of the dog's life, and is possibly coming to Laguna to try to buy him from her. But Arnie would be *very* interested to know that one Dan Strickland of Apex Self-Defense claims the dog is named Joe, too, and has belonged to him until a year ago. That he, Strickland, was here in town just yesterday, asking to see Felix.

And, of course, Dan Strickland would want to know that the DEA is asking questions about Joe.

Her second instinct tells her to keep her mouth shut on all counts.

Felix was Joe, she knows, right down to his random ears and the locations of the ovals on withers and back. She sighs and admits as much to obnoxious Arnie.

Arnie levels his Crumley eyes on her. His easily read face is 100 percent judgment. "Has anyone else been asking questions about Felix, Bettina? Other than me?"

Bettina has always been a good liar, so it's an easy question to answer. "No. No one."

"You sure?"

"Don't call her a liar, brother," says Billy. "You don't get to do that."

"Sorry."

A long, uncomfortable silence. Bettina watches the waves breaking down on Main Beach, sees the gulls wheeling and squabbling over Rock Pile. She looks south to the dim cliffs of Dana Point. Hears the plastic flags of the art gallery snapping in the breeze behind them. Catches Billy studying her and wishes he'd stop.

"Bettina," says Arnie, "it looks to us like your Felix—the DEA's retired Joe—was being misused by some very bad actors. I'm relieved to see that he's happy and well cared for here, by you, Bettina. He's lucky to have a human like you."

"You can't have him."

"We certainly can. He's federal property. But we don't want him. What we do want, is to verify what we now suspect—that he was being used by a drug cartel in Tijuana, where he nearly died that night. Specifically, that Joe was being deployed by the New Generation Tijuana Cartel to rob the Sinaloa Cartel of its drugs and money. We believe that Joe was handled by a New Generation thug known as El Romano—the Roman. To say that he's a person of interest to us would be an understatement."

Bettina remembers the clinic's Dr. María Lucero's tale of the cartel wars in Tijuana, and the violence back in early February.

"Ms. Blazak, let me cut to another important chase here: if Joe was sniffing drugs and money for the New Generation, that makes him an enemy and envy of the Sinaloans. They might want him for themselves. Or worse, he might be a target to be, well, retired. To you, he's just a cute little dog, but the cartels get competitive and vengeful with each other. They go to extremes. They love extremes. Joe's a rainmaker, a good one. And you, young lady, because of your stories and video, have located Joe for them. Sent them an invite. Putting him and you in a potentially dangerous position."

She exchanges looks with Billy. She knows he's remembering their words in Tijuana from the day before. Just as she is:

I'm not just telling stories about a dog and a boy.

They're only parts of a bigger story, Bettina. Or what happened would not have happened.

"Would they come up here?" she says.

Arnie Crumley stares at her flatly, offers a nearly silent huff and a quick shake of head at her absolute ignorance. He folds his hands on the table. "We have credible but unverified information that El Gordo has sent two ranking representatives across the border. A man and a woman. A Thoroughbred horse trainer and a hospitality executive, but cartel operatives through and through. Dispatched to kill or perhaps kidnap your dog? Maybe. They're money people, not exactly who the Sinaloans would use for simple revenge on the New Generation. So, questions abound but our sources are good. Nobody in Mexico invokes El Gordo's name lightly. He's a folk hero and a cold-blooded killer. Alejandro Godoy? You have heard of him, I take it."

"Everyone has. Gordo means 'fat' but he's not fat."

Bettina has that hollow-in-the-chest feeling she gets when she paddles into a big wave, or speeds down Coast Highway on her lightweight road bike, the wind whistling through her helmet, the bike's skinny tires her only connection to Earth. Or when she used to take Sawblade through the barrels back home in Anza Valley, his ton-plus body working under her like a machine. It's an eye-widening thing, this feeling, and it makes her vision sharp, and it lets time slow down until she locks the moment to herself. Owns it.

"You and Joe should move around if you can," says Arnie. "Vary your schedule. Stay two or three days with friends or family, then two or three days with others. Out of town would be preferable. Work remotely from wherever you are—you and Joe are exposed in your office on Coast Highway. Motels are cheap and pet friendly these days. Just a few days, until we get a bead on El Gordo's friends in Laguna. They might not have been sent here regarding Joe. They might not be here at all."

"Wait, Arnie, what about a safe house?" asks Billy.

"They're not designed to be occupied for more than a couple of days. We'll put you in one, but only in a pinch."

"This isn't a pinch, brother?"

"Not by DEA standards. It's a credible suspicion, a rumor—not an actionable threat."

Bettina sees the anger in Billy's usually pleasant eyes. "Bettina, we can trade apartments off and on. And I'll help cover Felix if you need me to."

Bettina reaches down and runs her hand over her dog's smooth round head. Feels his ears soft and relaxed as her palm glides over them. Strangely, since his reunion with Dan Strickland yesterday, Felix has been particularly relaxed and affectionate.

"They can't take him. He's mine."

"That's the spirit," says Arnie. "I'm going to give you both my secure numbers. Use them. Text is best. Tell me if you see or hear something that doesn't seem right. Be reasonable, though. If you start feeling like you're paranoid, you probably are. We're working on conjecture here. Rumors. Imaginative informants. Call me if you need me, but be reasonable. I can't answer you a hundred times a day."

"I understand," she says. "Felix will protect me."

"Not necessarily," says Arnie. "He wasn't trained for protection or patrol. He might attack if you say *Fass*, but he might not. Never had the killer spirit, did you, Joe? Dogs can't tell the difference between the good guys and the bad guys. They just do what they're told."

"They sense intent," says Bettina. "Maybe even character."

"Oh jeez," says Arnie. "Dog worshippers."

Billy looks at her, lips pursed and steady in the eyes. Bettina wonders how can Billy and this asshole can be brothers.

"Let's get you packed and out of your apartment for a while," Billy says. "We'll sit down Jean Rose, tell her you're fixin' to work from home—wherever that may be. Don't worry, Bettina. Felix is going to be fine. You're going to be fine too. Everything's going to be okay."

"I feel like I'm in a story instead of writing them."

"You've felt that way since you rescued Felix."

She rubs behind Felix's up-flapped ears the way Billy Ray Crumley and Dan Strickland did. The way she used to do when they had the bird dogs and terriers.

Joe glances back at Arnie and Billy Ray, then turns his pleasured attention to Bettina. After listening to every word of this conversation, he's sure that she's Bettina and he's Billy.

Besides hearing his own name again, the word DEA has conjured in

Joe a long chain of memories of Aaron. Some of his memories are good: they were a Team and Joe worked hard for Aaron and DEA, though he was not sure exactly sure which person DEA was. Some memories are bad: Joe remembers going very far to find Teddy, and the great sadness he felt when Teddy wouldn't come to the door and Aaron leashed him and walked him to his car.

Because in Joe's dog mind there are not stories, but only one story. There is no beginning, middle or ending. Just one story, ongoing, connected firmly to itself. His story. His People. His Team. There are no surprises to Joe. He knew he'd hear his name again, even if Bettina thought he was Felix. He knows he'll be with Teddy again and with Dan. He doesn't want to be with Aaron, or with the mysterious DEA, though they are part of his single, enclosed story.

What Joe feels most strongly now is that he will be with Teddy and Dan again.

And that Bettina might be an important Woman in this story, this world of his experience.

14

By evening Bettina has checked into a motel in Dana Point, the Queen Palms. It's on Coast Highway and there's a dog-friendly dirt and pee-burned grass "play area" with three shaggy queen palms growing close together. Not only that but room 212 has a microwave and mini-fridge, in-room coffee, and free internet.

She pays extra for a king bed so there's plenty of room for Felix and Thunder. Thunder being her trap gun, a Winchester Model 12 with a high-profile comb and a cheek rest and a good recoil pad for the days she'd shoot a hundred, two hundred rounds in tournaments. Heavy as a tank but smooth of swing, and the pump action effortless. Her best friend for years. Her dad, a terrific shotgunner, shortened the stock and gave the gun to Bettina for her twelfth birthday. It was an old gun, one of the pre-1964s. When she outgrew it, she helped Dad put the cut-off piece of butt back on, helped him glue and sand and refinish the whole stock. Blued the steel too. Better than its former glory. Thunder shoots like a dream and kicks like a mule.

In room 212 now, Bettina checks the breach then shoulders the weapon, wondering how many hundreds of thousands of times this makes. She feels the weight and balance, the perfect fit to her face. Even feels a little of that spark inside, the danger and excitement. She tracks an invisible clay pigeon flying through the room. Clicks her tongue to simulate the trigger pull, and swings through the target to lengthen the shot string—trap 101.

She figures she'll be sleeping with Thunder beside her, no plug in the gun, six shells in the magazine, barrel pointed to the foot of the bed, slide open, ready to be racked and fired. Safety on, too, in case of an active dream or a sudden move by Felix. He hasn't chosen to sleep with her yet, but he could change his mind while she's in dreamland.

She feels somewhat overequipped for this DEA "rumor," but the "better safe than sorry" cliché offers her a mostly believable rationale.

"They better not try to get you," she says to him. He's lying just inside the doorway of the bedroom, watching her as always.

She wonders again if she should let him go back to being Joe. He's responding to Felix by now, and Bettina likes the name, because it tells a story.

"So, Felix or Joe?"

He sits up and stares at her. He almost never backs off a stare-out, unless he gets distracted, which for Felix is not difficult. Any small living intruder in his world—an earwig on the kitchen floor, a fly on a window, a fence lizard on Bettina's Laguna deck—is enough to snap his reverie and send him tearing off after it. The terrier in him, Bettina knows, bred for hunting and barnyard ratting, bred to kill pretty much anything smaller than himself.

But nothing distracts him now.

"Felix or Joe?"

His brown eyes are intent and intelligent looking, but she has no idea what he's thinking.

"How can you have thoughts if you don't have words, little dog? I know you have thoughts, but what form do they take? Do you hear them? Maybe you see them. Or smell them."

He lies down like a sphinx, paws out and head up, not breaking eye contact with Bettina. Still staring back, Bettina extends her left arm, makes a fist and says "Joe." Then holds her right arm out in a fist and says "Felix."

The dog considers each fist, then lets out a faint whimper as he lies back down. Lays his head on his paws and looks at her with what Bettina thinks is profound frustration. He wants words, she thinks.

Give him words.

"You are Felix," she says. "The best dog ever in the world."

He cocks that head and taps his tail unconvincingly.

Settled.

After dark she drives to the market for provisions. Parks up close to the entrance and leaves Felix crated in the locked Jeep, a window cracked. She's nervy about this, checks the Wrangler through the supermarket windows twice, but she's back to it in less than eight minutes. Realizes she'll need a service-dog license so he can go everywhere. Hell, she thinks, maybe Arnie can get me a DEA K-9 vest, scare the hell out of everybody.

Felix is asleep when she gets there.

She heats up two high-quality frozen dinners, cuts a pear and some goat cheese for sides, pours two fingers of bourbon in an old-fashioned rocks glass from home. Adds an ice cube and a slice of lemon rind.

Checks her messages and social buzz. Views and responses to "Felix: The Rescue of a Mexican Street Dog"—both print and video—continue to multiply. Even her scantily illustrated article about the boy who saved Felix, "Hero Without a Face," has gotten major traction. There's a voice mail on her work line from a literary agent and another two from Hollywood agents, all wanting to talk. She feels her heartbeat speed up but she's not surprised at all. People love stories that matter.

The dog lies under the little table, at her feet, working on a cow's hoof.

She puts Billy Ray Crumley on speaker and tries to eat the turkey and stuffing dinners without making noise.

"That was kind of ugly today," says Billy Ray Crumley. "I would have warned you what was coming about Felix, but I didn't know what Arnie had up his sleeve."

"Arnie did the right thing. I have to be careful."

She glances at the long tapering lump under the bedspread.

"Arnie likes the tough-guy Federale act," says Billy. "When he'd catch me in baseball, he'd pop that ball back hard if he didn't like my call or my pitch. Him throwing runners out was a thing of beauty, though."

"Brothers," says Bettina, thinking of her own. What a tangle of testosterone they were. "Talk about competitive."

A beat, then: "Thanks for helping me today, Billy."

"Anytime, anyplace."

"You've got a big heart."

"Just trying to be a friend."

"You miss your life in Texas? Your friends and job, and the way everybody knew you were a major leaguer?"

"Hmm."

Bettina hears a muffled gulp, figures he's drinking a beer. And having a chew, which he tries to hide from her. But you have to spit it out somewhere. Smells like mint.

"Sure, yeah. The friends mainly."

"Are you still friends with your ex?"

"No, ma'am. It got ugly in the divorce, and things got said that weren't true. In a small city like Wichita Falls, everything's everybody else's business."

"Laguna too."

"Laguna's about as different from Wichita as you can get. It's great here. A great place to start over. I was damn lucky to have an uncle on the PD or I'd probably never have got an interview. Everybody wants to be in a cute town on the California coast. I ride a bike around and help tourists for sixty grand a year and bennies. That's not bad."

Another pause. Bettina sips the bourbon.

"Where'd you put the shotgun, Bettina?"

"Under the bedspread. Thanks again, Billy. For everything."

"I am more than happy to be there for you," he says. "I'm pissed at Arnie for scaring you, then cutting you loose."

"That means a lot to me, Billy. I'll call you if I need you."

"Anytime and I'll be there."

"Later gator. Felix says good night."

Bettina pours another bourbon, adds ice, wipes a fresh lemon peel around the glass and puts the lemon in the tiny fridge. Straightens the kitchen, checks the door, leaves the lights on and gets into bed with *Papi*. That Rita Indiana is one crazy-good writer.

Tonight, though, Bettina can't lose herself in Indiana's funny-desperate phantasmagoria. The bourbon makes her think of Keith, and the occasional too much of it they drank together. Keith would have liked *Papi*, she thinks. It has his loopy humor, his wide-eyed hunger for the unexpected, his love of words and language.

Here's to you, Keefo.

Propped up in bed, here on the second floor of the U-shaped Queen Palms Motel, she can see the far parking stalls and the face of the building. Felix lies across the wide-open doorway, angled into the bedroom to keep his patient brown eyes on her.

She thinks of Billy Ray Crumley and how he reminds her of someone she knows but doesn't want to know. But she won't say who. She *could* say who, but she won't. Some people are better off unnamed. What a terrible time to remember all of that, Bettina thinks, but sometimes a second bourbon breaks things loose inside. Once her memory starts in, it's as unstoppable as a freight train going down a grade.

It was her freshman year at UCI, and she was living on Balboa Island with roommates and she went to a party over on North Bayfront. Some drinking going on and she did her part to represent the Hamilton High School Bobcats, did some tequila shots, got maybe a little more than just happy but still way under control. Way. Went upstairs to use the bathroom. Some boys in the bedroom drinking and talking conspiringly, scratchy phone music, so she had to wait. Made bitchy small talk

with them. One said she had a pretty face and asked what her major was. And out of the bathroom came J from Hamilton High, a familiar face to Bettina but only an acquaintance—a jock quarterback with aw-shucks manners and an easy smile—and he was weaving drunk, wiping his mouth on the back of one hand, gripping a champagne bottle by the neck in the other. A cliché drunk. Grinning when he recognized her and swayed to a standstill. Blubbered a greeting, stuttering through the Bs: "B-b-bettina B-blazak the b-beautiful . . ."

"You're drunk, J," she said, a ripple of worry when the music went louder and the lights went out. She turned for the stairs. Motion from the bed, men climbing off, then J pushing her onto it, one strong hand over her mouth, cramming her head back into the pillow, the other hand yanking her belt open. Then the zipper of her jeans got pulled down hard. "Go for it, J," slurred someone from the corner and the door closed so even the light from outside was gone. Bettina bit J's palm and clubbed him on both ears with her fists, and kneed him in the meat of his thigh, and then again. But J forced her back flat, and clamped her wrists to the bed. He was heavily on top of her and thrusting away even though her pants were still on and so were his as far as she knew. Then he was panting and telling her he loved her and trying to kiss her but she head-butted his nose, blood spraying into her face. Then the lights come on and J froze for a second and six-foot Bettina was strong enough to reverse the wrist-locks and use her weight to twist the big man away and off her. J sat on the foot of the bed looking bewildered, and Bettina kicked him hard in the face. J collapsed to the mattress. The guy who had turned on the light, a capable looking dude in an Anteaters Lacrosse hoodie, asked Bettina if she was all right. She nodded, not knowing, zipping up her jeans, looking down at J and wanting to hurt him badly again, right then. Just crush the bastard. Instead, she wiped her face with a pillow, looked the lacrosse guy in the eye and nodded. Then carefully went down the stairs, a trembling hand on the banister.

She walked back to her apartment in the dark, arms crossed around herself, heart pounding, crying without sound. Throat sore and body hurting. Coppery smell of blood. Made it to her bathroom without being seen by the roomies, took a long shower, put on clean clothes and laid herself on the bed.

Wondered what to do.

Much later when the first light came to her windows, Bettina knew, all right: endure it. Avenge it if you can, someday, somehow. But for now, no police. No denials. No he said, she said. Nothing of tequila shots and tight jeans and were you flirting? No reports, no charges, no testimony, no public anything.

Let it become something buried down deep. Like a diseased corpse that she knew, even then, she would never forget.

Which brings her full circle to the Queen Palms Motel on this March night to wonder: What did that have to do with Billy?

She knows damned well what it has to do with Billy.

Nothing and everything.

The nothing part is easy to understand because Billy has nothing to do with what happened. The first time Billy walked into her cubicle at *Coastal Eddy*, however, she thought of J: a faint physical resemblance, the athletic stature, the easy face. She didn't want Billy to remind her of J, but he did. That was the limit of Billy's culpability—he walked into her cubicle.

The everything part is harder for her to deal with because it's not a memory, not a piece of personal history, but her own reaction to it: J had stolen not only her once-easy trust of men but also her natural affection for them, her empathy, her spiritual attachment. J had spoiled half the world. Spoiled all the Billys and the Toms and the Tylers, the Nathans and the Marks and the Juans, the Albertos and Kendricks and Jamals. All of them.

Spoiled any chance of friendship with the lacrosse player, John Torres, who had offered to talk to the police about what he'd seen, and tried to keep in touch with Bettina after that night.

J had even spoiled Bettina's brothers and father, forced them to be a part of a separate vile gender.

Felix comes to her bed and jumps aboard. A first! He licks her face and Bettina sets her left hand protectively over the trigger guard of the Winchester.

Later she turns off the lights. Propped up in bed with the gun on one side and her dog on the other, Bettina looks out at the parking lot and the other units, two stories of them, facing her from just a few hundred feet away. Everybody in everybody's face. Some with lights on inside, most not. Faint lights over the doors, flecked by moths. A compact car arrives; a van departs. Doors open and close and voices drift through the damp March air. English. Spanish.

At the sound of the Spanish, she goes to the window and finds the source: two men at the door of a downstairs unit directly across from her. They look old and tired. One has trouble with the card key, in and out and again, and the door finally opens.

Shame on you, thinks Bettina: these guys are workers.

Back under the covers she can't sleep. Can't believe how good it feels to have a dog in bed again. Can't believe that just yesterday life was more than good, but now she's trying to protect a former DEA drug dog from the Sinaloa Cartel, which is possibly in Laguna right now, looking to dognap Felix, or worse. Or so says a pain-in-the-butt DEA agent with "credible but unverified" evidence.

She checks her laptop with the free Wi-Fi, sees the pictures of Felix's "relatives" still coming in. Some of them really do look like him.

She closes the computer, wondering if it might be time to open the box in her brain, give J his name back, let him be a real man instead of a living curse, time to deal with him face-to-face, once and for all and forever.

Bettina strokes the top of Felix's perfectly round head, the "doggen noggin," as her mother would say. Then she works his funny ears with her fingers, scratches under his front legs, feels his heart beating deep in his chest. She can't quite believe how much she loves him. How easy it is to fall in love with a dog. You just do. They make you.

Her last thought before tumbling into sleep is about Felix: You can't take him.

He's mine.

Joe lies beside Bettina, his back flush to her. He feels the faint thump of her heart and the sounds inside her, draws in her river of smells. He thinks of his mother and the sweet milk and the other puppies all around him jostling each other for position and the way she would suddenly get up and go away, yanking that wonderful warm tube from his mouth and leaving him rolling and roiling with his brothers and sisters in the sudden emptiness of their crate. It's one of his best memories, being buried in live, warm, friendly bodies that smell good.

He thinks of swimming in the pool with Teddy, and at the beach with Dan.

Remembers the mouse he killed working with Dan before they shot him.

Thinks of the boy holding him tight and running to where he was taken care of by Good Man and Woman.

He knows this Woman Bettina loves him. He sees it on her face and hears it in her words. These are clear and unmistakable signs. Faces are easy to understand; words, too, if you go by sound. When she looks at him in that certain way, Joe is starting to love her back.

He doesn't know the word for love. Just that it's all good feeling and happiness. For sleeping next to.

Six Months After Joe's First Visit to Excalibur K-9 Training Center...

15

On a bright spring day, Teddy, his father, Wade, and year-old Joe got ready for a mock Class I detection exam at the Excalibur K-9 Training Center. It's a present from father to son in reward for good grades in fifth grade. Teddy has been talking a lot about being a dog handler when he's old enough: for rescues, maybe, or tracking lost people, or maybe catching criminals or terrorists. His dad wants him to get a taste of what it might be like.

Joe knew none of this. He was happy to be here at a place he loves, doing things he loves for people he loves.

This test was an edited version of the detection test that Wade would give any Excalibur candidate headed to the ranks of federal, state, county, and municipal officers, or private citizens willing to pay top dollar for a top dog—minus the drugs and dangerous opioids because of Teddy's age. If a dog passed all four parts of the real Class I exam—detection, security, patrol, and protection—the next step was to place this "green" dog with his handler-to-be for a week of compatibility-training to assure a good canine–human fit. And if that happened,

Wade would sign away yet another of his beloved dogs for five years of hard and sometimes dangerous work.

If the dog didn't pass, Wade always tried to find a good owner, hopefully a family, and passed his failed friend into a safer world. It was a little tough sometimes, since many of the dogs were patrol, security, and protection trained, so prospective civilian owners could be liability-shy, if not downright afraid to bring a trained attack dog into their home.

The three of them—and occasionally Dad—had been here Tuesdays, Thursdays, and weekends for six months now, and Wade wanted to see how Joe could do on a timed, intense examination with steep scoring penalties for false and missed alerts.

They started with on-leash obedience—hand and voice directed—at which Joe had always excelled. They did it right out in the grassy park with the dozens of other dogs and handlers. Half the battle for a dog was distraction.

Joe was distraction-prone, to say the least, but that day he sensed the gravity of what they were doing in Teddy, whose voice was stern and hand signals more forceful than usual. Joe saw that Wade's wrinkled old face was serious, and that he carried a flat black slab with a screen that tilted up, and, as many people do, was poking it with his fingers. So Joe tried extra hard—sitting extra fast, keeping still as a rock as Teddy circled him, going down hard with a *humph,* rolling over completely, and raising his paw the second he heard Shake or Teddy offered his hand.

Wade marked down Joe for anticipating commands rather than waiting for them, something else that Joe had also always excelled at. Joe lost his self-control and broke for a spotted towhee flitting in a hedge of pink oleander, but when Teddy called him off, Joe came sprinting in, flipping onto his back at Teddy's feet, butt swiveling on the grass and tail wagging desperately.

Looking up, Joe saw the anger on his Boy's face, and heard it in Wade's big voice: "That's going to cost him, Ted!"

Joe knew that they were unhappy and that it was his fault—I did it,

I did it, *I did it*!—but the bird was right there in the bush and Joe badly needed it.

He calmed himself down, and the off-leash field work went nearly perfectly. Their expressions inspired him. Wade's big gnarled hands worked the black Slab.

They did the detection test in a modest 1950s stucco house relocated to the Excalibur for just this purpose. It was smaller than the warehouse and Joe had never been inside.

"Unfamiliar territory," said Wade. "To make it as hard on them as we can."

Joe had no idea what that meant, and hoped that Teddy did.

"He'll do good, Mr. Johnson. He knows when things are important."

Joe followed them up the steps to the front porch, his nose keen to this new world.

Over the months, Joe had learned his basic discard odors well: human and dog food, dogs and other animals, tennis balls and plush toys, chews and tugs, small amounts of currency. And many other things that Joe enjoyed smelling but brought him no reward at all. Only sharp words and mean faces. Joe thought Bacon should get him a reward, but he'd learned that it wouldn't.

Joe's detection command was one holy word: *find*.

Which would be issued by Teddy, as he let Joe whiff a sample of a target item that Wade had hidden somewhere in the house.

They stood in the entryway of the house, Joe's nose in the air, drawing in the river of scent. He whimpered softly.

Teddy smelled the strong Lysol and the bleach used to disguise the scents.

Wade gave Teddy a salted-in-shell peanut.

"Go to, Teddy," he said looking at his watch.

Joe watched Teddy's face, shivering. This was the most important thing in the world. He was so excited he believed he could jump up and bite the ceiling if he wanted to. Then Teddy held out the thing, his voice an urgent whisper.

"Find the peanuts, Joe! Find peanuts!"

A scent drew him forward into the living room, but he stopped and put his nose to the hardwood floor, then abruptly retreated back to the hat rack in the entryway.

Where he sat, looking up at the hats and umbrellas and raincoats. Went up on his hind legs, braced his paws on the entryway wall, nosed the pocket of a windbreaker that was streaming scent into his quivering muzzle.

Peanuts!

In his peripheral vision Joe saw Wade doing something on the black slab.

But he focused on Teddy, reaching into the jacket pocket and pulling out a clear bag of peanuts!

Teddy smiled as he held up the small plastic bag and Joe's receptors nostrils bristled with an irritating scent.

Teddy brought the bag to his nose. "They used ammonia on the bag, Joe. But you found the peanuts anyway. You found them!"

His Boy gave Joe two small kibbles from his pocket. "How did Joe do? Did he get a fast time?"

"Yes, sir, Ted. It took Joe eight seconds to find his target, inside an ammonia-wiped plastic mini-bag."

"You're the best dog in the world," said Teddy. He only said that sometimes, and Joe loved the sound of it. Joe knew the word Dog, of course, and he's pretty sure that "best" is a very good word.

Joe watched Wade give his Boy another item and Teddy let him smell the small blue rectangle. It smelled like Teddy after getting wet in the rain box.

"Find the soap, Joe. Find soap!"

So Joe stepped forward into the living room again, feinting left and right, then came another sudden stop. His nose dropped to the floor like something weighted.

Again, he backtracked into the entryway. Sniffed the old rug, then dug a corner up and over itself, revealing the still-wrapped piece of chewing gum underneath.

Teddy brought it to his nose. Smelled the cinnamon, but Joe smelled the little shard of soap.

"Took eleven seconds to find a slice of soap hidden in a cinnamon gum wrapper," said Wade.

Joe's tail wagged hugely as his Boy gave him a treat from his pocket. "You're the best dog," said Teddy again and Joe knew exactly what he meant. There was something on his Boy's face that made Joe feel love, though he had no word for his strong, good feeling.

Joe was really getting this game: Wade gave Teddy something for him to find, and he found it with his nose and Wade did something with his black slab and everyone was very happy.

Suddenly Joe was off again, after another peanut smell, but Teddy sternly called him back to the entryway. Joe bolted back and sat, scanning both faces with bright worry. Teddy's voice had gotten lower lately and when Teddy was stern he was very stern. It surprised Joe. He thought he was playing.

"In a timed test, you have to start from the same place," said Teddy, but Joe understood not one word.

Teddy looked at Wade for the next item.

Joe took in the grassy smell, not the yard grass where they played but like it.

"*Find, Joe!*" Teddy whispered intensely. "*Find the spice!*"

Joe quartered the living room in three short bursts, which brought him to the old fabric couch along the far wall. Like a lure enticing a fish, the scent drew him to the seam between the back cushions and the seat. He sprang up and buried his thick Labrador muzzle in it. It took him four quick, tingling snorts to confirm his find. He pulled his snout out, looked at his Boy.

Teddy ordered Joe off the couch and down. Joe watched him pull away a cushion like at Home.

Joe's nostrils were bristling as he watched Teddy lift a small box that emitted this important smell that he had never smelled before. He watched his Boy open and look into it.

"Twelve seconds for half an ounce of dried oregano," said Wade. "Packed in a freezer bag, stashed in a cigar box slathered in hot sauce."

Teddy praised him and fed him more treats. Joe was happy. Teddy was happy. Team happy.

It was all so easy and fun. Joe got treat after treat, good face after good face. Praise from Teddy.

Joe found the cotton ball wiped with antiperspirant in a wastebasket in the bathroom; the breath mint inside a jar of peanut butter; the pinch of laundry soap sprinkled in the opened pack of smokes; an apple in the lidded toilet; a fragment of lemon peel wrapped in scented tissue wrapped tight in a sandwich bag.

"The drug traffickers will try anything to hide the scent of their product," said Wade, working his tablet. "But the scent almost always ends up on the container, no matter how they try to wipe them down or stink them up."

Joe listened intently to Wade, but didn't recognize one word in all those sounds.

The bigger stuff was farther back in the bedrooms and bathrooms: a shoe high on a closet shelf, part of a jacket, a nautilus seashell still smelling faintly of the ocean.

The grand finale was a handful of wild bird feed in a small plastic food container with a toilet puck and six naphthalene moth balls inside.

"Eighteen seconds," said Wade.

Joe followed Teddy and Wade into the small dining room and sat next to Teddy's chair. No more Play. He heard Wade tapping the Slab.

"Pretty much what I thought," said Wade in his rocky old voice. "Joe just did a slightly modified Class I detection course almost twice as fast as it's ever been done. No false positives, not one miss. I've been doing these tests for thirty years and Joe's the best I've ever seen."

Joe heard his name in a good way. Lowered his proud body to the cool floor and fell asleep.

Joe lay in the back of the Delgado Heating and Air van, with Dad at the wheel and Teddy talking loudly and excitedly. This was the best day of his life.

He listened hard to his people, as always:

"And then in twelve seconds, Joe found the oregano!"

The shelves of parts and tools rattled and clanked all around Joe, and he was extremely happy.

At Home he slept on the Team Bed for three straight hours, dreaming of what he'd found, hearing the praise and excitement, smelling in his dream the specific, discrete, wonderful scents.

That evening Joe's dad and mom would be going out to dinner to celebrate their twelve-year anniversary. Teddy thought they looked happy. Tony and Alicia all dressed up. His dad said they'd be with Uncle Art and Aunt Nancy, at Mister A's in San Diego. Shelly from down the street would be here with him.

"There's leftovers in the fridge," he said as they were walking out the door. "And a new tub of ice cream. Shelly, help yourself to dinner and that ice cream if you want."

"Thank you, Mr. Delgado."

"Good, Dad."

"Teddy, you and Joe were fantastic today, just fantastic."

"Joe was."

"You, too, son. We won't be late."

Joe took all of this in but didn't understand much. He linked "ice cream" to the sweet Food that Teddy gave him sometimes after dinner.

When Teddy gave him a spoonful of the sweet Food, Joe wolfed it down and took off after his tail in a frantic, cyclonic whir.

He fell asleep that night alongside Teddy, who was watching TV on the living room couch with the Girl.

A big day, and Joe out cold.

He dreamed of all the things he'd found that day.

The best day of his life, again.

Much later the doorbell blasted Joe into an ear-shattering bark, and he was at the door growling before his Boy could get off the couch.

"No, Joe! Come! Down! Stay!"

Joe stopped growling and came and hit the floor by the couch, as ordered. Shelly took him by his collar.

He watched Teddy look through the small hole in the door, then open it.

Joe saw people in the porchlight. A man who looked like Dad and a woman Joe remembered. Also, a man and a woman wearing dark shirts and pants, with tools and guns and things wrapped around them like some of the people where he played today.

But what Joe saw and heard most clearly was their sad faces and the very sad voice of the man that looked like Dad.

"May we come in, Teddy?" he asked.

"Come in," said his Boy.

Teddy's voice was afraid. Joe felt the fear and was ready to fight. You can't hurt him, Joe thought. He's mine.

They came in and the woman with the man who looked like Dad rushed in and threw her arms around Teddy and held him like wrestling in the grass.

Joe growled but Teddy wrestled himself away from the woman and looked at the Dad-like man.

"Teddy, please sit down. We need to talk."

"No," Teddy said to him.

"I think I should drive myself home now," said the girl.

The man who looked like Dad gave her something from his pocket and the girl went outside.

The wrestling woman's face was wet and the man like Dad's voice trembled.

"It's your father and mother," he said.

"No," Teddy said again. "No."

The man and the woman with the matching shirts and guns stared at Teddy but said nothing.

Joe had never heard such sadness in Teddy. Growling almost silently, he leaned against his Boy's legs, using all his weight to protect him.

Joe looked at all these sad, ugly faces and growled louder. He understood that they had hurt his Boy and were hurting him now.

Teddy ordered him to down and stay, then knelt beside Joe.

"Something terrible has happened to Mom and Dad," he said. Joe only understood the words Mom and Dad, but he got the meaning of the rest of them, thunderously loud and frighteningly clear.

His growl became a whimper.

16

Teddy spent the twenty-three hours waiting to be "placed" with Art and Nancy Delgado.

Most of those hours he was in a room in a cottage in San Diego's Polinsky Children's Center, attended by a doctor and several child Welfare Services workers.

He cried himself to sleep but woke up after a few hours, then did it again. He ate once and vomited. He agreed to a medication that would make him calm. Most of the time he stared at the TV screen, eyes closed, trying to will away what had happened, like he would sometimes will himself out of a bad dream. He wanted to be over all of this, or dead, but he didn't want to kill himself. Wasn't sure how.

The only shred of good news was Joe, who was at Art and Nancy's home in La Jolla while Child Welfare Services made sure that Teddy would be well cared for and happy with his aunt and uncle. They sent pictures of Joe to one of Teddy's caretakers' cell phone.

Teddy didn't know how much had died inside him but it felt like almost everything but Joe.

Uncle Art's and Nancy's home in La Jolla was up in the hills. From his room, Teddy could see the Pacific below, blue water and white foam on black rocks. Seals and sea lions lolled in the choppy cove. To Teddy, Joe was just as solemn and unhappy as Art and Nancy seemed to be. His uncle and aunt argued. Nancy blew her nose a lot. Doors slammed.

These Delgados were very different people from his father and mother. Their house was gigantic compared to Teddy's former home in Otay Mesa—three stories of old-looking furniture and paintings. A white grand piano. There was a four-car garage with a gleaming concrete floor.

His uncle Art had sold his air conditioner factory and chain of dealerships, and retired early. Kensington Air. Now he managed his "modest fortune" from his home office, and by frequent travel.

Teddy's dad and uncle Art hardly ever got together. Teddy had been only faintly aware that his father and uncle were in the same business. Kind of—his dad installing and servicing air conditioners and heaters, some of which were made by Uncle Art. Uncle Art was sharp faced and high voiced and always in a hurry. Joe didn't like him. Nancy was blond-haired and beautiful and always dressed up.

Three days after arriving here, Teddy was out in the backyard with Joe, throwing the tennis ball. He saw the big white SUV with the Excalibur K-9 Training Center emblem pulling into the Delgado driveway. When Teddy saw Wade Johnson get out of the SUV, he felt a warm feeling in his heavy heart; but it was followed by a cold one when Uncle Art came striding across the rose-lined driveway toward Mr. Johnson with a smile on his face and his hand out for shaking.

A moment later, Uncle Art led Mr. Johnson from the house into the backyard. Joe bolted for Mr. Johnson and immediately dropped to the grass at his trainer's command, rolled over once, twice, then hopped up into a sit and looked up at him with that expression that Teddy knew and loved. Joe didn't look at Uncle Art at all.

They sat in the shade and drank iced teas that Nancy brought on a tray. She sat beside her husband at the round table, and through the glass Teddy saw them take each other's hand. Joe sat between Teddy and Mr. Johnson.

Uncle Art and Mr. Johnson talked about the Padres and Nationals coming up that night from Washington, then Uncle Art looked at Teddy and said:

"Teddy, I'm sending Joe away to live with Mr. Johnson out at the training center."

"No."

"It's totally my fault," said Nancy. "My allergies are really doing a number on me, and the meds make me drowsy. I've always been that way with dogs. I've never even been able to have one. I am so very sorry, Teddy. I tried. I thought I could do it."

Teddy didn't know whether to grab Joe and run for it, or scream at his uncle and aunt, or just go to that quiet place inside and accept this horrible thing.

"I'll keep him in my room."

"The hair, dander, and bacteria won't stay in your room," said Uncle Art. "And I agree with Nancy, the dog will have a much better life out at the center. You can go visit him anytime you like. Heck, stay all day if you want. Mr. Johnson told me on the phone that he's serious about continuing Joe's training. Right, Wade?"

Mr. Johnson looked pale and solemn. "You know I'll take good care of Joe," he said. Joe's tail thumped at the sound of his name. "You're always welcome at Excalibur. You can help me with the dogs. I can use a good assistant. And I think I can put Joe to work someday. For real. As a detection dog. I know a handler who wants a small dog with a big nose. I hope that cheers you up."

"I'd be happy for Joe but not for me."

"You can still see him until he's ready for work," said gray-faced Wade Johnson.

"No," said Teddy, rallying his will, tears running down his face. "He's mine. Uncle Art, Aunt Nancy, I'll buy one of those air filters and keep my door closed and run it all day. None of Joe's germs will—"

"That's an awful lot of electricity," said Uncle Art. "And those filters really don't do anything a good air conditioner can't. A Kensington, of course."

"Excuse me just a minute," said Teddy. There was a lump in his throat so big it hurt, and his eyes were blurring and burning.

He called Joe to heel and headed up the stairs to his room, leashed the dog, made sure he had his wallet and the twenty-six dollars in it, grabbed Joe's half bag of kibble, and went out the front door.

Bag under his right arm, dog leash in his left hand, Teddy ran down long, steep Avenida de La Jolla all the way to Girard, downtown, to a sandwich place that allowed dogs on the patio.

He sat there, heart pounding, wanting to cry but sucking it up, an eleven-year-old boy in mute agony. The waitress brought water for him and for Joe.

Ten minutes later Teddy saw his aunt and uncle patrolling down Girard in their Range Rover with the blackout windows and the DELGADO 100M plates. Turned away and stared at himself in the café window. A few minutes after that, the Excalibur SUV came by the other direction. Teddy turned away again.

He ate the cheapest sandwich and looked out at the crowded, bustling city. Everybody was beautiful and rich. Dogs all over, and cars so rare he didn't even know what they were.

Teddy didn't know squat about La Jolla except that he had to get out.

He didn't know the best way to the freeways from here. He had another uncle, his mom's brother Phil, in Yuma, which he remembered from last year's visit was, like, three hours from here in a car.

So, take a bus, he thought. Right?

He waited half an hour for his aunt and uncle and Mr. Johnson to give up looking for him. It only took him twenty minutes to get to a bus stop.

He stood there looking up at the maps on the signs, Joe sitting at his feet. He didn't know La Jolla and its surrounding cities at all, and wasn't sure which bus would get him and Joe to Yuma. Didn't think the buses took dogs anyway.

He was still looking up at the sign to divine when the next bus would stop here, when a La Jolla cop car pulled up fast, lights flashing, and stopped right in the street. A big man in uniform got out of the car and came toward him.

"Teddy Delgado?" he asked, stopping a few yards away.

"Yes, sir."

"Is your dog friendly?"

"Yes, sir."

"I want you to come with me."

"To where?"

"Get in the car, son. You're going home."

"They're going to take my dog away."

"They'll do what's best for you, Teddy. You've been through a lot. But don't argue with me."

17

Bettina wakes at sunrise in the Queen Palms, Felix warm on one side of her, the Winchester Model 12 cold on the other.

Just three hours of sleep, haunted by J, and by spooky *sicarios* possibly dispatched to kidnap Felix, and by Daniel Knowles Strickland.

She cracks open a curtain on dark storm clouds and a breeze through the three wretched queen palms in the courtyard. Gets dressed to run, leashes Felix, and peeks out the window again. Imagines herself slipping into the near dark, heading for the Dana Point marina.

God, it would feel good to move, to *run*. But good enough to risk being seen by the two cartel representatives that Arnie Crumley's DEA says might be here?

She backs away from the curtain and detaches Felix's leash.

"Sorry, pup-pup," she says. "No run for us out of an abundance of caution. I hate that shit, caution. But I'm worried about you."

Angered at being a captive of her fears, she makes some coffee in the rinky-dink drip maker, props the Winchester in a corner, and checks her email and text messages.

She's got twelve new Felix emails and twenty new text messages to her phone. Some are accompanied by pictures of Felix's "relatives." Some want Bettina to return him to them, the rightful owners. Some offering to buy him, just as Strickland had done.

Five of the new emails are pleas from Teddy Delgado, reiterating his story of raising "Joe" in Otay Mesa for a year when he was a puppy. That Joe worked for the DEA for four years and was about to retire but he either ran away from, or was stolen by his handler, Aaron. So Teddy says. Teddy has eighty-five dollars and he won't take no for an answer and he's trying to get to Laguna but he can't drive yet.

The same basic story Arnie Crumley gave her, she thinks.

It further annoys Bettina that three of Felix's alleged "owners"— mysterious Dan Strickland, grating Arnie Crumley and now this pushy Ted Delgado—all want to see the dog. Not just see, but two of them want to take Felix away from her. To *own* him. A thought: Are they working together to get him away from me?

If you start feeling like you're paranoid, you probably are.

On the other hand, others online have claimed that his real name is Max, Spots, Jason, Scout, Magnum, Streak, Andy, Falcon, and on and on. One said that Felix knows over a thousand Russian words. One said she had raised Felix from birth, feeding him baby formula with an eyedropper. Another said he'd taken Felix skydiving when the dog was Murphy, his puppy. Another said her dog had been featured in a traveling circus and could answer addition and subtraction problems by raising and lowering his right front paw. Some wanted their dog back; others only to be featured in one of her videos.

Such as "Felix: The Rescue of a Mexican Street Dog," which is now just over a week old, and still getting lots of views and likes. There are more hustlers, liars, and cheats after her dog than ever, she thinks.

Annoyance rising, Bettina tells Ted that she understands his feelings for his former dog, but can't sell her Felix back to him. I'm really very sorry, she says, and she is. But not sorry enough to sell Felix.

Blood pressure high, as usual—she can feel the blood surging in her veins and arteries, trying to get through—Bettina updates next week's *Coastal Eddy* calendar from her voluminous emails and press releases.

It takes over an hour to replace the outdated listings with the new ones. It's nice to have something distracting to do.

She's just pressed the Send button on her laptop when she decides what to do about Strickland.

Writes her message and sends it off:

Hello Dan Strickland.
I have important news and some questions for you. I'll be walking Felix at Alta Laguna Park at one this afternoon.
Bettina Blazak.

His answer comes thirty seconds later:

See you then.

She wonders if she's making a bad decision. Maybe even falling into a trap. But she knows it's paranoid to think that a war hero, ex-cop, self-defense teacher would steal a well-known journalist's dog in a popular public park in broad daylight.

Paranoid indeed.

But after her meeting with Arnie, Strickland has some explaining to do.

She thinks of calling Billy Ray, maybe he could just sort of glide by and keep an eye out for her and Felix. Decides not to.

Strickland's résumé proves he's on the up-and-up, right?

And she'll have Thunder with her in the Wrangler.

Dan Strickland rises from one of the picnic tables as Bettina approaches. She notes the cardboard box on the table. She drops Felix's leash and he sprints to his former owner, who takes a knee and lets the dog lick his face, then rolls Felix over and scratches his underside.

"Mr. Strickland . . ."

"Dan."

"Bettina."

They sit.

"Dan, you were right. Felix was a DEA drug-sniffing dog until six months ago. His name was Joe. I've seen pictures of their Joe and he's definitely Felix. Joe was about to be retired for poor behavior and depression. He either ran away from his handler or was dognapped. Shortly after that, DEA thought that their retired Joe was being used by the New Generation cartel to locate drugs and cash belonging to the Sinaloa Cartel. Up until the time he was shot last month. Possibly by the Sinaloans. Who have possibly sent two of their people to Laguna to deal with Felix in some way."

"Deal in *what* way?"

"They don't know."

Strickland stands, brushes the dirt off his pants. His smile is slight. "Jesus, are you serious?"

"I'm scared. They told me to vary my patterns. Stay with friends or in motels."

"That's big of them."

"That's what I thought."

"No safe house for you and Joe?"

"Felix and me. No. They're interested in a guy called the Roman."

"The what?"

"He handled Joe for the New Generation. Nobody seems to know his real name."

Strickland shakes his head and meets her stare, no amusement in him.

Bettina is proud to have better information than this know-it-all self-defense genie. And she must ask the big question, because that's what she does, that's how you find stories that matter.

"Maybe *you're* the Roman?" she asks. "Technically, you could be."

His expression is tight and unreadable but she sees anger in his eyes and hears it in his voice.

"Well, actually not, Bettina. I run a successful self-defense company. I've never used or sold drugs. I don't have time to be running all over Tijuana with a dog, putting my gringo head in the crosshairs of cartel soldiers. But mainly, as I already told you, I lost Joe over a year ago and haven't seen him since."

Bettina vets his story and his tone. Does the math. "I had to ask. People surprise you, sometimes."

"You surprise *me*, Bettina. With your naïveté and gullibility. Where's that great reporter in you? Open your eyes and use your brain. Don't make me up. If this Roman is a gringo, he's more likely undercover DEA than a small businessman like me."

Which makes sense to Bettina as she thinks of Arnie Crumley's appearance and arrogance. Arnie as undercover Roman? Extravagantly far-fetched, but possible. Loyal to DEA or the New Generation, or only to himself?

Felix looks up at Strickland, ears limp with submission.

Bettina sees the worry on his face, knows that Felix has picked up on his former master's anger.

But Strickland's reaction helps a weight lift inside her, because she wants to believe that Strickland is a decent guy. Maybe more than decent. He gives her a somber glare.

"Okay," says Bettina. "All right. My eyes and brain are not perfect, but they work just fine."

"Well."

"Pardon my questions and suspicions. The DEA has me rattled. I don't rattle easy, but my imagination does have a mind of its own."

"It sure does."

"Reset?"

"I'm happy to. Let's sit."

Felix gives Bettina a hopeful look.

"Thanks for meeting me here on such short notice," she says. "You barely had time to make the drive from San Diego."

"I'm staying at the Montage here in town."

"Why?"

"I wanted to be close to Joe and you. I was hoping you'd call."

"Nice hotel."

"It's the ocean you pay for."

"I stayed there once to write an article about it. Felt like a princess."

"You'd be good one."

"What do you mean?"

"You're uncommon."

"Don't flatter me. I know who I am."

Strickland purses his lips and nods, gives her a gaze. His anger is gone and his eyes are gray and cool.

"You might not like what's in this box," he says.

Bettina has already registered the curious items, the most puzzling of which is wrapped in clear plastic and propped in a corner of the pasteboard box on the picnic table.

"Flowers?"

"I thought you'd like them."

"You have the manners of my grandfather." It looks like Strickland blushes but the sunlight through the clouds is strong right then.

"There's also food and some things for Joe."

"Felix."

"Joe to me."

"This is not a date, Dan."

"No, it absolutely is not."

Bettina shakes her head.

Strickland's face is a map of contradictory lines. Something in his posture, as he pulls what looks like a Montage hand towel out of the box and covers the dumbass flowers against the sun, makes Bettina see him as not just another egocentric, self-obsessed man. He looks embarrassed.

"Let's take a walk," says Bettina.

They take the trail that leads down from Alta Laguna Park into Laguna Canyon. There are enough hikers and bikers and dogs to further dilute Bettina's paranoia that Strickland is going to take off with her dog.

The canyon views are beautiful: gray clouds, winter-green hills, a peek of the silver Pacific. Felix zigzags the narrow trail ahead of them, nose up, nose down, nose up again. Bettina is sorry for lecturing Dan Strickland on his manners. She wonders for the millionth time in her life why she's so quick to take offense, and so quick to anger. But sometimes accepting of risk and willing to face danger. *Wanting* to face it. Like she gets things backward. Her mother used to tell her to slow down, Bettina, take a pill. But which one?

"I love my grandfather," she says, the stiff canyon breeze in her face. She likes the way the wind snatches the words from her mouth, like they're valuable. "I shouldn't have bitched you out."

"I've never done that before. Flowers."

"In your whole life?"

"Whole."

"Why today?"

Strickland stops and turns and the breeze moves his hair. "As a kid I thought I was just simple-minded. It took me forever to read and write. When I got to high school, I saw how different I was. Different shrinks had different names for it. ADHD was the one I heard most. I knew I didn't have certain feelings other people had. Certain behaviors. Certain fears. I heard, 'high risk tolerance' a lot. I heard 'impulse-driven' a lot. 'Low dopamine, high adrenaline.' But when I looked at other people, I seemed to be as good as them. Sometimes better. I closed off my mom and dad and sister. I never asked anything of them or anybody. But the flowers were asking you to like me, and to thank you for letting me see Joe."

Bettina considers his handsome, matter-of-fact face. "Felix. But what a beautiful confession."

A small smile from Dan the man. "I don't talk much about myself, so that'll probably be it for a while."

"I don't either," Bettina says. "I can go on and on about myself with Felix. People are a little tougher."

The trail is steep and narrow, with long switchbacks down the flank of the canyon. Felix puts up a covey of quail from a big patch of prickly pear, and Bettina's heart jumps as the birds tear into the sky. She picks one out and imagines her shotgun lead, and her squeezing of the trigger, regretting having shot so many of these quirky little birds when she was young. She calls her dog back.

"I used to hunt those when I was a girl."

"I hunted snakes and lizards."

"There's lots of those in this canyon. Two kinds of rattlers."

"Mom found my snake collection in my toy chest when I was ten. Crawling around the balls and helmets and in-line skates. I drilled holes in the back for air."

"We had snakes in Anza Valley but I never liked them. One of our Labs got bit and it almost did her in."

"Tell me about Anza Valley," says Strickland. "I've never been there."

Bettina's Anza Valley monologue carries them almost all the way down to the Laguna Canyon Road, then back up in a long gradual loop that brings them back to where they started at the park.

They sit facing each other across the picnic table, Felix at their feet.

Silence settles over them. Bettina gets water for the dog, then watches the tennis players and listens to the pop of the balls on the rackets. Watches Strickland as he sets out the cheeses and grapes and chocolate and two cans of fizzy water.

One thing about having lunch with a hunky self-defense guru, Bettina thinks, is you feel safe. Even if you hardly know him. Even if he inappropriately brings flowers. The flowers are actually pretty nice: sturdy protea and eucalyptus shoots. Strickland carries a gun in the small of his back, but a sweater mostly hides it. Maybe not a surprise, she thinks, given his occupation.

"Tell me more about how you got Joe," she says.

Felix raises his head at his name. Bettina sees him looking at her from down by her feet. He studies her, then he plunks his chin back down to the ground.

"When he got retired from DEA, a friend called. He knew I was looking for a dog. Joe and I took to each other immediately."

Bettina finds Arnie Crumley's forwarded DEA photos of Felix, hands her phone to Strickland.

Who looks up from the screen to her. "It's him, all right."

"Yes, it is."

"Apparently the Sinaloans hate him," says Bettina. "He's cost them millions of dollars with that nose of his. DEA says two Sinaloans have possibly been dispatched from Tijuana to California, possibly to steal him. Senior people, heavies. So I'm living away from home for a while. Different places every few days. Working remote. Not going out in public or falling into a pattern."

"They should offer you a safe house."

"They only use them on actionable intel. The intel they have on Felix is unverified. They said the Sinaloans want him, not me."

"That's the most gutless thing I've ever heard."

"Yeah. But there's no arguing with them."

Strickland hands back Bettina's phone. Shakes his head and squints out at the hills.

"I know people who can protect you and Joe," he says. "Professionals. I trained some of them. They'll give me a good rate, and I'll pay for them."

"No, you're generous. But no."

"They would have to be in your life twenty-four seven, until this resolves. They'll keep you and Joe safe. It's what they're trained for."

"No. I said no."

"I don't understand you, Bettina."

"Felix and I are moving targets in a state with twenty-three million people in the lower half, and God knows how many dogs. I have my Model 12. And Felix was trained for attack by the DEA, even though he wasn't real good at it."

"You're stubborn and naïve."

"Just stubborn."

"They'll kill you to get the dog, if they need to."

Bettina feels that spark starting up inside, the one that so easily kindles her instincts for fight and flight.

"Flowers," she says. "A free protection team for me and Felix. What do you want from me besides my dog?"

"All you offer."

The words land like a blow. "That's a creep-show thing to say to someone you don't even know."

Bettina flashes back to those strange first minutes with Daniel Strickland:

You made my day.

"You know what I think? I think guys like you almost always get what they want. And if they don't, it's no big deal."

"I'll do anything to protect you and Joe. I'll put you through my Apex program, no charge. Joe likes watching the training. You can bring him."

"Where you can take him off my hands, for his protection?"

"It could come to that."

"Not on my watch, Dan Strickland," says Bettina, rising. "Thanks for lunch but I'm going now."

Strickland takes a knee beside the picnic table, rubs Felix's ears with his big hands. Mutters his name while he pets him. Bettina feels like a villain.

"I'm sorry," he says. "But I feel strongly about things sometimes."

"We shouldn't do this again," says Bettina, surprised how bad she feels about what she's decided. Like she's lowering blinds on a sunny new morning.

Strickland stands and holds out the leash. Bettina takes it, studying his fine, hard-to-read face.

"You're new to me," he says. "I'm not sure what to do or say."

She nods and leads the dog away through the park, Felix trying to get back to Dan Strickland, whining as Bettina pops the lead smartly, bringing him to heel.

18

Strickland doesn't get off Interstate 5 until he passes his exit for home, then stops in San Ysidro. He fills the Quattroporte's tank with premium, pushes the cheese and protea flowers into the trash can, washes the windshield, and crosses the border into Tijuana.

Less than an hour later, he's drinking a beer in the great room of Carlos Palma's beachfront compound near Rosarito.

Through the enormous picture window, the sun is sinking into the Pacific. Orange ribbons on black water. Men with machine guns stroll the property, loiter in the arcade and gardens. There's a helicopter draped with camouflage net not far from the swimming pool. And a private marina made of enormous boulders, in which a gunship bobs, the guns themselves stowed on board for secrecy and quick deployment.

Here in the gaudy, over-furnished great room that reminds Strickland of a Miami hotel, the muted big screen shows recorded *fútbol*.

Strickland knows that Palma is unusually old to be running the Tijuana plaza of the CJNG—the Jalisco New Generation Cartel. Carlos was born in Veracruz, so he's not just old, he's a fish out of water.

Midsixties; thick gray hair; a suspicious, doubting face. Strickland has seen cartel life eat its young members alive. Yet Palma soldiers on. His wife, Camille—svelte and beautiful—reclines in a bowl-shaped rattan chair on a pedestal, her legs crossed under a white linen dress.

The men weave back and forth between Spanish and English, Strickland nearly fluent after classes in high school and a semester of college, and living in Mexico months at a time. Palma is conversant after his years at San Diego State University, and nonstop American movies and TV here in Mexico

Palma listens intently as Strickland reveals the rumors about Sinaloans dispatched to Laguna Beach to deal with Joe.

"Deal with him in what way?"

"Not clear yet, but I imagine they'll kill him." Strickland feels the cold plunge of his heart. "Kill a dog, for Christ's sake," he says.

"I want Joe back to work as much as you do," says Palma. "So, yes, if you want my men to steal him from the reporter, I can do this."

"And protect her from the Sinaloans?"

"Yes. Why don't you steal the dog yourself?"

"Joe is with the reporter twenty-four seven."

Palma squints at Strickland. "I have Frank and Héctor in San Diego. They are my best Californians. But you should know that this is an expense and a risk."

"I think Joe's worth it, for our business," says Strickland. "Thank you, Carlos."

"But while we try to claim your Joe and protect this reporter, we must get back to work. We are losing opportunity. We have good intel but no good dog."

"Benjamin has good dogs," says Camille. She's got the face of a princess and the wary eyes of a street fighter. Strickland knows she's from Hermosillo, daughter of a supervisor in the Ford Factory. Palma and his lieutenants always have new Fords but Camille hasn't gotten her license, though she just turned nineteen. Strickland knows that old Palma doesn't want her going anywhere.

"He will give me any dog you wish," she says.

"I don't trust him," says her husband.

"He's a good friend."

"Then I trust him less."

Strickland has observed a few dogs trained by Palma's men—three pit bulls and a Malinois—and found them unprofessional and churlish, more interested in fighting than finding drugs and money. There is no comparing them to Joe in either skill or spirit.

Palma speaks into a remote, and the TV *fútbol* becomes boxing. Strickland watches a series of lavish knockouts going back decades—a highlights reel apparently curated by Palma himself.

Strickland watches the colors play off the faces of Palma and Camille, burnished by the glow of the setting sun.

The boxing becomes cockfighting, staged atrocities that Strickland can hardly watch. Strickland has always hated cockfighting.

Then bullfighting, which he's always hated even more.

Palma senses Strickland's mood and gives him a cagey glance. Speaks into the remote. The TV shows Bettina Blazak and Dr. Rodríguez at the Saint Francis of Assisi Veterinary Clinic in Tijuana.

Strickland is startled by this sudden, larger-than-life image of her, by the zoomed-in details, her hopeful eyes, the dark waves of hair breeze-blown in the cloudy gray day.

Palma stares at him, eyes magnified by his black-framed glasses. "Have you talked to her?"

"I drove to her office as soon as I saw her video."

"My Frank and Héctor will move quickly."

"That's what I'm hoping. Carlos, make it absolutely clear that they cannot hurt her."

"Do you like her face?" asks Camille.

"Not particularly, señora."

At Palma's command, the TV now offers dogfights, bloody spectacles that Strickland ignores in favor of the darkening western sky. The sun dips into the ocean while in the periphery of his vision writhing forms thrash in silence.

"Señor Strickland, you and Joe have made me money," says Carlos.

"And humiliated the Sinaloans. It was your idea. To work for New Generation. And I thank you for bringing your idea to me."

"Yes, sir," answers Strickland, sensing bad news. He remembers that first precarious meeting with Palma, brokered by one of Strickland's Apex Self-Defense clients—a wealthy Mexican resort developer with a love of horse racing. Everybody knew that Carlos Palma owned stables. Back then—just over a year ago—Palma had seemed smart and businesslike. He had taken Strickland's outrageous proposal to use his exceptional dog to find Sinaloan loot with a dark sense of humor and a glimmer in his eye.

No humor in him now, Strickland sees, just business. He begins to admit how foolish he was to think his relationship with Palma could lead to trust and friendship. How foolish it was to reveal his real name, his real history.

Palma fingers the remote and in the window reflection, dogfighting turns to human pornography.

"So, I will return Joe to you so that we can continue our important work," he says. "But now I find it necessary that we change our arrangement. My risks grow higher as the Sinaloans send in men from the mountains. And my costs grow higher as I bribe the Policía Municipal for our freedoms here."

"Carlos? *Change* our *arrangement*?"

"You are a businessman. You surely see this."

"I see that I am about to be robbed."

Strickland turns and sees the TV obscenities flickering on Palma's dark glasses.

Then pivots back to the window and looks down at Rosarito, the hotels and restaurants, their lights twinkling like jewels. Two men with guns slung over their shoulders look up at him from the arcade. He's never wanted out of somewhere more than here, right now, once and forever.

"Daniel," says Palma. "I have paid you thirty percent of what Joe has found—of the money and the products. Now, I am asking you to work with a new dog until we get your dog back. And, to accept twenty percent, as a way of supporting the New Generation Tijuana Cartel against the Sinaloans. Against the world. We are like the Corleones. A family against the wicked and the corrupt."

Palma speaks into the remote again and *The Godfather* starts up, a man's face in the darkness:

I believe in America . . .

"Take the new arrangement," says Camille, not moving her eyes from the screen. "It will guarantee that Bettina Blazak is protected. You surely see this too."

Strickland nurses a glass of wine through dinner in the formal dining room. Conceals his lifelong indifference to alcohol with colorful stories of his time in Sangin Valley, Afghanistan; learning Krav Maga from badass Israelis in Tel Aviv; his headline-making rescue of the congressman in the restaurant assassination attempt. What he wants most in life right now is to kick the shit out of the old man and get back to San Diego. But if he leaves now, proud, vain, pathetic Palma will take it as an insult.

After dinner, they all return to the great room for cigars and brandy and more TV entertainment.

Strickland agrees to his new pay scale.

Agrees to audition three more of Benjamin's miserable dogs.

Professes his fierce loyalty to New Generation and makes another earnest request that Joe be abducted safely, and the *Coastal Eddy* reporter be spared violence from either side.

Palma tells him that Frank and Héctor are honorable men, and not to worry so much.

Later, awash in tequila and red wine, growing sentimental about his native Veracruz, where he plans to retire, Palma falls asleep on the cowhide couch, his head lolled back on a cushion and muted *Scarface* scenes playing off his glasses.

Camille leaves the room without a word or a look.

Strickland goes to the big window again and looks out at the heaving sea. Faint music drifts to him from somewhere deep in the house.

Strickland sees himself as a man who has never hesitated to take what he wants, never wavered in the face of acceptable risk, never cowered from threat or danger. He eats such things for lunch. But here right now, in this gangster's compound by the sea, he feels fear as never before. It's not from something out there, coming at him. It's gotten *inside*, pushing away the adrenaline, coloring his thoughts. He thinks part of it might be the three men he shot down in the Calderón factory and warehouse. They fall through his dreams. He's seen this same fear in his students at Apex, especially in the fighting rings, that knee-wobbling, heart-pounding shutdown of confidence that turns scared humans into easy targets.

He box-breathes for a minute, feels his pulse slow down and the fearful static in his mind begin to quiet.

Glances back at snoring Palma, at his slipped eyeglasses and slack mouth, which strike Strickland as the perfect rewards for human lust and vanity. He wonders if that could be him someday, decides it most certainly could. Wonders if he would regret his life. And admits now that he would probably regret all but a few relatively minor moments of it. The rest just meaningless pursuit of things. Reflex, distraction.

He feels himself changing and isn't sure he likes it.

He looks through his reflection on the window glass, all the way to the dim line where the twinkling black ocean meets the dull black sky.

These sudden notions of fear and regret are new to Strickland, and they gnaw at him.

But what's bothering him just as much is Bettina Blazak and his unprecedented desire to give her what he has. All he has. His protection, attention and consideration. His words and emotions. His past; his stories. His occasional smiles and laughter. All his cool stuff, all the things he's collected from all the places he's been. And, of course, there might also be things they'd acquire and the places they'd see, together. All they would make together. He wonders for the thousandth time what exactly has been happening to him since he first watched her Felix video online and saw his Joe in the company of a beautiful bright woman who reminded him of someone, or some *thing*. He's never used the word *love* in any but the most mundane way, and never regarding a whole, fellow, human being. *I love a rare ahi steak. I love the way the Quattroporte grabs the road and won't let go. I love the smell of money and the things it can buy. I love her legs.*

So when Strickland tries to solve himself, he sees that fear plus regret equals his desire to give. Not to take. To give. That is love, correct? To give all.

He remembers asking the same of Bettina Blazak:

All you offer.

He feels a cold shudder down his back as he considers the "honorable" Frank and Héctor. Has he loosed the hounds of hell on Joe and Bettina? Or found the most expedient available way to keep her and Joe from being harmed by the Sinaloans, and getting Joe returned to his rightful owner?

The light from the TV suddenly changes. Strickland turns to find the *fútbol* on again and Camille in a green satin robe, her sleek black hair up, regarding him. She looks empty and exhausted.

She sets the remote on the couch and walks out, glancing back at Strickland before heading into a dark hallway.

Back home, Strickland sends a text message to Bettina Blazak's *Coastal Eddy* number:

Sorry for "all you offer" this morning. I can't get you out of my mind.

19

Tough titties, thinks Bettina, reading the text twice, then deleting it. In fact, she's having trouble getting Strickland out of *her* mind, and she cusses herself for this. She wishes he'd never seen her video, never walked into the *Coastal Eddy*. But then, well, she's kind of glad he did. And did she have to be a bitch? Bust his ass for flowers?

It's late now, the Alta Laguna Park playdate with Felix and Dan Strickland is a full twelve hours old. She's got her work laptop set up on the small Queen Palms desk, the Winchester Model 12 propped in the corner, and a bourbon glass sweating into a paper towel beside the computer.

Felix has been morose since the park, where she dragged him away from his former master. He rests his head on his front paws, eyeing her, his forehead creased. She wonders why she feels so bad about keeping him when she has every right to—moral, ethical, financial. God-given and approved by fate. *Finders keepers.* Did she believe for one second that Strickland would give the dog back to her if their roles were reversed?

Being locked in this tiny motel room for two nights and a long day and a half has given her more than enough time to interview the Laguna Beach Art Festival directors by phone, and get their bullish chamber-of-commerce-ish thoughts on this year's event. It has taken her some hours to write it up, though, earnestly boring as they are. The fact that people use reporters to further their own agenda is her least favorite part of the job. Turns her into a flak. She'd love to work for a paper or a show with enough weight and independence to just tell the truth about stories that matter.

Today has been one of the longest of her life, and she sees by the bedside clock that it's become tomorrow.

She's about to pour a nightcap when a new message lowers into her email feed.

She doesn't recognize the sender:

La señorita Bettina Blazak,

It is very good to meet you. I very much love "Felix: The Rescue of a Mexican Street Dog." I am almost certain that this dog has been robbing me. My soldiers have witnissed him doing this. Therefore, will you please sell the dog to me? I have already dispatched two friends to Laguna to pay you $200,000 for Felix. If you will not give him up, I must order him to be confiscated, of course. And, Señorita Blazak, they will pay you another $200,000 if you can identify the dog's handler. He is known to us only as the Roman. I believe if he has seen your happy story about the wounded dog he will contact you about getting him back. You should understood that I am a kind man and prefer the way of peace to the way of pain. I have a family and many dogs for my children. I believe in the Father, the Son and the Holy Ghost. I would consider you a friend forever and I do not make friends with lightness. I would not harm the dog, of course. Only to use him against my enemies as they have used him against me.

With Sincerity,
Alejandro Godoy
El Gordo

Five black-and-white photographs are attached. They're all of the same subject, likely taken on a cell phone with a rapid-snap setting.

They're dark, fuzzy shots of a black-clad man in a black ski mask, gun in hand, caught mid-stride along railroad tracks in what looks to Bettina like a switching yard. Taken from behind and aside, at night.

A medium-sized dog carves a path out ahead of the gunman, his body pale, his saber tail raised, his head down.

Felix, she sees, her heart in free fall.

The man has his gun in one hand, raised high and pointed slightly down. Man and dog are at some distance from the photographer.

The man could be any race, any nationality, anybody. The Roman, Bettina can only assume.

But the dog is Felix, no doubt.

My new friends, thinks Bettina—El Gordo and the Sinaloa Cartel.

Who now know where their devil dog is, and what I look like, and where I work.

Two of my friends are in Laguna Beach now . . . and if you will not give him up I must order him to be confiscated. . . .

Her heart thumps and sweat cools her forehead.

There's a giant miracle in all of this, though: Godoy wants to buy Felix, not kill him!

She checks the curtains and turns off all the lights except the small desk lamp. Surveys the Queen Palms Motel and the parking lot and the cars sliding up and down Coast Highway in this dark early morning.

Forwards El Gordo's message to Arnie and Billy Ray. Thinks of sending it to Dan Strickland but she doesn't quite trust him. She *wants to*, just can't.

Billy calls immediately, tells her to pack, and that he'll be there in twenty minutes.

She checks the window again, pours out the bourbon, and packs her things. Felix sits up and watches, sensing her worry and change of mood.

She hears a car pulling in below, then car doors closing. And, a moment later, footsteps on the noisy, wobbly concrete-and-steel steps that connect the motel floors.

Then voices: alcohol-slurred English and laughter. She tiptoes closer to her gun and the hackles on Felix's back lift like spines. He stares at the door in hypervigilant silence. The men pass by her window, blurred shapes through her curtains.

She sits up in bed in the dark, the gun across her lap and the dog sitting bolt upright at the foot of the mattress, full attention on the door, no more than twelve feet away.

Billy's text message pings in.

Besides the cars outside, the next sound she hears is Billy coming up the stairs.

Six Months After the Deaths of Teddy's
Mom and Dad . . .

20

On a cool October Saturday, Teddy Delgado sat in a small aluminum grandstand alongside grass arena 2 at Excalibur K-9 Training Center. Joe was among those dogs taking their final Class I certification tests—a formality, really—before being officially placed with their new handlers. With Teddy were his adoptive parents, Art and Nancy, and his siblings Jorge, Angela, and Beatrice.

Teddy sat apart from them, up on the empty top row for a better view of Joe and his soon-to-be handler, Aaron. Teddy looked out at the training center grounds, where other K-9 dogs were testing, before being paired with their new handlers. There was a sense of celebration in the air; even the dogs sensed that good things were happening here today.

Teddy felt none of it. He had not had a haircut for the last six months, and now his mother's shiny black hair dangled from under his Padres cap. His jeans were worn at the knees and his Excalibur windbreaker was big on him. He was eleven when they died. He was eleven now. He hated eleven and thought he might be stuck there forever.

Teddy knew that Joe would go home with Aaron today and begin his

Class II training at a DEA facility. No visits allowed at the Class II—guns, controlled substances, dangerous drugs such as fentanyl, heroin, and cocaine—all of which would become target scents for Joe to learn. Which meant that, after the graduation today, this was the last time that he would see Joe until his tour of duty was over, and Aaron's DEA could retire him back to Teddy.

He also knew that between now and then, a lot can happen.

Things could go well for a working detection dog. There could be success, heroics, even awards.

But also, there could be injuries, accidents, fearfulness, over-aggression, and burnout. Even handler problems. Wade told him that it can be as hard for some working dogs to live with a demanding law enforcement professional as it can be for some handlers to live with a dog. They were "in each other's snout twenty-four seven, three sixty-five." It was all about limits, discipline, and unconditional obedience, as Wade had told him again and again.

Despite all of that—everything that had happened and could happen—Teddy did not regret handing Joe over to be fine-tuned for actual K-9 work. Teddy's heart was broken by this, but it was already broken, and he in fact had broken it himself, knowing that he was doing the right thing for Joe, and for the people that the DEA and Joe would save from addictions and deaths.

So you have no regrets, he told himself.

No regrets.

No regrets.

He was still numb over Mom and Dad. Less sadness since that night, but more numbness. And this pending loss of Joe felt like an even heavier layer on top of it all, a cast iron lid, unmovable.

The pills were helping. They kept his emotions in boxes that Dr. Reyes urged him to "take off the shelf and open" anytime he wanted. Anytime he felt ready.

He liked his cousins/siblings okay.

Art and Nancy too.

There was a girl at school who smiled and sometimes touched his hand when no one was looking. Anastasia.

Teddy drank a soda and watched Joe doing his off-leash obedience. He was great. No mistakes, no anticipated cheats. Crisp timing, perfect body language. Joe was always so great at this, unless he ran across a lizard or a bird or a low-flying butterfly, even a distant rabbit. Teddy could always feel Joe's happiness, and he felt it now.

He knew that Aaron was a strong, firm handler and he tolerated no errors, no variation. Aaron rewarded Joe very sparingly—words only—never food. Unlike Teddy, who gave Joe endless kibble treats for practically anything he did, and sometimes just to feel Joe's whiskers and tongue on his hand.

Really, thought Teddy, Joe's the one thing that hasn't changed since Mom and Dad. Joe was still his dog and he was still Joe's boy. Joe was the only thing in his world not numb and flattened by antidepressants.

Which was why—when Teddy suddenly remembered that today was the last day he'd see Joe for up to five years—he felt his heart sink, all the way to the center of the earth. Then he felt his medication rushing in to cushion its fall. DEA rules: no visitation between past owners, handlers, or breeders and deployed dogs.

But Teddy had gotten his uncle and aunt to okay Joe's return to La Jolla when his tour of duty was over. When Teddy would be old enough to really take care of him properly, they suggested. Art was going to install a special HEPA HVAC system that would remove 99 percent of the allergens released by Joe in the La Jolla mansion. This, dependent on Teddy getting his grades up. They'd been going down since his mom and dad.

Down in the ring, Aaron waited for Wade Johnson to enter something on his tablet, looked up at Teddy, and nodded.

Teddy nodded back. That was about as much positive emotion as Aaron showed him. Aaron was one serious guy. Teddy knew that Aaron hated criminals, especially drug sellers. Hated what they did to innocent people. Loved his job. Loved a perfect dog. When he wasn't at work, he was in his home gym. Not married.

Teddy watched as a well-padded man strode into the arena and faced off Joe and Aaron from fifty feet away. Teddy could see the man's eyes, alert behind the protective bars of his helmet. The man would have been big even without the pads but now he looked like some upholstered mega-villain. He spread feet for balance.

Teddy had seen a lot of this in the last six months, out here several times a week, eating up his allowance money for bus fares back and from La Jolla. Joe tried hard but he didn't have the weight to match his bite, and the two-hundred-pound men usually battled him to a draw. Joe didn't have a mean bone in his body—except for small animals, which was different from aggression—until he came here for good six months ago. They'd tried to mean him up, but Teddy had seen little improvement in Joe's protection and apprehension skills. Although Joe would do anything to make his master happy. His master's command was his Bible. Teddy hated the thought that Joe's new master might not be able to be happy, and that Joe could only fail.

Joe sat and watched the man, his quirky ears erect.

Then Aaron yelled, *"Fass!"*

Joe's lithe body and long legs gave him acceleration that none of the other Excalibur dogs could match. He was across the grass like a cream-and-tan spear, teeth bared, hackles high, silent, as trained. He launched himself from ten feet away and latched on to the thick arm of the back-pedaling man. Then his snarl erupted, and his head shook and his body curved and snapped back and forth sharply in midair and the padded man managed to throw him to the ground. Joe rolled and charged and got thrown down again. It hurt Teddy to see Joe so overmatched.

Aaron ran into the fray, calling Joe off, making him sit while the padded villain ran off, lumbering slowly.

"Fass!"

And off again went Joe, a pale blur across the green. The man threw him down again and Joe charged again and this time the big enemy went down and Joe got a foot and thrashed it for all he was worth.

Aaron got there a moment later.

"Aus!"

Teddy saw Wade Johnson make an entry on his tablet. His face had a neutral expression. These apprehension drills were always Joe's worst scores. Teddy had long thought that a small detection genius like Joe shouldn't have to attack and apprehend. But who knew? Maybe he'll have to defend his handler someday. Or an innocent bystander.

When all the trials were over and Joe and Aaron stood amid the small crowd of attendees, Teddy went to the front and knelt down in front of Joe.

Jorge, Angela, and Beatrice were with him, and they knelt, too, and Joe went from face to face licking them, then back to Teddy, at whom he smiled pantingly and lay down then rolled over at Teddy's command.

They all rubbed his belly, which he'd always loved, and his right rear paw scratched the air around their small hands.

Teddy was going to tell Joe he loved him and would see him soon, but his throat clenched in a painful knot and his eyes burned and he said nothing.

Sitting alone in the far back seat of the big Sequoia, he stared out the window but saw nothing. Thought thoughts but felt nothing. Wondered again what it would be like to be dead, and how you could do it quickly. Thought of Anastasia but felt nothing. Thought there was a lot of nothing in this world.

Jorge reached back and swiped his hand through Teddy's burning vision.

"Cheer up, little brother."

"Okay," said Teddy. "I will."

"We got Hawaii tomorrow, you know."

Yes, he thought: the vacation. A week of nothing on an island in the middle of nothing, without his dog.

21

Billy Ray picks up Bettina and Felix at the Queen Palms in the black March morning. She seems anxious and distracted but Billy understands that she just wants to write her stories and have a normal life again. The dog seems on edge too, hypervigilant and all business. Billy has traded shifts to watch over and help Bettina through the day.

So he gets her home to sleep for an hour and a half, sits in the living room while she showers and gets ready, then follows her to the *Coastal Eddy* building for her usual 8:00 a.m. start.

He goes to the Havana Café across the Coast Highway, where he can see her small cubicle window above the thickening traffic. The coffee here is strong and he pours in lots of warm milk. There's only one door in and out of *Coastal Eddy* offices, and Billy's eyes are glued to it.

"Nice morning," he says to the guy a few stools down. Barely looks at him he's so intent on that door.

"Perfect," says the man.

"Boy, this coffee *con leche* is strong," Billy says, sizing the guy up before refocusing on the *Coastal Eddy* front door. "You a tourist or a local?"

"Just visiting. I live down in San Diego. You?"

"I live here now."

"I hear some Texas in there."

"Wichita Falls."

"Never been."

"It's a great town."

Arnie finally calls back. "You're damn right the message is real," he says. "It's El Gordo. We've got everything from text intercepts to voice recordings of him."

"That's a pretty risky thing to do—threaten someone and sign your name."

"He thinks he's immortal."

"Maybe he is," says Billy. "He's been a fugitive from you guys for fifteen years."

Silence. "We want Bettina to help us nail the visiting Sinaloans."

"You've already left her in danger. Why should she risk her life for your career?"

"We'll certainly protect her, Billy. We're not cold-blooded."

"If you don't quit being a condescending asshole to her, she won't help you one bit."

"Can you get her to my division office in San Diego? Say noon? I've got a plan and some people I'd like you to meet."

Billy pays up, nods farewell to the stool guy, and jaywalks back across Coast Highway for Bettina.

Less than an hour later, Bettina, Billy, and Felix wait at the entrance gate of the San Diego DEA division office on Viewridge Avenue.

Bettina looks up at the pale flank of the building, almost entirely hidden by a tree-lined battlement studded with forward-pointing steel spears. Wonders why federal buildings have to be so macho. It's nice to have Billy here.

"Good morning," he says to the guard. "We're here for an appointment with special agent Arnie Crumley."

The guard has an armored DEA Police vest, a buzz cut, and what looks to Bettina like dark snakes tattooed around his thick arms. He eyes them one at a time then takes Billy's badge wallet and Bettina's driver's license back inside the booth.

A short minute later, he's back with a placard for the pickup truck. "Visitor parking up by the stairs."

This conference room is small and windowless. White walls, three long tables in a horseshoe, plenty of steel-framed chairs that slide easily on the short green carpet. Bettina notes the clean whiteboards and the many electrical outlets on the walls and floor. There's a big monitor on a stand at the open end of the horseshoe.

Arnie comes in ahead of a stocky Black woman in a dark suit and a middle-aged white man wearing chinos and a golf shirt and carrying a laptop. Bettina notes that Arnie has traded his undercover border badass look for business casual and a shave.

He introduces his confederates, joining them to face his brother and Bettina across the horseshoe.

Felix lays himself at Bettina's feet, head up, alert.

The middle-aged man is digital forensic examiner Dale Greene. He has plenty of silver-gray hair, and a face that Bettina instinctively trusts. He opens his computer, taps a few keys, then starts things off.

"This threat would terrify most civilians," he says. "So Ms. Blazak, I'm glad you have the courage to trust us and help us. Mr. Crumley, thank you for being here too. My section recovers and analyzes digital evidence, determining authenticity for the courts. The first thing I should say is this message was surely written by Alejandro Godoy, Mexico's most wanted *narcotraficante*. We've been surveilling him, and intercepting some of his digital mail, for years. It's him, all right, right down to his word choice and misspellings. Some of his recurring favorite topics are here—the Holy Trinity, his family, the high value he places on friendship, the way of peace and the way of pain. We know he's serious about cash for the dog because four hundred grand is serious money, especially for Godoy. He grew up poor in the Sierra Madre and is a legendary tightwad."

Chuckles.

Greene touches his computer screen and Alejandro Godoy's face appears on the big monitor.

Bettina is surprised by how young he looks. His face is impish and his wavy dark hair needs a cut. "How old is he?"

"Forty-eight or -nine. He was born in a clinic that kept poor records. Don't be fooled by his cute face. We've tied him to over a dozen murders, personally. And almost a hundred more, as a coconspirator. The tonnage of illegal drugs he's freighted into the United States is unknown. What we intercept is impressive. What gets past us is incalculable."

Bettina watches the slide show with fascination and revulsion:

Alejandro Godoy as a schoolboy, 1983.

In a Culiacan *fútbol* uniform with a group of other boys, circa 1985.

Teenaged Alejandro Godoy in a panga, holding up a dorado.

And on a horse, with the enormous Copper Canyon behind him, a place Bettina recognizes from having been there just after college.

El Gordo in the mountains, skinny and shirtless, cradling an AK-47, his narrow shoulders draped with ammunition belts, a cigar in his mouth.

Young El Gordo in a wedding photo with his young wife.

"Now, this is Godoy christening the school he built in Creel, not far from where he grew up," says Greene. "Taken just a couple years ago. He's been grooming his Robin Hood legend with the locals since his first crimes, which were robbing tourists in the Copper Canyon railroad on horseback—outlaw style—I kid you not. He's built two schools, a medical clinic, and a church—all in towns high in the Sierra Madre. He's also got modest homes and small compounds throughout the Sinaloa mountains. He moves around a lot. He's not flashy. It's safe to say he believes his own myth."

Bettina feels an uncomfortable silence in the room as the slide show abruptly shifts to carnage:

Bloody bodies heaped by a roadside.

Piled in a van.

Stacked like cordwood in a lake of blood on a dirt road.

Headless bodies.

Bodiless heads.

Plastic drums with their lids off and vaguely recognizable human parts suspended in liquid.

"Hydrochloric acid doesn't eat the plastic," says Arnie. "They use steel drums for burials at sea, because HCl disintegrates the metal along with the body. All evidence destroyed. But really, they're happy to litter the country with bodies. It sends the right signals."

"Why show me all of this?" she asks.

"So you know who you're dealing with," says Arnie.

Bettina feels not just revulsion but sharp fear that El Gordo's people are in Laguna, waiting to buy Felix and vanish with him forever. She feels the horror of having been personally contacted by a monster, El Gordo himself. She feels like he's invaded her. Can feel him inside, jagged and breath-robbing, like the virus in her dad. Which makes her remember the bagged bodies in the refrigeration vans and the mass graves and the flaming pyres in India during the worst of that year.

"Um, I need to step out for a sec," she says. "Felix, sit and stay."

"Come with me, Bettina," says Special Agent Ladonna Powers, who rounds the tables through Felix's soft whimpers, takes Bettina by the arm, and steers her to the bathroom.

Where she makes it to the closest stall, throws up, lowers the lid, sits down, and tries to breathe slowly and deeply. Tries to slow her galloping pulse.

"I'm okay, Agent Powers."

"It's Ladonna, and you are definitely not okay."

"I'm better."

"Sit and breathe, girl. I won't leave you alone."

Bettina's heart beats shallow and fast. "I don't know how I'm going to help you, but I'll do anything on earth to keep those people away from my dog and me."

"That's why we're here, Bettina. We exist to make that happen."

"I have never once backed down from a fight. I like fights. But what I saw in there scared the living shit out of me."

"Me too. It always does. Sometimes I look at that stuff just to remind me who I am and why I do what I do."

"I want to be a special agent too."

"We're hiring."

"Nah. No. I want to be a writer more."

"World needs writers too."

"Okay. I'm okay now. I'm coming out."

Back in the conference room, LaDonna takes over.

"Our counter-op starts when El Gordo contacts you again," she says. "He'll do it soon. And so long as he believes that his pen pal really is you, Bettina, and you're playing fair with him, he'll keep his people under control."

"Who are they?" asks Bettina.

"Joaquín Páez and Valeria Flores," says Arnie. "A horse breeder and a hotelier. Married, a handsome couple, good English. Way up the Sinaloan chain, close to Godoy. Charged with international narcotics distribution five years ago, both acquitted. They're money people, not in the muscle end of things. They launder cash, make investments, create and disband entities and accounts, as needed. They've got Southern California connections in the horse racing and hospitality industry. Horses and hotels. We're a little surprised that they've been dispatched here to buy your dog."

Felix looks at Bettina.

"They've been on our wish list for years," says Arnie. "They'll follow El Gordo's orders until they get Joe. After that, anything can happen."

Bettina's foggy shock has lifted and she's starting to feel the old fight coming back, her spark and flame and fire. "What do you mean by *anything*?"

Hearing her change of tone, Felix sits and looks up at her.

LaDonna is blunt and to the point:

"They might already be under orders to kill you both rather than pay the money. Godoy says he wants to use the dog against his enemies, but really, what does that mean? It's the weakest part of his pitch. Whereas killing Joe is satisfactory revenge, and much easier. He can post it all on the *Blog Narco*: 'The Robin Hood of Sinaloa Bares His Fangs!'"

Again, Bettina feels that light patter of heart, chokes back her disgust. "El Gordo would do that? This God-fearing family man, dog lover, friend maker? Slaughter a woman and a dog for revenge? For his losses? His hurt pride?"

"We can't know what he'll do," says Arnie.

"I agree," says Dale Greene.

"We have to assume the worst," says Powers. "So our job is to make El Gordo believe that Bettina trusts him, is motivated by the money, and willing to deliver Joe to them. When you get your orders from El Gordo, we'll be locked, loaded and everywhere. This is what we train for."

Billy gives the agents a skeptical once-over. "Why can't you keep Bettina out of this, just handle it yourself? Use an agent as a stand-in. She isn't bait."

Bettina sees the emotion on his face. And she knows that Billy—all of them—see the emotion on hers. She's still clammy and cold from vomiting and fear. Weak. She breathes deeply, trying to will herself into calm action, as she so often has. "I'm all the way in on this, Billy. You know that."

"Yeah, I do."

"We can't fake you, Bettina," says Powers. "You're a known quantity, recognizable. You are our voice, and our face. You can control Felix. We're honored you brought this to us. We're honored to be trusted by you. Mr. Crumley, we'll guard this woman with our lives, and we may need your help."

"You'll have it."

"El Gordo will contact you," says Powers. "Bettina, let's get some numbers into your phone. I don't have to tell you to keep it charged, on, and on you every second of your day. It's good to move around, and stay away from home and work. It's good to assume that Joaquín and Valeria are waiting and probably watching. Don't be more than an hour away from home by car. When El Gordo moves, you will need to be close."

On the drive back to Laguna, Billy offers three times to "shadow" Bettina whenever he's not on duty. He doesn't want her alone for a second.

"No," she says. "I can't have you breathing down my neck, Billy. I can take care of myself. I do appreciate your concern and I promise not to do anything stupid. So thank you."

"Okay."

"You'll try to shadow me anyway, won't you?"

"Well, I just might."

"Thanks for your honesty. But don't."

Joe feels the intense seriousness between Bettina and Billy, but he can't understand their words.

All he gets is that something is going to happen and it could be a bad thing or a good thing, and there would be seriousness in it.

Work, like with Dan or Aaron.

Work, like when it was loud and his leg was hurt and the boy carried him to the Good Man.

Something is going to happen and Joe understands that he and Bettina will be a part of it.

Earlier That Day...

22

Strickland has guessed right, twice.

I should be in Vegas he thinks, watching as Bettina and Joe walk into the *Coastal Eddy* newsroom at eight o'clock sharp.

Escorted, as before, by the same Cowboy in the same brown blazer, whom Strickland found on the Laguna PD website. Billy Something, who patrols town on a fucking bike.

And now takes a stool at the Havana Café coffee bar on PCH, three empty stools away from Strickland himself.

"Nice morning," says Billy.

"Perfect," says Strickland.

They converse, then Strickland orders up a Cuban breakfast sandwich to go with his *café con leche*. Calls Charley Gibbon and gets him to teach the Apex class today: it's heavy on hand-to-hand, right in Charley's wheelhouse.

He reads the print edition of *Coastal Eddy* while through the noisy clatter of dishes and conversations, he eavesdrops on Billy the Bike Cop.

. . . a fugitive from you guys . . .

Why should she risk her life for bureaucrats?

. . . quit being a condescending asshole . . .

Then Billy pays up, gives Strickland a nod, and dashes across Coast Highway and into the *Coastal Eddy* offices.

So, Billy the Bike Cop is putting Bettina in a risky situation, Strickland thinks. Involving *you guys*, who include at least one condescending asshole, probably in law enforcement. To do what? Take down the two Sinaloans allegedly in Laguna Beach right now? What else could it be?

Billy, Bettina, and Joe are a fairly easy follow down Interstate 5. Strickland knows from his Strickland Security days that it's easier to tail yapping distracted people than a solo driver. Off and on, he sees the back of Joe's head and his outstretched ears, or his powerful, ingenious snout taking in the world through the cracked 4X4 windows.

Strickland is thinking the obvious—DEA—and when Billy takes the Balboa Avenue exit in San Diego, Strickland feels like he's just put three rounds through the heart of a moving silhouette at a hundred feet.

Billy's pickup pulls onto Viewridge Avenue. As he drives by, Strickland sees the guard booth and the flank of the DEA building on a tree-lined rise beyond it. Would like to be a fly on the wall in *that* place, he thinks. He wonders if Bettina Blazak is bonking Billy the Bike Cop. Cute couple. Hope not. He tells himself to keep his eyes on the prizes: Joe and Bettina.

Strickland U-turns at the next light, wishing he could tell her that Carlos Palma has sent two of his best men to protect her from the Sinaloans, but of course he can't.

Strickland reminds himself to be patient, let Frank and Héctor swipe Joe as planned, then he can get out of Laguna and back to work. He doesn't want to leave Bettina to deal with El Gordo's people—or Frank and Héctor—but he's got no choice. He could shoot all four of them dead before they touch Joe, but that would draw replacements from both Godoy and Palma. The key is El Gordo, he thinks. The Fat Man holds the cards.

He parks where he can keep an eye on the Viewridge exit.

Asks Charley Gibbon to cover his Apex classes for the next three days. Strickland shoves a lot of money at him to make it happen. Charley is not a people person.

A long three hours later, Strickland has tailed Joe, Bettina, and Billy back to the Canyon View Apartments in Laguna Canyon. The onshore afternoon breeze has kicked up, and the eucalyptus trees shimmer in cool sunlight.

He parks at some distance and watches them walk toward the building. Stopping at a cluster of mailboxes, Bettina hands the leash to Billy, then removes a thick handful of flyers and envelopes.

Then they head up the stairs, Joe apparently happy to be here. Strickland tries not to let this trouble him. Jealous of a dog? Joe's got good taste, he thinks: Bettina Blazak is beautiful.

He walks briskly to the mailboxes, gets her apartment number, then continues on to her red Wrangler in the parking garage. Attaches the Mole GPS vehicle tracker under the rear bumper. It jumps to the chassis with a magnetic clunk.

He's back to his car in three minutes. A beat later, Billy comes back to his truck, climbs in, rolls down the windows, but doesn't start the engine. He leans his head back on the rest, facing Bettina's apartment. Strickland waits a couple of minutes, wondering if Billy the Bike Cop will make him from the Havana earlier today or not. Strickland has to figure, yes, a cop will remember him, that's what cops do.

Strickland uses his distance from Billy to sidle along the Stan Oaks storefronts and take a different, out-of-Billy's-view stairway up to Bettina's place.

Looking into her Ring camera, Strickland knocks. Hears Joe woof softly, then footsteps, and the door opens a little. Joe squeezes through and leans into Strickland's leg, wiggling like a puppy.

"This is strange," says Bettina. "You just keep showing up."

"You're not safe," he says, his voice soft but urgent. "Let me help. I'm legally armed and can protect you until professional bodyguards can get here. I trained them and they're good. No expense to you, as I said. Or you and Joe can come with me back to Apex. There's a secure guest flat on the second floor. The building is full of weapons and people learning how to use them. Door number three, we can get separate hotel rooms anywhere that takes dogs. I'll have your back, believe me. Bettina, I'll do anything to protect you and Joe. If you're working with DEA to set up El Gordo's people, you need a man with a gun by your side. I'm offering my services to you."

"Why?"

"I like you. And I love Joe."

Bettina isn't just tongue-tied; she's heart-tied too. She can't quite believe this guy is as generous and protective of her as he seems. Is all of this just to get his hands on Joe? Strickland has given her no reason to doubt him. *Yet . . .*

She orders Joe back inside and speaks through the cracked door. "No. El Gordo will contact me soon. DEA says he'll keep his people on a leash until then. I really do appreciate what you've offered. You are very generous."

Strickland puts his foot between the door and the jamb. "Are they going to let you deal with El Gordo's people directly?"

"Yes, and they've guaranteed protection for me and Felix."

"Guaranteed? God, woman, be careful. El Gordo never stops and never loses his nerve or his luck."

This guy's more worried about me than Billy, she thinks.

Through the cracked door, she holds his look.

Then nudges his foot out the door and shuts it.

23

Watching Strickland walk away on the Ring screen, Bettina feels the dangerous, powerful thrill of flirting with disaster. The spark that makes the flame that becomes the fire.

Door number three was tempting. Separate rooms in a beachy hotel sounded good. Her and Felix and a self-defense guru who carries a gun. Finding out what makes him tick. There's a story in him.

From her patio now, she watches Strickland get into a green Italian-looking luxury sedan so subtly unusual she doesn't even know what it is. She can see Billy's truck on the other end of the parking lot, and Billy's shape just visible through the dark window glass.

Bettina feels that spark, still burning, still calling her.

The spark has to do with Strickland and it has to do with J. They are parts of the same larger thing inside her, separated only by time.

The spark has to do with Felix, too, and the calm and courage she needs to get him through this "deal" with El Gordo.

So, even if this is an odd time to deal with J and what happened that night, she knows she has to. She has to give J a name, unbury him from the tight folds of her memory, let him stand and become whole, so she can knock him out. Or cut him down. Or whatever she'll do. She knows he's settled in their hometown and started a family. Sells real estate in Anza. She's seen his Facebook crapola and she knows where his office is.

Joe whimpers when Dan leaves.

A few minutes later, as he watches Bettina slide her gun under a beach towel in the back seat of her Jeep, he knows that something big and serious might happen soon.

Which makes him think of the loud noises in the building when he was working with Dan, his hurt leg, and the stone crate where he lived with the Good Man and Woman and the big cone over his head.

Joe remembers the pain and the fear.

An hour and a half later, Bettina is entering Anza Valley, a world away from Laguna, Felix in the passenger seat and the Model 12—loaded, a misdemeanor—hidden in the back. She's just a bit outside the DEA-recommended one-hour-away-from-home curfew, and she's given Billy the slip by using the frontage road exit from Canyon View instead of Stan Oaks. She half wants to see the sleek green beauty of Strickland's car in her rearview, but hasn't yet.

She looks out at the darkening, unspoiled, high desert valley, plains of grass, green meadows of flowers getting ready for spring, rock out-croppings and a warm orange blush around the setting sun. She hasn't been back here since last Christmas and she feels that singular content-ment of being home again. Laguna Beach is great, but Bettina's roots are still in this sturdy, rural, unspoiled place, populated mostly by sturdy, rural, unspoiled people. Such as her mom and dad. Her brothers and friends from school.

She cruises past Inland Frontier Realty just off Highway 371 in Anza, population three thousand souls, many of whom Bettina has known for years. Anza is that rare California town that has actively resisted development, so it looks pretty much as it did when she was a child.

Through the windshield she sees the Inland Frontier Realty OPEN sign, but her smartphone says it won't be open for long.

It's a newer building but made to look like an 1800s saloon. There's even a hitching rail out front. Pictures of homes for sale in the windows. There are six parking spaces, one of them sporting a late-model Escalade, possibly J's vehicle for lugging clients to Inland Frontier properties.

She parks on the street, far enough away that J won't recognize her.

But plenty close enough for her to recognize unmistakable J as he stands in the open doorway, reverses the OPEN sign, then comes through the door and locks it. Tall and heavier, with the same jock carriage he had in high school—the Hamilton Bobcats QB, of course. He was toothy, blue eyed, and happy-go-lucky. He's her age but his hair is thinning and he strides chest out with his belly sucked in. His feet look small even in the cowboy boots.

Jason fucking Graves, thinks Bettina as he points a fob and the Escalade lights come on.

Good: you have a name again.

She tells Felix to stay. Lowers the windows, locks the doors, and trots across the parking lot to the Escalade, into which Jason Graves has climbed with the help of a custom chrome grab bar. She notes the Inland Frontier Realty signage on the driver's door, a rearing horse and a wrangler mid-throw, his rope forming letters in the sky.

He smiles heartily at Bettina and rolls down his window as she approaches.

"Evening!"

"I'm Bettina Blazak."

His smile freezes in place. "Pleased to meet you."

"Don't try to bullshit me, Jason. You know who I am and what you did."

He blushes deeply. "I'm sorry but . . . we've met?"

"Eight years ago, at Hamilton. Then UCI. Balboa Island party on

Bayfront. You tried to rape me and I got you off me and a lacrosse player named John Torres watched me kick you in the face. You cried and blubbered."

"No, I'd sure remember *that* if it happened! I went to Hamilton for sure, but I don't remember you. Your name again?"

"You know my damned name. I came here for an apology, not to play some pathetic head game. You can't Kavanaugh *me*."

"Oh jeez, lady. You've got to be kidding. I am not about to apologize for something I didn't do!"

"You did it. You yanked the zipper of my jeans down. Hard. You had it out and you were limp as a noodle. I know you did it. John Torres knows you did it."

Graves starts up the SUV, which bellows to life with what sounds like a thousand powerful horses. The entire vehicle rocks.

"If you come out here again to harass me about some weird fantasy of yours, I'll call the police."

"I know you, Jason Graves."

"You don't know shit, lady."

Felix is all ears as Bettina pushes the keypad on the gate box, then starts up the long driveway of her family home. She's still trembling. "Here I am," she tells the dog quietly. "This is me."

Dad and Mom greet her on the veranda; Gene has lost the weight that Barbara has gained and they both look healthy and right. Her dad had gotten the virus pre-vaccine and ridden it out at home with Barbara's help. Bettina has shelved her memories of the brief minutes she spent in his cool room while he breathed fast and light, slept, shook and sweat profusely. She was terrified for him and for herself—sure she'd get the plague through her suffocating double masks and the faceplate, but committed to see him through this hell. And him trying to make light and cheer her up. Two generations of Blazak fight. After a week in bed, he was up and around, wobbly, but better. The balance came back over the next two months, and he was fully himself by his fiftieth birthday, which the family celebrated by riding a bit of the 1,200-mile Juan Bautista de Anza Trail, blazed in 1774 by a Spanish explorer, which ran, more or less, through their backyard.

It's a wonderful feeling for Bettina to sink into the old couch, between her mother and father. After minor turf disputes with the bird dogs Minnie and Marge, Felix backs into a corner where he can watch her. Bettina feels her nerves settling, the warmth returning to her feet and hands.

When the conversation pauses, her father asks the obvious.

"What's up?"

Bettina gives them an edited version, leaving out El Gordo and his soldiers awaiting orders in Laguna. She just tells her folks that her *Coastal Eddy* video about Felix has brought some real creeps out of the ether, people who think the dog is theirs, even a dumbass threat to dognap him, so she's moving around some.

"I wanted to tell you both that I love you very much," she says, setting her hands on their knees.

She looks across the room to the hearth and the family pictures framed and propped on the mantel. Knows those photos by heart, of course: Mom and Dad, brothers and dogs. Keith and her as ten-year-olds, dressed up like Superman and Wonder Woman for Halloween.

"You can stay here with us, Betts," says Barbara. "Or leave Felix. Any dognappers dumb enough to come out here will be greeted by Ma and Pa Kettle with shotguns. We've been shooting trap again lately. We both hit twenty-five straight last weekend."

Bettina squeezes their knees. "No, Mom. It's nothing that serious."

Yet, she thinks with a quick shiver, wondering if El Gordo is really able to control his soldiers—the alleged horse breeder and the hotelier.

What if his offer is just to make her believe that Felix is going to be okay? To make Felix an easier mark for a dognapping, or worse. . . .

Is El Gordo really going to pay good money for something his actors can just steal?

———

After dinner and a long talk in front of the fire, Bettina and Felix board the Wrangler and head back for the coast.

She smiles to herself when she makes Strickland's car, falling in behind her on Highway 79.

She's got a room reserved at the La Quinta Inn and Suites in Irvine, off I-5 and not far from Laguna. It's a converted commercial granary, with the old silos for guest rooms. She stayed here two nights nearly a year ago, while waiting to move into her Canyon View apartment.

Searching her rearview for Strickland, she almost misses the exit, has to gun it across two lanes of interstate. But the traffic is light and she accelerates up the ramp toward the hotel.

She walks Felix and a small rolling suitcase across the parking lot. It's pushing midnight.

Felix growls, bristles, and stops short as a couple emerges from the restaurant. Midforties, Bettina guesses, the woman has bouncy red hair, the guy has nice clothes and a cool-looking straw fedora.

"Good evening," says the woman. An accent.

"Hello," says Bettina, then to Felix, firmly: "*Quiet.*"

"He is well behaved," the woman says into the sudden silence.

Bettina notes that Strickland hasn't yet cruised into the parking lot. Wonders if that last-second exit surprised him. Gives the leash a curt tug. "*Heel.*"

She begins a wide detour around the couple, Felix silent but riveted on the pair.

"You are Bettina Blazak, and he's Felix," says the man, his voice smooth and his Spanish accent strong. His trim dark suit is cut European-style and his tieless spread-collar white shirt looks Cuban on him.

"This is us, all right," says Bettina.

They stop between her and the lobby, which brings her to a stop too.

"I loved the Felix video," says the woman. Bettina sees that she's pretty and wearing an expensive-looking black dress, black leggings, and silver-studded black ankle boots.

The woman takes a white paper bag from her purse, kneels, and offers Felix a piece of meat. Food-motivated to a fault, he wags his tail but stays put. She tosses it to him and rises, putting the napkin back in her purse.

"For our dog at home," says the woman. "But I want the famous Felix to have it."

If these people are who I think they are, thinks Bettina, and if Strickland comes flying in now, my cover is blown and my dog and I are in deep trouble.

But how did they find me here?

Arnie: *Horses and hotels.*

No. Impossible. They're just well-dressed *latinoamericanos* who liked her Felix video.

Arnie again: *If you start feeling paranoid you probably are.*

Still, what she wants most right now is to be on her way with Felix before Strickland circles back on her after the sudden high-speed exit.

"Good night," she says, then cinches Felix up tight to her calf and walks past them.

Catches the woman's perfume and the man's thin smile as he takes the redhead's arm.

Bettina can hear them, heading down the walkway behind her, not talking.

When she looks back again, they're getting into a shiny black Blazer.

At the front desk, she taps her credit card and watches the late-model SUV heading away.

No Strickland.

Her feet and hands are cold again. Felix stares through the glass doors toward the parking lot.

She takes a second story silo room with a view of the parking lot. Felix hops onto the bed and watches her. She has just gotten the curtains open for a look outside when Strickland's green Maserati pulls into a space.

She feels a ribbon of relief unwind inside, which surprises her. Especially after trying to play brave to Billy.

Texts Strickland:

Think I just got cased by Joaquín and Valeria.
Black Blazer?
Yes. Didn't look like narcos.
Did they threaten you?
No. They recognized me and Felix. Gave him some leftovers.
I'll be out here until sunrise Bettina.
Thank you, Dan.
You doing okay?
I'm a bundle of nerves but I think I'll be able to sleep.
I'll be here. No one will bother you and Joe.
Felix.
Sleep well.

Joe's First Day on the Job

Six months after the deaths of Teddy's parents...

24

This is nothing like playing with Teddy, Joe thought, nothing like training with Wade.

Aaron was strong with the leash and his voice commands were angry and loud. He was quick to yank, quick to curse. The way he said the word *fuck* made Joe flinch, though he had no idea what it meant. He'd been on the job for the last hour here—a crowded strip mall in Yuma, Arizona—and he hadn't gotten one kibble treat, even though he's finding Drugs.

But Aaron seemed more angry than happy. Work faster. Bigger drugs! The other DEA men and women didn't speak to him or pet him. The other DEA dogs—big German shepherds and surly Malinois—either snarled at Joe or ignored him completely. Joe wasn't quite sure what DEA meant, but the letters were emblazoned on his mind early this morning, when Aaron pulled his gun and yelled *DEA, hands up!* at a Man coming out of a bus station. Joe quickly guessed that DEA meant either angry, or stop, or both. The sound of the letters had raked across his nerves like the stiff steel brush that Aaron used to get the foxtails off him.

Joe had never felt so hesitant, but more eager to please.

The strip mall shops were small and crowded with smells: spicy food like Teddy's mom cooked, sharp hair- and nail-salon chemicals, swimming pool chlorine, new clothes and shoes, pizza.

In the back room of the pool supply store, he went from one nose-quivering carton of plastic jugs to another, as Aaron snapped the lead and tried to force Joe to the holy smells. Joe wanted to follow his nose instead, but when he found a scent cone, Aaron cursed and pulled back. Joe heard voices in the front of the store, commands for another search Dog.

He heard Aaron and the Man talking, though most of their words were lost on Joe:

"There are no drugs here, *señor*. And our small amount of money is in the cash register."

"That right? Let's see what my dog says."

"The chemicals might damage his nose."

"Damage that nose, and I'll kick the living shit out of you, amigo. He's got the best nose of all time. It's the only reason he's here."

"There are no drugs."

"Find the drugs, Joe! Find the money!"

Even though his nostrils were stinging, Joe pressed on into the storage room, investigating the boxes of new pool sweeps and skimmers, the floating toys and air mattresses, the water thermometers, the basketball and volleyball playsets. Nose up and down, short four-beat sniffs, receptors bristling.

He soon caught the scent of Drugs, just a trickle of scent at first.

But the scent got stronger and the cone narrowed into a cluttered corner of broken-down boxes and empty plastic containers, recycle bins and garbage cans filled with rubbish.

Joe's tail was wagging big by then, and he stood still in that river of smells, nose to the floor, nose to the air, then to the floor again, across which the smell of Drugs drew him, like a fish to an irresistible lure.

The drugs brought Joe to the deepest part of the corner, where the stained white walls met the concrete floor and a rodent bait-station waited, bolted to the concrete to keep the rats from spilling the bait.

"The poison will kill him," said the man.

"Joe, *down!*"

His belly on the cool floor and his ears cocked upright and out, Joe wagged his long saber tail, happily fixed on the big, black bait station. Drugs, he knew: *Drugs.*

"Unbolt that thing and set it on those boxes."

"The poison is strong. I need my gloves."

"Get your goddamned gloves, Enrique."

Joe listened to Enrique walking away but he didn't take his eyes off the Drugs.

Aaron knelt and called Joe over, gave him a stern *down*, and a milder *Good Dog.*

Which sent a jolt of love through Joe, panting happily, still staring at his find.

Enrique came back, escorted by another DEA agent and his German shepherd. Enrique knelt by the bait trap with his gloves on, unbolted it, and set it on the boxes.

Joe sat up but stayed in place as the other dog growled at him. The other agent gave Joe a hard look but did nothing to silence the shepherd.

Aaron opened the black plastic box, froze for a long moment as he looked down at it, then lifted three locking plastic bags, each half-full of pills that looked gray to Joe but were in fact gray-green.

"Fent, amigo," he said to Enrique.

"I have never seen it. I do not deal in narcotics. The cartel has put it there."

"You're under arrest anyway. Your memory might improve in prison."

Aaron stepped quickly toward Enrique with the plastic cuffs. The other DEA agent aimed his pistol at Enrique with both hands, his dog growling with intent to kill. Joe knew from training that this was a very serious moment, and he was ready to bite the man and tear away at whatever he got hold of. Joe didn't like the bite command, because the padded men tasted bad and usually threw him down, hard. Joe growled at Enrique too.

Then two more DEA men came in without dogs and took Enrique by both arms and led him out.

"Shut that fucking dog up," said Aaron to the other agent.

Inwardly, Joe cringed at the sound of the word.

The agent ordered him down and quiet, and the shepherd obeyed with a baleful stare at Joe.

"You did okay, Joe," Aaron said, "but I need more out of you."

That night Joe lay in his Crate in Aaron's Chula Vista living room, while his handler lifted weights. The big screen was on, flashing the usual uninteresting pictures and the mostly incomprehensible words and music. Every once in a while , a Dog would appear and bark, and Joe would perk up. Most of his nights here had been like this—Aaron grunting and talking to the TV, Joe curled in his Crate and waiting for Aaron to move it into the bedroom for sleeping. Joe slept in his locked Crate. He had not yet slept in the Aaron's bed. It was not a Team Bed.

But that night, Joe's neck was sore from Aaron's muscular leash-work, and Joe's heart was heavy with his failure to please Aaron. Joe was beginning to see that Aaron was almost never happy. He was all work. He was no play. He was alone. No visitors, no family, no Woman. Teddy and Wade had friends and family. They smiled and touched him and gave him kibble treats all the time. Sometimes he didn't know why. They threw the Ball and the flying disk and wrestled Joe on the grass, on the carpet inside, anyplace where wrestling seemed like a good idea. Aaron only touched him to brush out his thin undercoat and to leash and un-leash him, which was more of a tug on his collar than a real touch.

Tonight, for the third time in two weeks, Aaron fell asleep lying on the couch while the TV played.

Joe went over and looked at him, then smelled his hand, his face, feet, knees, crotch, his face again. Little four-count breaths. Touched him with a whisker, just once. Coming from his nose, Aaron's breath was sharp with the smell of the liquid he poured from a large gray bottle that said BOMBAY on the label, if Joe only knew how to read.

So he thought of Teddy's Dad, who had bottles like that and seemed unhappy a lot of the time. And he thought of Teddy, his wonderful Boy, after Art and Nancy had taken him away from his Mom and Dad, which made him sad, strongly sad, like he had been taken away too. Back then Joe knew that there were things that would make Teddy happy again, but he didn't know what they were. He tried. Teddy was always very good giving him commands so things were clear and Joe had no doubt what was wanted of him. He smelled Aaron's breath again. There was so much hardness to his face and voice, so much hurry. There was no way Joe could see or hear through the hardness to understand what Aaron wanted. Other than more Drugs. More Money.

So Joe knew that he had to do better. Aaron had even said so, at the strip mall today. At least that's what Joe had heard.

Joe went through a doggy door in the kitchen into the backyard. It was a small yard with a six-foot chain-link fence and a tall hedge behind it, but plenty of room to poop and pee. He knew he could dig under that fence and get out. Or climb over it. Some inherited confidence told him it would be easy. And some inherited thirst for freedom told him go, dig out or climb that fence, run free in the world, eat what you find, and mate.

Back inside, he curled up in his Crate in the living room, where Aaron was making the loud growl of sleep. Joe dreamed of his mother and siblings warm in the darkness, of her wonderful milk and how she licked him over and over. Dreamed of wrestling Teddy on the grass. And the plastic pool he splashed in. Dreamed of the metal paper he'd chewed to bits and how Teddy was mad at him for that. Dreamed of the kibble he'd found in the inner tube, how pleased Teddy was when Joe smelled the wart on his foot that hadn't appeared yet. He dreamed of hashish and mothballs hidden in a plastic container, a rock of methamphetamine hidden under a floor, heroin in a hat, fentanyl hidden in a stick of chewing gum—all things that Aaron had taught him and were now his target smells. Very important. The most important smells in his world.

Dreamed more of Teddy, always Teddy, his first Boy.

Woke up an hour later, checked on Aaron, went into the backyard again, and climbed the fence.

An instinct and some inherited urge told Joe that his last home with Teddy—the one high up with the ocean below, and Art and Nancy—was right this way.

Food. Water. Mate.

Find Teddy.

25

Bettina is up at sunrise in her silo room at the La Quinta Inn in Irvine, with maybe two hours of actual sleep the night before. Dreamed she was shooting an Olympic trap qualifier and Keith was there, watching from the stands.

She's starved and foggy brained at the free breakfast, which she takes outside by the pool with Felix at her feet. The guy sitting at a table on the other side of the pool gives her a brisk nod. Looks like Dan Strickland because it is. A little chill runs the back of her neck. He may be generous and interesting, thinks Bettina, but he's so focused on her and Felix it creeps her out. She tightens up on the leash and gives Strickland her back.

She's just slipped Joe half a sausage link when the email arrives:

Good morning Señorita Blazak. I watched your old videos on the *Coastal Eddy* web page. You have always good stories. You have facts. When they write about me in the American newspapers it is always lies. Blog Narco is better. Maybe you should interview me for the truth. Besides "Felix: The Rescue of a Mexican Street Dog," I liked the one about the whale that was freed from the fishing nets in your beautiful Laguna Beach. And the girl who got bit by the shark.

I am now confirming that you will sell Felix to me. As you know, my offer is $200,000.

Bettina gets right back:

Dear Mr. Godoy,

Yes, I will sell him to you but you have to promise to treat him well.

Bettina

Bettina forwards Godoy's email to Special Agent Powers, who calls immediately and orders her to stay where she is and wait for instructions.

Unfortunately, El Gordo doesn't get right back.

So she sneaks off with Felix to the nearest Turner's Outdoorsman, where she buys a "point and fire" pepper gel pistol with a special trigger and a grip "deployment system" that will allegedly deliver maximum strength pepper gel bursts at fifteen feet. Plenty close for Valeria and Joaquín. It's a stubby little thing, black with an orange slide, and small enough to fit into her purse.

El Gordo gets back fourteen hours later, at 10:00 p.m., by which time Bettina is crazy with frustration in her grain silo hotel room.

Dear Señorita Blazak,

I am very happy. We will be very kind to Felix.

Please bring him to the famous lifeguard tower of Laguna Beach in one hour. At eleven. You must be alone and have no weapon. Make sure your phone is on, as there may be changes. The dog must be on a leash. When you have passed the leash to my companero, Joaquín, then his wife, Valeria, will give you her fashionable bag. It will contain the money and will weigh over two pounds. Go back to your car immediately. Do not look into the bag until later. If any of these laws you break then there will be no money and maybe bad consequences. Very simple.

Of course, if you have had contact with the Roman and can supply us with his name, my friends will deliver to you $200,000 more, once we have verified your information and his relationship to the Jalisco New Generation Cartel.

With Sincerity and Friendship,
Alejandro Godoy

El Gordo

Bettina answers:

Yes, Mr. Godoy, I will do that, exactly. You have promised me you will take good care of Felix. I need the money. But I don't know who the Roman is.

Bettina

All of which Bettina sends to Powers, who tells her again to stand by and wait.

One thing that Bettina hates almost as much as being told what to do, is waiting.

But Powers is soon back to say they'll have their people in place. All Bettina has to do is follow El Gordo's instructions exactly. When she gets back to her car with the money, drive to the Laguna Riviera motel on Coast Highway, where a room has been reserved for her. Paid for, of course. The DEA will deliver Felix to her.

"Don't let them take my dog."

"They won't get your dog. They won't even know what hit them."

This late, she easily finds a spot in the Laguna Beach Library parking lot, leashes up Felix, and crosses Coast Highway to Main Beach. The coastal eddy is in, and the night is misty and chill.

Nearing the lifeguard tower, Felix looks up at her three times. Sensing her nerves—Bettina guesses—that are surely running down the leash from her unusually jerky hands.

"I love you, Felix," she says. "Don't be afraid. I'm going to protect you."

Which makes her think of the DEA, Billy Ray Crumley, and Dan Strickland, all offering to protect him. Her too.

"You have a good team on your side," she says, and Felix looks up again, cocking his head intently.

The boardwalk foot traffic is light. The beaches are open until 1:00 a.m. Bettina watches the people coming across the sand, their bodies faint at first, then solidifying as they approach the lifeguard stand and its floodlights. A helicopter cruises by. Voices and bits of conversation drift past her as she joins the northwest bend of the boardwalk, headed for the big white plaster Laguna Beach Lifeguard tower, with its well-lighted emblem:

Laguna Beach

LIFEGUARD

Dept. Est. 1929

Her phone says 10:52 p.m., so she passes the tower on her left, heading toward the hulking black outcropping known as Rockpile. The waves are throwing up so much white water against the rocks that she can see the spray from a hundred yards away.

A runner pads by in big foamy shoes; a Dalmatian stops Felix for a friendly sniff; Bettina smiles faintly at the guy while she studies the faces coming past—no obvious Joaquín or Valeria among them, that she can see.

"Is this Felix?"

"Yes."

"I loved that story. Really moved me."

"He's a terrific little guy. Night."

"Good night, Ms. Blazak. I'm a big fan."

"Thank you."

"Richard."

"Richard. Come on, dog!"

She takes a bench, studying faces, phone out, checking the minutes. Felix studies faces too. The March night is cold and Bettina buttons her wool duster all the way up.

At 10:59, she's standing at the far inland side of the boardwalk, twenty feet or so from the lifeguard tower, Felix sitting at her feet. Bettina turns a slow, casual circle, degree by degree, meeting each oncoming face with a steady deadpan.

Sees Powers out on the grass, dressed in running clothes, stretching.

And Arnie Crumley sitting on the boardwalk facing the ocean, wearing an Angels jacket and cap, a white fast-food bag open on his lap.

Bettina's really hoping and praying there's not another Richard out here tonight, who might somehow foul the takedown. She wonders if Valeria will maybe pull a little gun from her purse, and if Joaquín will pull something bigger and more deadly. She knows that they were the ones at the La Quinta. *Knows.* Fingers the pepper gel gun deep in the pocket of her coat. Felix looks up at her with a mixture of concern and trust that breaks her heart. What have I gotten you into? she wonders.

"It's going to be okay."

Five minutes. Ten.

Then a woman's accented voice by phone:

"Go back to your car and drive the dog to Moulton Meadows Park. When you get to the parking lot, park but do not get out of your car. Make sure Felix is on the leash. Control him."

The park is in the hills above South Laguna, a tidy little place where Bettina filmed part of her video special on the club she belongs to, the Biker Chicks. Bettina drives toward it just under speed limit, hoping to give her confederates an easy target to follow.

Moulton Meadows Park is long closed tonight and the lot is empty. Bettina pulls into a space facing the street, cracks the windows and kills the engine. Up here, the fog is lighter. Felix sits in the Jeep's passenger seat, curious as always, ears up, flaps out.

"They're probably checking us out," she says softly. "I didn't see our federal friends, but I texted them. You heard me. We're not on our own, little dog."

Feeling that first little spark of hers, Bettina reaches into the back, flips the beach towel off the Model 12, and, hand on the grip behind the trigger, draws it carefully beside her. Wedges it barrel-down between the console and the floor.

She watches Capistrano Avenue, and the parking lot, and the homes across the street. Occasional cars. An SUV. Could that be her cavalry? Then a throaty, exotic-looking thing that looks green in the misty streetlights, and very much like Dan Strickland's ride. Her wannabe guardian angel? Somehow, she's not surprised. And she's glad her self-defense guru is here.

Bettina feels the spark trying to light the flame that can become the fire inside her, the fire that stokes her excitement, lets her accept the danger, and, say, race down Coast Highway at forty miles an hour on her Cannondale with the Biker Chicks. Or, all alone, lets her drop into a marching six-footer at Brooks Street, the entire Pacific behind her, pushing her like a giant's hand. Or stand in front of a video cam and let the world see her for what she is, a former shy tomboy who has become a reporter with a good story to tell, has her own show, and a possible Pulitzer in her future.

But the spark feels different to her now.

Like it's damp. And it can't get her flame going, because she knows that using this big shotgun on the Sinaloans would be dangerously stupid.

So she moves the Model 12 to the back seat again, and covers it with the beach towel, her heart thumping hard and her fingers growing cold.

Which is when a woman emerges from the foggy dark of the park and starts across the parking lot toward Bettina. She's in jeans and boots and a black leather moto jacket, with a big red bag over one shoulder. A blonde. Looks nothing like the woman at the hotel.

Felix sees her first and growls low.

"Quiet."

He whimpers, his attention on Capistrano Avenue now, where motion catches Bettina's eye as a man crosses the street, coming toward her from another direction. He's carrying a metal catch pole with a noose at one end. He's older and smaller than the man at La Quinta.

"Quiet, boy. Mama loves you," says Bettina, lowering the front windows half a foot.

Bettina feels like crying.

Then retrieving the shotgun and blowing them both away.

Calm down, she thinks. Down . . .

Valeria stops six feet from the driver's side and Joaquín six feet from Felix's window.

"Good evening, señorita I am Joaquín."

The dog growls and Bettina hushes him again. She can't believe how heavy she feels, almost numb, her hands and feet frozen.

Good evening, she hears herself say.

Bettina raises her open hands, then lowers them slowly, her right pressing deep into the duster pocket.

"Hello, Felix," says Joaquín, peering in. "I see you are wearing a leash. Señorita Blazak, open the door and bring now the dog to me. When I have the leash, Valeria will give you the money."

Something tells Bettina that this is going too fast, that her defenders have not gotten into place, that if she obeys Joaquín, Felix will be on his way back to Mexico in a heartbeat.

"I want to see the money first," she says.

"You must trust us, as we trust you."

"What if it's just a few hundred dollars in that bag? Or bottled water?"

"It is all the money. Why are you not obeying my orders?"

Suddenly the dark, misty night is shot through by bright lights from all directions. Bettina, one cold hand on the door pull, squints into the beams, sees figures advancing, heavy-booted, military-looking people in black tactical wear, hung with weaponry and gear, night vision machine guns raised. She sees them through the windshield and both side windows, even in the rearview, an eerie war party on attack. A big white SUV comes slowly down Capistrano in the mist. Strickland's exotic green sedan glides the opposite direction, slowly.

Bettina sees Valeria, blanched in the high beams, marching with her hands up toward the nearest phalanx, the bag dangling from one shoulder.

Then turns just as Joaquín pulls a pistol from his coat and muffled bullets rip the life out of him before he even hits the ground, his catch pole twanging on the asphalt.

Felix whimpers now, confused and eager to do something but no idea what. He looks at Bettina for guidance.

"We're alive," she says. "That's all I know. We're alive, Felix."

She doesn't move. Maybe *can't* move with feet this cold. She hugs her heavy coat tight and watches a black helicopter descend from the darkness and touch down on the grass, not fifty feet away. No emblem, no ID, landing lights only.

The door opens and two tactical warriors drop to the ground then pull out a gurney. Its hinged legs automatically deploy when they clear the fuselage. A third man climbs out, covering his soldiers with a tactical shotgun. Bettina notes the slender red canister dangling from a carabiner on his chest.

One of the men toes Joaquín Páez's head, which turns, then lolls life-lessly back into place. They lower the gurney and get him aboard while the cover man blasts the blood off the asphalt with the fire extinguisher, then hustles back to the chopper.

Bettina times this op on her phone. The reporter in her, always gathering information. Fifty-five seconds later, the machine corkscrews into the night in an unlit, ascending roar.

She pets Felix's round little head and feels the warmth of him coming into her fingers.

Watches Powers and Arnie Crumley approach.

26

Six hours later, Dan Strickland is at Adolfo's in Laguna, sitting in a back booth of the restaurant with OGs Frank and Héctor—Carlos Palma's Barrio Logan diplomats.

Frank is skinny and tall, and has the weirdest golden eyes that Strickland has ever seen. Héctor is thickly muscled. Both wear chinos and hoodies against the early March morning.

Strickland understands that when El Gordo learns what happened to his ambassadors last night—the guy with the dog noose and the stylish blonde were pictured in *Blog Narco* feature, "The New Sinaloans," almost a year ago—he'll send in reinforcements for revenge on Joe and Bettina. Bettina has obviously betrayed him to the DEA, costing him blood and treasure. Joe's been targeted for death since the Sinaloans first saw the odd little dog humiliating them in their own city.

Strickland also knows it will take El Gordo days, not weeks, to deduce what the DEA has done with his people and his cash. Silence is all the feds will give him now, letting him dangle in the quiet wind. El Gordo will turn to Bettina for information, soon.

Strickland checks the booths around them—just a couple of surfers, blue-lipped with cold—then leans in and keeps his voice low. The kitchen roars with breakfast orders just a yard or two away.

"Joaquín is MIA and Valeria is under federal arrest," he says. "It happened a few hours ago. So our job just got easier. For now."

"Good," says Frank.

"They'll send better people next time," says Héctor.

Strickland sips his coffee. He has spent every minute of the last few hours letting his ideas run off-leash, imagining alternatives, measuring risks, comparing angles, and forecasting consequences. All in service of making the world safe and right for the three things he loves—Joe, Bettina, and himself.

And he's done it.

He's found a way. It's going to take all his skills and luck. It's going to cost him some treasure. But he's found a way to protect his family.

First, he'll have to pitch his deal with El Gordo, pretty much immediately.

Of course, El Gordo's first reaction will be to have Strickland killed along with Bettina and Joe. But El Gordo is smart too. He'll take the deal because it's a good one.

Because he'll be able to inflict the same costly embarrassment to the Jalisco New Generation Cartel that it has inflicted on him—the great El Gordo.

Because he'll be able to get his money back, plus interest.

Because he will be able to feel powerful, by rescuing an innocent young woman.

There are three downsides to his plan that Strickland can see.

One is that he'll have to arrange Joe's kidnapping from Bettina without her knowing he's behind it. Easy enough. But it will pain him to hurt her like that. He cares for her in a way he's never cared for anyone. Except, of course, himself and Joe. He needs Joe back, but not just for business. He loves that dog.

The second downside has settled to the bottom of Strickland's soul like a frozen anchor: after he and Joe are reunited, any future with

Bettina may be doomed. But maybe, just maybe he can make it work. There has to be a way. He must remain positive and optimistic.

And count his blessings, such as having Joe again, and all that solid, Joe-generated cash coming in from *both the New Generation and the Sinaloa cartels*. He's got no choice really—it's not like he can give Carlos two weeks' notice.

Which leads to downside three: Carlos will find him out someday. But Strickland is already working on a plan for that.

He really can't believe he didn't think of this sooner. He doesn't have any problem with the audacity of it. He's taken risks before that have worked out in his favor *because* of their audacity. Such as hiring out himself and his dog to help one cartel rob another in the first place.

Working for two cartels and running Apex, he'll amass a fortune, he thinks. A small fortune—nothing like his father and mother's—but enough for him to live out this precarious, adrenaline-crazed, take-what-is-offered life he was apparently born for.

"So, my good hombres, Joe is fine and I'll be handling things here for myself. You can go back to San Diego now."

"C won't like this," says Héctor.

"I've already talked to him," says Strickland. "He's on board."

This "on board" claim of Strickland's is not purely fictional. Just half an hour ago he talked to Carlos, who sounded old and hungover and foggy about why he'd ordered his men to Laguna in the first place.

"We didn't come all the way up here just to turn around and go home," says Frank.

"Why not?" asks Strickland. "Breakfast is on me."

This draws a strange, golden-eyed stare from Frank. "You want the reporter as much as you want the dog."

"Leave her out of it. Joe is a talented animal, and getting him back to work is what C wants. I'll see to it."

"Your Tijuana enemies call you *loco*," says Héctor.

"So do your Tijuana friends," says Frank.

Strickland sets three twenties under his half-finished breakfast plate, stands, and walks out.

27

One of Strickland's first Apex clients, Mike Lineberger, is a successful young captain with a gleaming 46 Billfish docked in Dana Point. The sleek, blue-hulled *Game On* is outfitted for big-dollar marlin tournaments. It rolls gently in the water, bristling with antennas and outriggers.

Like Strickland, Lineberger is a gringo who has spent years in Mexico, building his fishing skills, winning more than his share of the lucrative Mexican and US West Coast contests. He's around a lot of cash—the marlin tournament hunters are by definition well-off and careless with their money. There's always the latest robbery in the host port, sometimes violent. And no end of desperately poor men willing to stick up a wealthy, distracted tournament angler obsessed with catching the biggest fish. So some years ago, Strickland showed Lineberger how to defend himself if things went truly, well, south.

One night in Cabo San Lucas, things went very south, but Lineberger was able to get himself out of it, thanks to Strickland's brand of hyperefficient Krav Maga.

Which left the captain indebted to his self-defense instructor.

So now they sit on the deck of *Game On*, the dark afternoon clouds admitting just enough sunlight to put a shine on the calm harbor water.

They've had a beer and caught up on their few mutual acquaintances. Strickland has filled him in on the Apex Self-Defense improvements; Lineberger has admitted that the virus knocked his tournament business down for most of 2020. But things are roaring again now.

Lineberger asks how he can help.

"Something you said one day after class," says Strickland. "We were with Christy and Gayle at Morton's, and you were talking about the big Bisbee win you'd just had in East Cape. The winner was a Mexican guy from Los Mochis but you wouldn't say his name. Said you couldn't say his name. Los Mochis is on the coast of Sinaloa, so I got a strong whiff of narcotics."

"Miguel Villareal," says Lineberger. "A serious angler, and a very badass man. He's the only narco I've captained who doesn't touch drugs or alcohol. We were the two Mikes in that tourney. We hit it off *and* won the contest. He took to me, bragged about his murders over seafood and fizzy water."

"Can you put me in touch with him?"

Lineberger frowns. His face is leather dyed by the sun. "Jeez, Dan."

Strickland says nothing for a long moment, letting the captain process.

"You don't mean talk to him in person, do you?"

"Just phone, Mike. Then, if it goes well, face-to-face."

"He'd put the screws to you," says Lineberger. "I mean, you'd be helpless down there."

"I have something good for him."

"You better."

"Something he'll appreciate. No screws required."

"Dan, I don't want to read about another gringo from San Diego missing in Mexico. I don't want to be the guy who hooked you up down there. You taught me a lot about protecting myself. We had some cool times with the ladies. I like you. Maybe I'm helping you protect *yourself*."

"Tell him I have some information about El Romano of Tijuana. This is very important, Mike, El Romano."

Lineberger gives Strickland a dispirited look, shakes his head. Stares at the brooding sky for a moment as if it might offer some advice.

"I'll make some calls," he says. "No promises. Miguel could have been . . . retired since then. Four years is a long time in that business."

"Thank you, Mike."

"Can I tell you just one thing, Dan? Some things aren't worth risking your life for."

"Amen to that," says Strickland, thinking: Joe and Bettina Blazak are.

By evening, Lineberger has given Strickland a number for a Miguel Villareal lieutenant, one Jesús Narciso.

Sitting in his living room on the third-floor suite of Apex, Strickland uses a Walmart burner, claiming to be the infamous El Romano, the scourge of the Sinaloans in Tijuana.

He gives Narciso a partial rundown of what he hopes to soon be pitching up the chain of command to Miguel Villareal, then to El Gordo himself.

Minutes later, Narciso gets back with an okay: he'll meet El Romano at the train station in Los Mochis tomorrow afternoon at two.

Strickland books an aisle seat round-tripper on Volaris out of Tijuana, departing 7:21 a.m.

Then, roaming his living suite with its views of the big harbor hotels and the Coronado Bridge and the silver Pacific beyond, he calls Bettina.

"I saw you last night in that green show-off car of yours," she says. "Up at Moulton Meadows Park, where the DEA blew away Joaquín Páez. And made off with Valeria Flores. They picked up Joaquín like a piece of litter and washed his blood off the road with a fire extinguisher. I didn't get the impression they were going to book the woman into the Marriott. Where's the nearest federal lockup?"

"Santa Ana," says Strickland. "But they'll question her in San Diego."

"Nobody will know what happened up there, will they? Unless I tell the story."

"Why do that? Bad things happened to bad people. They might have killed Joe, you know. And possibly you."

"Things like that don't happen in this country, even to cartel thugs. We have due process. People have the right to know. It was murder by government agents, Strickland. They used silenced guns. They shot him down without even an arrest or charges. You think he didn't have a family? People he loved and was good to?"

"But did he draw a weapon?"

"With twenty commandos coming at him, and snipers in wait."

"Well . . ." Strickland feels little real sympathy for Páez. About the same as he felt for the three men he killed that night in Furniture Calderón. Or the fighters in Helmand. They were in the line of fire by choice. Live by the sword.

As Strickland listens to her silence, he pictures Bettina driving her Jeep from the La Quinta to the Laguna Beach Library parking lot, Joe in the front seat beside her. He remembers the joy that was in him then, the way it came over him suddenly, just seeing them. Now he watches the matchbox cars creeping over the Coronado Bridge.

"I'll be out of the country for a few days," he says.

"I'll miss you following me everywhere I go. But thank you for last night. It made me feel safer. It meant a lot that you'd risk yourself like that. You did kind of creep me out, there by the hotel pool."

"I told you I'd do anything in the world to protect you and Joe. Personally, I'm glad Joaquín is out of business and Valeria Flores is being detained by DEA. They'll squeeze her dry, try to set her up as an informant and deport her."

Another silence from Bettina.

"Put the phone to his ear, please," Strickland says.

He hears the shuffle and scratch of contact, then tells Joe hello. "Hope you're taking good care of yourself and Bettina. She's a good reporter with lots of talent, and she'll probably be on TV someday. I hope to see you again soon. And your woman too. So long for now."

"He listened," she says. "And so did I."

"I'm glad you did."

"Who are you and what do you want?"

"I told you all of that."

"Your life was on the table last night, just like mine."

"You need me by your side."

"You're a story with holes in it," she says. "Intriguing and mysterious."

Strickland's silent time now. He's in his bedroom—the view of the harbor and a bit of the Gaslamp, the cool photos on the walls. The unmade bed. Joe's crate and all his plush toys.

"I can tell you that story."

"Okay."

"Good stories aren't short," he says.

"True."

"We have time. We're young," he says.

"Women dis twenty-six, but I like it."

"I'm fine with thirty-three," says Strickland. "I see a good future out there. Just now shaping up."

Bettina sighs. Just kind of can't believe this guy, but likes him.

"Strickland?"

"Blazak."

"Safe travels."

28

Jesús Narciso is waiting for Strickland at the Los Mochis train station. He's short and wide, wears jeans and cowboy boots, a black felt cowboy hat, and a big white-and-black tooled belt. Old-school Sinaloa, thinks Strickland, not the paramilitary stylings of the New Generation.

The terminal is crowded with tourists taking the Copper Canyon train through the rough and scenic Sierra Madre Occidental, which traverses Sinaloa north–south. Strickland rode that train years ago, on a summer study program in Mexico through Newport Harbor High School.

Now he puts his overnight duffel on the back row seats of a dusty white Ford F-250 Lariat Super Duty.

"Nice truck," he says.

Narciso nods but says nothing.

The Lariat rides loud and sits high, and Strickland can see that Los Mochis hasn't changed much. It's still a sprawling city, upwards of three hundred thousand souls living in the crowded *central* and in houses sprinkled throughout the dry green hills. It boasts a modest sportfishing industry, and is known for producing champion boxers. Strickland remembers from his study program that the city was founded by American utopian socialists hoping to make their fortune in sugarcane. But today it looks like most of the tourists are here for the dramatic railroad trip through the canyon.

Narciso steers the grumbling truck into the hills, passing small farms and houses. Not a word. A boy in sandals and shorts leads a horse through a ribbon of greenery running along the edge of the asphalt.

Then they take a wide, well-kept dirt road lined with tree-branch barbed wire, behind which slender cattle graze in sparse grass.

A mile in, Narciso turns into a dirt driveway blocked by a very tall wrought iron gate. Brick columns frame the gate and are home to an intercom and keypad. The fencing is black industrial chain link, ten feet high, topped by three rows of electrical wire.

Narciso gets out, presses some numbers, then speaks into the mic.

The house and outbuildings are another quarter mile in, tucked beneath native fan palms and paloverde. It's rocky and rough and hot. A rugged-looking place to Strickland's eyes, nothing on the order of Carlos Palma's oceanside compound. Miguel Villareal—if that's who lives here—has less ornate tastes.

Back in the truck, Narciso slams the door. "Go to the house."

Strickland gets his duffel from the back, salutes grim Narciso goodbye.

The man who answers the door is a much larger version of Narciso, but similarly proportioned: big from the waist up but short legged, with a bullish neck and head. A cousin, thinks Strickland. He's got two days of whiskers, a bushy mustache, and a satellite phone clipped to his belt. He points a black automatic pistol at Strickland's chest.

He's as tall as Strickland and now stares at him with small, hostile eyes. "Who are you?"

"I am El Romano."

"I should kill you and get the reward."

"Yes, you should, Señor Villareal. But alive, I can bring you a lot more than money. I can get you revenge on the New Generation. I can replace *el señor* Godoy's dollars lost in California. And if you are smart enough to help me bring this deal to El Gordo, he'll be very pleased with you. May I come in?"

Villareal pushes open the door and moves back, waving Strickland in with his weapon.

Strickland steps in with his duffel and shuts the door. The inside of the house is nothing like the outside. It's cooled by a quiet air conditioner and furnished with some of the nicer furniture Strickland recognizes from Furniture Calderón factory-warehouse in Tijuana. The tile is the good stuff from Saltillo. And there's Taxco silver all over the cool orange walls—crosses, candelabra, scones, hummingbirds, quetzals, crocodiles, and fish, fish, fish, some life-sized. The only thing on the walls that isn't handcrafted silver is the enormous big-screen Sony.

Villareal's wife, Anay, has Native blood, Strickland sees. She's on her way out with their four children, to church—Villareal explains in his poor English—because Anay speaks no English at all. She and the kids look scrubbed clean and are dressed nicely. Through the open door, Strickland watches the black Suburban back out of the garage.

"Explain everything," says Miguel.

It takes Strickland all of five minutes to explain his plan. He holds back a central premise—that it's a trade for a young reporter's life—because he knows it's a possible dealbreaker. And if it is, then El Gordo's *sicarios* would eventually find Bettina and Joe, while Strickland feeds the Sierra Madre vultures for a brief time. He feels a shiver of fear as he again considers that this whole precarious idea depends on rational decisions by violent men.

When he's done, Villareal stands and slides the pistol into the waistband of his jeans.

"Stay. I call."

Strickland can hear Villareal's low rumbling voice from another room. As best he can tell, Miguel has a series of conversations with different people. Strickland can only make out occasional words: *El Romano . . . sí, todo loco . . . Badiraguato o Creel? . . .*

Strickland listens and looks out the windows at the dusty, rock-strewn compound outside. Rusting metal drums. Red plastic gasoline cans lined up in the shade of a palapa. The cars. Only the fishing boats and the black family Suburban look cared for. He wonders why Villareal spills living human blood for so little in return. Maybe he's a simple man. A man who likes to do his work and go fishing rather than fuss over his material possessions back home.

For a long moment, Strickland feels amused at his situation here, trying to arrange a long shot deal with one of the most powerful narcos on the planet. He isn't even carrying a gun—it's impossible for any civilian to bring a handgun or ammunition on a commercial Mexican flight. His self-defense skills are nonapplicable. His phone won't work outside Los Mochis. He's got two changes of clothes, a shave kit and $5,000 from his cash stash. What's so amusing about that? He wonders. But it is.

He thinks of Bettina, how this is almost as much for her as it is for him and Joe. Bettina will be safe, and maybe there's some way he can get her back in his life. Make a future with her. If not, maybe there will be another Bettina out there for him someday. He wonders. Do you find more than one woman like her? Why not? But he has no interest in this now; he's sure of that much.

Yes, he knows this is the right thing to be doing, edgy as it is. Edge is good. Edge is an advantage.

His father, Dyson, used to say that.

Sitting in Miguel Villareal's silvery living room, Strickland thinks of his family. Dyson is sixty-three now and remarried. As a father, banker-turned-investor Dyson was distant and judgmental, limiting his lessons to son Daniel to the pursuit of (1) money and (2) women. He encouraged little else, was intensely humorless and drank a lot. So Strickland and his friend Rupert Summerville had taught themselves how to surf, fish, backpack, shoot, box, and make minor, conservative investments through a discount stock broker, while their peers played team sports and competed for cheer- and song-leaders. Strickland had graduated solidly near the bottom of his class; Rupert Summerville near the top.

Strickland's mother, Jennifer Knowles, has been single since the divorce, and apparently happy to be that way. Strickland remembers her as an emotive but largely absent mom. By mid-career, she had become a high-end defense attorney, having worked her way up in the Orange County District Attorney's office before making her move to the dark side. She was an undemanding woman, but busy, too, favoring independent Dan over her shy and sensitive daughter, Allison. Strickland still can't remember his mother ever asking him where he was going or when he was coming back. She liked her martinis. When Dyson announced his intention of divorce—called in by phone from the high-rise offices of a Houston oil company—Jennifer had thrown his clothes, jewelry, and books into the swimming pool. Then plowed Dyson's beloved Bentley through the classy white estate fencing around the back forty, and driven it into the pool too. She jumped out at the last second but broke an ankle.

Strickland hears Villareal in the other room. His fourth call? Fifth?

He checks his phone: no reception, no messages since the airport.

Sits up straight in the cowhide armchair, closes his eyes, and commences his box breathing. Four, four, four, and four. Immediately feels the static in his brainpan start to recede. An ancient breathing method, he knows. Wonders what it would be like to be a swami. He's read that CIA officers are trained in the box method too.

Strickland banishes thought and lets his unconscious take over. Sitting here in this dangerous place reminds him of his earliest hero dreams—beginning around age ten—in which he found himself on the campus of whatever school he was attending at the time, armed with a good .38-caliber revolver, trying to protect a popular girl from several much older, much better-armed bad guys who were after them.

It was always a weekend or holiday because they'd be alone—Strickland and the girl—scrambling past the lockers and the empty classrooms, diving and rolling for cover, Strickland holding the girl's hand and returning fire. He'd kill their attackers one after another, but he'd always get hit himself, somewhere in his torso, no pain but lots of blood and he'd know he was a goner as he shot down the last guy then slumped against the wall and held the girl's hand and told her he loved her, and she kissed him and then he died. But even in the dream he knew his death wasn't real. Which allowed him to dream the dream again, right then, that same night sometimes, up through elementary and junior high and his first two years of high school—at which time the hero dreams ended and never came back.

From this pleasant reverie, Strickland is yanked back to reality by bullish Miguel Villareal, reclaiming the living room.

Strickland believes that Villareal will either march him outside at gunpoint and shoot him dead, or have wonderful good news to share.

"We go to El Gordo in Badiraguato," he says.

Strickland looks out the window of Villareal's Escalade. He has never been as deep into the mountains of Sinaloa as the municipality of Badiraguato, but he knows it as Alejandro Godoy's birthplace. Its people are poor and the land rugged. There are farms and cattle and small towns, but mainly heroin poppies. It is the birthplace of the Sinaloa cartel. Mexican military and law enforcement give the entire state a wide berth. Godoy began calling himself El Gordo—the Fat—out of respect for his mentor, El Chapo—the Short—himself a product of nearby La Tuna. Strickland and the US government know Godoy as the cartel's next generation, fighting hard to hold on to a once-great drug-trafficking empire with its founder, El Chapo, doing life in a Florida federal prison.

Strickland has the recurring, uncomforting thought that, because of all the Sinaloan cash and product that he and Joe have shoplifted in Tijuana, Godoy might just kill him and enjoy the vengeance.

The light is fading. The mountains have steep flanks and rocky gashes, blanketed by a verdant canopy of trees. The Escalade's outside temp readout is 32.2 Celsius, or 90 degrees Fahrenheit, Strickland calculates, looking down at the sun-grayed asphalt with the faded yellow ribbon running its middle. No wonder these people are strong, he thinks.

The farms and fences get fewer, and the houses larger, lots of reds and blues and festive lime greens. Many are two stories and most look old. An occasional new valley-tucked estate peeks from behind the thorns of acacias and ceibas and paloverde, and Strickland knows that these belong to the narcos.

As the Escalade shifts down and climbs in elevation, the punishing coastal thorn scrub gives way to coniferous pines and firs. The road gets steeper and the switchbacks tighten and only an occasional truck or horse trailer sweeps past them, heading for the coast.

"I've never been this far up," says Strickland.

"I don't know," says Villareal.

"No, I didn't think so."

"El Gordo will to hear of your plan."

"Do you think he'll like it?"

"I don't like it. You go fish in California?"

"Sometimes. Tuna, off San Diego when the water warms up."

"*Buenisimo.*"

Soon they come to a narrow dirt road on which await a flatbed truck, and what looks to Strickland like a homemade tank. The flatbed has a .50-caliber machine gun mounted in back, manned by a youthful gunner. Two more narcos in the cab are eyeing the Escalade, and one of them nods. The tank is a bulbous tan contraption, and splotched with rust, with tiny slots for windows, immense tracks, and a short cannon barrel housed in a dented turret.

The truck and the tank lumber slowly onto the asphalt, surrendering the rough washboard road to Villareal and the Roman.

29

The ranch is a full mile in, centered in an expansive meadow surrounded on three sides by sheer rock palisades topped with pines that have the last of the sun on them.

Strickland looks out at the big, sturdy house, newly built with the indigenous pine and fir. The lumber has been finished clear so the grain and color show. There are two barns, a smokehouse, a horse corral and stables, and a fenced pasture for the healthy-looking Criollo cattle. El Gordo's builders have left some of the big trees for shade and privacy. Under a long low sunscreen hung with camouflage netting, SUVs and late-model Chevrolet sedans are neatly parked, with plenty of room for more. There's a big grass lawn with an aboveground pool, covered by a blue tarp. Small bikes and trikes, red wagons and rocking horses litter the grass.

Villareal pulls under the sunshade. Strickland steps from the truck, noting the camo green Boeing Apache helicopter hiding in plain sight on a green asphalt landing pad not far from the house.

Strickland gets his duffel and follows Villareal to the shaded front porch of the house.

A tall man in jeans, his shirttail French-tucked behind a large silver belt buckle, waits in the open doorway. He's got the sinewy face and suspicious eyes of a mountain rancher used to dealing with rustlers. Steps outside and gestures.

"*Adelante.*"

Strickland follows Villareal in. Sets down his duffel and turns slowly, admiring the classic Mexican mountain lodge great room: hardwood floors, rough-hewn beams, three majestic fir candelabra hung from black iron chains, white plaster walls, still life paintings of flowers and fruit, three brutal crucifixes. The furniture is simple, rustic, and inviting, leather mostly, and draped with blankets. There's some Calderón furniture, too, Strickland notes. Maybe collected for Godoy's "protection" of the family-run business. Villareal has stationed himself in a cowhide chair.

Godoy enters the room through the front door, just as Strickland and Villareal had, moments ago. So he got a sneak preview of me, thinks Strickland. Where was he lurking?

Godoy is tall and trim, with an ascetic face and a head of black curls. The opposite of fat. Jeans and white canvas slip-ons, an open-collared white shirt, worn out, with a pack of cigarettes in the pocket.

He inspects Strickland, ignores his lieutenant.

A long moment, Strickland inspecting back.

"Please sit."

"Thank you."

Strickland takes one end of a long black sofa and El Gordo the other. He lights a cigarette, sets both feet on a large vintage trunk with iron latches and leather bindings.

"Make me believe in you," he says.

Strickland intends to give the best sales pitch of his thirty-three years. He's been thinking about what to say, and rehearsing it for twenty-four-plus hours now, ever since watching the DEA bag Valeria Flores and drain Joaquín Páez's pond up in Laguna.

"Joaquín is dead and Valeria is under federal arrest," says Strickland. "I was there. I saw it happen."

The anger is visible on El Gordo's slim, boyish face. "I send them to buy a dog, and the Americans kill and arrest them."

"The government is not releasing information," says Strickland. "When and if DEA is asked about two possible cartel soldiers in Laguna Beach, they will refuse to comment. But you must have suspected what happened, Señor Godoy. Have you sent *sicarios* to Laguna for revenge on the reporter?"

"This is not your business."

Strickland hears the cool threat.

He lets the words hang in the air a moment.

Then nods and continues his pitch with a brief bio: growing up in Southern California; early interest in nature, guns, and self-defense; college; military service; a year of San Diego PD; Knowles Security; then later, Knowles Academy of Self-Defense in Los Angeles. He's not going to spill to Godoy what he so innocently spilled to Carlos Palma—his real name. So he uses his mother's. If El Gordo decides to dissolve him in a vat of acid, at least Strickland will have kept one of his secrets.

Next, he confesses his part in the looting of Godoy's treasures in Tijuana over this last year. He apologizes and admits how wrong it was.

Then he goes quiet for just a beat to let his mastery of the Sinaloa Cartel sink in. To let Godoy imagine such mastery over his enemies.

With growing excitement, Strickland explains the almost unnatural nose possessed by the mongrel Joe, presently known as Felix in the *Coastal Eddy* video. That Joe is formerly a DEA detection K-9 who was retired early because of poor performance and depression.

Godoy frowns at this.

"I know," says Strickland. "But it happens to one in ten law enforcement K-9s. They come to dislike the work and the constant pressure."

"Now the dog is yours?"

"Not yet." Strickland explains the situation with Bettina Blazak and the dog, together 24/7.

"How did you come to have the dog in the beginning?" asks El Gordo, still frowning.

Without giving up Aaron's name, Strickland says that Joe's last handler was a former client of his who thought that he, Strickland, might enjoy Joe as a pet. The handler got the DEA to re-home unhappy Joe, whose work ethic—and work itself—had slacked off.

He wants Godoy to know that Joe is formerly DEA. It makes him more valuable, and it adds weight to Godoy's desire for vengeance over the Americans.

"It hit me one day that he'd be a real weapon in Tijuana," says Strickland.

He's on thin ice now, about to tell two absolute lies.

One:

"Through friends, I contacted one of your Tijuana associates and offered him Joe's nose for a cut of New Generation cash and product we would discover. He told me he'd kill me and my dog if he ever saw us in his plaza again. I felt lucky to be alive."

Two:

"So I went to the New Generation and Palma took my offer immediately. I'd get forty percent of all the cash Joe found, and a forty percent cash equivalent for drugs. I have no interest in selling or using drugs, Señor Godoy."

"Who of my men said no to you?"

"Rubén Cortázar," says Strickland, who has never met the man but read about his grisly end in *Blog Narco*.

"Killed by Palma's men in Hermosillo last year," says El Gordo.

"They tortured him, first. They taped it. Gloated over it. I heard them."

"But maybe you are lucky he's not here. For to tell the truth of your story."

"My story is true."

"Go on."

Strickland moves into what he believes is his sales pitch wheelhouse: the millions of dollars in cash and drugs that he and Joe can—over time— bring the Sinaloa cartel; his willingness to return Godoy's $200,000 lost to the DEA in California *plus* $50,000 in "restitution." Next, he's willing to reduce his take to 35 percent for Godoy. Very important, he knows the New Generation plaza in Tijuana like the back of his hand—its properties and alliances, its bribed police, its warehouses, brothels, safe houses, its tunnels and caches. He even knows the passcode for the vehicle tunnel running underground from Otay Mesa to Tijuana.

"Palma's goods are waiting for us, Señor Godoy."

After what he hopes is a loaded silence, Strickland plays his trump card in a soft, solemn voice. He's rehearsed it. A lot.

"Señor Godoy, I would enjoy helping the Sinaloa Cartel regain the plazas and prestige you once enjoyed in Tijuana. As you enjoy now, here in these mountains, where the people respect and protect you. I would enjoy helping you unmask your enemies for what they are: greedy animals, beneath your dignity."

Of course, Strickland withholds the fact that he intends to remain in the employ of the New Generation too. For a time.

"What did they do for you to betray them?" asks El Gordo.

Strickland gathers his words. "Revealed themselves to me. The torture of Cortázar. Rotting old Palma and his child bride. Their military equipment and desire to destroy every other cartel in Mexico. Their selling of central American immigrant girls as slaves."

"Has Palma cut your pay?"

"Yes. And—"

"What do you want from me beyond thirty-five percent?"

Strickland stands and goes to a window. Looks out at the vertical escarpments rising in the near dark. And at the faint scratches of the switchbacks, leading from the valley floor higher into the Sierra Madre. All the way to the clouds, he thinks. Mother mountains, help me now.

He hasn't rehearsed this, and it's the only part of his deal that isn't a flagrant upside for El Gordo. He's told himself it's best to speak man-to-man, to tell Godoy the simple truth.

"I assume you have already dispatched men to avenge Joaquín and Valeria," says Strickland. "To kill Bettina Blazak. I want you to spare her life."

Sitting in his cowhide chair, Miguel huffs quietly, shaking his head.

"The reporter betrayed me," says Godoy. "She cost me a life and much money."

"The DEA used her, sir. They told her that Valeria and Páez would be detained, questioned, and deported. Bettina is an innocent young woman, Señor Godoy. She tells good stories for her newspaper. You've seen them. You know."

"Yes, I know. She is honest in the stories. She is smart, and when she talks to the camera, you believe her."

Strickland nods, letting Godoy steep in his own words. He himself couldn't have said them any better.

"Is she special to you, Mr. Knowles?"

"Yes."

El Gordo smiles a dry, unemotional smile, an ascetic's comment on Strickland's weakness for romantic love.

Miguel chortles.

"I like her," Godoy says. "But she has cost me very much."

"Which I will pay back, with interest, as I've stated," Strickland says with earnest enthusiasm. His next lines are rehearsed too: "I can't give Joaquín Páez his life back. But I can become him. I can bring you the loyalty and money that Joaquín did."

Godoy deadpans Strickland, who doesn't know if his melodramatic pitch has hit the drug lord's soul, or baffled the man, or maybe just pissed him off.

The only thing Strickland can do is to believe it all himself, and he does.

"Bring your people home, Señor Godoy," says Strickland. "Tell them not to harm Bettina Blazak. Not to touch her. Joe and I will pillage the New Generation plazas for you, and we ask a fair thirty-five percent. I will pay you the two hundred thousand dollars you lost and another fifty thousand as a symbol of my loyalty to the Sinaloa Cartel."

Strickland tries to read El Gordo's expression but can't. Just dark eyes and a firm set of jaw. Something about his shock of curls suggests innocence, but Strickland doubts that there is any of that at all in Godoy.

"I accept your offer," says El Gordo. "You and the miraculous Joe will work for me. I will bring my assassins home. They will not harm Bettina Blazak. You will reclaim Joe."

Strickland feels his heart rate climb, feels the heavy weight of Bettina's life on a line partially controlled by himself.

"Please, Señor Godoy, do it now."

Again, Strickland sees the anger flash across Godoy's face.

"Do it soon. Please."

Godoy eyes Strickland with some finality. He's clearly a man used to having the final word.

"When you and the dog are together again, ready to work, call Miguel. Of course, you must get the money to me before anything can happen. I will need it quickly. I have couriers in San Diego."

"Yes, sir," says Strickland.

"With respect, Alejandro," says Miguel. "I must speak. A traitor once is a traitor twice. This man is a *norteamericano* thief without loyalty or soul. Let's kill him now. Do our business as we have always done it. The reporter *no es importante*. I think this is a mistake."

"You are not to think," says Godoy. "You are to take *el señor* Knowles back to Los Mochis for his flight home."

"Yes, sir. I will guard your traitor with my life."

Strickland, light-headed with triumph, shakes Alejandro Godoy's hand and follows the hulking, broad-backed Villareal into the Sinaloan night.

Runaway Joe,
Searching for His Boy...

30

Joe got himself from Chula Vista to La Jolla the same way any dog would—through a series of miracles that God only performs for the innocent and the pure of heart.

Along the way he ate fairly well, raiding garbage cans and pilfering from pet bowls left outside. He had especially good luck at those food places with the yellow arches, following his instincts and nose to the rear kitchen doors, into the kindness of the employees taking out trash, rinsing mop buckets, breaking down boxes for the dumpster.

He drank from streams and flood control channels, ponds and fountains, sprinklers, gutters and leaking hoses, swimming pools and drive-through car washes.

He mated three times in his first five days, all with beautiful females that would remain emblazoned on his memory forever and he would like to mate with again.

He slept in parks and yards, under freeways with tattered human beings and their fragrant belongings, in the median shrubbery of drive-throughs, where he fell asleep to the sound of idling engines and music and orders being placed.

The hardest part was taking long detours to avoid the cars that roared at him from all directions, while he tried to remain on course. At least what he thought was on course. Those cars could come at you so fast you didn't have time to think, just *Go!* Sometimes he'd focus on one car, while another car came charging up behind him like a wild monster. Some were almost silent.

He hated the screeching brakes, but something told him it was good, that he was still okay and on his way to Teddy.

Three people tried to get him by his collar, but Joe skittered away on his dainty feet, and disappeared as fast as he could. One evening before sunset, three coyotes trailed him across a soft grass meadow with ponds and people with sticks hitting small pale balls, and one of the men chased away the coyotes in a small car.

Progress was very slow. Sometimes he'd have to go far out of his way to get on the other side of a freeway or a crowded city. Sometimes he'd go backward, then way around, just to get a little bit farther ahead. It felt safest to travel at night. He had to find places to hide and sleep during the day, and the hunt for food and water was constant and time consuming.

But somehow, Joe knew what to do. How to survive and how to get where he was going. It was like he'd done this before, or maybe had dreamed it, or maybe his mother had taught him, though he couldn't remember that ever happening. Maybe the father he'd never met was good at these kinds of things. Or his father's father. Somehow, navigation and street survival had gotten into his mongrel blood.

On his sixth day of travel through the most crowded half of the most populous state in the republic, Joe found himself on the shoulder of La Jolla Boulevard. The cars thundered past him and the gravel was salted with broken glass. He'd gone long without water, and this morning's raided trash cans had given little but chicken bones, carrot peels, and lettuce.

But as he lay in the shoulder dirt, his nose to the air, Joe was reminded of where the policeman put him and Teddy into his car and took them back to Art and Nancy's big house on the hill. The more he looked around, the more sure he became that this was the place. Joe's inner navigator told him he was close to that house now. It was higher up in the sky, right under the cloudy sun.

It took him just a few minutes and a few steep side streets to find his big house with Teddy. Sitting on the sidewalk, Joe looked up at it, remembering Art and Nancy and the children. Remembered Wade coming here, and the serious meeting. And going with Teddy for sandwiches in town and how sad his Boy was because Dad and Mom had left them. Then walking all the way to the freeway where the policeman put them in his car.

Joe walked the fence line past the garage to the backyard. It was a tall black fence with pointed spears, impossible to climb. He could see through it to the grass and the pond where the children used to scream and play. The old smells flooded back to him—the grass with Teddy, the strong water in the pond, even the salty odor of the beach, which was not far away. He dug hard to get under the fence but hit concrete.

He followed the spears to the front gate, which people opened by pushing a small black box on a brick stand. Raised his nose toward the house and let the river of scent wash into him, smelling for Teddy.

No Teddy.

Then, just a hint of him. . . .

Joe stood on his back legs and put his paws to the bricks, and found him, finally, his Boy, Teddy, right there on the black box with the numbers on it!

Art was there too. And others, and Nancy, the strongest scent of all, like Mom smelled before she and Dad left him.

The front door opened and Nancy stepped onto the porch and turned to lock the door. She wore her big white padded shoes and pink sweats and a small pouch around her waist, like he remembered.

Joe whimpered and yipped and wagged his long saber tail, his happiness breaking inside him like a warm wave.

Nancy looked at him, then came over. She never touched Joe and she didn't touch him now.

"Joe, how did you get here? After four years! I can't take you in again. I don't want to put Teddy through losing you again after so long. I know you don't understand."

Joe looked up into her sad face. Then Nancy hurried back inside. Joe heard the dead bolt clank. Was she going to get Teddy?

He knew that Nancy would come out soon, but she didn't. He lay down on the warm bricks and waited, wondering if Teddy was inside or if he'd gone off to school with the other children like he usually did.

He didn't understand why Nancy didn't come out. What was she doing? What was she waiting for? He felt sad, and like something bad was going to happen, but he didn't know what or why.

All he could do was wait.

Half an hour later, Aaron parked his truck along the curb and got out.

"Joe! Joe, *come!*"

He had the leash in one fist and he was not happy.

The drive to Chula Vista was almost silent. Aaron's anger came off him in noiseless waves and Joe could smell his sour bad temper. Joe felt punished by the silence and believed that once again he had failed to do the things that would make Aaron happy. He'd never done any of those things, except for Find Drugs and Find Money. And even those didn't make Aaron really happy. They were not enough. Aaron wanted more. So Joe wanted more.

Aaron touched some buttons on his dashboard display and Joe heard the funny sound, then a voice.

A Woman talking with words Joe didn't recognize:

"You have reached Apex Self-Defense. If this is an emergency, please call 911. No one is available at this time. Please leave . . ."

Joe yawned and closed his drowsy eyes.

"I'm returning Dan's call about a dog," Aaron said, though Joe only understood Dog.

Joe would have asked Aaron for water but had no way of doing that.

So many things a Man or a Boy needs to do without being asked, Joe thought. If he wants a Dog. Like Teddy. Like Wade.

He felt the road bumping under him, wondered why Nancy hadn't told Teddy that he, Joe, had come home.

Back to work, he thought.

Find Drugs. Find Money.

31

After work, Bettina straightens her apartment, propping up Thunder, the Winchester, room to room as she dusts and wipes and sweeps. She's got the pepper gel gun in her purse, and her purse on the kitchen counter.

Felix follows her, lying in protective positions in doorways, ears up, chewing his now bedraggled turkey.

"We're a good team," she says. "And you are a Guten Doggen."

She's in the kitchen, putting cut flowers in the yellow vase she bought at the border the day she brought him home. Felix cocks his head and wags his tail at the word *team*, as he does every time he hears it, in any context. It's just as meaningful to him as *treat*.

Even with the sudden death of Páez and the detention of Valeria, Bettina's weighted fear of the Sinaloa cartel has lifted by not one gram. She knows that Godoy can send new soldiers to capture or kill Joe and, while they're at it, why not kill her for setting up his people and costing him $200,000? Powers and Arnie Crumley have told her it's possible but unlikely, saying that Godoy's risk–benefit equation won't pencil out, given what happened up in Moulton Meadows Park. Thus, no full-time protection—only intermittent, unscheduled surveillance. Continue to vary your routine, they said. You can spend some days at home and some at work, but use hotels too. Federal witness protection is disruptive and long term and used only as a last measure, generally for people who appear in court. You would have to give up your byline and your video shows, Arnie reminds her. Basically, your career.

Thanks, guys.

Billy has offered to be with her every second he's not working. Good of him, but she doesn't want anybody crowding her like that.

And she doesn't want witness protection anyway. What she wants is her old life back, even just a little at a time.

El Gordo has been silent since that brutal, surreal night. Through Powers, Bettina knows that the DEA has paid an informant to post on *Blog Narco* a speculative, "eyewitness" account of a kidnapping and murder of Sinaloan Cartel soldiers in Laguna Beach, California, possibly by rival Jalisco New Generation gunmen. This, to put El Gordo in his place.

Bettina assumes that, as of two nights ago, Godoy has been expecting to hear the good news that his associates had purchased Felix—the costly, humiliating, New Generation mutt made into a celebrity by *Coastal Eddy* reporter Bettina Blazak.

"I'd kill me, too, if I were him," she tells the dog in her blackest humor.

Felix considers this, springs to his feet, drops the turkey, and chases his tail in a circular, whirling blur.

At exactly 6:00 p.m., the dog goes to the security screen door.

Seconds later, Strickland appears behind it, as promised. Felix wags his tail dramatically, whimpering.

Bettina unlocks and opens the heavy steel door, Felix throwing himself against Strickland's knees as he tries to come in.

He downs the dog, who immediately flattens out at his feet, then rolls over. Bettina watches Strickland's face as he quickly scans the living room and kitchen, holding up his empty hands.

"No flowers." He turns a 360.

"Enough of that. I'll take your jacket if you'd like."

"No thank you."

"The gun doesn't bother me," she says.

"It should, a little."

"I have bubbly water, wine, and bourbon."

"Bourbon, please. Straight, with a dribble of tap water."

Strickland locks the security screen door.

From the kitchen, Bettina looks at Strickland and Felix as she makes two bourbons. The man looks bigger in here, or maybe her apartment looks smaller. It would be very difficult to escape if Strickland tried what Jason Graves tried. She hates that thought and everything behind it, and everything it leads to. She wonders again what to do with Jason. Hates *that* thought even more.

Concentrate on the here and now.

The three of them join Canyon Cocktails around the firepit. Bettina feels safer—maybe even bolder—with Strickland at her side. The evening is cold for Laguna but the swimming pool is heated. Two of the Canyon View residents talk and tread water in the deep end, the recessed light illuminating them from below. Legs like pale fish. The whirlpool is crowded, steam and words rising above the noisy bubbles.

Bettina introduces Strickland around; Felix takes a chaise lounge for himself, sitting upright, eyes on them, raising his nose to the cool canyon breeze.

Bettina likes Strickland's manners, slightly formal, controlled but genial. He answers questions about himself and his work with ease and apparent honesty, though he's quick to redirect his questioners back on themselves. Bettina is exactly the same way: the first thing she learned to do as a shy girl was to let people talk about themselves, which 99.9 percent of the time is what they wanted to talk about anyway. Which, years later, made her a natural reporter. Questions as a profession and a defense. Questions as armor.

She watches as Felix suddenly jumps from the chaise and, nose high, wends his way around a group of people standing near the pool. His limp hardly noticeable, he weaves his way along the water with his nose down, following a scent trail through the faint mist rising off the heated pool.

He angles away from the water, into a cluster of chaise lounges and patio chairs, to a round glass table on which purses and bags have been stashed. Sweaters and heavy jackets and scarves hang from the chairs around the table.

Bettina breaks away from the group.

"Felix, *sit!*"

He ignores her and, wagging his tail excitedly, drops back onto all fours and pokes his nose into the side pocket of a peacoat draped over a patio chair. Then he sits and looks at Bettina as she arrives.

By then the dog has everyone's attention, and some of the partiers have come over.

He sits now, a foot away from the coat, staring at that pocket.

"Whoa, dog, that's my jacket."

"Sorry about that," says Bettina.

Strickland arrives next with his practically untouched bourbon and an amused expression.

Peacoat swings the heavy jacket on. "Okay, dog. Good idea—this will definitely cut the chill."

Felix braces his little front paws on Peacoat's leg and jams his snout into the left pocket of the jacket.

"Felix, *down!*" Bettina commands. "*Down!*"

He pushes off and downs himself at Peacoat's feet, dropping a small plastic bag on the concrete.

Bettina sees the foil-wrapped item inside, the small pipe, and a box of wooden matches.

"*Leave it,*" says Bettina.

Felix looks up at her with glee in eyes, then turns his attention back to the bag.

Which Bettina picks up and hands to Peacoat, who stuffs it back into his pocket with a nervous grin.

By then every Canyon Cocktailer present tonight has gathered around.

"Bust-*ed!*"

"Don't let that dog into my place!"

"What is it?"

"What's it *look* like?"

Peacoat steps back, dangling the bag to the audience. "Anybody want some more hash?"

Felix jumps for it but misses.

Bettina snaps his leash on and walks him back over to his original chaise lounge, lets him jump back up.

"Sit and stay, dog," she says too harshly, regrets it because she knows he's only done what he's been taught to do. It brings him joy.

Bettina looks over at Dan, who has amusement on his face.

"Good dog," she says. "Now, sit and stay, will you?"

32

After dinner, Bettina and Strickland talk late, sitting on her deck over-looking Laguna Canyon Road. The Festival of Arts grounds below are dark, and the traffic in and out of town is light. Heat radiates from a steel chiminea.

Between them is a table for their cocktails and sherbet, and a cop-per hurricane lamp. Felix lies under the table, eyeing them through the glass top as he works on his plush turkey.

Strickland prods Bettina for her version of the death of Joaquín and arrest of Valeria, what Godoy has tasked her to do, how her DEA handlers had reacted.

Recounting some of what she saw that night, Bettina feels the dull fear returning, sees Joaquín punched dead by silent bullets, sees the agent toeing his head to see if he was still alive.

"Did you see much?" she asks. "I saw you zooming around in your fancy green car."

"Some."

"I'd rather not remember that right now."

"Please don't."

She looks out at Laguna Canyon, tries to let the remembered fear pass through her. She points out the once-notorious little cluster of homes nicknamed Dodge City, for the drug dealers who lived there in the sixties, and the cops who happily raided them, sometimes with guns drawn. Bettina has written articles and done videos on those wild days, and she's always felt some affinity for those hippie outlaws.

"Why?" asks Strickland.

"I envy them. They were brave and half-crazy. Me, I'm just conventional."

"Wait, you surf and race up and down Coast Highway with the Biker Chicks. And you're good with a shotgun. Those aren't exactly conventional things. Maybe you're wilder than you think."

Bettina never could take a compliment. Not that she's ever been drowned in them, except for maybe the during her Olympic trials. "I don't mind being me. Mostly."

Strickland lets that one sink in. "You're a lot. You're good. You're solid."

"Thank you."

A beat, then:

"What happened to you, Bettina? I see it on your face. It stands between you and what you want to say."

The lamplight bevels Strickland's face into light and shadow. It's a hard face, but it says the man inside is smart and honest and trustworthy. Though appearances can be all wrong, she knows.

"There are two," she says. Takes a moment to look out the stars twinkling above the black ridge of the canyon. Feels Keith, alive inside her, pleased to be thought of, taking form in her mind's eye.

"My brother died of a fentanyl overdose when he was twenty. Keith. We were twins. He's with me everywhere I go. I try to let in the good memories and edit out the bad ones. Sorry I can't keep him off my face sometimes. Don't really want to."

"You shouldn't," says Strickland. She can tell by the gravity on his face that he understands. And is moved by what happened to Keith.

She goes inside, brings out her framed picture of Keith and herself as Superman and Wonder Woman, look-alike superheroes in happy times.

Strickland sets it upright on the table before them and studies it with a solemn expression.

"Tell me about him."

"There's so much. Maybe some other time."

Bettina can't talk about Keith on demand. Right now, can't really talk at all. She wipes a tear on a knuckle.

His gaze in the steady lamplight is penetrating. "What else, Bettina?"

"No," she says, wiping the knuckle on her jeans, toughening up. "Not a big deal."

"Big enough to keep eating at you."

"Avoidable," she says.

"All of life is avoidable if you just stay home."

"I was not asking for it."

"No, you weren't," he says. "And that's why you can't let it go."

"I don't want to talk about it now."

His gaze softens. He pets Felix. "I like that you don't give up things easily. Fine with me and Joe."

"His name is Felix."

"Joe."

"You hardly touched the bourbon all night."

"I don't really drink," Strickland says.

"I do, but not like I used to. You get high?"

"A few times. Never liked it."

"Losing control," says Bettina.

"And coordination and competence."

"Me too. I could barrel race Sawblade drunk on beer and bourbon, but not high on weed. Made me question myself and—oh boy, that's not what you need in a race."

Strickland's laugh is hardly audible. She watches him in profile, nodding. Likes his nose.

He tells her stories from Afghanistan. They're horrible but funny in that way that marines have. Like about the SAW gunner Tristen Chunn, who could foresee attacks and IEDs while they were on patrol, Chunn on point that day, lugging the heavy-as-an-anvil squad automatic weapon toward a Sangin footbridge and stopping dead in his tracks just a few meters short, one hand up for everyone to stop, like a cavalry captain.

Strickland tells the tale with a wry urgency that suggests both a happy ending and a sudden catastrophe.

"It's going to blow, Sarge," says Chunn. "I saw it happen already."

"When?" says Sergeant Abbate.

"In the future."

"Well, Private, our asses are in the wind right now. And we're not turning around. So, can we get over this damned bridge *before* it blows?"

So, in Strickland's telling, young Chunn takes off running as fast as he can, carrying twenty-five pounds of machine gun and two hundred rounds of belt-drive ammunition. He's a little guy, eighteen years old. So nobody can get around him on the narrow bridge and they're all cussing him to go faster and Chunn finally gets across and the men all surge past him and keep on going. Strickland hangs back because he likes Chunn and Chunn is still just a boy and he's got this beautiful, innocent smile on his face, Chunn does, and when Strickland grabs his vest to pull him along, the bridge blows all right, the middle section blasted to splinters high in the sky, both ends cut off in a jagged mess, shards of wood and concrete raining down on the Helmand River like a storm from hell.

"I saw it happen exactly like that," Chunn says.

"And I told him, Tristen, I think you should lead these patrols for the rest of your tour. And he did."

"Did he do it again?" asks Bettina. "See the future?"

"Twice," says Strickland. "One was a dug-in IED that nobody could see but Chunn 'saw' go off. The other was what happened to Carlson, who said Tristen was full of shit and he, Carlson, stood up from behind the HESCOS to demonstrate that Chunn could not see the fucking future and no rag-head sniper was going to kill *him* eating his goddamned lunch today. Carlson took a bullet to his head and collapsed on top of Tristen. And that was that."

"Awful."

"Too bad. Carlson was okay."

Later Strickland talks about Dyson and Jennifer and his sister, Allison. Dyson strikes Bettina as slightly monstrous; Jennifer as selfish and impulsive; Allison much too tender and gullible to survive the Strickland parents. Dan no longer speaks to them.

"Do you still have things to say to them?" asks Bettina.

"I'm writing a letter to each one. Have been for some years now."

"You could just bomb in on them."

Bettina imagines bombing into Jason Graves's office in Anza. Then what?

Well, she's actually thought about that a lot recently.

"I might," says Strickland.

They talk about tomorrow's duties: Bettina's at her *Coastal Eddy* cubicle for just an hour or two, Strickland's at Apex for a full day of classes.

Her message notification pings and she sees a health insurance solicitation. Finds this funny with all the violence she's seen, up close. Taps it into trash.

"El Gordo?" asks Strickland.

"No such luck."

"He'll contact you again. He'll have questions about his people and his money, and your dog. It's good to keep moving around, Bettina, vary the schedule. If El Gordo decides to punish you, or maybe make another grab for Joe, he'll send his roughest diamonds."

"Can't wait to meet them."

"It's okay to be afraid. Fear can keep you alive."

"That's why I sleep with my Winchester." She stifles a yawn. "I'm turning into a pumpkin, Strickland."

"I'll sleep on the couch if you want."

Felix moves from under the table and sits, looking at them expectantly.

"No, thank you."

"This was great tonight."

"Maybe I'll come down your way next time."

246 • T. JEFFERSON PARKER

"You'd like San Diego. It's full of surfers and bikers. We even have our own *Coastal Eddy*. It's called the *Reader*. It's got smart, sassy stories, like yours."

She's still not sure she trusts Dan Strickland enough to walk into his Apex lair. Can she trust her gut? If not that, then what?

All she knows right now about Dan Strickland is that her heart is in a big, hard-beating tangle.

Bettina forces herself to push him out the door. Felix tries to go with him, but she gets him by the collar and back inside.

She slides home the dead bolt, ear to the door as Strickland's footsteps diminish, then go silent.

She gets the picture of Keith off the deck and puts it back on her office desk.

As he walks through the parking lot to his car, Strickland is filled with two foreign emotions: love and guilt. He doesn't understand the love, how it can just arrive inside you like this, for the first time. The guilt he understands clearly. Tonight he's seen the consequences of his cartel adventures on a real person, with a real tear in her eye and a real wound in her soul. The look on her face is the saddest he's ever seen.

He realizes that after this is over—tomorrow, probably—Bettina will be freshly heartbroken again and worried sick at the loss of Joe. She'll blame herself and fear the worst. And he realizes that he won't be able to tell her that Joe is just fine, that he's back in San Diego with him, living a good life. No more than he can tell her that he uses Joe to make money in the trade that killed her twin brother Keith and tore her heart in half forever. Learn to live the lie, he thinks—it's the obligation you've taken on.

Right now, he feels like he's destroying the village in order to save it. In order to save her life, he reminds himself.

El Gordo has given his word and I've given mine.

He takes off his coat and lays it in the back seat of his car. The hour-plus drive to San Diego will give him plenty of time to call Charley

Gibbon, nail down details for tomorrow, upload his Mole tracker app to Charley's phone. Bettina told him she'd probably have lunch with Felix tomorrow, up at the park where they go all the time. Gibbon and Marcos—Charley's assistant dognapper—are here in Laguna already, resting up at a motel.

Strickland feels a strange, blue doom falling over him.

Billy Ray Crumley, feeling like a jilted suitor, watches from his pickup truck as Strickland walks toward the fog-windowed, green Maserati that's been there all evening and much of the night.

Billy's already recognized him as the guy from the Havana Café the morning they met Arnie at the DEA in San Diego. The guy who heard Texas in his voice. Watching out the window for Bettina too? Yes, obviously.

A good-looking guy, thinks Billy. Has to be the reason Bettina has been so quiet the last couple of days, busy and distant and cool toward him. He's been sitting here for hours, since texting her five times this evening, all sincere, caring messages, all unanswered. Ignored. As if she were otherwise engaged.

Which Billy saw was true when he looked in on today's Canyon Cocktails happy hour—to which Bettina had taken *him* not long ago—only to find her and Felix there with this Maserati guy who was spying on her at the Havana.

Billy writes down the plate numbers so he can get an ID on Mr. Maserati. Run him for warrants.

Then pass that name to Arnie, whose DEA analysts can spit out information on people faster than shit through a goose, as Arnie likes to say.

When Mr. Maserati takes off his coat and sets it on the back seat of the car, Billy notes the paddle holster at the small of his back.

Cop or robber? he wonders.

One of Arnie's guys?

33

The next morning, Bettina grinds through the entertainment calendar listings for this week's *Coastal Eddy*. She gives top billings to her favorite entertainers and artists, lets her not-so-favorites have the bottoms. Felix sleeps in his crate.

She feels lighter than she's felt since Arnie Crumley's "credible but unverified" warnings at the Cliff nearly a week ago. Since sleek Páez and stylish Valeria came to their grim ends. Since obnoxious Arnie turned out to be right, and his robotic DEA troops really did make short work of El Gordo's people here in Laguna. Scary short. And having Strickland around, even making him dinner last night, has made Bettina feel safer. She almost kissed him goodbye; glad now she didn't.

By ten o'clock, she and Felix are at the hilltop mansion of the retired MLB five-time All Star, two-time MVP, and the thirteenth leading home run hitter of all time, Rod Foster.

They conduct the interview on his putting green, Felix lying in the shade of a picnic table under a magnificent magnolia while Bettina asks questions, makes notes, shoots video.

The day is bright and cool and Foster is dressed like a tournament PGA player, right down to the white Titleist visor.

Foster putts and talks and intermittently drinks from a liter stein of iced lemonade so loaded with rum that Bettina can smell it, resting in the shade of a picnic table twenty feet away. Her stein is next to it, but she's just sipping. She notes that Foster's putts don't often go in, that he seems impatient. He talks about pressure being a privilege in sports, how the younger stars fritter away their time and talents on social media. He squats to line up a shot, misses it, claims his drink, and gulps it down to the ice.

The interview and video shoot go on forever. Foster's assistant delivers two more lemonades.

When it's over, Foster smiles and shakes Bettina's hand warmly, then pulls her in for nice wet kiss on her cheek, his lips cold, his breath sour-sweet with lemons and rum.

Felix growls.

By lunchtime, Bettina is walking Felix across Alta Laguna Park, on her way to her favorite concrete table, over by the playground. In a small cooler she's got take-out sashimi, a can of sugar-blasted iced tea, kibble and water, and Felix's shiny metal travel bowl.

There are people out and about, most of them in coats and sweatshirts against the chill. Brown women push white infants in elaborate, state-of-the-art strollers. Runners run and joggers jog and the tennis players whack away.

Bettina brushes fresh fragments of orange peel from the bench of her table and sits down.

She feels good right now. At least better. Foster wasn't so bad, and she'll get a decent story out of him, and she has the rest of the day off, and again she feels relief that Joaquín is dead and Valeria on her way to being deported. She knows that El Gordo might become vengeful when he learns what happened that night, and deduces her betrayal. She's got the DEA, Billy, and Strickland to call on, if needed. She tries to dismiss the possibility of revenge from El Gordo, get it away from this bright, clear beautiful day.

Feels good until she hears her phone ping and sees another message from Billy Ray. He's concerned, wonders if she might be free for lunch. She sighs, leaves the cooler closed, and sends back another message of her own, trying to sound pleasant. Sure, she tells him, I'm up at Alta Laguna right now if you can make it. Already have my lunch, though . . .

Billy's there ten minutes later, in his street clothes, a white bag in one hand. When he takes a knee in front of Felix, his face is heavy and his eyes are all worry. She hates to see him this way, knows it's her fault.

Billy does his usual thing with the dog—sit, down, roll over—then a vigorous belly scratch that gets the dog's right leg going, always the right leg when Billy does this.

He talks to Bettina the whole time, looking up at her with those beautiful eyes of his, explaining how he got today off, covering for Benson on patrol tonight, trying to keep the conversation light until she cuts him off.

"I'm sorry, Billy," she says. "I've been so distracted since that thing up at Moulton Meadows. I just need some trust and some privacy, that's all."

A doubtful look from Billy. "Okay. I get that, Bettina. I really do. And I don't mean to crowd you. I care about you, though, and I know you've been through a lot. Just trying to help, if I can."

"I know. I appreciate it."

He sits on the same side of the table as Bettina, at the end of the long, cool concrete bench.

"The canyon is beautiful today," he says. "Look at that sky. Who'd believe rain tonight?"

They eat mostly in silence, the cooler on the bench between them, Felix under the table.

When Billy's done with his dinky little burrito, he puts the foil in the bag, rolls it tight in his big hands, and rises.

"I'll see you around," he says.

She squeezes his free hand. "Good."

"Are you scared?"

"Some."

"Felix? You take care of Bettina. She needs you."

Felix is standing, tail wagging, but Bettina sees uncertainty in his expression when he looks at her. All the heaviness coming off me, she thinks.

She watches Billy walk away.

She sits a while, takes Felix down the canyon trail a few hundred yards, doubles back and heads for her Jeep.

When she rounds the Jeep to get the passenger door for Felix, he growls.

"Hola, Bettina! Hola, Felix," says the man. Thick accent, short, sunglasses and a Pacifico ball cap pulled down tight.

He arches something to Felix, who snatches it midair.

"And for you, Señorita Blazak—El Gordo forgives you."

When he extends a thick bundle of cash Bettina turns away, yanking the leash hard, and crashes into a big man in a black ski mask who twists her wrist back with instant, serious pain, easily prying her fingers off the leash.

"*Fass!*" Bettina orders, but it's too late.

Ski Mask is already leading him away, calmly ordering Felix to heel while Pacifico firmly grips Bettina's shoulder and drops the bundle of money at her feet

"*Come! Felix, come!*" she yells. He looks back at her, whimpering in confusion, tugging at the leash to come, his body twisting and his front feet off the asphalt, paddling air.

"Don't follow us," says Pacifico. "We will not hurt your dog. El Gordo is a man of peace and truth, and he loves dogs."

"Fuck El *Gordo*! I want my dog back."

"Give thanks for your life, *señorita*. Joaquín Páez has no life because of you."

Over Pacifico's shoulder Bettina watches Ski Mask yanking Felix into a white SUV. When Pacifico turns and breaks into a run Bettina stuffs the money in her purse, grabs the key fob, unlocks the doors, and clambers in. Across the lot she sees Pacifico climbing into the white SUV, which is already moving toward the exit.

Bettina cranks the Wrangler's engine but hears only the crisp click of a starter with a dead battery.

She jumps back out and grabs the Model 12. Her spark jumps to flame then fire. She's more than pissed. Slams the door shut and runs toward the white SUV, which by now is out of sight.

She makes okay time across the parking lot and starts down Rimcrest toward Alta Laguna Boulevard, wobbling in the low-heeled fashion boots she'd worn to be slimed by Rod Foster, the Winchester balanced in her hands. But she's fast losing hope because the white SUV has to be at least half a mile downhill by now, and her balance is bad in the boots, and Alta Laguna Boulevard is steep as hell and because running around in public with a shotgun is really, really dumb.

So she slows to a stop, breathing deeply, the shotgun butt to the ground and her hands on the barrel for something to lean on.

A guy coming up the road in a convertible slows and studies her. Two women in a Mercedes coming down from the park stop, and the driver's window goes down and Bettina meets the woman's stare, then the window goes back up and the sedan rolls widely around her, headed back to town.

She's traipsing back uphill, brimming with fury and adrenaline, when she hears the siren. She knows whom it's for but what the hell can she do now—run away from the cops with her shotgun?

She lays it down and stands panting on the shoulder of the road. Raises her hands as the cruiser approaches, siren off but the lights still on, flashing in the afternoon light.

"Police! Do not move. Do *not move!*"

Bettina just nods, hands still up, wondering if breathing counts as moving, telling herself there's no way this can turn into a cop shooting—she's just a local citizen out for a run with a loaded 12-gauge shotgun, right?

The two officers come crabbing out of the car, crouched low and weapons drawn. A man and a woman. Bettina recognizes both faces but doesn't know their names. Susie, maybe. Their gear jangles and the red and blue lights of the cruiser flash behind them.

"Step away from the weapon!" yells the man.

She does.

"Down on one knee, *keep your hands raised*!" he commands.

The shoulder gravel bites through her $300 suit pants.

"Bettina Blazak?" asks the woman.

"Yes, Susie?"

"Don't move," the man calls out. "Keep your hands up!"

He sidles out wide around her and she hears him come up from behind.

"Put your hands behind your back," he says. "Slow now."

Bettina lowers her arms. Feels his grip, then the tight cinch of the plastic.

"Bettina, what's going on here?" Suzie asks, holstering her gun. "Are you all right?"

"They stole Felix! Do a BOLO on him! Set up roadblocks on Coast Highway and Laguna Canyon Road!"

"Well, maybe, but . . . ," says Suzie.

Then a fresh storm of tears hits Bettina. She's not just humiliated by her own circumstances, but she knows—just *knows*—that those two assholes have probably already killed her dog, and Animal Control will probably find him in a ditch off Laguna Canyon Road when he starts to draw vultures, so Bettina cares not one bit what these cops think of her or what they're going to do with her.

"Please go after him! Find Felix! He's the famous one from the *Coastal Eddy* show. I'll walk to the cop house and turn myself in!"

"Is that your gun?" asks Suzie.

"I tried to make the Olympics with it. Can I stand up now?"

The man helps her up with a firm hand on her upper arm.

Bettina thanks him and bows her head and squeezes her eyelids closed and prays that this is not happening, has not happened, will not happen—her wonderful, loving, goofy, inspiring, historied, funny-eared Felix taken by cartel killers—and she, the great journalist Bettina Blazak, headed for jail.

34

An hour later Bettina is delivered back to Alta Laguna Park in a PD cruiser driven by Officer Susie Ortega. Bettina's hands are still shaking, her Model 12 locked in the trunk.

"I hope the BOLO for the dog and the Pacifico guy helps," says Ortega, opening the trunk and handing Bettina her gun and an evidence bag with the shells. "It's all we can do without the plates, or a good description of the SUV."

"White. Late model. Dark windows," says Bettina, dazed and tired of repeating herself. The surge and ebb of adrenaline has left her exhausted, like after a high-velocity bicycle ride, or surfing a six-foot day at Brooks Street.

"Don't be running around town with that gun again, Bettina. You could have killed someone. Or yourself. Are you going to do a story on this?"

"Absolutely yes, I am."

"I'll talk on camera if you need me to."

"I'm going to find Felix. My story's going to have a happy ending."

"Be realistic."

After Officer Ortega drives off, Bettina is not surprised to find the hood of her Wrangler ajar and the battery cables disconnected. She gets a wrench from the toolbox and hooks them back up, a sudden orange pop scaring the hell out of her and bringing fresh tears to her eyes.

She drives all over Laguna looking for Felix. Downtown, south and north, the hills, Dodge City and Canyon Acres, and Stan Oaks and Sun Valley. Can't believe how many late-model white SUVs there are, and how many dogs. How many U-turns and dead ends and fruitless drive-bys.

Gets her binoculars from home, trades her wobbly boots for athletic shoes, then takes Laguna Canyon Road to the 73 South, which takes her to Interstate 5 and the border crossing at San Ysidro.

In the dark, Bettina sits in a pay-to-park lot near the crossing lanes, scanning the cars heading into Mexico through a tall chain-link fence topped with gleaming coils of concertina. The binoculars are good ones and she feels like she's looking at these people from the back seats of their cars, not a hundred feet away. They talk on phones or with each other; they smoke cigarettes and pick their noses. Only one bouncy dog in a Chevy. No Pacifico ball cap. The powerful lights blaze down from their standards and the vehicles belch exhaust but hardly move.

And really, she thinks: just what the hell are you going to do if you spot him?

She knows she won't. Knows she'll probably never see him again. Faith unrewarded is a bitterness to the soul. Her dad used to say that. Much bitterness ahead, she thinks.

She feels the thump of her heart, heavy and broken.

She hasn't felt this bad since the frat party on Balboa Island, when Jason Graves ripped away her happiness and her trust.

He's still not done with me, she thinks. Hates herself for that as much as him.

And realizes that now, exactly right now—emptied of hope, filled with helplessness, and fueled by nothing that resembles reason—is the perfect time to get her revenge on Jason, forgive herself, and set things right.

She parks the Jeep across the street from Inland Frontier Realty in Anza. It's cold and late. She downs her 7-Eleven hot dogs, Funyons, and a decaf.

The back of the Wrangler is big enough for her to stretch out, so she takes off her shoes and gets into the sleeping bag she always carries. It's not exactly comfortable, but the folding pad helps.

Felix's hair is everywhere, which weighs heavily on her. In the weak dome light she counts the money thrust upon her by Pacifico Man—$10,000 in hundreds. She can't understand why El Gordo gave her this instead of killing her.

Her phone pings and it's a message from Strickland, saying he had a great time with her and Joe—let's do that again soon.

She texts back that Felix was kidnapped by two of El Gordo's killers up at Alta Laguna this afternoon. That she's talked to DEA and they're sending agents to Laguna to search for him. Says she's fine, don't worry. But doesn't have the spirit to talk to Strickland when he immediately calls back.

She texts Billy because she feels she has to:

So sorry for everything. Felix has been kidnapped by the Sinaloa Cartel, as you know by now. It happened just after we talked at the park. I'm about to square things up with a man who's been haunting me for years. You are a strong and loyal friend and I adore you. I'll be hard to get a hold of for a while.

Teddy Delgado's third email comes through a few minutes later.

Dear Ms. Blazak,

I'll be starting off for Laguna Beach in just a few weeks. A friend is driving me to the Oceanside transit center where I'll get the Coaster to San Juan Capistrano. After that it's still pretty far to Laguna but I have some bus money.

How is Joe? I know you're taking good care of him. I watch your video about him a lot. I contacted Joe's DEA handler, Aaron, just to make sure he saw your story, and he told me he'd seen it. Turns out, Joe was unhappy and ran away from him not once but twice, and the second time Aaron looked all over San Diego County but couldn't find him. Joe had a chip but nobody notified Aaron. Aaron thought he was dead. This was like over a year ago. Then you found him in Tijuana! I think God personally watches over Joe.

I have been enjoying your stories. When I get to Laguna I'll come to the *Coastal Eddy.*

Oh, if you want to play the game that Joe loves most, it's like hide-and-seek. You give him something to smell, then you make him stay and hide it in a really impossible place to find. Indoors or out. It can be something that doesn't have a strong smell. He'll find it, though. He always does, so you have to give him really good treats when he does. You'll see how happy it makes Joe to make you happy. I taught him that game. Back in our house before Mom and Dad. I was the first one who noticed that Joe has the best nose in the world. Even his trainers at Excalibur told me so.

Have you thought of a fair price I can pay for Joe? I'm hoping to leave Laguna with my dog back!

Sincerely,
Teddy Delgado

She watches the sunrise scrunched down in the front seat, head just high enough for her to see Inland Frontier Realty through the steering wheel. The western, saloon-look building sits alone on the outskirts of Anza, windblown tumbleweeds stacked against a chain link fence. Not much around. The Circle K is way down the road, the DQ half a mile away. She feels like a fool, hunkered down here, hiding from nobody. Her whole body is sore from the shotgun chase and the cold night in a steel Jeep.

Jason Graves's Escalade with the rearing horse and roping wrangler on the doors bellows to a stop in the same parking spot out front, just feet from the hitching rail. A moment later the door opens and he swings his pale boots to the ground. Dust rises from the gravel parking lot. Jason unlocks and goes in and CLOSED becomes OPEN.

She gets out and crosses the street, the heavy Model 12 cradled in her arms, fully loaded, a hand on the sliding forearm.

She marches past the hitching rail, up the steps, and onto the wooden porch. Throws open the door and steps in in. Jason's behind his desk. His mouth opens, and his face goes pale.

Bettina levels the shotgun at him. "You touch your phone, and I'll blow it out of your hand."

"Bettina."

"Correct. I thought your memory might improve."

Jason's wide-eyed face looks like a child's.

"I came here for an apology," she says. "And I won't accept a denial of the truth. If you can't or won't remember what you did, I've got John

Torres lined up to talk to the UCI campus cops. I've read his statement. It's detailed and graphic. It would also make a real easy post. Talk about viral potential. I even took pictures of the house, and the room where it happened."

Almost none of which is true, except that she *has* talked to John Torres and he's still willing to tell the cops what he saw that night.

"Please don't do that," says Jason. "I tried to put it out of my mind. For years I did. But I've been thinking about it a lot since I saw you. Thinking about it, like, every second. I'm not just sorry, Bettina—I'm really, really sorry. I was horrible and there's no forgiving what I did and I'm so sorry I hurt you. I won't ask you to forgive me. I won't even ask myself to do that. But don't tell the world. Don't tell my wife and children. Please. I beg you."

"I want you to feel like I did."

"I have money."

"You'll need it for the Escalade. Thanks for the confession and apology. Wipe the slobber off your lips, Jason."

Bettina kicks open the door and hustles back down the steps and blows out the right front tire of the SUV. Pumps the gun and destroys the left tire, then rounds the Escalade, steps back a few yards and blasts the Inland Frontier sign and its rearing horse and roping wrangler not just once but three times, the big 12-gauge, #6-shot pheasant loads crushing through the paint and bending the metal into a giant pucker that takes up almost the whole door.

She goes back inside, finds Jason still at his desk, trembling and loading a big revolver.

"No, please," he says, dropping the gun and cartridges to the floor.

"Stand up and kick it here."

Jason lurches up, manages to kick the gun on his second try. The revolver spins across the floor, cylinder free and two cartridges spilling out. It stops just short of Bettina's boot.

"I want to hear you apologize again."

"I did it. I assaulted you and I apologize!"

"Say 'rape,' Jason. Use that word."

"I tried to rape you but I didn't. I didn't."

She takes his revolver back outside, heaves it over the chain-link fence and into the tumbleweeds.

Quickly stashes her shotgun in the sleeping bag, jumps into her seat and fires up the engine. Stomps on the gas and fishtails out of the parking lot in a storm of gravel, sand and dust.

Screams *"Yeeesss!"* for her new freedom, for the improved, industrial-strength fire she believes is inside her now. For the burden of vengeance lifted. For the liberty to feel something for a man besides suspicion. All of this locked away by Jason Graves until today.

And most of all for her plan—hatched last night in a fearful dream in the back of the freezing Wrangler—to get Felix back.

A bold and beautiful plan.

If he's alive, she can get him back.

Home in Laguna, Bettina emails Alejandro Godoy:

Dear Mr. Godoy,

As you know your men kidnapped Felix in Laguna Beach yesterday. They treated him roughly but they were respectful of me and did not harm me or the Dog. I appreciate your $10,000 very much and would like to offer it back to you as partial payment for returning Felix to me.

Here is my offer: I will tell the true story about you—the one that you said the newspapers never tell. It will focus on you but also on your giving Felix back to me, to show your caring side, the side of you that loves children and dogs, as you told me once. But I have to be factual too. I will present you as a dangerous and sometimes violent man, and the leader of a powerful drug cartel.

I will also interview you on video for my newspaper, *Coastal Eddy*, so you can tell your story in your words. You understand that an interview with El Gordo would be picked up by probably every news outlet in the known world. So, if you don't want your face seen by millions and millions of people, then we'll just do the print and e-paper version of my story without pictures.

And as I said, I'll give back the $10,000. I'd offer you more but I don't have any more.

I love Felix and I want him back. You told me you were a man of peace. Please do the right thing and return this dog to his rightful owner.

Sincerely,

Bettina Blazak

She hits Send, knowing full well that El Gordo will probably not give Felix back to her for $10,000 and a *Coastal Eddy* story and video.

And that her editor, Jean Rose, will certainly frown upon a video interview with one of the most violent cartel traffickers on earth in her slick, puffy, paradise-flaunting *Coastal Eddy*.

And that Billy and her DEA handlers will feel betrayed.

She feels like she's betrayed everybody around her except Felix and Strickland. Felix she trusts. Strickland, close to.

Bettina, she thinks: these are the least of your problems.

Fortune favors the bold.

Sanity optional.

She stares across her home office at her beautiful blue swallowtail surfboard, can practically hear it talking to her.

Felix's abduction has kindled the spark that makes the flame that becomes the fire that now chews through her. Her wild. Jason Graves stood no chance against it, and neither will El Gordo or Jean Rose.

Or the March storm-swell that's pounding the Laguna coast right now in advance of the rain, the water a bitter 56 degrees and the wind whipping whitecaps into her face as Bettina drops in on a large and chaotic wave that encloses her in its spitting maw before dashing her into the water like a bathtub toy.

The guys in the water hold up, bobbing on the chop and watching her.

She takes another wave.

Back home, her teeth chatter and she's so tired and cold she can barely get out of her dry suit and thermals. It's five thirty and there's a light rain falling.

She looks at Felix's crate and starts bawling again. Takes a scalding bath, heats a frozen pizza, downs three neat fingers of bourbon, and falls asleep.

35

While Bettina snores, half a mile away, Billy Ray Crumley reads the "Inter-Agency Informal Dossier" on Dan Strickland, attached to Arnie's email.

Billy's in a Laguna Beach PD conference room with his laptop hooked up to the good department broadband, already in uniform for his Bike Team patrol downtown.

He's worried sick about Bettina: last night she left him a very strange text message about being haunted by a man. She's not returning his calls. But as of half an hour ago, at least, her Wrangler was parked in her Canyon View spot, right where it belongs.

It more than worries him that last night, Bettina was "about to square things" with this fellow who's been haunting her for years. *Years?* He feels her heartache, fear and anger as if she's sitting right here in the conference room beside him. Makes it hard to concentrate.

Billy reads that Daniel Knowles Strickland is thirty-three. He owns the apparently successful Apex Self-Defense school in San Diego.

Strickland has a rapid-fire past that includes some college, military service, law enforcement, and a now defunct private investigation company, Strickland Security.

An action figure, thinks Billy. A rugged war hero. It pisses him off that three days ago, he was with Bettina all evening and half the night. He's not the man haunting her, is he? What *is* he doing to her? Hustling her into hiring him to protect her and Felix? If so, then a lot of good *that* did. Was he just trolling for business—trying to convince a pretty young woman to take his course at Apex? Maybe just trying to get friendly with her? Billy Ray would love to ask her but he probably never will.

DEA hasn't included much in the way of pictures or videos of him, but there's no doubt this is the man he talked to at the Havana Café, and saw coming from Bettina's apartment. There's a high school yearbook picture, and a shot of Strickland receiving his Silver Star in 2011. There's a poor-quality picture of a young Officer Dan Strickland of the San Diego PD.

And a brief International Practical Shooting Confederation website video of a "Young Talent" shooter—a much younger Strickland—loping through a woodsy, two-minute course, nailing paper silhouettes with a Glock as he runs and fires, reloads, runs and fires. Billy notes that when Strickland is close enough, he shoots with only one hand—right or left—holding the gun a little higher than necessary, trading an easy sightline for Hollywood. Which is crazy in competition like this, he thinks.

But, as a cop who has to qualify with his sidearm every year, Billy can see how well this guy shoots. Crazy, maybe, but crazy good.

In the video, Dan Strickland reminds Billy of someone he knows, or maybe has seen before. A faint memory at best. Something about the way he swings his weapon on the move, the ease of gait and turn of torso. Like he's after style points. *Trying* to look graceful. Billy has shot on the run, in ranges such as this. They're difficult and this guy makes it look easy.

Billy thinks he might be remembering one of his fellow cadets in training. Why does that seem so long ago? Something to do with Lorna and their public secrets in Wichita Falls, no doubt. Too bad Bettina seems 100 percent not interested in going further. Because of Dan Strickland? Or is it just me?

He replays the IPSC video again, can't connect Strickland to anybody in his past. He's remembered dreams more clearly than this vague whisp of a memory. Maybe a memory. Or it might *be* a dream, for all he knows.

Billy can't get his mind off Bettina, but it's dangerous to be distracted when you're patrolling a crowded city on a bicycle. With a gun on your hip, no less. When the traffic is bad you have to dismount every other minute, cut between the cars, go another block maybe, then dismount again. When traffic is light the vehicles are moving fast enough to kill you and half the drivers are either looking out their windows at the pretty little city, or on their phones.

Billy soldiers through his beat, dodging the puddles from last night's rain. He checks the outdoor dining on Forest, going strong for March.

Gives directions to tourists; stops in at Bushard's Pharmacy and Tuvalu and *Coastal Eddy*, even though Bettina's car isn't in the parking garage.

Chats with Crazy Larry outside the Wells Fargo entrance, tells him to quit panhandling the bank customers on their way in and out. "But this is where the money is!" says Larry, his standard reply, and Billy usually thinks it's funny, but this morning it just gets on his nerves.

"Move along, Larry," he says. "You smell bad."

"Headed for the laundry right now, Captain. Got any quarters?"

In fact he has three, which he drops into Crazy Larry's very dirty hand while Larry stares at his gun, which always makes Billy nervous.

After work he changes into his civvies and drives to Apex Self-Defense, on Cedar in San Diego.

It's not easy to find, tucked into a labyrinth of squat brick industrial buildings, looming steel-and-glass concoctions and metro tracks, all webbed tight by telephone poles and power lines. The Apex building is a three-story brick structure with an address half-hidden in ivy and no ID other than the long-faded San Diego Sandblast sign above the front door.

Billy sits in his pickup truck on the uncovered roof lot of A-1 Parking, giving him a great view through his binoculars.

No Bettina.

No Strickland or green Quattroporte, no customers coming or going. But he sees motion through the small first-story windows. There's a hand-to-hand combat class going on behind one window, real nasty stuff, maybe Krav Maga. Everybody is in street clothes, practicing eye-gouges and throat rips in slow motion. No contact. The instructor—who looks shorter and wider than Strickland—wears a fencing mask with a full throat bib.

The third floor of Apex looks newer than the first two, with a slightly different shade of brick, and large windows on both of the walls that he can see from here. Through the fabric blinds Billy sees faint movement, someone deep inside, crossing the room maybe. Then none.

He watches the face rippers practicing their form. Eats his still-warm In-N-Out Burger Double-Double, fries, and the chocolate shake, always amazed you can get a dinner like this for less than seven bucks.

An hour later the Apex students come out. There are three men and three women, a variety of shapes, sizes, and ages.

No Bettina, but he didn't think there wouldn't be.

Billy wipes his fingers on the thin paper napkins and heads back to Laguna.

Bettina's Wrangler is in its usual spot in the covered parking.

Billy feels an uneasy relief settle inside. She may not want anything to do with me, he thinks, but at least she's alive and home and not with the crack-shot, pretty-boy, kill 'em with your bare hands Dan Strickland.

Strickland is still on Billy's mind later that night, as he sits at the chrome dinette in his tiny, furnished Laguna Beach apartment.

Specifically, Strickland's distinctive shooting style in the video, which has been running through his Bettina-distracted brain since he first saw it this morning.

Billy's got his laptop on the table before him, and a Coors Light sweating into a folded paper towel, as he opens the DEA link and again watches Strickland hustling, crouching, and blasting away at the International Practical Shooting Confederation match.

The video is from 2012 when, Billy notes, Strickland was twenty-two and working his brief stint at the San Diego PD. Billy has shot at ranges like this in the Texas Hill Country. Hitting something while you're running isn't easy like in the movies, but Strickland makes it look that way.

"*There,*" says Billy, pausing the video for a still shot of Strickland, his pistol up in one hand, caught mid-stride down a steep, curving slope, about to come into range of a paper bad guy crouching behind a small laurel sumac, gun ready.

I've seen this guy, he thinks again.

At the DEA office in San Diego with Bettina, Arnie, Dale Greene, and LaDonna Powers.

But it wasn't this IPSC video. It wasn't a video at all. It was a picture— part of Bettina's forwarded "offer" from El Gordo.

Which Billy calls up from his email and reads again.

The attached photos are of the black-clad gunman and his pale dog in what appears to be a railroad switching yard. He's got his pistol in one hand, like Strickland in the IPSC "New Talents" video. Felix is out ahead of him, his telltale brown ovals showing clearly, his nose down, his saber tail curving up.

Back to the man. Billy sees the same posture. Same turn of the torso, his hand raised, pistol pointed down. Not a classic shooter's stance. Not even close. More an improvisation? An efficient, necessary movement— maybe—but there's something else attached to it. What is it, he wonders. Performance? Celebration? Maybe even joy?

There's not much more tying this blacked-out, masked man to Strickland at the IPSC match, except for a general tallness, his medium build, and a somewhat long-legged carriage. Billy can't even tell what race he is, or the color of his hair.

But when he holds the printed dossier picture up next to the paused video he sees the same guy doing the same thing.

Is Strickland the Roman?

It makes no sense, but they sure as hell shoot alike. And, from what he knows of the Roman and of Dan Strickland, they share a keen interest in the dangerous.

Bettina, thinks Billy, what have you gotten yourself into?

36

Two nights later Strickland and Joe are back at work in Tijuana.

Finally, he thinks.

He feels like he's twenty again. Better. He's so pumped up to be the Roman, with his Glock 35 and his black tactical clothing and shiny boots and the black ski mask with the *R* hand-sewn in with indestructible white dental floss—a touch he added just yesterday after his Apex students had left. Joe watched him happily.

It's his first work since the Furniture Calderón shoot-out a little over seven weeks ago, though, of course, he's working for a different cartel tonight. Strickland has two employers now—Carlos Palma and Alejandro Godoy—sworn enemies. He knows he'll be twice as busy as before, will be making roughly twice as much money, and running a higher risk of exposure and death. Twice the danger, and twice the stone-cold, get-her-done excitement.

And he knows that sooner or later, Palma will catch wind of a rival handler and a dog, raiding his plazas in and around Tijuana. He might think they're knockoffs using his own ingenious methods, but eventually he'll wonder if it's Strickland and Joe. At which point Strickland will deal with Carlos, withdraw to his fortress of firearms and self-reliance in San Diego, ending his brief and spectacular career with the cartels once and for all.

To build a new life with Bettina Blazak.

The tactical question is how long can he work for Godoy without being seen by the New Generation soldiers that he, Strickland, will be stealing from?

Well, he'd been at it a year against the Sinaloans, and all they'd come up with were the uselessly grainy pictures of him and Joe in the Tijuana switching yard. If Joe hadn't been shot at Calderón that night, Strickland would still be just an unidentifiable stranger to everyone but his New Generation employers.

But realistically, how long can he make the big money by serving two masters?

Months he thinks. A year? Maybe, before Carlos begins to hear rumors of another rival handler and a dog.

Strickland doesn't care if it's only months. He's working on his exit plan. He's building his perfect fantasy with Bettina and Joe. It surprises him that they are no longer Joe and Bettina, but Bettina and Joe.

The Sinaloans are different from the Jaliscans. They're more rustic and cheerful than Carlos Palma's militarized New Generation. El Chapo may have built sophisticated smuggling tunnels under the US border, but many of his older men dress as if still in the Sierra Madre: *rancheros* and *vaqueros* and poppy growers in their straw Resistols and low-slung jeans and scuffed Tony Lamas. And their yoked western shirts, occasionally French-tucked behind big belt buckles. Crucifixes and mustaches. They drink beer and mutter among themselves as Joe tries to do his old magic.

Strickland and Joe are on airport property tonight, in an enormous aircraft hangar—Aviación Primero—one of several strung along the international runway. It's filled with airplanes, mostly private jets, some in varying states of repair. The overhead floodlights, high in the steel beams, throw a bright and even light.

Strickland could tell when they came into the hangar with six Sinaloans that Joe not only knew what they were going to do, but remembered what had happened the last time. Strickland had never seen a more honest expression of worry and trust in his life.

"It's okay, Joe," he'd said softly. "Find the Drugs. Find the money!"

Joe moves across the polished concrete floor, nose down, ears flopping, in the loose little trot of his that lets him angle left and right quickly, then turn on a dime.

Strickland's heart floods with affection for Joe, and the way he's put aside his fear in favor of doing what he loves.

This what you get for robbing me, Carlos, thinks Strickland. You greedy lecher, you and your captive child bride.

He imagines Carlos's fury.

But even this cautionary jolt isn't enough to kill the joy inside Strickland now as Joe zigzags through the Textrons and Boeings, Gulfstreams, Dassaults and Airbuses. The jets are all gleaming and pampered. They're as proud and strong as thoroughbreds and Strickland thinks he might just buy one someday.

He pictures Bettina and Joe, climbing aboard the handsome copper-and-cream Airbus ahead of him. He's carrying her big, heavy suitcase.

Strickland knows it's a preposterous and distracting fantasy, but it makes him happy.

On three sides, the perimeter inside the hangar is a long, continuous worktable with large, file-cabinet-sized drawers for components below and a six-foot-wide stainless-steel worktop. The workstations have all been left neatly abandoned at the workday's end.

Joe ambles along the west wall, then stops to face the tool bench, nose up, daintily sniffing. He does this for half a minute, which Strickland knows is a serious indicator: the scent is substantial and strong.

Then Joe goes to the worktable and rises on his hind legs to scan a certain drawer, propped on his front paws, drawing in scent with his four-part sniffs. Then the drawer next to it. No, Strickland thinks: not quite.

Still upright, Joe moves along the worktable with short wobbly steps, like he's learning to dance—but those steps get him where he wants to go. Then he drops and sits before one drawer among hundreds, his tail swishing across the polished concrete floor, smiling back at Strickland.

Who pulls open the drawer, smooth and heavy on its ball bearings. No tools here, just wooden cigar boxes, packaged neatly together in sheets of thick clear plastic and gray duct tape. They take up the entire space, neatly and efficiently.

Strickland lifts one out and sets it on the floor. Cuts away the plastic with his pocketknife. The smell of cedar is so strong Strickland can tell the boxes have been slathered in some kind of cedar oil concentrate. What a fool you are Carlos, Strickland thinks. After a year with Joe, you should know better.

He sets the box on the worktable and lifts the lid. The compressed disks of fentanyl bulge in the vacuum freezer bags, filling the cigar box.

Strickland has seen this before: pure fentanyl, created in a lab in Veracruz—Carlos Palma's hometown. Carlos is very proud of it. The fent is made with Chinese precursors, so its quality is very high and potentially very deadly. From here it will be shipped and processed in scores of labs scattered throughout Northern Mexico. Mixed with heroin, methamphetamine, and cocaine to create the most enjoyable, potent, addictive, and destructive narcotic cocktails on earth. No bulk, like marijuana. Cheap to make, easy to conceal and distribute. Just concentrated, powerful profit. Strickland knows American drug distributors who use fentanyl-sensitive test strips to prove to customers that their potential purchases *contain* fentanyl, so strong is its opiate pleasure and addictive grip. Many of whom overdose and die, which to some traffickers is a not really a tragic warning but an advertisement of good product.

Because the fentanyl is so powerful and cheap, its per-kilo profit can be exponential. Strickland counts twenty cigar boxes through the plastic packaging. He estimates that Carlos Palma has paid roughly $50,000 for approximately ten kilos. But these ten kilos of fentanyl, when added to the headline drugs, will net close to $15,000,000.

Which, according to his deal, means that he has just earned back

$17,500 of the $250,000 cash he's already delivered to Godoy's couriers in Tijuana, payment for sparing Bettina Blazak's life.

But, as Strickland looks down at this cigar box filled with misery and death, he doesn't feel thrilled at all. He knows he should be, but he's not. He loves the money he's earning, but now it feels different.

In the bright light of the hangar, he considers what he's looking at. What it all means, big picture. There's well over enough fentanyl here to kill every person in San Diego County.

His giddy, dangerous profiteering in the drug trade has never bothered him before, but now it does. He doesn't feel excitement; he just feels bad.

But it's not the big picture that's getting to Strickland now, it's much smaller and more personal.

He thinks of Bettina, that night on her deck in Laguna. Telling him about Keith, the brother she loved who died because of what he does. He thinks of Keith for what seems like the thousandth time since that night.

The picture of him as Superman. And of his twin, little Wonder Woman, so much like him.

Why this hits him so hard now, he doesn't know. Strickland has lived a life not examining his own mind, and this is not exactly the time to start.

"Good work, Joe," he says. "You are a good dog."

"He is a dog of genius," says Rudolfo.

"*El señor* Godoy will be very happy," says Jaime.

Joe wags his tail and, standing at almost eye level to kneeling Strickland, licks his face.

"Let's see what else is here, Joe," says Strickland, hearing the hollowness in his voice.

The Sinaloans' exit route into California isn't quite so swanky as that of the New Generation tunnel that originates under Superior Automobile Repair and Service in Tijuana. This tunnel is a simple rectangular tube, concrete floored, and secured by six-by-six beams and thick plywood. It is lighted and well ventilated, but no more than seventy-six inches high, Strickland calculating by the way the top of his ski mask brushes the ceiling in places. But the tunnel has two lanes, so two men can simultaneously pull two wheeled big-box store barges, piled high with whatever drugs need to go north and whatever guns and cash need to come south.

There's more than enough room for Strickland and Joe, off leash, trotting along happily through his world of smells, as he does everywhere he goes.

Strickland pulls off his mask as he climbs the stairs, then opens the office door of the Pacific Utility Supply warehouse in San Ysidro. Which is located all of a hundred feet from northbound lanes of Interstate 5.

Joe sits in the Quattroporte passenger seat, his head out the cracked window, squinting, nostrils flaring, ears blown back by the torrents of scent. He remembers riding in the back of Teddy's family car, doing the same thing. And in Aaron's car that smelled of the white tubes of smoke.

Dan plays the music too loud, a fast song with big booms and a human voice singing words Joe doesn't understand. Which reminds him that he used to howl with annoyance when Teddy played the shiny thing with his mouth that sounded like a coyote far away. Joe hates coyotes, has always hated them, always understood they were here to eat him.

He looks at Dan. He believes that this is the best day of his life. Being back with Dan. The Team. Playing Find the Drugs and Find the Money. Teddy will come back soon. He misses Bettina very much and believes she'll come back soon also. It makes Joe happy when Dan and Bettina talk to each other. Bettina is the first woman who didn't make him anxious and try to get Dan away from him. Break up the Team. Nothing in Bettina made Joe feel that way. She wanted him for herself! He could get right between them when they talked, and he knew they were both paying attention to him too. A new, bigger Team. Here in the car, the wind lifting his gullwing ears, Joe knows Dan is happy that he, Joe, brought Bettina to him.

Strickland is back home in the dead of early morning but text-messages Bettina anyway:

> Just wondering how you're doing. Anything about Joe? Do the police have any leads at all?
> I've been working a lot. And hoping that our dinner at your place won't be the last time I see you. I miss Joe but I miss you more.
> How about coming down my way tonight? I'm handy with the grill or there are some good restaurants. Seven?

He's pleased to see her reply just a few minutes later.

> The Strickland Grill sounds good to me. Seven's good. I expect my own room.
> Absolutely. With a lock that works and everything. I'm looking forward to this.

Later that morning Strickland gets Joe settled into Charley Gibbon's high-rise condo downtown. It has some of the same views as his penthouse in Apex—Petco Park and San Diego Harbor and the hotels.

Gibbon is a big man, an ex-marine who now runs the Peaceful Warrior Hapkido dojo out in Kearny Mesa. And moonlights for Strickland, as needed. He's a favorite of Joe's, who bounds into Charley's heavily inked arms before Charley gently lowers Joe the floor and pins him, his tail wagging.

Gibbon wants to know how Bettina is holding up. As mandated by Strickland, Gibbon and Marcos did everything they could to not terrify the poor girl while at the same time forcibly dognapping Joe from her.

"She left a message," says Strickland, more than a little preoccupied about how Bettina is doing. "But you can't tell with those."

"She was scared when we got close," says Gibbon. "Then furious when I took the leash."

"She loves this dog."

Gibbon pets Joe's smooth head. "You know, Dan, you can get them back together. Girl and dog. It would be easy enough to arrange without her knowing that you had him kidnapped in the first place."

"No," says Strickland. "Joe and I have contracted work to do. He can't be living up in Laguna with Bettina."

"You could pay Godoy for Joe's lost revenue. Use another dog."

"Not interested," says Strickland.

For all the icy blue distance in Charley Gibbon's eyes, Strickland sees the gentle spirit of the man he first met in boot camp. Gibbon is the only North American whom Strickland has told of his secret life as the Roman. And Charley *was* the only person whose judgments mattered to Strickland until just a few days ago, when Bettina had come barreling into his world like a boulder rolling down a mountain.

"But I'll consider that," says Strickland.

He sets up Joe's crate in Gibbon's living room, which has the great views. Joe loves windows. Strickland leans the bag of kibble against a wall.

"I'll see you soon, Joe," he says. "I'm going to go home and vacuum up all your dog hair so Bettina won't know I've got you."

Joe perks his ears at Bettina's name, then gives Strickland a hurt look when he pats his head and heads for the door.

37

Bettina and Strickland walk the San Diego Embarcadero in the blustery dark, spring rain tapping their umbrellas.

This touristy cruise ship hub is only lightly attended tonight, mostly groups of young people taking selfies under their umbrellas. The *Midway* looms at berth like a floating city, lights and towers and the huge runway jutting out over dark water.

They walk past the sculpture *Unconditional Surrender*, up-lit and monstrous to Bettina's eye. To her it looks more like a sexual assault than a kiss, and it makes her remember Jason blubbering for mercy in his office. But there's something almost comic about that now, she thinks, a reminder that she's free of him forever.

She takes Strickland's arm and squeezes in closer, their umbrellas bumping together above them.

"You know the thing I couldn't tell you about at my place that night? One of the things you saw on my face?"

"Sure, I do. Coming back to bite you again?"

"No, the opposite. I tracked the guy down and threatened to post the truth about him."

"Congratulations."

"I scared the bejesus out of him too," she says. "It felt so good. Now when I look at that poor nurse over there getting manhandled by the sailor, it doesn't remind me of what the guy did, only him breaking down like a child and admitting it. That's all it took. I carried that night around for eight years, in knots about what to do. And when I did it, it was so . . . liberating. Like being let out of a cage. And so easy! I was just a tad jacked up. I blasted his truck with my shotgun, though. It was either the truck or him, which I'd considered as a possibility, depending on how things developed. Really glad I didn't shoot him."

"Smart move, Bettina. We'd be talking through Plexiglas right now."

She glances at him, sees the wry smile.

"But you understand all of that, don't you?" she asks. "You understand the wild, and the thrill of throwing yourself in, and you know that beautiful calm it takes to size things up and act. And the way you feel when it's over. How full and alive you are for having done what you just did. A wave. A bike blast. A horse race. I'm sure you've got your list of wilds."

"You bet."

"What's on it?"

"War. Chasing bad guys. Protecting innocent people. Hand-to-hand stuff. Competition handgun shooting."

"Have you killed?"

No quick reply from Strickland. Bettina feels him sizing *her* up. She realizes how little she really knows about him.

"Sangin, Afghanistan."

"Jihadis?"

"To the core."

"How about as a cop?"

"Never drew my gun."

Bettina pulls Strickland to a stop, looks up into his sturdy, closed face. She studies that face a good long time, listens to the raindrops tapping on their umbrellas, picks a dog hair off the collar of his raincoat. One of Felix's, she thinks, heart sinking. From the old days.

Then she kisses Strickland briskly on the lips.

"You carry that, don't you?" she asks. "Sangin."

"I took pictures of their faces. Out of respect."

"Did you carry them in your wallet for a while?"

"I did."

"Creepy," says Bettina. "But I get it. It's like me taking pictures for my stories, or my videos—a way of preserving a moment. Making it important. Maybe even permanent."

"And it's about honoring what you take."

Drinks in the Gaslamp district, then back to the Apex Self-Defense building. Near the Apex entrance a bedraggled middle-aged couple sits on the curb near their white, blue-and-yellow Corona Light dome tent, a pale gray pit bull leashed to a street light.

"Good evening, Pam," says Strickland, leaving Bettina to approach them. "Evening, Roy."

They say hello. The dog growls.

"Lighten up, Wiley," Strickland says, and the dog's tail starts up.

"Where have you been?" asks Strickland.

"Rode out the rain in the shelter," says Pam. "Left a little early. What a hell hole that place is."

Bettina watches as Strickland pulls a folded-in-half white envelope from his wallet, slides the wallet back into his coat and hands the envelope to the Roy.

"Thanks, Dan," he says.

"You're the man, Dan," says Pam. "I'd get up and hug you if I wasn't so dirty."

"You can use the showers tomorrow when classes are over," says Strickland.

"Maybe," says Roy. "Hate to impose."

———

On the spacious third-floor penthouse deck, Bettina lingers upwind of the barbecue, where Strickland mans the meat, lobster tails, and asparagus wrapped in foil. He cooks with the over-seriousness of men. He's actually using a stopwatch. He reminds her of brother Nick. Something in the inner quiet he has. Maybe killing in a war quiets you down, she thinks, Nick having served in Iraq—Fallujah—and taken life there. She looks out at the harbor and the big hotels. The rain has passed and the low clouds are snagged on the sharp roof of the Hyatt.

She sips a bourbon, going very slow on it. Ditto Strickland and his wine.

"I miss Felix," she says. "I wonder if he's alive in Tijuana, working for El Gordo. Do you think that's possible?"

Strickland looks back over his shoulder at her, apparently unwilling to leave his demanding project.

"I do. El Gordo originally said he wanted to buy Joe from you, for revenge on the New Generation. People say he's a man of his word. Honest—for a drug kingpin. That's his myth, anyway."

"You know a lot about drug cartels."

"I have friends on both sides of the border. Mostly Apex clients. Some cops from the PD."

"And it was a DEA friend of yours who got you Joe."

"Yes, why?"

"Just curious. Do you think he was shot on accident?"

"Possibly," says Strickland, his back to her, consulting the stopwatch. "It's more likely the Sinaloans did it. Joe was certainly an enemy."

"That shoot-out must have been chaotic," says Bettina.

She flashes back to that cold day in Tijuana, interviewing the veterinary doctors and falling in love with the wounded street dog.

"The clinic where I got him was run by a married couple," she says. "Both veterinarians. He said the shooting was probably an accident, but his wife was absolutely certain it was an event directed by God."

"I think God's less interested in directing than in being entertained," says Strickland.

His pointed spiritual arrow sticks her. "I've thought that too. We sure provide a lot of entertainment. We human types."

Strickland pockets the watch, tongs the steaks and the lobster tails and asparagus to a large platter, lowers the grill top, and turns to her.

A small smile on his handsome face.

38

After dinner they sit side by side on a glider out on the deck. It gets to be another long talk, like the one at Bettina's house just a few nights ago. She feels great to be here on this cool spring night, breezy after the storm, clouds moving fast across the starry dark. She's got her favorite overcoat on, a red wool Navajo pattern with wooden toggle buttons and contrast stitching.

All of this—Strickland, the breezy night, the heavy coat, the smidgin of bourbon and the good food—makes her feel safe in a way she hasn't felt in days. Safe and trusting and very eager to break the news:

"I offered El Gordo a positive story and video in *Coastal Eddy*, and ten thousand dollars, in return for Felix. I haven't heard back."

Strickland wheels on her. "That's insane, Bettina."

In kicks Bettina's instinctive hatred of being told what she can and can't do.

"Why? I don't think it's insane at all. I go down there, do the interview, shoot the video and pay the money. Fly home with Felix. I've got the right papers from the clinic."

"Insane because El Gordo lost a good soldier and two hundred grand up at Moulton Meadows Park in Laguna that night. *Two hundred grand*, Bettina. And you think he'll trade the dog back for ten thousand dollars and a story? You surprise me."

Strickland's solid logic hits Bettina hard. She knows this is the fundamental flaw in her proposal.

"If I had more, I'd *offer* more," she says stubbornly.

Strickland abruptly rises, walks across the deck to the railing, and looks out.

An airliner lowers toward Lindbergh Field, and Bettina focuses on its blinking red lights. The jet is flying very low over the heart of the city. Bettina knows that Strickland is right, and all her worst fears regarding Felix come thundering down on her again. She feels cold sweat on her shoulders and back; it's like being dipped in the ocean.

Strickland turns to her and leans against the railing. "He won't take your offer."

Bettina speaks evenly to him, trying to ground her pitch in logic, not emotion.

"What if my story means more to Godoy than you think? What if he accepts my offer, not for the money, but for his pride? And vanity? To build his Robin Hood myth? His *brand*?"

"And you go off alone into the heart of the Sinaloa Cartel with ten grand and your camera?"

Of course I don't, she thinks. I'll need backup, and some Mexico savvy. Can't ask Billy because he's a cop.

"We go together and bring Felix back," she says.

"His name is Joe."

"His name is Felix and I'm bringing him back whether you help me or not."

Strickland stares at her in mute stillness. She can't tell if he's angry or ready to laugh. Over his shoulder, Bettina tracks the red lights of the jet over the building tops.

"I told you once I'd do anything to protect you and Joe," he says. "That offer hasn't expired, and it never will. It's possible. It's possible

Godoy will trade back Joe for his own pride and ego. If that's the case, we'll take Joe off his hands. You and me."

Bettina feels her heart filling with hope and gratitude. Surprise and relief. With other emotions, too, some contradictory or too muddled to decipher.

She pushes off the glider and joins him at the railing, turns and leans against it, facing what he's facing.

"Whatever I say will sound so corny," she says. "Thank you? I'm surprised at the depth of your loyalty? Holy crap, Batman?"

"Nothing corny about those. Except maybe . . ."

"I'm going to kiss you again but it's going to be a long one. If you don't, you know, faint or something."

She takes his hand.

Bettina finishes thrice with Strickland. The first is quaky and electrical; the second like falling through clouds; the third makes time either slow down or speed up, she's can't tell which.

Breath and sweat, heart and muscle.

As she drifts toward sleep beside him, Bettina thinks that Strickland is, well, mantastic. Maybe a little mechanical, but sound mechanics indeed. He's breathing deeply, not snoring but she can tell he's out. She smiles into the pillow, qualm-less for now, her world going dark.

Before sunrise she roams the penthouse, turning on lights and touching Strickland's things because they're his things and he's hers now, in some mysterious way she's never experienced. Which makes her interested in what interests him, curious about what he likes.

What a cornball notion, she thinks: You are the corniest girl of all time. You have your own category, the CGOAT—as she runs a hand along the top of his still-gurgling coffee maker, a twelve-cup programmable Cuisinart.

She hears him down in the gym, clanking away on the weights to what sounds like an old Western movie soundtrack, all big-sky strings, timpani hoofbeats, and languid rivers of pedal steel guitar.

She catches him downstairs on the bench press, waits for his last grunting rep, then slaps a kiss on his hot wet forehead. He stands and wipes his face with his workout gloves and kisses her forehead back.

"Soon," he says.

"Soon."

"Don't get your hopes up. One way or another we'll find a way to get Joe back home."

"Felix."

Getting into her Jeep, Bettina calculates that she'll be home in time to shower and change, and still make the *Coastal Eddy* offices by eight.

She feels lucky, confident, powerful. Because she knows that El Gordo is going to defy all odds and sell Felix back to her for a little money and a damned good story and video.

From hundreds of miles away, she can feel his acceptance starting to form in his mind, forged by her fire.

Bending to their wilds, hers and Strickland's.

She's halfway home, northbound on I-5, when her phone pings with a new notification: a message from Alejandro Godoy.

Dear Bettina,

I am considering of your desperate offer. It is very creative, like you. Your $10,000 means nothing to me but my true story if it made me more famous could be useful. Not only useful, but a chapter important in the history of my country, and yours.

Joe misses you. He loves my children and they love him. He will be going to work for me soon.

Sincerely,

Alejandro

Bettina reads the message twice, trying to vet Godoy's intentions and stay in her lane at eighty miles per hour.

She remembers his time-consuming caution while orchestrating his attempted purchase of Felix up in Moulton Meadows Park. All the waiting and changing of venues. All his crafty caution, turned to shit.

Costing Joaquín Páez his life, Valeria Flores her freedom, and El Gordo his $200,000.

She can't be sure, but Bettina thinks he'll be more decisive this time around.

Speeding for home in the bumpy Jeep, Bettina tries to send El Gordo the same kind of psychic vibes she was sending out to him less than an hour ago. She pictures her thoughts as bright monarch butterflies crossing the skies by the tens of thousands. Tries to butterfly-bomb El Gordo all the way down in Sinaloa. Like the prayers she launched at God from Anza Methodist when she was small.

Her phone pings again just as she's through her front door. Godoy:

Dear Bettina,

I will trade you Joe for a truthful story of me. The ten thousand dollars you offer back to me will be my bonus to you, if you make the story and video as great as it should be. It must be great. You can use the money for your expenses to travel of Sinaloa to pick up Joe.

Send me a message to this number when you reach Los Mochis. Remember the mountains can be cold and Joe will need his papers of vaccination in order to get into the Estados Unidos.

Sincerely,

Alejandro

She calls Jean Rose and says she needs a few days off. Promises to get the Rod Foster feature polished and the entertainment calendar updated for next week's edition before she leaves. Tells Jean she's going to bring her a story that will get picked up by every major news feed on the planet, and a video that will explode on the internet. Says *Coastal Eddy* will become a household name and she'll probably be shortlisted for a Pulitzer.

"Bettina, the editor in me loves it when you talk like this," Jean says. "But as a person, I tremble too."

"Trust me."

"I sense no choice."

Throat tight and heart pounding, she calls Strickland, who answers on the first ring.

39

Strickland listens in disbelief as Bettina tells him that El Gordo is willing to "trade" a great profit center like Joe for a *Coastal Eddy* article and video. And has waived her attempted regifting of his $10,000. Strickland asks Bettina to repeat Godoy's terms as his mind whirls, plotting his next move.

Which he manages to cobble together—loosely—by the time Godoy calls, five minutes later.

And orders Strickland to send Joe back to Sinaloa so Godoy can present the dog to his "lovely journalist friend" in return for fame in America.

"But he's not your dog to sell," says Strickland. "He's *mine*. And he's your business partner."

"She loves the dog very much," says Godoy. "Joe is what she is charging me for my place in history. Mr. Knowles, I'm asking you to do this to protect Bettina. So that she survives the Sierra Madre, after finishing my important story and video. We can't let anything evil happen to her."

"*You* promised to protect her!" says Strickland, his heart seething and his voice taut. "You accepted my money and my labor in return for protecting her."

"I keep that money."

"You rob me for your own vanity?"

Laughter. "But I continue to spare your lover's life. Páez is dead and Valeria is detained and my money has been confiscated by the American government. So we are even. Bring Joe to the *Factoria Calderon*. My people will find you. I trust you to get another good dog to work with. There are many. Joe is not the only dog, Mr. Knowles. And who knows? Maybe your creative Bettina will let him work for us again someday."

Godoy chuckles.

"I'll be with her in Los Mochis," says Strickland.

"It will be good to see you, my friend."

40

"Yeah, I remember Strickland," says Dave Bridgeman, the longstanding International Practical Shooting Confederation webmaster and historian.

Billy has tracked down Bridgeman through the IPSC website, all the way here to the Coach House in Scottsdale, Arizona. This morning he traded today's shift with another Bike Team cop, then made the six-hour drive from Laguna in five.

The Coach House patio is busy this March evening, cool though it is. A hangover from the plague years, thinks Billy, when the indoor drinking was shut down. Tonight it's mostly the snowbirds who pack Arizona in winter.

Bridgeman is early sixties, tall and well built, with humorful eyes and long blond hair.

"Dan Strickland was quite a talent with a handgun," he says. "Light on his feet for a big guy, like a dancer. And he had this graceful kind of approach to the sport. This could be him in the switching yard. The posture."

"But you're not sure?"

Bridgeman holds the picture up again, his fifth long look. "No."

"How many matches did he shoot?"

"Four, that one year he was with us. The big ones. Most of the shooters are regulars, you know? They grow up with guns and get good and win a few matches and they shoot almost every weekend, match or not. They're in forever. Not Strickland. He was in and out."

Bridgeman looks down at his notes. "He showed up back in '08, just out of high school, if I remember right. Good-looking young man. Quiet but confident. Seemed out of place. Not really like the gun culture folks we competition shooters typically are. But man, he could handle that Glock. Shot heavy loads, too, which makes your job *way* harder on a rough, running course. As a cop, you know that."

"How good was he?"

"He won the three regionals and the Western Regional finals in December. I remember he skipped the awards dinner that night. He had some young lady friends we called his blonde-tourage, so I figured they'd taken him off somewhere more fun. Never saw him again. Sent us a note in early '09, saying he wouldn't be competing anymore. Paid up his dues for the year, though. Said he was honored by the trophy. Asked us to put it in the headquarters trophy case, or change out the plaque and use it again. See some video of the finals?"

Billy squares Bridgeman's phone on a Coach House coaster.

Strickland looks a lot like he did on the IPSC website "Young Talent" clip that had reminded Billy so much of the shooter in El Gordo's photos. Billy thinks that the youthful Strickland had some extra intensity here in the regional finals. But still, plenty of that fluid grace that seems almost an affectation. A performance. Except that he's punching through the fifteen-centimeter bull's-eyes on the run, with heavy loads and an eerie, robotic precision.

Billy watches the rest of Strickland's brief, final championship run, pushes the phone back to Bridgeman. "Did you socialize with him?"

"Not really. It's all business at the matches and I don't remember but one time he joined us old people for dinner and drinks."

"Never met his friends or family?"

"The blondes."

"And that was all?"

"Well, that one time he came out with us socially was in San Diego. He didn't drink and he didn't say much except that he was going to join the marines. Said he was looking forward to shooting at targets that would shoot back. Said he'd been waiting since he was eleven and the towers went down."

"I knew a lot of boys like that," says Billy. "Hell, I was one of them when I was nine."

"I was a little old by 9/11, but I remember watching Saigon fall on TV when I was a kid. In my little suburban living room in Dayton, Ohio. I wanted to fight back but didn't know how."

A beat of silence for boys called to war.

"Did anyone ever refer to him as Roman? Or 'the Roman'?"

"Well, no. But he drove a new Ducati Monster S4R, so maybe he liked Italian things."

"A recent high school graduate with a new Ducati," says Billy. He remembers Strickland's moneyed upbringing, and his sleek Italian Maserati.

"Officer Crumley, I know you're a cop, but it's about time you told me what's going on. Why are you here? What has Strickland done? Happy to help you, but you do owe me answers."

"I'll buy you another beer and tell you what I know," says Billy.

Billy's back in the Viewridge Avenue DEA building in San Diego at eight sharp the next morning, watching Arnie's confederate Dale Greene digitally enhancing one of El Gordo's switching yard photos of the Roman and Joe.

It's a Sunday but Greene has opened up the forensic lab to do his magic on the picture. Billy has brought doughnuts.

Greene seems not at all put out to be working today, patiently cropping and enlarging, cropping and enlarging again, adjusting filters, zooming in and out on the Roman.

"This had to be shot on the run," says Greene. "The angle is funny, like the picture shooter isn't looking through the viewfinder, just firing away with his phone before he has to duck for cover. His motion accounts for the blurring."

Billy watches Greene slide the color control.

"It may look like it was shot in black and white," says Greene. "But that's the weak light. The shooter probably didn't want to use the flash. So, we'll add some color and see what happens."

"Nice," says Arnie, working on his second chocolate-on-chocolate with peanuts.

Billy watches as the seeming black-and-white photograph becomes, chameleonlike, colored. The hues are faint, but the Roman looks more like a man and less like a blurred sculpture.

"Now for some clarity," says Greene.

He slides the clarity control to the right and Billy watches the Roman, drawn into better focus. Billy recognizes his gun, a .40-caliber semiautomatic Glock 35.

"I'm going to peg the clarity, then the color," says Greene. "But this might be as good as it gets."

"Light-skinned," says Billy. "Look at the sliver of his left wrist, between his glove and his shirt."

"And pale eyes behind the mask," says Arnie. "Blue or gray."

Greene cues up the IPSC Young Talent video on the monitor, splits the screen and hits play.

Billy moves his eyes left and right, vetting the clip against the photo. He reaches into the doughnut box without taking his eyes off the screen. Takes a bite of what turns out to be a maple bar.

When the Young Talent clip ends, there's a moment of quiet, Billy guessing that all three of them are thinking the same thing.

"We can't ID Strickland as the Roman with just these," says Greene.

"No," says Billy. "But he's working with that cartel in Mexico, right?

So at least a few of them have to have seen him without his commando costume. They'd know what he looks like, maybe even his name."

"They won't give him up to us, that's for sure," says Greene.

"But we have our Jalisco informants," says Arnie. "Get them the Strickland video and the Roman pix, and the stills from our files, and let them ask around. No guarantees, but worth the time and expense. *Someone* at least knows what he looks like. If we've got a San Diego self-defense teacher and a former DEA dog making money for Jalisco, we need to know."

"The Sinaloans have Joe now," says Billy.

"Kind of beside the point," says Arnie. "The Roman probably already *has* another dog."

"Helping the fentanyl pour into these United States," says Greene.

Billy thinks of Bettina's brother. The way she teared up talking about him.

"I'll take this plan upstairs," says Arnie. "I think I can get them to bite."

Greene checks out, leaving Billy and Arnie with the coffee and doughnuts.

"You've got it in for Strickland," says Arnie. "All the way to Scottsdale to try to nail him down. All this. Is he cutting into your time with Bettina Blazak?"

"That's exactly what he's doing."

"You shouldn't mix professional with personal. What if this Strickland clown *isn't* the Roman? What if he's just who he says he is?"

"Then she can have what she wants."

"Big ocean out there, full of great fish."

"Sure, Arnie. Sure it is."

"You really do like her."

"I do."

41

The Sierra Madre Occidental is as forbiddingly beautiful as when Bettina saw it five years ago with a girlfriend—a college graduation gift from Mom and Dad. These rugged mountains are drier than her Sierra Nevada back in California, boulder strewn and not so green. Massive canyons and far horizons. The oaks and elms lean and twist. The red-barked manzanitas send their gnarled roots down through the rocks. Pines struggle up through the granite. A tougher world here, she thinks. She watches a Copper Canyon vintage Pullman train like the one she'd taken, gliding into a mountainside tunnel like an enormous steel snake, lit by the setting sun.

She steers the rental Chevy through the steepening switchbacks behind Los Mochis. Strickland sits beside her, regarding the fading orange evening through sunglasses, his Padres cap tipped low. From a friend in San Blas, Strickland has managed to obtain a .45-caliber semiautomatic pistol and shells, which is now in the glove compartment under which Strickland's knees barely fit. Bettina had watched him lift the rag-shrouded weapon from a rusted steel trash can behind a Pemex station, a cold chill running down her back.

With a nod to Mexican propriety, they take adjacent rooms at the rustic Creel Lodge. After dinner they retire to the nearly empty lobby and sip tequila under an immense, cascading chandelier of deer antlers. The fireplace burns hard against the cold Sierra night.

Strickland pokes the logs and adds another, then returns to his pine-and-cowhide chair and takes her hand.

"How are you feeling, Bettina?"

"Eager to see my dog. Anxious that I won't get a good story on Godoy. Afraid that something will go wrong. My nerves chilled when I saw what you did at the Pemex station. I thought: a gringo in Mexico is euthanasia."

"That's a bit of an exaggeration, Carlos."

"In the heart of Sinaloa? Maybe not."

The fire crackles and throws light onto the antlers massed above them.

"I have a favor to ask," says Strickland. "Don't shoot any pictures or video of me tomorrow."

"Why not?"

"I don't want to be seen down here. It could be misconstrued."

Which strikes Bettina as mysterious, maybe paranoid. By whom, she wonders, the cops he says he knows, on both sides of the border?

"No pics. No video. You have my word."

"Thank you."

She squeezes his hand. "It's so much colder here than I remember."

"It's still March," says Strickland. "Twenties at night. That's a good strong fire."

"What if my story flops? What if Godoy freezes up on camera? What if Felix has been abused or doesn't want to come home with me?"

"With us," he says.

"Us. He's still mine."

Strickland's hand is strong and dry. She appreciates his calm. She wonders if he maybe doesn't have her Polish-German-Irish spark, which turns to flame and becomes her fire. Maybe he's got cool water instead of sparks, she thinks. Cool water that turns to frost, then ice.

And the ice allows him to go forward, overcome fear and take risks, just like her fire does. Two different natures. Two different ways of getting to the same place.

"I don't see you as anxious and afraid," he says.

"It's not often," she says. "But when it hits, it's hard to shake. I'm prone to dread at three in the morning. I wake up afraid of everything. Hours go by. I can't sleep and every idea is a bad idea. Everything is doomed."

Bettina sips her tequila. Strickland has barely touched his.

"I picture you blasting the Escalade," he says. "Setting that boy straight. Or riding a wave. Or chasing the dognappers down the street with your scattergun."

"I hope I'm not just hot-tempered and stupid."

Bettina catches his minor smile. "Shut up," she says quietly. "All I want out of all of this is my dog."

"May I knock on your door later?"

"No. I want my own bed and body tonight."

"I want them too."

"Soon."

Strickland lies on his bed in the dark, blankets heaped against the cold and the wall heater glowing feebly.

He's having trouble believing how profoundly his life has changed since meeting Bettina Blazak at the *Coastal Eddy* in Laguna not even two weeks ago.

Nothing is the same.

Nothing feels real though he knows it is.

He's in love with her for starters, an emotion absent from all his thirty-three years.

He's pledged his hard-earned skills and his life to protect her, paying Godoy a hefty $250,000 to secure her safety. The money didn't break him but it did sting, Strickland being a lifelong penny-watcher except-ing guns, cars, and motorcycles.

He's told her things about himself he's never told another human being.

He's had sex with her, feeling different, and more strongly, than with anyone before.

He regrets his lies and trickery.

But more important than any of that, Strickland is giving Joe to her. It pains him, but his generosity feels whole and good. He'll get to visit. To Strickland there's nothing more generous a person can do than give up their dog.

Now we're here in the perilous Sierra Madre, he thinks, and his feet are cold and he can't sleep and there's just one wall between them.

He reaches one hand into the cold air, sets his palm against that plaster wall and wonders if Godoy will betray them.

The battered .45 and eight shells are all he has to protect them here in the beating heart of the Sinaloa Cartel.

So he prays, for the first time in his life, to a God he's never believed in. Even this feels different, feels true and real for the first time.

Feels his old light dimming and his new bright light burning strong.

42

"Three, two, one . . . ," she counts off. "This is Bettina Blazak, of *Coastal Eddy*, live with the head of the Sinaloa Cartel in the heart of the Sierra Madre mountains of Mexico. Shall I call you El Gordo, or Señor Godoy?"

"Alejandro."

"We're standing in front of the house you were born in, Alejandro, is that correct?"

"It was built by my grandfather with his own hands."

"And the nearest city is Badiraguato?"

"It is a small town."

Bettina has set up her video camera on its tripod, and positioned Godoy outside his birthplace. The house is a compact one-story, its stones rough and irregular, held fast by thick veins of cement. The roof beams look heavy and old, but their seams shine with fresh mastic.

Armed men loiter in the forest. There's a flatbed pickup with a mounted machine gun parked near a blue barn, the driver smoking a cigarette and the machine gunner seated at his weapon, watching Bettina.

She has posed Godoy in front of the eastern wall of the house to take advantage of the late morning sun, now coming over the ragged peaks.

Strickland stands in the sun of the eastern wall, too, well off-camera. Bettina thinks that Strickland is the opposite of boyish, well-coiffed Godoy. Strickland looks sullen. He really *doesn't* want to be photographed, or recorded, she thinks. A rare find, in her line of work. He also seemed unimpressed when she introduced him to El Gordo, refusing to use his good Spanish. She wonders if he's threatened by Godoy and his masculine supremacy here. The idea that Strickland is possessive of her feels good. Steam rises from his coffee cup in his gloved hands.

Bettina stands near the camera with her back to the sun, fingers stiff with cold, cussing herself for not bringing gloves.

She's annoyed that Godoy has refused to let her even see Felix until they're done with the interview. The interview which, if she's understanding his not-bad English correctly, will involve some mountain driving and take all day. She hopes Felix is inside the stone house, nice and warm. Sees the thick stream of woodsmoke rising from the chimney. Godoy wouldn't leave the dog in a freezing barn, would he? She keeps thinking Felix will hear her voice and bark, but no. Maybe he's been moved off-campus

Godoy looks younger than his forty-eight or forty-nine years. He's got a slender face, big eyes, curly dark brown hair with a forelock. Gordo he is not.

Bettina was more than surprised when he came to the door dressed in black boots, pressed jeans, a black wool blazer over a white, still-creased-from-the-package cowboy shirt, and a braided leather bolo tie with a silver cross outlined in turquoise. He looked like Springsteen on *Tunnel of Love*, her mom's and dad's favorite album when she was ten.

"What are your first memories of this place?" she asks.

"Collecting firewood with my mother. There is still no heating in this house other than the fireplace. I built my mother and father a new house lower in the mountains. For the cold. It has carpet and a heater–air conditioner."

"Did you have enough to eat when you were little?"

Godoy frowns. "Almost. There are good cattle here and fruit and beans in the markets. But there was no work. My father grew poppies and potatoes to survive."

"Can we see the poppy fields?"

Strickland cuts her a look.

Godoy frowns again. "I will show you the clinic and the schools I have built."

Bettina turns off the camera and unscrews it from the tripod. "Can I just see my dog once before we go?"

"He is with my wife and children in another *casa*."

"Is he happy here?"

"He is adored."

"Do you have lots of homes here in the mountains?"

"Yes, I am always moving. *Vamos*," he says, heading for a dusty white Suburban.

El Gordo does the driving, Bettina up front, Strickland and a gloomy-looking gunman behind them.

The Godoy Clinic on the other side of Badiraguato is a new-looking, boxy affair made of cinder blocks and topped with a still shiny aluminum roof. There's a shaded entryway and when Bettina steps inside, she sees the clean waiting room and the white-clad receptionist behind the counter, peering around a large clay pot of chipper, oversized paper flowers. The waiting room is furnished with rustic mountain furniture, a table stacked with newspapers and magazines, a large mural in the style of Diego Rivera, and is empty of patients.

Bettina pans this interior, then sets up her camera and tripod again and questions the receptionist, Leonarda Cuevas Escobar. The woman speaks almost no English, so Bettina coaxes her along in Spanish. Leonarda smiles shyly and says what she likes most about the clinic is all the free help they can offer to the poor. People with no money appreciate help, she says. Señor Godoy donated the land and the building, so the Clínica Godoy can stay open forever.

Bettina is aware of Godoy watching her. She can see him just at the edge of her vision, expressionless, his eyes rarely straying from her. She glances at him as she removes the camera from the stand, catches a hint of a smile.

Strickland strides between them to talk to Leonarda in his good Spanish, giving Bettina a brief cautionary look on the way. He's as on edge as I am, she thinks. She's not surprised he's this protective.

Next, El Gordo shows her the new church he's built near Divisadero (La Luz Sierra); the school in Batopilas (Universidad Godoy); the restaurant just outside Creel (Buen Vaquero) where they have a late lunch. Bettina continues her interview in the quaint cantina, where Godoy tells her his plans for the Hospital Godoy in Los Mochis, Godoy Primary school in Alamos, and a Thoroughbred training center outside San Bernardo.

Bettina changes the subject abruptly when she sees that Godoy isn't going to volunteer the part of his story that many *Coastal Eddy* readers want to hear most.

"Alejandro, some people in the United States say that money from the Sinaloa Cartel has paid for all these things. That the Sinaloa Cartel is one of the most powerful criminal organizations in the world."

She sees the flash of anger in his eyes, quickly muted into a warm smile.

"The appetite of *norteamericanos* for illegal substances is renowned worldwide," he says. "They flood our country with dollars. They flood us with guns. The Mexican cartels are greatly exaggerated. It is the police and the government who control the narcotics and the guns and the money."

"The Mexican government and police?" asks Bettina.

"Working with American government! Americans speak of corruption in Mexico, but look around you, here in the Sierra Madre, where the great Sinaloa Cartel is supposed to be all-powerful. Where is this cartel? Where?"

"With all respect, Alejandro, it is sitting right in front of me and my camera."

"Señorita Blazak, I have surrendered myself to you and your camera so the world can see the truth. I have taken you into my home and shown you the life of El Gordo. A life that began in poverty. A life of hard work. Yes, I have done business in the narcotics trade. I have sold illegal products to the United States. I have negotiated with Americans who are policemen in the day and traffickers at night. I have seen the slaughter their guns bring to Mexico. I have used those guns to defend myself. But I have always given much of my earnings to the poor of my country. As you have seen today. The clinic. The school and church. The cantina in which we now sit, where profits go to charity. I will build the hospital and the majestic Thoroughbred training facility."

Bettina knows that she's taken the accusations as far as she can go without pissing off Godoy and losing her chance to return home with Felix. Part of her responsibility is to please her subject. His breathtaking lies are walls that she can scale only at great peril to Felix, Daniel Strickland, and herself.

And yet there's some truth in them, she thinks. If you see things through his eyes. Through what he was given at birth and what he's done with it.

Either way, she's angry at herself for not digging in and getting the darker truths about this story—a story that matters. She's downsizing her professional integrity for ownership of a dog. For *her* dog, which means, for her*self*.

She looks out the window at the dirt street and the late daylight.

Realizes it's now or never to ask the biggest question she's wanted to ask Godoy since she agreed to profile him in *Coastal Eddy*. It's a way to rescue this story from being a one-sided puff piece. And to make it something that will matter to her readers and watchers.

She feels her heart beating fast and takes off on the wave:

"Alejandro, my brother Keith was twenty years old when he overdosed on a fentanyl-laced vape pen. So, what do you say to Keith, and the thousands of others who have been killed by that deadly drug you sell in huge quantities? Do you have anything you'd like him to know about why you do what you do?"

Strickland, arms crossed, looks down at the table, shaking his head.

"Do you have proof that this substance came from me?" Godoy asks.

"No, I do not."

"Or maybe from China, where fentanyl has for years been produced?"

"I can only prove that he died from fentanyl under a freeway in San Diego."

Godoy squints into the camera, his expression hard to read. Calm, certainly, but what else? Cold? Thoughtful? Measuring his words?

Then he nods and places his right hand over his heart. "I am sorry for what you did, Mr. Keith. I do what I do to provide for my family. That is all."

Bettina senses no falsehood in Godoy's words or voice or gestures. "But there must be more, Mr. Godoy. Can you apologize to him?"

"I am sorry what happened, Keith, but I will apologize for nothing. We choose our own roads. I am finished with this interview now, Bettina."

"May I ask you three more questions? One about giving and taking. One about killing and one about God."

He agrees to three more questions.

And answers them with a blunt honesty, his charm spent and his vanity exhausted.

When she's finished, she turns off the camera and returns El Gordo's troubled stare.

"I have enough for the story and the video," she says. "I'll need some time and privacy to write and edit them."

"I have an office in one of my homes. It is warm and quiet and you can work."

"When will I get Felix?" she asks.

"When I approve the story and video."

"Get me to that office, Señor Godoy. I need a shot of bourbon to get me started."

"You will have all the bourbon you need."

"One shot of bourbon is what I said."

"You loved this brother very much."

"Very much. He was my twin. The other half of me."

True to her word, it takes Bettina one shot of bourbon to get her through the five-thousand-word feature story on Alejandro "El Gordo" Godoy. Once she has that first line: *He was born on Christmas Day, so his mother was certain that Alejandro would become the light of the world,* Bettina is off and running on her laptop, fingers flying to keep up with the words racing into her. The story tells itself, as the good ones sometimes do. The layers build from Godoy's impoverished nativity, and he becomes a hero in his own eyes. She lets him supply the hyperbole and vanity, the braggadocio and narcissism. And the charm, too, his boyish pride in the illegal empire he's built from almost nothing, his self-promoting pro bono investment here in the Sierra Madre: Clínica Godoy, La Luz Sierra church, Universidad Godoy, the restaurant Buen Vaquero.

The piece is sympathetic and subtly flattering. Well written. But her last few questions—especially about Keith—keep it from being a puff piece about a self-righteous peddler of deadly drugs, a stone-cold killer.

But what will El Gordo think of it?

She saves and sends it to her desktop in Laguna for safekeeping, uses a cruddy old printer to make a copy for Godoy. Not much of an office, she thinks, but everything seems to work.

Her video, edited right there on the laptop, is also to her liking. The fashionably dressed Godoy loves the camera as much as Strickland hates it. Bettina's good eye for locations helps Sinaloa come alive—its rugged mountains and vast canyons, the humble, brightly painted houses, the towns, the silent regard of the Indigenous Tarahumara, who labor on foot on the dusty roads.

But most of all on Godoy and all his histrionic self-revelation.

Godoy's last words on camera: "I take and I give, in the eternal way of the Sierra Madre. I will leave this world a better place. If I have ridden with the devil, it was only to survive. God is my judge."

Bettina: "How many men have you killed?"

Godoy: "Only those who tried to kill me. This I swear, Bettina Blazak."

Bettina: "Are you afraid of the God who will judge you?"

Godoy: "I fear nothing."

Her rough edit now complete, all Bettina can do is pray that Godoy signs off on his story.

And that she can go home with Felix.

Godoy sits at one end of a long leather sofa in his living room, watching Bettina's *Coastal Eddy* video on her laptop, propped open on the old streamer trunk before him.

Bettina sits at the opposite end, nervously appreciating the artisan crafts and paintings on the walls, the handwoven Indigenous rugs and brilliant Huichol yarn art—an extravagant exhibition of color.

Strickland stands in front of the fire, eyeing her unhappily, silent. He's got the pistol jammed into his belt where everyone can see it, as he has pretty much all day. Godoy didn't seem to mind, which made Bettina wonder why El Gordo would trust the gringo Strickland enough to pack a gun in his presence. But more than half the men she saw today were armed with automatic weapons, so maybe a gringo with a pistol was small potatoes.

Godoy's man, Miguel, surly and still as an Olmec statue, faces Strickland from across the big room with a tactical shotgun slung over his shoulder.

Bettina is hopeful but worried. Going on scared. If El Gordo doesn't like both the story and the video, she'll have to try again tomorrow. And if he still can't accept the El Gordo that she has created, she may never see Felix again. Or worse.

Godoy has already read the article and offered Bettina only a long blank look, saying nothing about the piece.

Now Bettina hears the *Coastal Eddy* music outro, and hears herself signing off from Sinaloa, Mexico.

Godoy looks over the trunk at her.

"Excuse me," he says, standing. "I have some business to do."

Bettina looks in mounting panic to Strickland, then back at Godoy as he strides across the hardwood floor in his shiny black boots, his new western shirt with the big turquoise bolo tie, and his black blazer.

Then out the front door.

The thud of that heavy door sounds final to Bettina in a dreadful, numbing way. She tries to conjure her spark, the old Blazak spark, but right now her feet and fingers are cold with more than the freezing mountain night. She feels stripped of everything she knows, a visitor in a hostile world.

Strickland and Villareal still face each across the room, motionless but intensely attached.

"You guys ought to lighten up," she says, her voice flimsy. "We could play a board game or something."

She rises and goes to the fire and rubs her hands together in the orange glow. Strickland doesn't look at her.

She's back on the sofa when she hears muffled commotion outside, coming her way. She stands on wobbly knees.

The door opens and Felix flies into the room, Godoy behind him, slamming the door against the cold.

"Señorita Blazak, I deliver to you your dog!"

Bettina runs to Felix, catches him midair, and wrestles him to the floor.

Then he's off for Strickland, who takes a knee and spreads his arms as the dog launches into him.

43

The Volaris jet from Los Mochis lands Bettina and Strickland in Tijuana at noon the next day.

In baggage claim, they collect Felix, who peers hopefully from his battered plastic crate, a gift from El Gordo.

Charley Gibbon waits at the arrivals curb at the wheel of his new black 4Runner. He's got bottled waters in the cup holders, a large bag of popcorn, and a mesh bag of tangerines to pass around. A coffee cup for Felix to drink from.

Bettina sits in the back, feeding her dog popcorn and watching out for the San Ysidro Port of Entry signs. She finds Felix's vaccination papers from the Clínica Veterinarea San Francisco de Asís, stashed safely with her passport in the bottom of her bag.

When they get to the crossing, she sees by the line of cars that it's going to be another excruciatingly long wait. But she's never in her life been so happy to be almost home. She cups another handful of popcorn for Felix and scratches his ears.

They pull up into the lane and Gibbon kills the engine. Bettina sips the water and looks out at the hundreds of vehicles crossing north into the United States.

She realizes that she's got everything in the world she wants right now. A little talent, a great job, a man who interests her and likes her for who she is, a nice apartment in a cool town, and a terrific dog. A surfboard, a good street bike.

A future free of Jason Graves.

And maybe most of all, she's got the hard-won satisfaction that she's stood up to Godoy and finally told the world about Keith's unnecessary fate. Maybe his story will help to save a few of the thousands of people out there right now, craving just one more hit of relief as they blunder toward an early grave.

She also realizes that she's been a bundle of frayed nerves the whole time she's been following El Gordo's unpredictable orders. She still hasn't come down from her adrenaline-fueled reclaiming of Felix. She feels a deep exhaustion settling over her, knowing it will only increase the second they cross the border. It feels like her Olympic trials trap shoot, entire weekends of high-pressure matches in which one missed clay often made the difference between winners and losers.

"Hey, handsome," she says, leaning forward, a hand on the back of Strickland's seat.

"Ma'am?"

"Let's take a road trip. Just you and me and my dog. I want to be somewhere beautiful and safe, like the desert or the mountains or the beach or maybe all three. Where we can walk and hike with the mutt and enjoy the outdoors. No men with guns. No looking over our shoulders. What do ya say?"

Strickland releases the seat belt shoulder restraint and turns to face her. His expression is that of a boy considering an important invitation. He looks suspicious but tempted.

"I'm in."

"Can we go somewhere exotic and expensive? Just kidding. We can take my Jeep if you want. I just need one day at work to get the El Gordo story in the can, and edit the video again with Jean."

44

Jean Rose takes a seat in Bettina's cubicle. She's beaming.

"Bettina, I love the El Gordo video. And I love your print story even more. They portray a murderous man in a complex manner. The way you work in Keith is extremely strong. I didn't know, Bettina, other than . . . well, I'm so sorry. Our readers will be moved. Your fear of being there in those cold mountains, and of asking hard questions of a dangerous criminal, come through very clearly. Our readers and viewers will like that too. This is a story that matters, as you like to say."

Relief floods through Bettina like a strong warm river. She's done it. She's written a good story and filmed a good video. She's gotten Felix back.

Bettina looks at Felix on his pad in the corner, head resting on his front paws, his face furrowed and his eyes alert.

Jean Rose's expression confirms she has no idea that the *Coastal Eddy* stories were Bettina's ransom for a dog.

"I'm happy for you, Bettina," she says. "I know you had high hopes for those stories. Thank you. I've slotted in the Rod Foster piece for next week, so we can go with El Gordo in tomorrow's edition."

"I need a week off," says Bettina.

"Granted. Get some rest, Bettina. You look like you could use it."

45

The next day, a cool March morning in Laguna Canyon, Bettina and Dan Strickland load their luggage into the Wrangler. Felix's pad, food, and bowls go in last. When Bettina pulls out of her assigned parking place, Strickland backs in the Quattroporte, locks it with a chirp, and climbs into the Jeep. Felix licks the back of his head.

Bettina steers out Laguna Canyon Road to SR 241, bound for Highway 395 and, eventually, Mammoth Mountain. She's well rested but bothered by a nagging fear: What if Jean Rose changes her mind? Or her *Coastal Eddy* publisher kills the stories at the last minute?

Last night she and Strickland—trying to break her agitation—agreed that this Mammoth Mountain ski run should be relaxed and as unscheduled as possible, and dog friendly. They could go where they wanted, trying to enjoy the road and the motion and the freedom.

She remembers Felix's expression last night in her apartment, a look that said: *This is the best day of my life.* Bettina loved that a dog can do that, have one best day of his life, followed by another and another.

Wishes she were simple like a dog.

"I love this day," she says. "This moment with Felix and you. I'm trying to let go of the worries for now."

"Me too," says Strickland, setting down his phone. "Sorry—just checking with Charley at Apex."

"I'm glad he could cover for you."

"My clients don't mind. He's a better teacher than I am."

"Maybe I should take your course someday."

Strickland nods. "I was serious when I offered."

"What would you teach me first?"

He looks at her, then back out the window. "Risk assessment. When to de-escalate. How to avoid weapons and bear spray and breaking bones in the first place."

"But that's the fun stuff."

Strickland cracks a slight smile, takes his time replying. "There's some truth in that."

"That's why I packed Thunder," she says, the real reason being a very nice little trap range near Bishop where she's hoping to get in a few rounds, maybe show Strickland the basics.

"I saw that," he says in a casual tone.

Jean Rose calls and Bettina puts her on the speaker:

"Just wanted to tell you the El Gordo video has blown up and it's not even noon!"

Bettina's smiles, heart swelling.

Strickland watches the sere desert around Adelanto slowly scrolling toward him through the windows, a marching horizon of twisted yuccas and large stucco homes crammed wall-to-wall behind more walls.

Of course, he wasn't checking in with Charley at Apex, he was following today's *Blog Narco* story, in English and titled "Top Dogs the Latest Secret Weapons."

Blog Narco says cartel pit bulls, long used for ring fighting, have been bred into aggressive scent hounds. They'll fight any dog and anybody but their handlers to get to the dope and money first.

Thank God there's no mention of the Jalisco New Generation or Carlos Palma or El Gordo or anybody else Strickland knows. This blog is mostly Gulf Cartel and Zeta *sicarios* yapping about their enemies using dogs to steal their booty. They freely admit to using dogs for that purpose too. One Tijuana-based La Familia Cartel soldier describes a dog used by Sinaloans to raid their coffers. He offers no description of the dog other than "small," which sends a ripple of nerves down Strickland's back. The pit bulls can be small, he thinks, but what else might suspicious Carlos extrapolate from that word?

Strickland has always believed his training, nerve, and luck will prevail against his enemies. Lately, however, he's doubled his enemies by doubling his friends, and sometimes his everyday sense of threat is strong. If he thought that Palma had discovered his duplicity, he wouldn't be anywhere near Bettina Blazak. His vow is to protect her, not expose her to his professional risks.

Protect her. Through his sunglasses Strickland studies her in profile as she drives. This woman.

The fact is, Strickland is happier now than at any time in his life. He's got it all: a prospering dual career as a self-defense instructor and a thief; a great dog; a totally cool home in San Diego, and a woman who makes him feel needed and generous, and who apparently likes his heavily redacted version of himself.

And he's got this new thing in his heart, something MIA for most of his thirty-three years. It's almost certainly love, he thinks. What else but love could fill you with wonderful things that you can't wait to give away? Answer me that.

He's never seen a future until now, not even from the corner of his eye. But here it is, in the form of this beautiful being steering a red Jeep up Highway 395 with him in the passenger seat.

"I love this day, too, with you and Joe too," he says. "I don't know how I suddenly got to be so corny—to use your word."

Bettina refrains from correcting Felix's name. "You surprise me."

"And myself."

"Do you tell me things just to make me happy?"

"Now and then."

"Like last night?"

"That was all true."

"Do you even *like* skiing?"

Strickland laughs. "Well, I did fib just a bit about that. I've never tried it."

But he does fine on the beginners' slopes, and manages the intermediate runs with long-legged aplomb, some of that rhythm coming back to him from the International Practical Shooting Conference matches where he could glide and angle and sprint and never lose balance, punching out those targets with such unthinking, almost unconscious accuracy.

He follows Bettina down the Lower Dry Creek run, loves the sound his skis make in the snow, smiles as he watches her carving the turns, getting a little air, skis throwing off white sparks. When he dares to raise his eyes from the snow he can see for miles through blue sky to the jagged White Mountains.

He thinks of Joe at the dog-sitter's, pictures him curled up by that fireplace on his red plaid pad.

They eat an early dinner at Skadi, a skier's hangout that Bettina knows. A customer recognizes her and comes over for a selfie. Strickland feels mild annoyance that Bettina has been to this restaurant without him and knows how selfish and childish this is. He wants to own her past, present, and future.

The food is good. He even enjoys some wine. His legs feel heavy and his heart light and he can't wait to pick up Joe and get back to the rental condo and make love to Bettina.

Strickland gets his wish: Joe is chewing his ragged turkey in the middle of the living room rug when Strickland closes the bedroom door on him.

They heat up the bedroom so fast he has to turn the wall heater off. The windows sweat as Mammoth Mountain looks through the glass at them, a pale behemoth packed in stars.

Ski by day, love by night.

Best week of Strickland's life, bar none. Sounds like something Joe would say, he thinks.

Two days in Death Valley at the Oasis, the last of Bettina's vacation time. Gazing out at the sere majesty of Zabriskie Point that morning, Strickland lobbies for more days of this, but Bettina needs to get back to *Coastal Eddy* tomorrow.

"It's seven hours to your place," she says. "How about a good dinner in a dog-friendly restaurant?"

46

Back in San Diego, they dine in the Gaslamp Quarter at an outdoor table at Mikey's, heat lamps out against the chill, plenty busy for a blustery night.

Strickland feels proud, sitting across from Bettina Blazak. And happy to be seen with her in public. People here in San Diego don't stare at her like they do in Laguna. Here she's just another anonymous beauty. She's wearing a black knit suit and a silver-and-turquoise squash-blossom necklace, and her hair is up. He can't believe his luck.

He watches three men approaching on the crowded sidewalk—chinos and bulky leather coats. They're walking briskly toward the restaurant, hands in their pockets. Nothing unusual about them, but something isn't right.

They're two hundred feet away from Strickland, trying for casual, but he reads purpose in their strides. Before leaving for Mammoth, he checked the Jeep for a tracker, and twice more during their journey. But Strickland knows that Palma has allies in Barrio Logan, not far from here.

The three men spread out now, which is when he makes Frank—

skinny and golden eyed—last encountered that morning in Laguna, along with Héctor, the morning after the DEA gunned down Joaquín Páez.

Doing the math, Strickland turns a 180 in his restaurant chair, to find the hulking Héctor and two more intent young men coming from the other way, just a hundred feet behind him.

For a total of six gunmen, closing in on him like a vise. Palma has unmasked him, Strickland sees. Sooner than he had figured, much sooner.

He rises. So does Bettina, sensing his alarm, turning in the direction that Strickland was facing when the first wave of urgency came off him.

He turns her and hugs her lightly and whispers in her ear.

"Take Joe through the kitchen and out the back door. If they're not watching your Jeep, drive it to your parents' home in Anza Valley. If they're at the Jeep, walk until you find people and cops. These guys are after me and Joe. Not you."

"El Gordo's men?"

"No. *Go.*"

"I'm not going to leave you alone."

"You have to. For Joe. He's trained to defend, Bettina. If he attacks them, they'll kill him."

Strickland holds open the restaurant door and watches Bettina and Joe hurry across the lobby and disappear into the dining room.

He draws his weapon from the holster on the small of his back.

"Get down or get out!" he orders, sidling through the sidewalk diners, who lurch and scramble in every direction, one of them knocking down a heat lamp, which sparks and sizzles out. A waiter in a red vest with a tray of food over one shoulder stops mid-step, eyes wide and mouth open.

On the sidewalk, Strickland stays low, zigzagging through a gaggle of pedestrians toward big Héctor and his men. The crowd parts when they see his gun. A woman screams; a man yells, *"He's got a fucking gun!"*

A young couple holding hands cuts suddenly into the street, where a gleaming black Corvette skids to miss them as the driver rides the horn.

Strickland is fluid and loose but very clear on acquiring his targets early, like the IPSC pistol shoots he used to dominate. The adrenaline clears his vision and lightens his feet. Fuels his strength and purpose. He feels the danger bowing to him, feels the guidance and protection of his luck.

For Bettina, he thinks.

For Joe.

Strickland feels immortal on this mission—to protect and serve them.

He puts a bullet through Héctor's forehead and two more each into the chests of his two hapless friends, only one of whom even manages to get his gun up.

No collateral damage, but screams and curses fill the night, the slap of shoes and boots, the skidding and screeching of car tires. The wind blows a palm frond onto the hood of a pickup truck, which rear-ends a sixties hippie van in front of it.

Strickland wheels and reverses through the smell of gun smoke. Feels the strength of his legs, the invincibility in him. Pedestrians part and he sees Frank up ahead with his pistol drawn, taking a knee beneath a stylized Victorian streetlight, using a Gaslamp Quarter trash can for cover.

Bop, bop, bop!

One of the bullets snaps past Strickland's ear and another twangs off the brick building to his left, and again he zigs and zags toward the fire, dropping Leather Coat I with two shots to his chest, then crabbing farther toward Leather Coat II, feeling the bullets chewing through the air past his head. Strickland dives, rolls, rises, and fires off two head shots at fifty feet. A bony crack, and Leather Coat II collapses. Strickland angles off fast for Frank, who, to Strickland's satisfaction, is reloading. Strickland has thirteen rounds left and knows it.

He charges Frank, firing—twelve, eleven, ten.

Frank is frowning, a strangely patient expression. He slams home the magazine and points the weapon—*bop, bop!*—and Strickland feels the horse-kick to his left shoulder.

Fires off nine, eight, and seven. Feels the wet heat on his neck. Doesn't understand why he's missing shots he never misses. It's like damned Frank is too skinny to hit. The cars screech away and the pedestrians bolt and dive for safety and the sirens are screaming in the near distance, sapping Strickland's concentration.

Still he moves forward.

Focus, he thinks: eyes and feet, eyes and feet, eyes and . . .

Frank rises from behind the trash can, gun up in both hands. Strickland pulls into a modified Weaver stance for the easy torso shot, the one he has put into the center ring of fifty thousand targets. Squeezes off the round.

The last thing he sees is the orange muzzle flash from Frank's gun, and the last thing on earth he thinks is:

Bett . . .

Bettina jams Thunder between the passenger seat and the center console, barrel down. Felix is growling in soft, unrelenting fear of the gunfire, clearly remembering that night at Furniture Calderón.

She reverses out of the pay lot and takes L Street not toward the freeway but back into the fray outside Mikey's, where she absolutely intends to keep her outgunned Strickland from getting himself killed.

The sirens are howling by now, and with all the Gaslamp one-ways, it takes her forever to get back to Mikey's, where she sees the crowd gathered on the sidewalk under one of the Victorian-style streetlights.

She parks on the sidewalk, gets the pepper spray gun from the console, locks Thunder and Felix in the Jeep. Then runs toward the people who are lit by the streetlight, their coats and scarves rippling in the wind.

She crashes through the crowd, throwing curses and elbows all the way to the front, where she finds Strickland on his back with his throat half-gone, lying in a swamp of blood that drips into the gutter. She kneels and shakes him as she screams, rocking his beautiful head with her bloody hands and kissing his beautiful face with her bloody lips and this is not how it's going to end, you people, she thinks, you do not get to kill Dan Strickland, you do not get to kill him, you do not, you do not, you do not . . .

A boxy ambulance hunches to a stop in a flurry of red lights, and Bettina slogs through the crowd back to the Wrangler, where Felix is in the driver's seat, staring at Bettina and wagging his tail and still whimpering with fear and confusion as she opens the door and pushes him into the passenger seat. He licks Strickland's blood from her hand.

It takes her four turns in the Gaslamp one-ways to get back around to the fenced Metro Parking lot she'd left just minutes ago. She takes her old spot, hands trembling, back cold, the terrible metallic smell of Strickland all over her. But she's got a plan, a good one: these killers had to have followed them here, right? It's not like they just happened to spot them at Mikey's. So they know where I parked, right? *Right?* And they know I've got Felix.

Through the passenger-side window, Bettina sees a tall, skinny man in a leather jacket running toward her. He looks like the guy that Strickland recognized first. He ducks under the gate arm on the far side of the Metro Parking lot, and comes slinking through the parked cars toward the Jeep. Bettina hisses at her dog to sit and stay and he instantly obeys.

She lowers both front windows and slides from the Wrangler, drawing the Winchester along with her. Nudges the door shut with her hip.

"Stay," she whispers. "*Stay.*"

With her eyes on Skinny, she ducks and backpedals between an SUV and an enormous white Sprinter. Her heart pounds and her hands shiver on Thunder, but she's got a good view of the driver's side of her vehicle, and of Felix sitting in the passenger seat, and of the man still coming across the lot toward them.

He stops ten feet short of the driver's-side window, his back to Bettina. She sees the gun jammed into his waistband, the grip outside his short leather jacket.

"Hello, Joe," he says.

She can see Felix, staring at the skinny gunman.

Bettina steps from her lair and into the yellow security lights of the parking lot, racking the 12-gauge.

Skinny flinches.

"If you go for that gun, I'll blow you in half," she says. The pounding in her ears is so loud she knows he must hear it. So she says it again, louder.

The man raises his hands. "I don't have a gun."

"It's under your jacket."

"Are you Bettina Blazak?"

"I am her. Turn to me but keep your hands *up*!"

A lined face and a drooping mustache. His eyes are yellow gold and his face betrays no emotion. A face made in prison, she thinks.

"I saw what you did to Dan."

"He deserved his punishment."

"Who ordered it?"

"The Jalisco New Generation Cartel."

She spreads her feet and clamps the 12-gauge tighter to her shoulder. "Why?"

"He worked for them and betrayed them."

"Worked?"

"An arrangement."

Through the roaring in her ears, she hears Strickland's words that day in Alta Laguna Park: *I'll do anything to protect you and Joe.*

"Are you here to kill my dog too?"

"Yes. The order comes from Carlos Palma himself. His word is the law."

"I won't let you. I'll shoot you before you do that. I can get the cops here in less than a minute. They're all over the Gaslamp and my phone is in my pocket."

Listening to her own brittle, adrenaline-charged voice, Bettina believes almost nothing she has just said.

"But you don't want me dead or in prison," says Skinny. "If I don't convince Palma that Joe is dead, he'll send others to finish the job. And if they fail, he will send more. There's no end to men with guns, Ms. Blazak. Joe will certainly die. I can't save him if I'm in prison. Or a grave."

Skinny's logic is as dark as it is true.

"How do you convince your boss?"

"I am his son-in-law. And I am not only a fine *sicario*, I run the New Generation's business with La Eme—the Mexican Mafia."

"Why should I believe you'll lie for Felix?"

"Not just for your dog, Ms. Blazak—I would be lying for me and *you*."

"Why?"

"To keep my life and my freedom. My wife and children. My Javier is a soccer star and only twelve. I would be happy to let Joe live. He is cute. You rescued him and I like your videos. And to be honest, you *have* to let me go or the dog will be hunted down. I always liked him. Isn't that right, Joe?"

Bettina lowers the shotgun from Skinny's face to his chest. Past his shoulder she sees Felix, his funny ears alert, his expression intensely focused on the man just a few feet beyond her open window, so easily jumpable. She knows that the *Fass!* command will launch him like a rocket. Felix could take Skinny by the neck, all fang and jaw, like a hound from the underworld. But Skinny might just be fast enough to draw his gun and fire.

"You killed a man who loved and protected me. I will not let you go."

"You have to. My freedom for Joe's life. I can't bring—I'm sorry you lost a boyfriend. But maybe you're better off without a violent criminal in your life. Go find someone better."

Bettina's cold body has warmed; her trembling fingers and leaden legs feel strong and ready. No roaring in her ears now, just the steady rhythm of blood. Spark to flame to fire.

She will do what needs to be done.

"What's your name?"

"Frank."

"Drop the gun, Frank."

He sets it quietly on the asphalt.

"Now both hands up, Frank. Walk away slowly and Felix won't attack you. I'm tracking you with my gun until you're out of sight. Don't test me. I've hit a million clay targets a lot smaller than your head."

"I'll never get out of here with all these cops. My car's way down on Sixth. Give me a ride to Barrio Logan."

Bettina stands in the fire, the stubborn conviction that she's about to triumph. Feels capable and fated. She's clear on what she has to do.

"Kick the gun to me."

He does. Bettina keeps Thunder pointed at Skinny's chest as she picks up his pistol by the barrel end and drops it into her suit coat pocket.

"You drive and I'll keep your gun aimed at your kneecap," she says. "I'll take it home to match the cartridges you used on Dan tonight. Should that be required in court. Which it will be, if any more killers like you show up for my dog."

"You got some brains, *niña*. We could use you."

"Stay away from me at all costs."

As Bettina wends her way from Barrio Logan to Highway 163, Felix sits next to her, bolt upright, nose to the window crack, whining.

Where is Dan?

Who was that bad man?

Why does Bettina smell like bloody meat?

Where is Dan?

The sound of gunfire on the Gaslamp streets has brought him back to Furniture Calderón and the hot, thudding pain in his leg. He curls into the seat and starts licking the scar.

Thinks of Dan in warehouse, still doesn't understand why Dan left him there under that car.

Thinks of the boy holding him tight and how his leg hurt and the blood tasted, like Bettina's hand, and how the Good Man shaved part of his fur and stuck something in his leg.

Remembered the cold stone Crate that was his, and all the smells of

Tijuana flooding through him as he lay there day after day. Sad, and wanting Teddy and Dan, even Aaron.

He stops licking and looks up at Bettina, who looks at him with an expression so sad that Felix looks away.

But he knows she will not leave him.

Would never leave him.

Team.

47

In answer to the resounding silence of the Strickland clan, Bettina makes the death and disposition arrangements with the county. Charley Gibbon helps, dealing with the detectives and deflecting reporters from her. Besides a local self-defense academy owner, five known gangsters have been killed and two innocent bystanders wounded in the popular Gaslamp Quarter. The media is hungry for information on the dead self-defense instructor, a decorated combat veteran with no criminal record. But they haven't connected Bettina to Strickland or that night. She drifts around them like smoke.

It costs her a modest fortune to have Dan buried in a hillside cemetery up in Newport Beach, but she wants him close. Strickland's father and mother actually attend the service. At first they mistake Bettina for a mortuary representative, offering compliments on their son's appearance. They're two of the iciest and most charmless plutocrats Bettina has ever met, and she understands a little more of why Strickland was the way he was. Allison Strickland doesn't show but sends flowers. There are close to sixty people who file through the viewing, mostly clients and former clients of Apex, Bettina gathers. No extended family or close friends. She introduces herself to a series of attractive, mostly unaccompanied women, with an ache in her heart and a towering sense of gullibility.

She's in a state of mild shock before and after, spending most of her hours in her Laguna Canyon apartment, staring out the windows and talking to her dog. She cries and sleeps a lot.

Gets calls and emails about her *Coastal Eddy* El Gordo story and video from agents and publishers, producers, studios, networks, cable, and streamers. One from a human resources executive from *Los Angeles Times*, implying a job offer and inviting her to lunch. And, disturbingly, an email from a *San Diego Union* columnist who says two witnesses told her they had recognized Bettina dining with a man—and her dog—at Mikey's in the Gaslamp the night Dan Strickland was shot down. Did you know him?

She answers not one of them.

Her mother and father and brothers Nick and Connor come and go, as do Billy Ray Crumley and Jean Rose, and some of her *Coastal Eddy* coworkers, and the Biker Chicks. She realizes how alone she is—we all are—when it comes to being in our own skin, to putting one foot in front of the other.

She doesn't work. Doesn't ride. Doesn't surf.

Can't stay awake more than four hours at a time during day, can't sleep at night. Felix is depleted, eating less and sleeping more, looking at her lugubriously.

Alejandro Godoy:

Dear Ms. Blazak,

I am sorry to learn of the death of the señor Strickland. I knew him as the señor Knowles. He was a friend, and he believed very highly in you. I am pleased with your story and show about me in *Coastal Eddy*. I assume that Joe was killed with Strickland. Is this true? That is very sad but without his master a dog is just a dog. But you should always be watchful of the Jalisco New Generation Cartel. Palma is a rabid animal.

Vaya con Dios,
Alejandro Godoy

She writes El Gordo back, confirming Joe's death in the Gaslamp shoot-out.

Her life is an empty container.

The minutes take hours; the hours take days.

On her first day back at *Coastal Eddy*, Bettina meets Billy at Crescent Bay in Laguna. He's on bike patrol today downtown, but he's got his lunch hour free. He brings food from the French café on Forest that Bettina likes, and a couple of big gourmet treats for Felix. The plastic bag dangles from his hand as they walk across the beach. Felix bolts after a seagull, but Bettina calls him in. The tide is low and they choose flat rocks up by the sandstone berm.

Billy has been a rock of empathy and subdued good cheer these days since the Gaslamp. But today Bettina senses extra weight in him. The early spring day is cool and still, and they don't have a lot to say.

"Bettina, I'm wanting to bring up something that may not be pleasant for you. And I want you to know that I'll just cool it if you don't want to hear me out. And I'm not saying that what I suspect is absolutely true, but I have to say it. Say what I think is true, I mean. And there I go, tangling up my words again."

"Shoot, Billy."

"Dan Strickland was the Roman—the dog handler and shooter that El Gordo and the DEA talked about."

"No. Of course that can't be, Billy," she says. But her words sound weak. And it's not the ocean breeze just carrying them away. Once upon a time, she had thought that was a distant but actual possibility. But the idea of Dan as the Roman had gradually receded with his protection of her and of Felix, and his unwavering affection for both of them. And hers for him.

But now, Billy's words hit her heart with the heavy thud of truth.

"Prove it."

"The Tijuana Police cooperated with DEA, which ran the brass from Calderón against the gun that Strickland died with. It took some time with all the shots fired, but the toolmarks from six casings matched. Dan Strickland's gun was used to kill three men in Tijuana that night."

"And how did DEA think to do that?"

Billy sighs, nods compliantly. "Because I showed them the similarities between Dan as a competition gunslinger, and Godoy's photos of the shooter in the switching yard."

"I'm processing. I'm processing."

"He never told you?" asks Billy.

Bettina shakes her head, zips up her windbreaker, watches a couple of black-clad frogmen back into the surf. This kind of diving had never seemed scary to her, but now it does—disappearing into that dark black water with a bunch of lead strapped around your waist.

Everything seems scary since the Gaslamp.

Like when she's here on Laguna's beaches, looking at the waves, she imagines dropping into a Brooks Street barrel and feels cold fear.

Or in town, when she considers Coast Highway and imagines coursing down the asphalt into town with the cars whizzing past her, she feels fear.

And if she imagines guiding a big strong horse like Sawblade in a barrel race, she feels fear. Wonders how she ever did all those things in the first place.

Is this what Strickand meant when he said the first thing he'd teach her about survival was to learn when to back off?

She doesn't think so. She thinks if anyone needed to know when to back off, it was him, not her. Which was part of why she came to like and love him. Because they were alike.

Which does nothing to address the fear. No matter how still and open-minded, or how fueled by bourbon she becomes, since the Gaslamp shoot-out, Bettina has felt no spark, no flame, no fire.

"Bettina, I'm very sorry that you lost your friend like that. I've never lost someone I loved, in that way. It must be a heavy burden. So I'll do what I can to help you, be a shoulder to cry on, whatever you need. I won't crowd you like I did before, won't shadow or badger you. If what you need is less me, I'll clear all the way out."

"Don't clear out."

"I don't want to."

"Let's do this again next week."

"You got it."

After Billy leaves, Bettina and Felix linger at Crescent Bay. Today is her birthday. And Keith's. Keith's ashes were scattered at sea up in Dana Point, so Bettina figures that, technically, any part of the Pacific is somewhere some tiny molecule of Keith might be. So Crescent Bay's as good a place to think about him than any.

She strokes Felix's perfect round head and behind his gull wing ears, and memories of Keith come flooding out, good ones, only the good ones, only the good.

Here's looking at you, brother. Sorry the world wasn't enough. Sorry I wasn't.

Charley Gibbon holds open the Apex Self-Defense door, and Felix squeezes in first. Bettina nods at Gibbon on her way in. Charley has the same hardness, the same feral cool that Strickland had.

"Thanks for this, Charley," she says.

"I got some pictures and video for you on the desktop. Some letters I found in a file cabinet. Something for you from Dan."

"What do you know about his life as the Roman?"

Gibbon gives her a pained smile and a small shake of his head. "Let's sit outside in the sun for that," he says. "Beer? Bourbon?"

Gibbon's expression is a confirmation that Billy Ray was absolutely right about Strickland. This hurts—her last crumb of hope for Dan the Good Guy melting away.

"Bourbon," she says.

The April afternoon is sunny, neither warm nor cool, a representative San Diego day. Bettina sits on the deck exactly where she sat the night that Strickland cooked the dinner and told her about Sangin and later let her take him to his bed. The night she picked the short pale dog hair off the collar of Strickland's coat while they walked in the rain.

"So Felix was with you when I came here for the first time," she says.

"I was part of the conspiracy."

"To help me believe that my dog had been kidnapped by Godoy."

"Yes."

"When in fact Dan had him here all along?"

"He felt terrible about taking Joe from you. He knew how much you love him, because he loved Joe too."

"His name is Felix." Bettina reaches down and runs a hand over his fine round head, the doggen noggin.

"Of course," says Gibbon. "Felix he is."

"That was the only direct lie he told me, that I know of," says Bettina. "Him not being the Roman. The rest of his deceits were just errors of omission. Such as Felix not being here at Apex. Such as the women. Such as working for two cartels. Such as letting me believe it was safe to have dinner together in the Gaslamp."

"He underestimated the time it would take Carlos Palma to find him out."

"There's got to be a better word than 'underestimated.'"

Gibbon nods and sips his beer. "Dan's fearlessness is what made him a success. And got him killed."

"Yes."

"I get that way myself," says Bettina. "I've been reckless, too, in a much less spectacular way."

"The thrill of the hunt."

"Felix led Dan to the drugs and money," says Bettina, still having a hard time believing that he was the Roman. "How often?"

"In the old days, once a week, maybe twice," says Gibbon. "When Dan played both cartels at once, it got busier."

"How much money did he make, on a good night?"

"Fifty thousand."

"So he could take in a hundred grand in a week?"

"Some weeks not. Some weeks more."

"Was Furniture Calderón the first shoot-out?"

"Yeah."

"How many men did he kill that night?"

"Three," says Gibbon. "They were his first, outside of the war. It dimmed some of his light. The men he killed in Sangin, he chalked up to war—he was able to look back on them in a different way than the civilians in Calderón. I'd seen some changes in him over the last year. The crazier his escapades got down in TJ, the more troubled he was. Darker inside. Sometimes it looked like the risks he took for Palma were a way to keep that darkness away. Shoot his way out of it. Like the danger made him free."

"Why Roman?"

"He thought it sounded noble."

"Jesus." She can't quite laugh and can't quite cry.

"He told me once that he wanted to be remembered as a legend."

Bettina finds it hard to believe that this was the man she fell for and loved and surrendered her heart to. How could she have missed him by so far? Looked at one thing and seen another? How could she call herself a reporter when she got the facts of her own story so wrong?

"He loved you very much," said Gibbon. "In his way."

All she's been able to see for the last days is Strickland on the sidewalk in a lake of blood, his throat blown out and his beautiful dead gray eyes drying in the wind.

"I don't want to hear that now."

"He was driven by powerful things he didn't understand," says Gibbon. "He was misshapen."

"But in the end, what you do is on you."

Echoing what Godoy said about Keith. Reminding Bettina that Strickland was on the same side of history as El Gordo, for a time. Which makes her love him less and miss him more: People change, she thinks. He could have become a good man. Couldn't he? *Couldn't he!*

"I agree, Bettina. Dan would too. He liked to say, 'Wear the crown, wear the target.'"

———

Sitting at the big desk in Strickland's penthouse office, Bettina browses the pictures that Gibbon has curated for her. Felix lies in a rhombus of sunlight fading through a western window. Being in his former home has left him spiritless.

Bettina considers Strickland's birth certificate, issued by Hoag Hospital of Newport Beach.

Then a picture of Strickland as a first grader, bundled up in a preppy sweater, with a big gap in his smile.

And a *Daily Pilot* article about Daniel Strickland winning a Snowbird regatta at the Balboa Bay Club when he was ten. He looks like Hemingway, posed in the boat with a big smile and the wind in his hair.

There are family portraits in which Dyson's presidential bearing and Jennifer's composed beauty seem to drain the energies of their son and daughter.

Prom and beach pics.

A friend named Rupert.

Cage diving with white sharks.

Racing a Ducati into a perilous curve, if that's him inside the helmet.

Skydiving, solo.

Shooting competitions.

Strickland with unidentified girls—not many—and Bettina wonders if Gibbon has redacted the babe shots in consideration of her.

Sangin, Afghanistan: Strickland kneeling in front of a low mud wall, M16 in hand. He looks exhausted.

Shots of Strickland and his Apex students in action. He looks fierce.

A picture of "Wade and Aaron, Joe's trainer and handler at Excalibur K-9." With a proud Felix.

A close-up of a dark-haired woman asleep on a pillow, her face peaceful and pretty, which certainly annoys Bettina until she realizes it's her, in his bed, right here in this building.

Gibbon has arranged for the SDPD to transfer some of Strickland's phone pictures from their Mammoth run: ski shots and selfies of Bettina and Strickland and Felix before the condo fireplace, Death Valley panoramas, and them dressed up for dinner at the Oasis at Death Valley.

Enough, thinks Bettina, a hard, painful knot tightening in her throat.

Felix comes over and looks up at her. No limp. Licks her fingers and slides his noggin under her hand.

The letters that Strickland had once mentioned writing to his family are in a file cabinet folder labeled LETTERS, FAMILY.

One each to Dyson, Jennifer, and Allison.

They all say exactly the same thing:

I'm writing to explain to you some of the decisions I have made, and the unusual things I have done since I was a small boy.

And that's it, just this sentence, this huge promise followed up with nothing.

Bettina closes the folder on them.

She knows she's missed the truth of Strickland by a mile, and that there will be, in the end, no one else to know it except Charley.

She opens a big brown clasp envelope with her name written in Strickland's perfect, forward-slanting, all-caps print. It's been staring at her since she first sat down, and she's been dreading it.

No letter inside, just packets of new hundreds, packed with paper bands like they do at the bank.

Lots of them.

She and Felix roam Strickland's bedroom. Felix seems listless and uncertain. Bettina kneels and scratches behind his goofy ears, feels again the terrible responsibility for what has happened to Felix's former master.

I'll do anything to protect Joe and you.

"Maybe we'll all be together someday," she says.

What a strange thing to believe, she thinks, working Felix's ears. Not sure I do.

Throat lump and eye burn.

She slides open Dan's closet, looking for something of his to have.

Something she can take home, just a reminder. The clothes hang neatly. There are shelves with meticulously folded sweaters and knit shirts. She finds that dark sweater that Strickland was wearing when they met in the *Coastal Eddy* office. Takes it.

Joe sleeps in the Team Bed with Bettina that night, and by then he knows something is really Bad. He knows that the smells on Bettina that night of the guns were powerfully Bad. That the tall man outside the Jeep was Bad. That Dan being gone is Bad. Joe knows that Bettina's unhappiness is Bad.

But he knows that Dan will come back and they'll be a Team again. He thinks that was what Bettina was trying to tell him. Dan and Bettina and him. The Team.

And Aaron will come back, too, even though Aaron was often unhappy with him.

Teddy will come back, his first Boy, his first Team.

They will all be a Team. Together and happy.

Joe always looks forward, but he never forgets.

Especially his first human.

When she gets back to her office the next day, there's an older man in the lobby, and a boy, holding open the latest *Coastal Eddy* newspaper spread across his lap.

When he stands, Felix sails over the coffee table at him, leash trailing midair. The newspaper floats free and the boy catches Felix in the falling sheets of newsprint, then dog and boy crash to the blue leather sofa in a storm of crackling paper, canine caterwauling, and urgent human words: *"Joe, Joe, Joe!"*

Shit, Bettina realizes: Teddy Delgado.

48

Bettina sits with her back to her desk in the little cubicle, Teddy and Felix on the floor before her in an ongoing spectacle of affection. Wade Johnson stands at the entrance, arms crossed.

She composes herself as Teddy talks about how he kept the dog out of Mabel's surprise litter, named him Joe, let him live and sleep in his room, spent every second of time that he could with him, but he was in school so it was never enough. And how they played the hide-and-find game and Teddy saw that Joe had a great nose and memory, and even Wade at Excalibur K-9 who was a friend of his dad was impressed, and took him on for training even though Joe was small and kind of stubborn sometimes and didn't like to fight those big monster men with all the pads. But later he passed every Class I course, setting record times in his detection tests. And the reason Joe did so good, Teddy tells Bettina, is because he thought it was fun to make his humans happy.

Bettina feels her heart breaking off in slabs, like a calving iceberg. "That's so . . . beautiful."

Teddy smiles at her. He's a slender boy with straight black hair and a sweet, toothy smile.

"How old are you, Teddy?"

"Fifteen. I can get my learner's next month. How old are you?"

"Twenty-six."

He looks at her in apparent sympathy. Bettina doesn't know if it's aimed at her advanced age, or the fact that Teddy thinks he's getting his dog back.

Not without a fight, though, she thinks, telling herself that where Felix goes isn't up to her *or* Teddy. She considers Wade Johnson, standing just outside her cubicle with a look of forbearance.

"Do you know who Felix's father was?" Bettina asks. She won't call him Joe because Felix was never theirs—never Strickland's or the DEA's, or Aaron's, or Wade Johnson's or now, Teddy's.

"I think so. I saw this Mexican street-looking dog hanging around our yard when we got back from church one Sunday. He ran away fast and Mabel had dried slobber on her, and she was tired and acting guilty. I saw him again a week later but he wouldn't come or let me get close. He was wild, I could tell. No collar and some ticks around his eyes. I gave him some water and food but he ran off later. I didn't want him around Mabel. By the time Joe was a couple of months old, he looked like that Mexican street dog and Mabel put together. Mostly the street dog, though. He got Mabel's big head, and the curvy shape of the street dog's body. I guess his crazy ears came from both."

Bettina likes Teddy Delgado enough to hug him. The fact that Felix seems to love him more than he loves her breaks her heart a little more. Another piece of the iceberg sloughs off.

"What happened to your mom and dad?"

She listens to his story about the accident, and how it happened on the same day Joe shattered every Excalibur record in his mock Class I certification exam. How it was the happiest day of his life and Joe's, too, and they stayed home alone that evening with Shelly babysitting because Mom and Dad were out to celebrate their twelve-year anniversary with Uncle Art and Aunt Nancy.

Bettina feels ashamed that she's envious of Teddy and Felix. Wishes she could put her jealous heart in a box and chain it to an anvil and drop it off a pier.

"And the wreck happened on their way back," he says.

Teddy Delgado looks almost frail, but Bettina feels the emotional energy coming off him like electricity.

"And your aunt and uncle took you in, but not your dog?"

"Aunt Nancy has allergies, but Uncle Art said I was too young to take care of a dog. They wanted me to focus on school. Now that I'm older, I'll be able to do both."

"You've talked to them about this?"

"Kind of. If that falls through, Mr. Johnson will take Joe."

"Yes, I'm happy to," says Johnson. Bettina notes both the firmness and the kindness in the old man's voice.

Teddy gets up off the floor and pulls out his wallet. Felix sits at his feet, staring up at him. "I've got sixty-six dollars. Will you take it for Joe?"

Before she even speaks, Bettina knows she's going to lose him. Still, she will not be told what to do. "I'm so sorry, Teddy, but I can't. I paid for him and I own him and he's mine now."

"But he was mine first. I raised him and they took him away."

"It's not up to you if he goes or stays," Bettina says.

"Then it's not up to you either."

"You're right. It's up to Felix."

"Joe."

Bettina swivels her chair away from Teddy Delgado and her dog, pops a tissue from the box by her monitor, blows her nose. Gets a clean one and wipes her eyes. Pivots back to them.

"Felix, come."

He comes slowly, saber tail wagging humbly.

"Sit and stay."

He sits, looks back at Teddy, then Bettina.

"Teddy, please back away, go outside my cubicle."

Wade steps away and Teddy backs into the doorless entryway, his suspicious eyes on the dog and Bettina.

Felix watches Teddy, then joins him, sitting at his feet again.

"Felix, come," says Bettina.

He looks at her but does not come. Looks up at Teddy, tail wagging tentatively, shyly.

"Felix, *come.*"

He wiggles over to her, and Bettina leans forward in her chair and he licks her face.

"I love you, Felix."

Who now walks back to Teddy and lies down, puts his head between his paws, and looks up at Bettina with that same furrowed concern he'd first given her in the Wrangler on their way from the Clínica de Veterinarea to Laguna. And a hundred times since.

Hello and goodbye, she thinks.

"Teddy, keep your money. Felix is yours."

"He's Joe."

It is finished, she thinks.

"Yes. You and Joe."

"I don't know how to thank you."

"Let me follow you home and say goodbye to Joe there," Bettina manages. "I want to see where he'll be so I can picture him with you. I'll need to stop by my apartment first, then I'll follow you to La Jolla."

"Yeah, sure!"

Teddy cleans and jerks Joe off the floor—a lot of dog for a skinny boy—and Joe eagerly licks his face.

He looks at Bettina innocently. "You can come visit him anytime you want, Ms. Blazak. Either at my uncle's and aunt's, or at Mr. Johnson's."

"Absolutely," says Johnson.

"I'm going to take you up on that."

Teddy sets down Joe, who wiggles over to Bettina and lies down on her feet.

"We can all play hide-and-find," says Teddy. "Or go to the dog beach at Del Mar and let him run free. I'll text you every day to tell you how he's doing, and send pictures too. Thank you so much for giving Joe back to me. I'll protect him forever. He'll never get shot again."

And Jalisco New Generation won't know where to find him, Bettina thinks. Even if they don't believe Frank's lie about the Gaslamp.

Leaving Bettina's cubicle with Teddy, Joe moves forward on-leash in that small-footed way of his, almost a prance but not quite, checking out the floor smells, of course—dropped Food is always possible, maybe a crunchy dead fly—then looking up at his Boy as the air scents flow into his nose.

He recognizes the carpet cleaner and the random nameless smells that ride in on the soles of shoes, but the strongest scent is Teddy's, huffing out from his pant legs with each step.

Joe's heart is filled with love for Teddy and Dan and Bettina and his mother, even Aaron.

Catches the smell of Bettina behind him.

He's surrounded by some of his favorite things.

He trots along, reaching around to grab the leash in his teeth, one of his favorite games with Teddy. Teddy yanks at it in small but increasingly strong pulls. Elated now, Joe lets go.

He's going home, the happiest day of his life.

Again.

He tries to celebrate by chasing his tail but gets caught up in the leash and Teddy has to untangle him.

49

Bettina follows Wade Johnson's truck under the sweeping porte cochere of the Delgados' La Jolla mansion, and all four travelers disembark.

"My uncle and aunt are in Hawaii," says Teddy with a glance at Mr. Johnson. "Want to come in? Our nanny won't mind and my cousins are cool."

"No, thank you."

But she kneels and lets Joe clamber up against her; he leans in, full body weight, licking her temple and hair, favorites of his for the forty-odd days he's had her in his life.

A boy roughly Teddy's age comes to the front porch, a skateboard in one hand. Joe bounds over to greet him, then back to Teddy.

Who comes to Bettina and gives her an awkward hug. "Please visit soon."

"I will."

"You won't be sad forever."

Blubbering unrepentantly, Bettina picks up the freeway, heading not north for Laguna but south for Tijuana.

———

Half an hour later, she's parked across the street from the Clínica de Veterinarea de San Francisco de Asís, adjusting the rearview for a look at her face, dabbing away the smeared mascara. Her blouse is damp at the neckline, and she's got Strickland's fifty grand in her purse.

They have good dogs here, she thinks:

You can do this, Blazak.

ACKNOWLEDGMENTS

True respect and gratitude to the many authors who have written beautifully about humankind's best friends throughout the ages. I humbly submit this novel to the canon. There is simply too much "dog lit" to mention here, but Jack London's *The Call of the Wild* is an invaluable touchstone, as is James Herriot's *All Creatures Great and Small*. Our modern-day writers have contributed entertainingly and insightfully to the party. To name a few—*A Dog's Purpose* by W. Bruce Cameron, *The Art of Racing in the Rain* by Garth Stein, and the wonderful Chet and Bernie mysteries by Spencer Quinn. Special thanks to Robert Crais, whose wonderful novel, *Suspect*, inspired me to throw my hat into this timeless ring.

True gratitude to Kristin Sevick at Forge, no stranger to dogs and dog books, for her incisive editing and insight into all things canine, human, and literary. You made this a better book in a thousand ways.